for the staff
at ICU at
FAH – great
work with
Sylvia!

Naomi H.

CW01573215

BLUEBELL

NAOMI HUDSON

Pixeltweaks
PUBLICATIONS

Published in 2015
© Copyright Naomi Hudson

ISBN: 978-0-9934679-1-2

Second Edition

Book interior Design by Russell Holden
www.pixeltweakspublications.com

Cover Painting by Tamara Newton

All rights reserved without limiting the rights under copyright reserved above, no parts of this publication may be reproduced, stored in or introduced into a retrieval system, or transmitted in any form, or by any means (electronic, mechanical, photocopying, recording or otherwise) without the prior written permission of both the copyright owner and the publisher of this book. All characters appearing in this work are fictitious. Any resemblance to real persons, living or dead, is purely coincidental.

The author can be contacted at bluebellnovel1@gmail.com
or on Facebook under Naomi Hudson

Pixeltweaks
PUBLICATIONS

For those who have touched my life

CONTENTS

PART ONE
1970

CHAPTER ONE
SATURDAY 21 MARCH

The car eased to a halt by the zebra crossing, the beacons flashing weakly in the steady drizzle. Two giggling girls, trying to keep dry under their single umbrella, ran across the road. The car moved on, heading for the outskirts of Leeds.

"Open a window, Dave," came a request from the back seat, "I'm choking back here".

"I'm only going to open it a bit, otherwise I'll get bloody soaked".

Mike, seated behind Dave in the back seat, took another drag on his cigarette. "Me too".

"Look," said Dave, "we've got a long way to go, and it's a foul night. You'll have to ration your fags, Mike. It won't kill you, but if you keep puffing away at this rate, you might kill us".

"OK. I'll stub this one out, but get a move on. I'm freezing back here. Have you got the heater on?"

"Yes, I have, but I don't think it's working too well".

"You should get yourself a decent car," quipped Pete.

"Beggars can't be choosers, Pete, so button it. I'll get there as fast as this old girl will allow. Now shut up while I look out for the signs to the motorway. The Leeds section has only been open for a couple of years, and I haven't used it before. Just relax, you buggers. We've got all night to enjoy ourselves."

Before long, the city lights were behind us, and the car's headlights flickered on the Yorkshire countryside. It had been a long winter, and patches of snow lay in the fields and on the distant hills. Dave wound the window back up.

Pete tapped me on my shoulder. "Tell me again what we're doing tonight. I don't want to end up being a prat, apart from looking like one."

"Actually, you look more like a pirate to me!"

Pete Trevelyan was the seriously good-looking one of us, with long dark hair, blue eyes and a cheeky smile. A Mancunian, he was never short of female admirers, and there always seemed to be a queue of girls lined up who wanted to go out with him. Tonight, however, he *was* dressed as a pirate, with a plain shirt, dark jacket, typical hat, boots and a toy sword.

"Alright," I said, "I'll run through it again. Jackie Cameron is the fittest girl on our course. She's got the kind of figure that would make a bishop kick a hole through a stained-glass window." The others laughed as I turned round and glanced at Pete. "But she's got a steady boyfriend. It's her twenty-first birthday this weekend, and we've been invited to her party at Rotherham. She's decided to have a fancy-dress party, and as her parents are away, it's going to last all night. A few more students from our English course may be there, but Jackie has a younger sister and lots of her friends from Rotherham will be there too. You should have a field day, Pete."

"It had better be a good night, John, otherwise your head's on the block," Pete replied, as he pulled his jacket tighter around him.

"I'm not bothered what the party's like," said Mike, "so long as it's warm, and there's plenty to eat and drink." Mike Grant hailed from Morpeth in Northumberland, and he was the quiet one of our group. He was tall and wiry, with tight, curly hair and he wore rimless glasses. He hadn't needed to think too much about his costume. A white lab-coat and a few basic accessories made him look the perfect 'mad scientist'.

We were now heading south along the motorway, and Dave kept the car at a steady fifty. He was the only student I knew who had his own car. His Austin A40 was over ten years old, and he was always worried about breaking down in the middle of nowhere. It was now after eight o'clock, but, hey, the night was only young.

I glanced across at him, and picked out the large S on his t-shirt. Dave had decided to be Superman for the evening, and he had managed to find some black leggings and a cape in one of the local second-hand shops. A pair of brightly-coloured briefs completed his costume. I was feeling quite warm, as I was dressed in a full-length fur coat, with a track-suit underneath, a long scarf and a Homburg hat. Nobody had a clue who I was supposed to be, and neither did I.

It was now raining steadily as we passed Barnsley, and soon we saw the exit signs for Rotherham and Sheffield. Before long, we left the motorway in the direction of Rotherham and found ourselves passing rows of grubby terraced houses, and industrial areas with lots of factories and mills. "This looks grim," said Mike, "do you know the way to Jackie's house?"

"John's got the directions," said Dave. "Jackie lives in a big, old house on the outskirts of Rotherham, and she said it's quite easy to find. I hope it isn't too far, as we're getting short of petrol and the garages all seem to be closed."

"Great," moaned Pete, "out of petrol and we're all dressed like this!"

Jackie's house was easy to find. There were a few other large houses in the area, but hers was the only one with most of the lights on. Dave parked the car a short distance down the street, and the four of us piled out onto the wet pavement. "Let's go", muttered Mike, "I'm still bloody freezing." I hated wearing my specs in public, so I popped them inside my tracksuit pocket. We dashed along the drive, and I rang the doorbell. Nothing happened, so I rang the bell again and kept my finger on it. The door swung open, and Jackie and two of her friends stared open-mouthed at us, then burst out laughing.

"Bloody Hell," said one of her friends, "is this the cabaret?" More of the guests gathered by the door to gawp at us. Most of the girls were dressed in mini-dresses. Nobody was in fancy dress. We plodded into the hallway.

"Hi, Jackie," said Dave, kissing Jackie on her cheek

and handing her a carrier-bag of cards and gifts, “Happy Birthday! I think we might be over-dressed,” he said, looking around at the crowd in the house.

“Well, I did briefly consider having a fancy-dress party, but most of my friends weren’t keen. I don’t know where you got that idea.” *Pete glared at me. “Anyway, the kitchen is through there,” she pointed, “so just help yourselves. There’s a loo in the hallway and another upstairs, and you’ll soon find out what’s going on in the other rooms. Have fun!”

“I need a drink,” said Pete, looking embarrassed, and the three of us followed him into the kitchen. There were two kegs of beer on the worktop, bottles of beer, cider and wine around the kitchen and in the fridge, and a good selection of sandwiches and nibbles. We quickly helped ourselves to drinks, grabbed a few bites to eat, then we had a look around the downstairs of the house.

“Well, at least it’s warm in here,” I said, smiling, trying to make amends for arriving in fancy dress.

“Nice place,” said Dave, wandering through the dimly-lit lounge to a large conservatory. A Rolling Stones LP was playing loudly in the corner, and a few people were dancing under the coloured light bulbs. The doors were wide open, and several guests were smoking outside. Despite the drizzle, a few were dancing on the lawn. I saw Jackie’s friend Liz, and stepped outside to speak to her.

“Thanks a lot,” I said.

“What for?” she replied, smirking.

"Come on, Liz, you told me that this was going to be a fancy dress party."

"Oh, you obviously misheard," she said, with a mischievous grin. "I only said that it might be fancy dress! Anyway, you're quite shy, so now you've got an easy introduction to all of the girls".

"Cheers," I said sarcastically. I squinted back towards the conservatory, where a group of girls were huddled in a corner. "Who are they?"

"The one wearing the red top is Sandra, Jackie's younger sister, and the others are her friends. I can introduce you if you like."

"No thanks," I muttered, "I'll see you later."

I made my way back to the hallway, where Dave and Pete were talking to three of Jackie's friends. "Where's Mike?" I asked.

"I think he went through there", said Dave, pointing to another lounge. I went in, and saw Mike flicking through a selection of books on some shelves. He turned around as I tapped him on the shoulder.

"What do you reckon, Mike?"

"I'm fine, John. It's warm, there's plenty of refreshments and who knows, I might even pluck up the courage to chat up a girl?"

"Fat chance! I'll believe that when I see it. I'm going for another drink," I said, draining my glass. More people had arrived. I pushed my way back to the kitchen, and poured another glass of beer.

"Who are you?" asked a tipsy girl with long dark hair.

"I'm called John," I replied, manoeuvring her into a corner. "I'm a friend of Jackie's from Leeds. There are three more of us somewhere."

"So you're the lads wearing strange costumes?" she asked, eyeing my fur coat and giggling. "Why are you dressed like that?"

"It's a long story. We all share a house in Leeds, and Dave and I are both studying English with Jackie. She invited the four of us to her party, but somebody – mentioning no names – told me that we had to wear fancy dress."

"Who are you supposed to be?"

"Good question! I haven't a clue. Are you OK for a drink?"

"Yes, thanks. My boyfriend is in the back lounge."

"Oh well," I sighed, releasing her from the corner, "nice to have met you," I said, and went to find the others. Dave was sitting at the foot of the stairs. "How's it going, Dave?" I said, shoving him over to sit down.

"Good, but I think I'd have to be the real Superman to get fixed up here. Most of the girls seem to be paired up already."

"Well, it won't be the end of the world if you don't find someone. You've got Katherine waiting for you in Leeds." Katherine worked in an office in the city, and Dave had been seeing her for almost a year.

"Have you seen anyone you fancy?" said Dave, draining his glass.

"That dark-haired bird is nice, but she's with her boyfriend."

"You're too fussy, John. Just have a bit of fun." Dave got up and headed for the kitchen. I picked up my glass and made my way back to the conservatory. Somebody had put a Doors record on the player. The Doors were one of my favourite groups. "That's better," I thought, and found a comfortable chair. The drizzle had eased, and a few more drifted out into the garden as I listened to Jim Morrison's vocals.

"The Doors are performing at the Isle of Wight this summer," remarked a passing girl, heading for the garden. "I'm hoping to get tickets."

"You'll be lucky!" I called after her.

Time drifted on. I hung around to listen to part of a Jethro Tull LP, then squinted around and noticed that the room was less crowded. I guessed that more people were in the garden, or had found their way to the upstairs rooms. I got up, collected a bottle of Newcastle Brown from the kitchen and did some exploring. The bathroom door was open on the first floor, but all of the bedroom doors were closed. I opened one of them just enough to see a half-naked couple getting into their stride. The bloke looked over his shoulder, and I quickly closed the door. I glanced around the landing and saw a narrow flight of stairs in the corner. They led to a large attic room, and I could hear loud music playing as I walked up the stairs. The room was dimly lit, but I soon recognised Jackie's sister in a group of girls and blokes. I sat in the corner for a while, decided that the music and the scene wasn't for me, finished my beer and descended the stairs. Two couples were going into one of the bedrooms, as I made my way to the kitchen. Liz, her boyfriend and Dave were there, placing a few nibbles on their paper plates.

"Hi, John," smiled Liz. "Are you having a good time?"

"Well, it's a bit cliquey and most people seem to think we're aliens. You have a lot to answer for!"

"Relax," retorted Liz, "everyone's friendly down here, and after a few drinks they'll speak to anyone. If you need any introductions, just shout out."

"She's right," said Dave, grabbing his food and another beer. "Let's go back to the lounge. Have you seen much of Mike and Pete?"

"No, I haven't. Mike was looking at some books ages ago, but I haven't seen Pete since we arrived."

I told Dave about the attic room, and we grabbed a couple of bottles of beer and made our way up there. Sandra and most of her friends were still there, so we chatted to them for a while. Sandra was keen to know about her sister's life in Leeds, but we had little to tell her. We didn't see her out very often, and she never came with us to watch Leeds United at Elland Road.

More time passed by. Later on we went back downstairs and walked through to the lounge, then into the conservatory. Most of the guests were dancing to a Herman's Hermits record, some outside in the garden. "The music's shit, Superman," I said. It started to rain lightly again. Two girls were seated in the corner.

"What about those two over there?" Dave asked.

"Go on then, but I don't fancy yours!" I said.

We chatted to the girls for a few minutes, then they told us they were leaving. They moved back into the lounge.

"I told you I didn't fancy yours," I said, "and I think you would have had to be "Superwoman" to get anywhere with them!"

A number of the guests seemed to be heading for the hall, where a few were carrying their coats. Jackie was amongst them, hugging and kissing some of the girls.

"What's going on?" Dave asked her.

"Well, it's a quarter to one, and my parents will be home soon, so the party's over," replied Jackie.

"Oh God," I muttered, "we thought this was an all-nighter."

"Well I never said anything about an all-night party," said Jackie. "The neighbours would complain if we carried on much longer. It was always going to finish at one o'clock."

"We'd better find Pete and Mike," I nodded to Dave. "Mike was in that other lounge earlier on." We walked through and spotted Mike by the bookshelves, but this time he was deep in conversation with a long-haired girl who was wearing a long flowery skirt.

"The party's over, Mike," Dave said, "we've got to go."

"I already know, fellas. Alison told me earlier that the party would finish soon after midnight. Where's Pete?"

"We don't know," Dave shrugged. "We'll have to go looking for him. I bet he's with a bird somewhere."

Jackie and Liz were ushering more of the guests outside. "We've lost Pete," I whispered to Jackie. "Do you have any idea where he might be?"

"I did notice him chatting to one of Sandra's friends, but that was ages ago. She's got short, blonde hair."

"And big tits," Dave poked me, "I do remember seeing her earlier on."

Liz ran upstairs to check the bedrooms, while Dave and I searched in the garden. Mike, meanwhile, continued talking quietly to the long-haired girl. Within minutes, we were all back in the hall, shrugging our shoulders.

"They're nowhere to be seen," I said. "Perhaps they've gone to her house?"

"No way," said Jackie, "she lives on the other side of town. Has anyone checked the garage, because ... "

"Shhh," I said, pointing to the hallway cupboard, "I think I heard a noise coming from over there." I crossed over the hallway, and gingerly opened the door. A narrow shaft of light nestled on a naked arse at the back of the cupboard. "It's time to go, Pete," I shouted, and closed the door.

A few minutes later, Pete stumbled out of the cupboard, followed by a blushing blonde girl, who quickly made for the loo. "We were looking for buried treasure," Pete muttered bashfully, as he adjusted his sword.

"Well, you certainly buried something," I remarked. The others laughed.

"What's the big hurry?" said Pete, glancing at his watch, "it's not even one yet."

"My parents will be back soon," said Jackie, "everyone has to go."

"You're fucking joking, aren't you? This was supposed to be an all-night do, wasn't it, John?" Pete shouted in my direction. I looked away.

The four of us thanked Jackie, then left the house and walked down the driveway.

"Are you OK to drive, Dave?" asked Pete.

"Yes, but remember we're very low on petrol. We'll have to kip in the car until the garages open."

"Yes, and as it is Sunday morning, you'll have an extra hour to cuddle up to Mike in the back," I remarked, grinning widely.

"Lucky me," said Mike.

"When we get back to Leeds, John, you're dead," shouted Pete.

I just laughed at Pete. It had been a good night, with a few laughs, and I would get a decent sleep in the front seat, with my fur coat to keep me warm. I was really looking forward to seeing the garage attendant's face in the morning, when he filled Superman's car with petrol!

CHAPTER TWO
THURSDAY 26 MARCH

Dave Carson and I had been friends since October 1967, soon after beginning the English course at Leeds University. I shared a room in one of the halls of residence during my first year, and Dave shared a room with Pete on the floor above. Mike shared another room further down the corridor. In our second year, we decided to go for single rooms, but for our last year we thought it might be fun to share a house. So we found a large, rambling four-bedroomed house in Headingley. It suited our purpose very well. We all enjoyed each other's company, but had some privacy when it was needed. We tried to share the chores for a short time, but it soon became obvious that Pete, in particular, was not very domesticated. After a while, the rest of us decided to ignore Pete as far as housework was concerned, and only insisted on action when the mess from his room spilled over into the lounge. Our house was quite close to the bus routes to the university and the city, as well as within easy walking distance of our favourite pub, the Original Oak.

Dave Carson and I had a lot in common. We were both of medium build, had long hair, enjoyed both playing and watching sport, and didn't take life too seriously. We both wanted to do well at university, but were not prepared to slog away every day. We tried to keep a balance between what we needed to do to stay on the course, and to take advantage of the varied social scene at Leeds. Dave was an organiser, and was generally more outgoing and confident than me.

Dave came from Kendal, close to the Lake District, and he and I shared a love of football. He was a skilful player, and had trialled for Carlisle United before starting at university. He used to travel to watch league matches at Carlisle and Barrow, and occasionally travelled south to Preston, where I lived. Oh, I'm John Newby, by the way, Preston born and bred, a genuine Lancashire Lad. I had been a fanatical Preston North End supporter from a boy, but my team had struggled in recent years and this season was facing relegation from Division Two.

We both now followed Leeds United, and were enjoying the success that the manager Don Revie had inspired. He had built up a formidable team, and last season United had become First Division champions for the first time in the club's history. Dave and I managed to get to most of the home matches at Elland Road. Pete came with us occasionally, but he supported Manchester City, and often travelled back to Manchester at weekends to take in a match and to take home a bag of dirty washing for his mother! Mike was more studious than the rest of us, and certainly wasn't interested in football.

It was late, and Dave and I were in good spirits as he drove us back from Bolton, where we had watched Leeds defeat Manchester United 1-0 in the second leg of the FA Cup semi-final. The first leg had finished 0-0, so it had been a tense match, but now we could look forward to the Wembley final against Chelsea.

"What a game!" I said, turning to look at Dave's outline in the darkness. "Bobby Charlton, George Best and the rest of them couldn't even manage a goal against us in two matches. That was a gritty performance tonight, wasn't it?"

"Yes, it was a tough game, but we deserved to win. Billy Bremner played great, and after he scored that early goal we just hung on until the final whistle."

"Well, the lads can lick their wounds and relax tomorrow, before the next match on Saturday."

"I don't feel that optimistic," said Dave thoughtfully. "It was a great win tonight, and Leeds are having another fantastic season, but I think we're going for too many trophies and might end up with nothing."

"Yeah, you could be right, I suppose. We've got about nine matches in only eighteen days, and that includes a European Cup semi-final with Celtic. We're still in with a chance of winning the league again, as well as the FA Cup, but it might just be too much. Let's hope for the best, and a bit of luck."

It was past midnight when we returned home. Pete was in bed, alone for a change, but Mike was still up, doing some work.

"Was it a good match, lads?" asked Mike.

"Yes, we played well and hung on for the win," I said. "Now for the final. What are you doing?"

"Just some revision. Exams are only a month or two away, remember," Mike cautioned.

Yes, I did remember. I hadn't really enjoyed the course since the first year, but hoped that I would be able to do enough late revision to gain a reasonable degree. I wasn't looking forward to the final examinations but, hey, I would be alright. I just needed to stay positive.

CHAPTER THREE
SATURDAY 28 MARCH

It was another drizzly evening. Pete and I were walking the short distance to the Original Oak on Headingley Road. Mike was away for the weekend and Dave was seeing Katherine, so Pete and I decided to go for a late pint or two.

"How was the match?" Pete asked, moving away from me slightly.

"What do you think? It was a bloody disaster. Fancy losing 3-1 to Southampton. Dave said the other night that we have too many matches to play in a short time. It looks as though the league title has gone, so I hope we can still win one of the cups, or both."

"Well, I'm a City fan, so I was delighted when you knocked Man U out of the FA Cup, but I'm not really bothered if you win anything this season. Mind you, if I were in your shoes, I'd be absolutely gutted to be the bridesmaid in every competition. Anyway, not to worry, you still have Preston to follow. How are they doing?"

"Don't ask," I grunted.

We were now waiting to cross the road. I took off my specs and put them in my pocket.

"I love it when you do that, John. Girls are usually in pairs, one stunner and one ugly duckling, and you won't realise that you're with the ugly one until it's too late!"

We stepped into the pub and headed for the noise in the

bar. Pete ordered a pint of bitter for himself, and a Newcastle Brown Ale for me. I poured my drink, and squinted around the room. It was smoky, but I could see groups of students chatting and drinking. Pete spotted a group with two girls from his History course, so we shoved our way over to them. After a brief introduction, Pete focused his attention on one of the girls, and the conversation with the rest soon became dominated by exam revision and life after university. I switched off, and quickly swallowed my drink.

"Another, Pete?" I asked.

"Please," he nodded. I went to the bar, bought the drinks and returned to the group. I passed him his pint and glanced around the room again. A group of girls had taken over a table in the corner. They suddenly broke into laughter. Two blokes brushed past me. I peered again. The girls were huddled together, chatting among themselves, but a sudden movement caught my eye, a flash of blonde hair, a face turned my way, and I moved across the room.

"Hello," I smiled at her, "what's the big celebration?"

"Oh, it's Carly's eighteenth, so she's enjoying her first legal drinks."

"Do you ... ?" I pointed at a spare seat next to her.

"Yes, squeeze in. What's your name?"

"John, and you?"

"Mary."

"I like that name." She smiled. "Do you all live round here?"

"Most of us do, apart from Carly's cousin over there. She

lives in Ilkley. She's staying over at Carly's tonight." Mary had beautiful large eyes, and I smiled and looked at her full in the face.

"I guess you're all still at school?"

"Yes, upper sixth, we're taking our A-levels soon."

"I remember them well. I'm studying at the university, but I'm in my final year. I share a house near here."

"What are you studying?"

"English." I paused "You look really nice, Mary," I grinned. "I love your hair."

"Thanks," she replied, a shy smile on her face.

Two or three of the girls were putting on their coats. "Mary, we're leaving," one of them called over. "Are you coming?" "Shit," I thought, "I'm just getting in here".

"Yes, just give me a minute." Mary turned to me, her large blue-grey eyes drawing me like a magnet. "I'm sorry, John, but we're moving on."

"That's a pity," I said, thinking quickly, "but I'd like to take you out sometime, Mary, perhaps for a meal."

"That would be nice," she smiled widely.

"Have you a phone number?"

"Mmm, just a minute. Dawn, have you a pen or pencil?" One of the other girls passed over a pen. "Thanks." She wrote a number on a beermat. "Here you are, John."

"Cheers," I said, grinning. "I'll call you on Tuesday."

"Great," she flashed a smile, getting up from her seat. She bent over and kissed me briefly on the cheek. "See you, John."

I stood up and watched her leave, her long blonde hair blurring in the smoke. She turned as she reached the door, waved and left.

I sat down for a few minutes, closing my eyes, thinking. "Wow, what a stunner! Fingers crossed." I got up and finished my drink. Pete had joined another group of friends, and he was in close conversation with a leggy girl in a miniskirt. I tapped him on his shoulder.

"Where've you been?" he enquired.

"Just avoiding the ugly ones," I smirked at him. "It's your round."

CHAPTER FOUR
FRIDAY 3 APRIL

I paced up and down at the bus stop. It had just turned seven o'clock, and I was early.

I had phoned Mary on Tuesday evening. Her mother answered the phone, and called Mary down from her room.

"Hello," she said.

"Hi Mary, it's me, John. Did you have a good time on Saturday evening?"

"Yes, it was great. Carly was a little worse for wear, but we got her home safely. How are you?"

"Fine, I'm good. Can you come out this weekend?"

"Yes, I've already cleared it with my parents."

"That's great. How about Friday evening? Would you like to go for a meal somewhere in town?"

"Mmm, yes. That would be different. Where do you suggest?"

"I haven't a clue, but we can meet up and have a look around, see what we fancy. I don't think I'll need to book anywhere."

"OK. I probably live further out of the city than you, so I'll take the seven o'clock bus. It goes down Headingley Road, and we can meet on the bus. I'll be on the top deck."

"Good. I'll look forward to it, Mary. I'll see you on Friday, on the bus."

"Yes, goodnight John." I put down the phone.

So here I was, excited but waiting nervously for the bus. The others had asked where I was going, but I was non-committal. It was too early to tell them that I had a new girlfriend, just in case I hadn't. First dates could turn out to be a no-show, or just a one-off. Pete hadn't even seen me talking to Mary on Saturday evening. I glanced up the road, then paced a little more on the pavement. I checked that my specs were in my pocket. I wanted Mary to get to know me better before I started wearing them in her company. The bus appeared in the distance and soon drew up at my stop. I quickly mounted the stairs. I reached the top of the stairs and looked around. Another passenger was right behind me. I edged along the bus, looking for blonde hair. There was none to be seen. "Shit!" I'd been stood up. I sat down on an empty seat, and looked around again. A pretty brunette smiled at me. Her large eyes looked familiar, and I realised it was Mary. I crossed over and sat down next to her.

"God," I gasped, "you had me worried just now. I was looking for your blonde hair."

"Sorry," Mary laughed, "but sometimes I like wearing this wig for a change. I could see you looking puzzled."

"Panicky, more like. I thought you had stood me up!"

We chatted as the bus neared the centre, then we got off and walked along Briggate. I put my arm around Mary, and we looked around for a restaurant.

"This is actually the first time I have taken a girl out for a meal," I confessed. Mary smiled widely.

"Really?" she asked. "I'm honoured."

"It's not the first time I've taken a girl out, you understand?" I added hastily. She laughed. "I haven't a clue where we're going. What kind of food do you like, Mary?"

"I'm not used to eating out. I've only really eaten Wimpy burgers in town. This is a new experience for me too. No, I'm telling a lie, I have had a Chinese meal before, but just with my family."

"So have I. One of my uncles lives in Hong Kong, and when he comes back to England on business he often takes my cousin and me out for a Chinese meal. Let's see if there's a restaurant nearby."

We walked for a while, then Mary spotted some lights across the road. "Is that one over there?" I squinted in the direction of the lights. We held hands, crossed over the road and headed for the door. "It's an Indian restaurant," I said, turning round to look at Mary. "I haven't been in one of these before. What do you think?"

"I'm game if you are," Mary laughed. I opened the door. A middle-aged Asian man wearing a suit greeted us and ushered us to a table near the window. He took our coats and hung them up. A few other couples were scattered around the restaurant. Mary was wearing a green jumper and jeans. She looked really attractive, despite the confusing wig. The waiter gave each of us a menu.

"Would you like a drink, Madam?" he asked, then turning to me, "Sir?"

I smiled sheepishly at him, whispered to Mary, then I asked for a beer and a glass of lemonade. The room was dimly lit, and strange music was playing. We peered at our menus. It all looked very weird to me, as there weren't many Indian restaurants around. I had enjoyed chicken curries in Chinese restaurants, so I decided to order one of those.

"I have eaten hot Chinese curries, so I think I'll have one of those, probably chicken," I said, hoping to impress Mary. "How are you getting on? What would you like?"

"I think I'll have a mild prawn curry, that one," she pointed at the menu. "A korma."

The waiter came with our drinks, and we gave him our order.

"Which curry would you like, Sir?" he asked.

"Oh, a hot one, I think, perhaps a vindaloo," I said, smiling at Mary.

"That's very hot, Sir," the waiter cautioned.

"That's fine," I said confidently, "I'm used to hot food."

He suggested poppadoms to start, so I ordered those as well. We chatted as we waited for our food, asking questions about our families and the kind of music we enjoyed. We were getting on well, and had a laugh or two about the weird décor and music in the restaurant. The waiter arrived with our poppadoms and dips, and we quickly demolished them. I ordered more drinks, and then the main course arrived. I looked at the whole chicken leg in the sauce in a dish. "That's odd," I said, transferring the chicken onto the rice on my plate. "I thought it would be pieces of chicken in a sauce." I cut a small piece of chicken, added some rice and placed it in my mouth. I chewed for a few seconds.

"What's it like?" asked Mary, who was clearly enjoying

her prawn korma.

I reached for my drink. "God," I gasped, "I think I'm on fire." I downed half of my pint. "Wow! That's hot." Mary stared at me, quite concerned, then I relaxed and we both burst out laughing. "I think I'll have some ice-cream after this," I muttered, mopping my brow with the serviette. Mary was looking at me, and giggling.

"Is everything alright, Sir?" the waiter enquired.

"Delicious, thanks."

After a while, the fire in my throat subsided, and we enjoyed the rest of our evening. We left the restaurant hand-in-hand, and looked for our bus stop. I offered to stay on the bus until Mary's stop and then to walk her home, but she told me that her father expected her to phone him just before taking the bus. He would meet her at the nearest bus stop to her house. We cuddled on the return journey, and I asked Mary if she would like to come to a dance at the university on the following Saturday. She told me that her parents were quite strict, and were making sure that her A-level work was a priority, so we agreed to phone on Tuesday night and check arrangements then. I left her with a passionate kiss, waved as the bus drove away, then ran home as quickly as I could. I hoped that nobody was in the bathroom!

CHAPTER FIVE
SATURDAY 11 APRIL

I had quite a busy week. I went home for a couple of days to celebrate my mother's birthday, and to catch up with family news. I had a younger brother and sister, Ian and Susan, so I took them into town and asked about friends and school. They quizzed me about my university work, but more about my social life. I told them that I had found a new girlfriend, but did not go into details.

I phoned Mary from home on Tuesday evening, and confirmed Saturday's dance. I asked her to catch an earlier bus, so that we could have a drink before going down to the university union building in town. We agreed a time, chatted for a few minutes then said goodbye. I caught sight of my brother and sister eavesdropping at the top of the stairs. They dashed into their rooms.

I returned to Leeds on Wednesday, and tried to concentrate on some exam preparation for the rest of the week. On Saturday afternoon, the four of us went to a friend, Andy's house to watch his television. Leeds and Chelsea contested the FA Cup final at Wembley stadium. Leeds were ahead after twenty minutes, but Chelsea equalised just before half-time. Leeds continued to have the upper hand, and we were jumping for joy when Mick Jones scored with only six minutes to go, but Chelsea equalised again a couple of minutes later. Extra time could not bring a result, so the match ended in a 2-2 draw, with the replay set for Wednesday 29th April. Dave and I were gutted, as we hoped Leeds could win at the first attempt. Now another match had been added to an already over-full calendar.

I had a bath after returning to our digs, excited at the prospect of another date with Mary, though not about the dance. Dancing didn't really appeal to me, apart from the fact that it provided an opportunity to chat to a girl. Dave and Katherine were staying in, as was Mike, who planned to work. Pete was taking another victim out.

"Who is it this time?" I quizzed.

"Spanner." Pete liked to use nicknames for most of his girlfriends.

"What kind of name is that?" Dave had come into the lounge.

"A bit unconventional, I suppose, but I really like this girl. 'Spanner' ... well, every time she's near me, my nuts tighten."

I nearly choked on a drink. "Bloody Nora, whatever next? When you're old, you can write a book about all of your ex's and their pet names."

Time was moving on. I fetched my coat, and walked to meet Mary at the bus stop. The bus was on time, and she waiting on the platform as the bus slowed to a halt. She was wearing a light coat and white boots. I smiled and helped her off the bus. We kissed.

"Would you like to see our house, Mary? You can meet the others and see my pigsty!"

"OK. Is it far? Are we still going to the dance?"

"Yes, but it won't get going until later in the evening. We

can have a drink at my house."

We soon arrived at the house, and I took Mary's coat and hung it up in the hall. She was wearing a blue mini-dress, and with her blonde hair and white boots she looked stunning. "You look great, Mary, really nice." She smiled and blushed. "Come and meet the others."

I opened the lounge door, and we went in. Pete, Dave and Katherine were there, having a drink and chatting. Mike was still in his room. "Folks, this is Mary," then turning to her, "this is Dave and his girlfriend Katherine, and that other creature is Pete."

The others smiled and nodded to Mary, and she turned to chat to Dave and Katherine.

"Mate," Pete came over and whispered in my ear, "you're punching above your weight. If you get too busy ... "

"I won't. Go and get your nuts tightened!"

I asked Mary about a drink, and brought two beers and a Babycham from the kitchen. "Right, Mary, come and see my den." We went upstairs and entered my room. I switched on a reading lamp, and pointed to my collection of LP's. "I've mostly heavy rock, I'm afraid. Doors, Cream, Led Zeppelin, some Traffic too, perhaps a Beatles LP if you dig deeply enough, but I have one or two classical records, if you prefer that?"

"You choose, John," she said, taking a sip from a small beer. She hopped onto the bed, and I caught a brief glimpse of white as she did so. "This is tidier than I expected," she commented, looking around at the bookshelves above my desk and posters on the walls.

"Well, I have made an effort," I confessed, putting Mr Fantasy on the turntable. "This is a Traffic LP. I don't know if you've heard Stevie Winwood before?" I asked. Mary shook her head. "He's got a great soulful voice." I drank my beer. "I feel scruffy compared to you, Mary. I'm sorry, but I've always been a casual dresser."

"Don't worry about it, John, you look fine – at least in this light!" We both laughed. "I do like your long hair." I sat on the bed beside her.

"I like yours too." I took her drink and placed it on the floor next to mine. I put my arms around her, and we kissed tenderly, then more passionately. I eased her down and we shuffled along the bed. We kissed again and I ran my hands up and down her hair. She turned and held the back of my head, pushing her fingers into my hair. I moved my hands again down her hair, and felt the softness of her breasts as I moved to her waist. She twisted and eased on top of me, and I was drowning in her kisses and her hair. I held her more closely as our bodies slowly moved together. I was drifting in the music and the passion as we moved more quickly. It was getting warm, but I didn't want this moment to stop. We shifted again and I eased Mary onto her back and gently caressed her face, her neck, slowly moving down ...

"John, we've decided to go into town." Dave was tapping the door. "Do you want a lift to the dance?"

We suddenly parted. "OK, thanks," I shouted, "we'll be out in a minute." We looked at each other and laughed, hugging each other again.

"Saved by the bell, eh?" Mary whispered.

"There'll be other times," I said, "let's dust ourselves down. You look great. You shall go to the ball, Cinderella," I joked.

We had an enjoyable evening after that. I introduced Mary to Mike before we left, and she and Katherine chatted as Dave drove us into town. As for the dance, the less said the better, but I kept smiling as Mary received several admiring glances from the other blokes. "Why do you keep smiling?" Mary whispered as we gyrated to a slow number. I could have told her that I often wondered why some ordinary-looking guys had stunning girlfriends, but I didn't. It was my turn tonight.

"Just happy," I muttered. "I was feeling down this afternoon when Leeds only drew the Cup Final, but now all of that's forgotten. Football isn't everything."

I think the evening ended too soon for both of us. "I know you have to work again through the week, Mary, but would you like to go to the cinema on Friday?"

"Yes, that would make a nice change. Please call me just to double-check," she said, as we looked for a phone-box. "I'll have to phone Dad, as usual." Mary smiled apologetically.

"He's very protective, isn't he?" I commented.

"Yes, but it's dark, and I have a short walk from my stop," Mary explained. "It's quite secluded where we live."

I wasn't complaining. I had a nice warm glow inside, and after I got off the bus and waved to her, I felt as if I was walking on air. Everything seemed to be going well, so far. The darkness didn't bother me.

CHAPTER SIX
FRIDAY 17 APRIL

I caught the bus on Headingley Road and joined Mary upstairs. It was rather chilly, and she was wearing a coat and jeans. We kissed. It was good, really exciting, to be together again.

"How has your week been?" I asked.

"Oh, just revision and more revision, very boring," she replied. "I'll be glad when my A-levels are over."

"And after that?" I continued.

"University, I hope. I've been accepted at both Manchester and Newcastle Universities, as long as I achieve my grades. I'd like to study History or Archaeology, or a combined course. I'll know better in August, when I get my results."

My head was swirling. My course was almost over, and I hadn't decided what to do next. Some of my friends, including Dave, were considering teacher training, but I didn't feel ready for that. I wanted to look at other options, but at that moment the possibility of looking for a job in Manchester or Newcastle was more appealing. I turned and smiled at Mary. "I thought we could go to the Odeon – "Butch Cassidy and the Sundance Kid" – you haven't seen it, have you?"

"No, I haven't been to the cinema for ages. What's the film about?"

"It's a Western, with Paul Newman and Robert Redford. It's had great reviews."

We got off the bus, walked round to The Headrow and joined the queue for the cinema.

"Well, did you enjoy the film, Mary?" I asked, as the bus drew up.

"Yes, it was exciting, but sad at the end. I suppose it's just a story, isn't it?"

"I'll have to ask Pete. He's our house historian. I think the film is based on real people and a real story. By the way, mention of Pete has just reminded me. United are playing Manchester City tomorrow at Elland Road. Pete's a big City fan, and this will be the last time we'll see the two sides meet while we're at university. Would you like to go?"

"To a football match? My parents will think I've gone mad, but I'll ask them. How will we get there?"

"Easy. Just come down on the bus to our stop, and Dave will give the four of us a lift to the ground."

I kissed her, and stood up. "I'll ring you in the morning," Mary said.

"Bye, Mary," I made to go downstairs.

"John," I turned back, "you looked great in your specs." I smiled bashfully.

I waved as the bus moved up the road.

CHAPTER SEVEN
SATURDAY 18 APRIL

Dave eased the car through the busy city-centre traffic, and followed the main road to Headingley. Pete, in the front, was in a buoyant mood, having just seen his team win 3-1 at Elland Road.

"Sky blue, Mary," Pete chirped, turning round to look at her, "get John a sky blue scarf, then he can follow a good side!"

"Bog off, Pete," said Dave, "OK, you won well today, but United were understrength and tired after playing so many matches. The League had already gone, so the match was meaningless for us."

"You're just a bad loser, Dave," retorted Pete. "When you beat us at Maine Road last year I didn't moan." He laughed.

"Did you enjoy the match?" I asked Mary.

"Yes, it was quite exciting, much better than on television. There was a good atmosphere, very noisy, but there were a lot of rude comments and bad language as well."

"That's football," called Pete. "Now let's get home, Dave. I'm going out to celebrate tonight."

"Just drop us at the bus stop, Dave. Thanks." The car eased to a halt.

Pete moved his seat and opened the door so that we could get out. "Bye," Mary called, "thanks for the lift, Dave."

We held each other as we waited for Mary's bus. "My

parents would like to invite you for a meal next Wednesday evening," she said. "I didn't want to mention this in front of your friends. I thought they might tease you about it."

"Thanks. Great, I'd love to come. What time do you want me there, and how do I find your house?"

"Take the six o'clock bus from town, and I'll meet you at the Alwoodley stop. That's the nearest to my house."

"What shall I wear? I don't have a suit or anything like that."

"Just dress casually, John. I've already told them what you're like!"

The bus appeared and stopped. I hugged and kissed Mary and she hopped on the platform and climbed upstairs. I waved at the bus as it moved away. "Meet the parents", I thought as I walked home. I felt as if I was going to be put on trial. I reached our house and opened the door. Mike was in the lounge.

"Good match?" he asked sarcastically.

"No, but Mary enjoyed it. I've been invited to her house for a meal."

"Getting your feet under the table, eh?"

"I'm not sure about that, but Mary must be a little bit serious about me. We haven't been going out together for long, and I can't remember the last time I took a girl home in Preston. Perhaps this term is going to end on a high." I grinned at him. "Don't tell Pete about this, Mike. He's already had his fun today."

CHAPTER EIGHT
WEDNESDAY 22 APRIL

I had found it difficult to concentrate on anything since Saturday afternoon. I moved from one emotion to another as I anticipated an evening at Mary's house. Excitement dominated all others, but nervousness and anxiety followed close behind. I had to make a good impression, I thought. I had been out with a number of girls since arriving in Leeds, and a few in Preston, but none of them had involved a home visit. Well, it had happened once in Preston, but that was only because our families knew each other.

I was encouraged by the fact that Mary's family wanted to meet me so early in our relationship. It said something for Mary's feelings for me, but I knew there was something special about our relationship and meeting her family just seemed a natural progression. Even though we had only recently met, I felt strongly that Mary was the only interesting girl I had met in Leeds.

On the other hand, perhaps Mary's family wanted to meet me because her father wanted to lay down some ground rules. I already knew that he was strict and protective, hence the 'chaperone' service he provided for her bus journeys. Perhaps he felt the need to meet me face to face, to winkle out some of my intentions regarding his daughter and to assess my prospects in life after university. God, I was starting to assume that I was about to face the Spanish Inquisition on Wednesday evening.

“Calm down”, I told myself. After all, Mary’s parents are probably just curious. She’s only eighteen years old, and I may be the first serious boyfriend she’s mentioned to them, or even the first boyfriend she’s ever had. I didn’t even know if Mary had any brothers or sisters, so in some ways they were bound to be interested in a potential addition to the family. I just needed to relax and enjoy myself on the night. If nothing else, I was confident that I would be well-fed!

I knew that my dress sense would not win any awards, but thought that a gift or two for Mary’s mother would gain some brownie points. I went to the local florist’s in the afternoon, bought a small bunch of freesias and left them in water in the sink. As an afterthought, I purchased a box of Maltesers at the newsagents. They would make a good impression on arrival, I thought. I had a good soak in the bath, then changed, putting on my best polo shirt and clean jeans. I was hardly dressed to kill, but it was the best I could do. I still had some spare time before catching the bus, so I went to relax in the lounge. Mike and Dave were there, playing a game of chess.

“Are you ready for your big date?” asked Dave.

“When are you getting changed?” Mike added sarcastically.

“Give me a break, lads. This is my best shot. I don’t want to fuck up, I need everything to go right tonight.”

“Relax, son,” Dave pointed in my direction. “You’ll be fine. Mary seems a nice kid, good-looking too. I’m sure you’ll be comfortable with her family. It’ll be a piece of cake.”

"Cheers, pal," I said, springing up from the sofa. "Time to go." I nipped back into the kitchen, collected my bunch of flowers and went out and put on my coat. I took a couple of paces, then went over to the mantelpiece to pick up the box of chocolates. "Nearly forgot," I laughed nervously. I shoved the box into a pocket and made for the door.

"Good Luck," the others called in unison. I grinned back at them, then opened the door. I almost bumped into Pete.

"For me, darling?" he chuckled glancing at the flowers. "I didn't know you cared."

"I don't," I said, pushing past him. "See you," I called back, then hurried along the street. I had plenty of time for the bus, but didn't want to linger to listen to more of Pete's sarcastic comments.

Alwoodley is a well-to-do suburb in northern Leeds. I hadn't visited the area before, but I expected to see well-spaced estates of semi-detached houses, with a sprinkling of detached bungalows and larger detached houses. I wasn't disappointed, as I peered out of the grimy side window of the bus. As it neared my stop, I could see Mary waiting for me – alone. Good start, I thought, no need for a paternal escort, but, of course, it was still light. I picked up my flowers, and skipped down the stairs. I curled my spare arm around Mary, and we kissed. "Are you ready for the condemned man?" I quizzed. Mary laughed.

"Take it easy, John," she said, "they're all looking forward to meeting you."

"All", I thought, sounds like a crowd. I took her hand

and we walked away from the main road. "Is it far, Mary?"

"No, just over ten minutes."

"Are the flowers for me?" she grinned.

"What do you think? I hope your mother likes them."

"She will love them. You're very thoughtful, John."

We chatted about our past few days, and before long we were in front of a large semi-detached house with a manicured garden.

"This looks nice," I remarked, eyeing the front lawn and well-stocked flower bed, "somebody has green fingers."

"That's Mum." She opened the door. "Give me your coat, John, then I'll do the introductions." I placed the flowers gently on the hall carpet, took out the box of chocolates and handed my coat to Mary. She hung it next to others, then turned and gave me a peck on my cheek. "Come on," she smiled, as she pushed open the lounge door. I picked up the flowers and followed her into the room.

A tall man, probably in his late forties, rose from a chair and extended his hand. "Dad, this is John."

"Pleased to meet you, Mr Hodgson," I smiled nervously, but shook his hand vigorously.

"Welcome," her father said, then he turned to a slim dark-haired lady who was coming out of the kitchen. "This is my wife Sarah." I smiled and mouthed Hello to her. Mary took over again.

"Finally, this is my older sister, Theresa." A pretty brunette stood up and shook my hand. I smiled again.

"Oh," I gasped, "these are for you, Mrs Hodgson," and

handed her the freesias.

"How lovely," she said, "I'll just pop them into a vase."

"These are for you, as well," I muttered, handing the Maltesers to Mrs Hodgson.

"I'll look after them," said Theresa, with a cheeky grin. "Please sit down, John."

I sat down next to Mary's father on the larger sofa. The two sisters sat on the other sofa. "Mary tells us that you're studying English, John?" asked her father.

"Yes, I'm in my final year, taking my exams soon."

"What would you like to do after university?" he quizzed.

"I'm not sure at the moment. I always thought I would be a teacher, but I haven't really enjoyed the last couple of years, so I may look at journalism or something else. I'll get my exams out of the way, then have a proper think about it after my results. What do you do, Mr Hodgson?"

"I'm a civil servant. I work in Leeds City Hall, in the Social Services Department. I've been there over twenty years."

"That sounds interesting. Do you ... " Mrs Hodgson emerged from the kitchen, wiping her hands on a pinny.

"I'm doing stew and dumplings. Will that be alright for you, John?"

"Brilliant!" I rubbed my hands, "one of my favourites. My mother makes a good stew, but I haven't had one for ages." Everyone laughed.

"The stew will be ready in a few minutes," Mrs Hodgson announced. "Go through to the dining room. John, would you like some wine or a beer?"

"I'll have the same as your husband," I smirked.

"Beer it is, John," came the reply.

We all got up. "Are you OK?" whispered Mary.

"Fine," I said, feeling more relaxed, "I'm enjoying myself."

Mary led the way to the dining room and I moved aside to allow Theresa through, but she waved me on and followed closely behind. The meal was delicious and the conversation flowed as we moved on to desserts – apple crumble and custard. I was feeling "at home" and very relaxed. I looked around the table. "Did Mary tell you about our first date?" I asked.

"Oh yes," replied Theresa, "she told us that you went to an Indian restaurant. Very unusual."

"Yes, it was, I hadn't been to one before. But did Mary tell you about the bus?" They shook their heads. "Well", I continued, smiling at Mary, "we had arranged to meet on the top deck of the seven o'clock bus. I'm quite short-sighted, but I hate wearing glasses, so I kept them in my pocket. I bounded up the stairs and peered around for a pretty blond-haired girl sitting alone. When I couldn't see one, I thought that I had been stood up. Then I saw a drab-looking brunette sitting on her own, so I decided to sit next to her – and it turned out to be Mary!"

Mary prodded me. "Pig" she said, grinning. The others laughed.

"Actually," I went on, "I bet that you and Theresa look almost identical when you wear your wig. Or is Theresa really a blonde who is wearing your wig tonight?" They all laughed again.

We had all finished now, so I helped carry some of the dishes through to their spacious kitchen. "Tea or coffee, John?" asked Mrs Hodgson.

"Tea will be fine, thanks," I called back as I joined the others in the lounge. "I notice that you are married, Theresa," I said, nodding at her rings.

"Yes, just over a year ago," she replied, "my husband Brian works for Leeds United, but not as a player," she hastily added.

"Great", I said, "I follow United, as well as my home team Preston North End. Do you like football, Mr Hodgson?"

"I'm more of a rugby man."

"Rugby Union?" I fired back, tongue in cheek.

"Hell, no, Rugby League."

"Apologies, Mr Hodgson, I was only teasing you." The others laughed. "I live near the rugby ground in Headingley. I've been to a few games during my stay here, but I grew up with Union. Preston doesn't have a Rugby League team. I suppose I could drive down the motorway and watch Wigan."

"Have you not been educated over the past three years, John?" Mr Hodgson spluttered, laughing. "Support a good *Yorkshire* side, lad."

His wife saved the day carrying a tray with tea and coffee, and a selection of cakes. She put the Maltesers on the table. "Help yourselves, everyone."

Once drinks had been poured and everyone had taken something to eat, I sat back and spoke directly to Mary's parents. "I'd like to ask your permission for something, Mr and Mrs Hodgson." Mary and Theresa looked at each other, then at their mother. They all held their breath. "My best friend Dave has an aunt and uncle in Richmond, and he and his girlfriend are visiting there a week on Sunday. Would it be alright if Mary and I go with them?"

Everyone relaxed, and Theresa said: "Good God, I thought you were going to ask for permission to marry Mary!" We all laughed heartily.

"That's next week," I joked. The laughter continued, then I explained: "Apparently she is Dave's favourite aunt. She's his mother's youngest sister and only about ten years older than Dave. I thought that while he and Katherine go on their visit, we could explore the town. I've been told that Richmond has an interesting castle, church and market place and there are some nice walks nearby."

Mr Hodgson looked at his wife, then back at me. "Sarah and I visited Richmond many years ago," he said. "It's an interesting town. You'll enjoy it there." He glanced again at his wife. "Make some arrangements, John, but remember that Mary is in the middle of her exam schedule. It's a very important time for her. If you return for tea-time, she can do some revision in the evening."

"Thank you," I said, smiling at Mary. Theresa winked at me.

The evening was over all too quickly and Mary and I walked together through the dark avenues to the bus stop.

Her father lingered back in the distance. “That went well,” I thought as I kissed Mary goodbye and made arrangements for the following Saturday. I was back at our house in no time, and retreated to my room, lost in thoughts of the future.

CHAPTER NINE
SATURDAY 25 APRIL

The past two days were uneventful, but as Saturday morning dawned I was looking forward to spending some time with Mary. I joined her on the bus at Headingley Road, and we carried on to the city centre. Shopping is not my forte, but I was happy to visit the fashion shops with Mary, to grunt favourable comments when required and even to carry her bags. She found a flowery mini-dress which I really liked, particularly as it was starting to feel like spring. I bought her a small bottle of deodorant, and treated myself to some Old Spice. We found a café, and I bought two coffees and two different cakes. "Are you trying to fatten me up?" she grinned.

"Fat chance," I fired back, "though if I did you would find it difficult to run away from me. By the way, I really enjoyed Wednesday evening. You have a nice family, and your mother is a great cook."

"I'll tell her you said that. They all liked you, and my sister thought you were quite dishy."

"She must have had too much to drink," I commented, smiling. "I did really feel at home."

Before long we were strolling along the street to my house. "Are you OK with this, Mary?" I asked. "This may be the last get-together the four of us have before we leave university."

"It's fine by me, John."

I hung up our coats in the hall, and we entered the lounge. Dave and Katherine were there, along with Pete and a dark-haired girl I didn't recognise. That wasn't surprising, as most of Pete's girlfriends didn't last very long, so we knew very few of them. He had only brought three of four of them to the house over the past nine months.

"Hi everyone," I gazed around the room, "I think you have all met Mary."

Not quite," said Pete. "This is Lindsay." She got up and spoke briefly to Mary. Is that 'Spanner'? I mouthed at Pete. He shook his head, and grinned.

"Have a seat, Mary," I pointed at a spare place on the sofa. "What would you like to drink?"

"Just a small beer, please."

"Anybody else?" I asked. They all shook their heads. I went into the kitchen and poured a couple of beers, and gave one to Mary.

"Cheers."

"We have a little surprise for you," Dave announced, then standing up he shouted up the stairs. "Mike!"

A minute or two later, Mike appeared, followed by the long-haired girl from the "fancy dress party" at Rotherham.

"Bloody Hell," I gasped, "you've kept this secret well, Mike."

"This is Alison, everyone," Mike announced. "She's staying over the weekend."

I checked that everybody had a drink, and moved a couple of beanbags by the sofas, so that we all had a seat.

It was a pleasant evening. It was rare for the four of us to have an evening in the house, and I think it was the first time that all of us had female company together. We chatted most of the time, Mary and I played cards with Mike and Alison for a short time, and we took turns in choosing the music. I made some hot drinks after nine, as Mary would have to leave soon.

"Why do you have to leave so early?" Pete asked.

"It's my Dad," Mary replied. "We live on a dark, quiet estate and he likes to meet me off the bus."

She phoned home just before we left the house, and we discussed the week ahead. She had lots of revision to do, so our trip to Richmond with Dave and Katherine would be the next time we could meet. I was looking forward to the time when all of our respective exams were over, then we could have some quality time together. I was quiet as we neared the stop, and said:

"I wish we could see more of each other, Mary. I miss you during the week." She smiled and hugged me.

"I do too, John. Cheer up, soon we'll have all the time in the world." She kissed me and dashed up the stairs. I waved to her as the bus drew away.

CHAPTER TEN
SUNDAY 3 MAY

I had an uneventful week, apart from Wednesday evening when we listened to the FA Cup replay between Chelsea and Leeds. The match was played at Villa Park, and as we expected Leeds went down 2-1. That was the final nail in the coffin for the teams we followed. Leeds had finished runners-up in the League, had lost the FA Cup final in a replay and had been knocked out in the semi-final of the European Cup. A season full of promise had brought nothing. To cap it all, Preston were relegated from League Two. Nevertheless, we could still look forward to the World Cup. England, as champions, were going to defend their trophy in Mexico, and the first matches were early in June. We did not have long to wait.

Putting aside patches of revision, my thoughts were mainly with Mary. We had phoned each other three or four times this week, simply to catch up with any gossip and to confirm weekend arrangements. I always enjoyed hearing her voice, albeit briefly. We both eagerly anticipated our visit to Richmond.

We made an early start on Sunday. Katherine had stayed over, and so the three of us had a light breakfast, then we drove to Alwoodley where Mary was waiting at her stop. We shared the back seat. It was warm, a beautiful spring morning, and though we both had light coats, we did think we would need them. Mary looked really lovely. She was wearing the flowery mini-dress she had bought the previous Saturday, and I couldn't help glancing at her shapely legs. We smiled at each other. It was going to be a great day.

Dave headed out of Leeds and made for the A1. Richmond is north of Leeds, in the northern Yorkshire Dales, and we expected to reach there in around ninety minutes. "Have you been to Richmond before, Mary?" Dave asked, glancing in his driving mirror.

"No," she replied.

"Neither have I," I added. "What is there to see or do?"

"Well, as you know, my aunt and uncle live there, so Kath and I will spend most of the day with them. We'll have a coffee with you both and point out the main places, then we'll leave you to your own devices. We can meet in the market place around four-thirty, and head home."

"Sounds good," I said, smiling at Mary.

"As it is Sunday, most of the shops will be closed," Dave continued, "but there's lots to do. You can visit the castle, Trinity Church or the old market. They usually have craft fairs and things in there. If you want, you can just wander round the medieval streets. There are plenty of pubs. If you get fed up of sightseeing, as it is so nice today, you could walk down to the river. Some of the narrow streets are very steep, so don't tire yourselves out before you make the walk back." He turned and grinned at me.

"Don't worry," I grinned back, "we'll try not to do anything too energetic."

I relaxed as Dave kept the car at a steady pace. Katherine

and Mary chatted for much of the journey. I was quite happy to half-listen to them, as I knew that Mary and I would have a few hours alone. Before long, we were leaving the A1 and heading along country roads to Richmond. Soon we could see the castle keep, standing high and proud above the town. Dave followed signs for the town centre, and easily found a parking space on the cobbled market square. We got out of the car and Dave pointed out the main landmarks. The castle occupied the key site, high above the river, but most of the other attractions were fairly central, apart from the walk down to the River Swale. We found a café and enjoyed some coffee and toasted teacakes. Dave and Katherine got up and pushed their chairs under the table. "OK, we're leaving you now. We'll see you both back on the square around four-thirty. Do you want to keep your coats?"

"I think we will, "I replied, looking at Mary. "They're only light and you never know, we may get a shower or two this afternoon."

Dave and Katherine waved as they left the café. I sat back in my chair and thought: "gorgeous girl, great location, beautiful weather. Life can be so sweet sometimes!"

"Shall we explore?" I grinned at Mary. She smiled and nodded. I took her hand and we stepped out onto the cobbles.

We wandered round for an hour or so, window-shopping, exploring narrow alleys and admiring the variety of quaint cottages that had been built into the fabric of this old town. We decided not to visit the castle, but had a brief look around Holy Trinity Church and browsed around a craft fair which was in a building close to the old market hall. I bought an attractive embroidered centre-piece for a table for Mary's mother, then minutes later spotted a lady making jewellery with semi-precious stones. A lovely green heart-shaped pendant caught my eye and I pointed it out to Mary. She loved it, so I asked the lady to attach it to some thin leather, and the purchase was made. We moved away from the stall and found a little space. I parted Mary's golden hair and fastened the pendant around her slim neck. "Now you have my heart," I whispered in her ear, then kissed her. We made our way out of the building.

There was hardly a cloud in the sky, and little breeze. It was quite warm, so we found another café and had a cold drink. "Let's go down to the river," I suggested. "It's still early, we have plenty of time and there should be some nice walks down there."

"Good idea," said Mary, finishing her drink, "it will be cooler there as well." We left the market place and edged our way gingerly down Millgate. The street was very steep in places. "Little wonder that this place was so difficult to attack!" We finally reached the bottom of the narrow street and found ourselves in an old square, with a green in the centre. A sign in the corner pointed the way down to the river walks. We were fortunate in visiting Richmond on such a beautiful day. The cottage gardens were full of spring flowers, stretching to take in the early sunshine.

Soon we were near the River Swale. Couples and small family groups were also taking advantage of the glorious weather. The river was in full sway, and we paused to admire the water gushing through the rapids. There were several well-established pathways, and we sauntered along one of them, clinging to each other and laughing as the path became rougher. There was no need for conversation, just being together in this lovely place was all we needed. The path now meandered as the woodland came close to the riverside. It was shady in places. We paused again, kissed and turned to watch the water rushing close by. I turned, and peered at the woodland behind us. As usual, I wasn't wearing my specs, but through the darkness there seemed to be a hint of sunlight. I gently nudged Mary, and we stumbled our way through the grass, pushing aside the occasional low branch, heading for the sunlight. Clumps of bluebells appeared, resplendent in the warm spring weather and they grew more densely as we neared the shafts of sunlight. They almost formed a blue carpet as we came into a small clearing, brightly lit in places when the sun drilled through the trees. We moved around slowly in the centre, taking in the beauty of the scenery. How fortunate we were! It was the perfect day, the perfect place and it was just for us.

A fallen log, bathed in sunshine, lay on the edge of the clearing. I placed my coat over the smoothest part of the log, and we sat down, breathing in the pleasure of this golden site. "This is heaven," muttered Mary, and I drew her face towards mine. We kissed, gently at first, but soon with more passion. I caressed strands of her hair, gently felt her neck, her ears, her face, then I kissed her lightly on her face and her neck. We were holding each other more tightly.

She clung around my neck as I found her breasts and caressed them through the soft fabric of her dress. I freed my head and kissed her neck and her breasts. I eased Mary off the log and pushed my coat onto the grass and bluebells. We continued kissing, touching each other's bodies as we lay on the coat. We were in a haze of gold and blue. It was warm, I was warm. I moved my hand down to Mary's thighs. Her dress had shifted upwards and I could feel her soft and cool flesh. I could feel a growing longing, a throbbing inside my jeans as my erection became obvious and slightly painful. I thought that I was going to burst through the tight fabric. I slipped my hand down into Mary's panties and teased my fingers gently through her soft hair. As I caressed her mound she moaned and our kisses became much more passionate, more violent. She fondled the hardness in my jeans, then slid down the zip. I quickly eased her panties down and slipped them off her legs. Mary put her hand inside my pants, reached for me and we guided ourselves into each other. Gently at first, then with more confidence I began thrusting deeply into Mary as we made love on our bluebell bed. It was a frantic passion, born out of our mutual longing and excitement, and being able to seize the opportunity. We both moaned and sighed as we came to a climax, and gradually the thrusting and movement slowed down. My head was buzzing, a kaleidoscope of colours. We came to a stop and we clung to each other, now limp and exhausted.

"Hello. What you doin?" enquired a small boy from the path near the log. We sat up by the log, and hastily rearranged our clothing.

"Just playing," I called to him.

"Jonathan, come out of there," shouted a female voice in the distance. A young mother appeared by a tree. "Come over here, right now!" she ordered, and the little boy ran to her. "Sorry," she shouted in our direction, as she led her child away from us.

We looked at each other incredulously, then fell back, laughing. We clung to each other, then Mary reached for her bag and passed me some tissue. "Be prepared," she pointed her finger in my direction, "I was in the Guides." We cleaned ourselves and I buried the tissue under the log.

"We'll look for that in twenty years," I said, and we giggled with embarrassment. We straightened our clothes, I shook our coats and we gazed back at our bluebell "boudoir". We held hands and slowly made our way back along the riverside towards town.

Later that evening, Dave and I were chatting in the lounge. He had dropped the girls off at their homes after our return from Richmond. "Well," he enquired, eyebrows raised, "what kind of day did you really have?"

"Fantastic," I replied, "couldn't have been better. Thanks for the day out. Richmond is a special place, very special to Mary and me now. We got really close down by the river."

"You can't have shagged each other out in the open, surely to God. You'd have frightened all of the little children and embarrassed their Mammies."

"No, not quite, but we found a secluded bluebell glade and, well, enjoyed ourselves for a while."

"Oh yes," said Pete, who evidently had been busying himself quietly in the kitchen, "so finally shy and bashful John gets lucky with what's-her-name – "Bluebell" – that's what we'll call her."

"Mary is her name, as you know, and anyway we've been close for some time. I just don't go about crowing like you."

"Whatever," said Pete, "Good Luck with her, mate. Anyway I can't stay wasting my time talking to you sad gits. I'm taking 'Polaris' out tonight."

"Polaris – which one is that?" asked Dave.

"Lindsay. She was here the other night – remember? I'm staying over at her place tonight."

"Go on, then," I quizzed, "why Polaris?"

"Simple – she goes like a rocket!"

CHAPTER ELEVEN
SATURDAY 9 MAY

It was the exam season. Some of our university friends had already taken one of their final exams, and students in other years had first-year examinations to take. Others had assessments to prepare and hand in. Mary's first examination, one of her French exams, was the following week. Social activity was at a low. As always, however, Mary and I had been in regular contact and had arranged to meet that afternoon. We had agreed to spend some time in the city centre, then to go to the cinema. We still had to decide on a film. We passed some time looking around the shops, and enjoyed comparing our likes and dislikes in a record shop. Later on we went to a café for a drink and a snack. It was our first opportunity to discuss last weekend's passion in private.

"I'm going to remember our visit to Richmond for a long, long time," I whispered to her. "How do you feel about it, Mary?"

"It was lovely, really lovely. I think we were both ready to get closer to each other," she smiled.

"If that's your nice way of saying I really enjoyed making love with you, well I feel exactly the same," I grinned. "You are very, very special to me, Love. I'd really like to talk about our future this summer and beyond, but we've both got a lot to think about with our exams. Let's wait until they are all finished, then we can concentrate on us."

"Yes, I agree, that's the sensible thing to do. I've still got lots of revision to do, as well as the exams themselves, and my Mum and Dad are so anxious for me to do well. In the meantime, which film do you fancy seeing tonight, John?"

"Well, I've looked in the paper. I won't bother mentioning the kiddies' films or grannie's black and whites that neither of us will watch – or would you?"

"No, of course not," she laughed. "What are the other choices?"

"Another western – 'The Wild Bunch'. It's directed by Sam Peckinpah, and his films are generally violent, but it has some good actors."

"Next, please."

"A war film, 'Where Eagles Dare', with Richard Burton and Clint Eastwood. It's had good reviews. A couple of other films that I have seen some time ago, but would watch again are 'If' and 'The Graduate'. 'If' is a sort of fantasy about a group of senior pupils taking over a Public School, and 'The Graduate' is ... "

"I've seen it. It's quite funny and quite romantic, with Dustin Hoffman, but I don't like re-watching films."

"I don't mind really, and the film has some great music by Simon & Garfunkel, but the choice is yours. I think it's got to be something like 'Bambi' or 'Where Eagles Dare'."

"I always used to cry in those Disney cartoons, so let's see the war film."

"Good. That's the one I fancied!"

"Oh, I almost forgot. Theresa and Brian would like to

come along too. Is that alright with you?"

"Of course, I would like to meet Brian."

"Good. I'll phone Theresa and we'll meet them outside the cinema."

We had a quick drink with Theresa and Brian after the film had finished, then Mary and I walked out of the centre to catch our bus.

"What did you think of the film, Mary?"

"Well, there was plenty of action and the scenery was impressive. I thought Clint Eastwood was cool. It's nice to see him in a film that isn't a western."

"I agree with everything you've said, Love, but I did think the action was a bit far-fetched in places. They'd have needed a massive amount of luck or had help from Superman to achieve what they did."

"Yes, but it's just a film, remember. If it was just ordinary people doing ordinary things, it would be pretty boring!"

"OK, Mary, you're right of course. Now, can you come out next Saturday evening?"

"What's happening?"

"As it's nearing the end of term, or rather the end of university, some of our friends down the street are having a leaving party. It might go on quite late, but I know we'll have to leave early. What do you think?"

"I think it should be alright. I'll check my exam timetable, and we can make arrangements during the week. Oh, here's our bus."

We found seats on the top deck as usual, and we briefly hugged and kissed before I got off. "Just a few more weeks," I thought, "then our exams will be over and we can spend lots of time together." I watched as the bus disappeared in the distance, then walked home.

CHAPTER TWELVE
SATURDAY 16 MAY

The week had dragged. There's not much less exciting that re-reading notes, having the occasional tutorial, glancing through old exam papers, studying sections of books that you have studied 'x' times before, and so on. I had spoken to Mary three or four times, and had been along to the Oak for a pint with friends, but other than those rare interludes, little had broken the monotony.

I had been looking forward to Saturday, of course. Mike was away for the weekend, so the three of us met up with other friends in the city and just chilled out for a couple of hours. We were all feeling the stress of the exam preparation, yet at the same time the future after university was beginning to loom larger in the backs of our minds. I asked Dave if he had come to a decision about teaching.

"Yes, I think I have. I've discussed things with Kath, and I'm going to stay in Leeds to do my teaching training course. I might look at the option of going to Carnegie College, more for a change of scenery than anything else, but at least I can stay in the city. Kath and I may rent a house or I could stay with her family to keep the costs down. We haven't decided yet, in fact she hasn't even mentioned any of this to her parents, so we have a few decisions to make pretty soon. How about you, Pete?"

"I'll probably do the same as you, Dave, teacher training, but I'll go back to Manchester to do it. I don't know if I really want to teach, but it makes sense to get the qualification now. It might be fun, anyway. I guess," he smiled, turning to look at me, "that you'll be sailing into the sunset with Bluebell before marrying, getting some boring job and having lots of kids?"

"Ha ha," I muttered, "very funny. In fact we've agreed not to discuss the future until after our exams have finished. I must admit that I haven't made up my mind about a career, but Mary and I will look at everything together once she decides which university to attend. Now, what about tonight, who's going to Andy's party?"

"I think it's going to be boring," Pete yawned, "but Polaris and I will probably look in for an hour or so. We might as well have some free booze before moving on. Her parents are away for the weekend, so we might watch a bit of telly."

"And the rest," Dave said, with a knowing look. "The four of us are going, aren't we, John?"

"Yes, Mary's catching the seven o'clock bus, so we'll have a drink at our house and go along to the party when it's warmed up."

Mary and I had just walked from the bus stop. She was wearing white boots again, with a mini-skirt and top and, as always, looked great to me. I kissed her before entering our house. "It's great to see you again, Mary. I've really missed you this week."

"Thanks. I've missed you too, John. It's just been work, work, work this week. I've been so longing to be with you again. Are we staying here?"

"Yes, but not for long. Dave's gone to collect Kath, then the four of us will go to the party later. Drink?"

"Please. Oh, here they are now." Dave and Katherine came into the lounge. I brought some drinks through and handed them out.

"Thanks," said Katherine. "Is this party going to be any good? The last one they had was rubbish."

"Well, let's see. We can always come back here if it's boring," I said.

True to form, it was boring. There was little atmosphere, and even less food and drink. It seemed to me that Andy had expected his guests to bring everything. All he had provided was the venue and some music. Pete didn't show, and Dave and Katherine decided to move on to another party hosted by one of *her* friends. It was bound to be an improvement. Mary and I quietly slipped out and returned to my house. I fetched a couple of drinks from the kitchen, and we went up to my room. I didn't switch on the lamp, but left the door slightly open to that a faint glow of light drifted in from downstairs. I opened the curtains as well to catch some of the moonlight. "We haven't got a lot of time before you have to go for the bus, but at least we have more time that we did at Richmond," I laughed.

"True, "smiled Mary, "and it's more comfortable, but not as romantic."

"Nothing will be quite like our bluebell glade, "I whispered, "but you're talking too much," as I dragged her onto the bed.

"Why are we whispering?"

"It's more atmospheric," I lied. I didn't know why we were whispering.

I kicked off my shoes and pulled off my t-shirt, then eased Mary's top off and unfastened her bra. We kissed and held each other, and I drew her long hair around us like a cloak. She sat up and unzipped her white boots.

"Are you prepared today?" she gazed at me. I nodded, and we helped each other out of our remaining clothes. It was heaven to finally lie naked together. We continued to caress each other, to kiss gently and to let our hands explore each other's bodies. There was no frenzied rush this time, we had more time and privacy to enjoy the closeness that we had with each other. I kissed her breasts and eased myself into her, slowly increasing my thrusts as we reached for each other in the darkness. I could feel her nails in my back as we moved together, more quickly now, more urgently, more eagerly as we moved to a climax. I could feel the sweat on Mary's brow and we kissed around our faces, holding each other's head, as we gradually slowed down, thrusting gently now, moving slowly to a standstill. Our breathing slowly returned to normal as I eased Mary onto her side, gently running my hands up and down her back.

"I love you, Miss Hodgson, "I whispered playfully.

"Yes, I know," she grinned, "but I love you a bit as well."

We continued to wallow in our intimacy, almost like being in our own little bubble, until all too soon, it was time to get dressed and to walk for the bus. It was going to be another long week of separation, of snatched phone calls and of tedious exam revision, but at least we had the memory of our precious time together this evening to help us through the week.

CHAPTER THIRTEEN
SUNDAY 24 MAY

The week had passed more quickly that I had expected. My parents drove through to Leeds on Wednesday, and we managed to have lunch together and some time to catch up on recent events. I had packed some of my possessions before they arrived, so we loaded their car before they returned to Preston. Mary had some free lessons around lunch, so she managed to get out of school to come and meet my parents. She had changed out of her uniform into jeans and a top, and as usual she looked very smart in casual clothes. Our meeting was short, and Mary caught the bus back to school. My Mam and Dad seemed very impressed by her, but soon it was time for them to return to Preston, to be home when my brother and sister came home from school. I felt a little sad and lonely when everyone had gone.

Friday afternoon was another bonus, however. Mary had an exam in the morning, but afterwards she and a group of her friends caught the bus to the city centre. I met them in a café on Briggate, and it was fun to see a couple of her friends giggling quietly behind Mary's back. Mary and I left them in the café with their milkshakes, and we spent a couple of hours wandering around, window shopping, going nowhere in particular, just relaxed and comfortable in each other's company.

We made arrangements to meet again on Sunday. Mary's aunt was travelling from Doncaster on Saturday to see her sister and nieces, and apparently I was welcome to join them and meet another member of the family. "I think I'll give it a miss," I told Mary, "I'll feel like a gooseberry. I'm sure there will be other times when I can meet your aunt." I preferred the Sunday option. We were going swimming in the morning, then spending some time at my house afterwards. I wasn't sure what the others were doing, but it didn't matter. We still had the privacy of my room.

I caught the ten-thirty bus on Sunday morning and joined Mary upstairs. She was dressed casually in jeans and a sweater, looking great, and had a large bag with her swimwear and towel. I just had mine in a carrier bag. We kissed and chatted until we got off the bus and went to Bramley Baths. I hadn't been there before, not being much of a swimmer, but Mary knew it quite well. I paid for our tickets and we went to get changed.

I was the first out. It wasn't too crowded. Three or four serious swimmers were doing lengths of the pool, and a few lads were huddled by the steps near the shallow end. I hovered around the middle of the pool, treading water with my back to the pool edge. I knew that Mary had appeared before I saw her. The lads were nudging each other and making comments as Mary dived in and swam over to me. She was wearing a tiny bikini and the top had come loose as she dived in. The group of lads hadn't missed a thing. Mary stayed close by me as she adjusted her top. "This is last summer's bikini," she spluttered, "I must have grown a bit since then."

"I don't know about that," I smirked, "but those boys

know exactly how big you are now!"

"Shut up!" she laughed, as she poked me in the ribs. "Let's do some swimming."

We swam around for a short time, and I teased her by grabbing her foot or tickling her waist. She wriggled away, then we swam together again, kissing as we moved along. We paused and Mary put her arms around my neck. I gently squeezed her bottom and pushed it towards me. I was becoming aroused and Mary could feel my erection. "Ooh, I can feel something gruesome down there, "she joked. I pushed one of her hands down to my trunks.

"Feel again, "I whispered in her ear, "it's just grew some more!" We clung to each other, laughing heartily.

We stayed in the pool for another half hour or so, but by that time we were both feeling so horny that we decided to shower, get dressed and head off to my house – as quickly as possible. I bought some crisps and a couple of sandwiches while I was waiting for Mary. She appeared, her golden hair now frizzy. "You look like a mermaid," I grinned at her as we left the baths and looked for a bus.

The house looked empty when we arrived. I wasn't sure what the others were doing, but just at that moment I didn't care. We dropped our bags in the hall, I poured a couple of lemonades and we dashed up to my room. I locked the door, and closed the curtains. I put on a Doors LP, Strange Days. We stood in the centre of the room and put our arms around each other's necks. We kissed passionately. "Now you're going to find out what happens to careless mermaids who get themselves caught," I joked, as I took hold of clumps of her hair. It seemed twice as thick as usual. Gentle slivers of light filtered through the curtains.

We undressed each other eagerly. I sat on the bed as Mary tossed her clothes onto a chair. The green heart pendant swung between her breasts, as she turned a couple of paces towards me. I held her bottom and buried my face in her groin, kissing her pubic hair. "You're wearing our heart," I gasped, as I moved on my back.

"Always," she said, "always."

She leaned over and kissed me passionately. We broke off and took turns in kissing each other's bodies. Her nipples were hard against my face and I nibbled them gently, playfully. She kissed and tickled my back, scratching as she became more aroused. I was briefly aware of Jim Morrison's voice in the background, then nothing, back to our bubble. I tickled the top of her thigh, then teased my fingers gently through her pubic hair and beyond. Mary moaned and shifted her position, kissing my chest and belly, moving down and sucking gently. Now I was moaning, I think, as I turned to kiss, lick and nibble the top of her thighs.

We were both moving more urgently, clinging on to the ecstasy until Mary sat up and pushed me onto my back. She straddled me and began moving up and down, forwards and backwards, slowly at first, but increasing in pace as the passion gripped us both. Now she was riding me wildly and I held her bottom to make sure that we kept together. I knew I was near so I switched her onto her back and took charge of the final proceedings. I was vaguely aware that the last Doors track, The End, was also coming to a climax, as I thrust and thrust as if my life depended on it. My head was exploding. Mary was rolling from side to side, stifling a scream, as she finally gave in to the relentless pressure from above. The music was throbbing on, as mercifully we reached our climax together, shuddering, clinging to one another, moaning softly, slowing down, easing to a gentle stop. We broke away from each other, gasping for breath, sweating, exhausted from the love between us. We lay side by side on the bed, totally spent, as our breathing became more normal, and I opened my eyes and turned slowly to face my woman. The music had stopped.

"I'm glad that's over," I grinned, "there's something on telly that I want to watch." Mary laughed and slapped my chest.

"You aren't going anywhere, John. Just stay right here, next to me."

I reached for our drinks from the bedside table, and we took a sip. I drank more thirstily, then put my glass under the bed. Mary finished her drink. Conversation was not necessary. We relaxed and lay back on the bed, touching each other, occasionally kissing. I tried to rearrange Mary's hair. She turned to me and covered us both with strands of her golden locks. I ran my fingers up and down her bottom. She touched my face and my chest, pinching and tickling. I prised us apart a few inches and began kissing her breasts. We intertwined our legs and moved our thighs slowly. The touching became a little more intense, as our kisses lingered and I felt movement down below. Mary broke off a kiss and looked down.

Again? she mouthed. I gave her an astonished look and shrugged my shoulders as we continued kissing and moving our pelvises. We were soon ready for an encore, but this time our love-making was gentler, less frantic but satisfying in every way.

Mary glanced at her watch. "Wow!" she gasped, "I have to go." We reluctantly got dressed and had a final kiss and cuddle. I grabbed the empty glasses and we moved down the stairs. Dave and Katherine were seated on the sofa, Pete and Mike were standing near the kitchen.

"About time," said Dave, "we thought there was a hurricane going on." Katherine smiled knowingly at Mary.

"You're wearing him out, Mary," laughed Mike.

"It's true, Bluebell," Pete pointed at Mary. "Christ, John looks totally whipped!"

Mary was blushing heavily as she moved into the lounge. I put my arm around her and looked around at the others. "We were only reading Shakespeare, weren't we, Mary?" She nodded sheepishly. "We've got to go," I announced. We paused at the hallway to collect Mary's bag, and turned and waved.

"I'll be surprised if you can walk down the street, John," called Pete. The others laughed.

CHAPTER FOURTEEN
SATURDAY 30 MAY

The university examinations were in their final stages, in another week or so it would all be over. Mary's A-levels exams, however would not finish until later in June, so she still had lots of home pressure to keep the revision maintained at a high level. We had managed to meet briefly twice during the week, once in the city centre, the other time at the Original Oak, where we had a drink. It was nice to have a little quiet time in the location where we had first met. I told Mary that the four of us were planning to meet with our partners and have a pub meal somewhere. It would probably be our last getogether before going our separate ways. As usual she needed to check with her parents, but she thought that there would not be a problem. Only Dave had a car, so I thought the meal would be somewhere in the city. I phoned Mary on Friday evening to ask her to catch the seven o'clock bus tomorrow as normal, and we would meet the others in the centre.

I joined Mary on the top deck and we smiled and chatted on the way to the city. We did not speak about the passionate Sunday afternoon that we had enjoyed nearly a week ago, but our smiles revealed that we had a shared secret. The closeness between us was now very strong. I knew that now we did not have too many days to wait until our exams were through, and we could relax and make plans for our future.

We met the others in a pub in the centre. Alison had

come through for the weekend to stay with Mike. Her examinations were almost over too. Pete and Lindsay were the last to arrive. We found a table and Dave and I went to the bar to order drinks. We brought the ladies' drinks over first, and I was pleased to see that Mary was involved in the conversation, even though she was the youngest of our group. Pete and Mike fetched the remaining drinks, then we settled down and studied the menus. Mary and I quietly discussed the various options, and we both decided to order chicken. A few minutes later a waitress came over and took our orders. Pete winked at the lads.

"Who is she? "Mike asked.

"Just a girl I took out last December. "Lollipop"."

Mary opened her mouth to ask Why? I just looked at her and said: "Don't bother."

We ordered desserts after our meal. I thought that the conversation would be dominated by our futures, but we had talked about nothing else as the exam season wound to a close and the girls seemed reluctant to talk about something which might not involve them. Predictably, we chatted about football, in particular the impending World Cup in Mexico and England's first group match against Romania on the following Tuesday.

"Look," said Pete, forcefully, "we are the World Champions and shouldn't be frightened of any other team."

"Yes, but am I right in saying that we have to play Brazil in our group, and they have Pele and all of those other wonderful players?" commented Alison, looking at Mike.

"Don't look to Mike for support, Alison. He knows

bugger all about football," laughed Dave.

"Actually," smirked Mike, "I happen to know that Brazil are the favourites to win our group, but that two teams are promoted to the quarter-final. So England have an excellent chance of getting through."

"Correct," I said, quietly clapping Mike.

"My Dad says that Brazil are going to win the World Cup, but that England could get to the final," Mary chipped in, looking very knowledgeable.

"And a lot of people would agree with your Dad, Mary," said Pete, nodding, "but personally I still fancy England."

"Anyway," I held up a hand, "we need to decide where we're going to watch the Romanian match."

"Oh, that's easy," smiled Dave, "we'll go to Andy's. His parties are shit, but there's a big telly in his house. We'll get a few beers, and call round."

"And if he won't let us watch his telly?" I enquired.

"We'll just sit on him!" smirked Pete, with his cheeky grin.

The rest of us laughed.

CHAPTER FIFTEEN
WEDNESDAY 3 JUNE

Tuesday evening had gone well. I called round to see Andy on Monday and he had no objection to the four of us watching the match, as long as we brought plenty of beer and snacks. He told me that a few other friends were planning to come along, so the atmosphere ought to be lively.

It certainly was lively. About twenty-five of us crammed into Andy's lounge to watch the game, and the banter was noisy from the start. All of the windows had been opened to clear the smoke. I'm amazed that we didn't have any complaints from the neighbours. Perhaps they were just as noisy in their homes watching or listening to the match. Andy had invited a friend called Wolfgang to join us. He was a German student on Andy's course, but he promised to support England. He didn't have much choice. We would have thrown him out if he tried to cheer on the opposition!

The game was tight. England won 1-0, with Geoff Hurst scoring the vital goal in the second half. We stayed at Andy's until the beer ran dry in the early hours.

It was late afternoon. I was doing some packing in my room when the phone rang in the hall. "It's for you, John," bawled Mike. "Sounds like Mary."

I came down the stairs and lifted the phone. "Hello."

"Hi, it's Mary," she said, in a quiet voice.

"Hello, Love, this is a ... "

"John, I'm sorry, but we're going to have to stop seeing each other."

"Speak up, Mary, what did you say?" I had a puzzled and worried look on my face.

"I'm sorry, but my ex-boyfriend has been to my house, and he wants to go out with me again. I'm sorry, John, but I still love him so we have to finish."

"Ex-boyfriend?" I muttered.

"Yes, Paul. We split up at Christmas, but he's finished university now and wants us to get back together. I do as well."

"What about us, Mary? Do the past few weeks mean nothing to you?"

"It's been really nice, John, but I'm sorry and I've made up my mind. You're leaving Leeds soon, and I'll be going to university, so it's for the best that we finish now." She was still speaking softly.

"I can't believe I'm hearing this, Mary."

"I'm sorry, you're a nice bloke, but you'll meet someone else. We're over, I'm going out with Paul again. I'm sorry, Good Luck."

The phone went dead. I placed it back on the hook, and slowly walked into the lounge. I felt shell-shocked.

"What's up, mate, you look as if you've been hit by a bus," said Dave, and he came and put his hand on my shoulder.

"Mary's finished with me. I can't believe it," I said glumly, sitting down on the sofa, head in hands.

"That can't be true, John. The two of you have so much going for you."

"Well, that's what I thought, but she said that her ex-boyfriend has come home from university and wants to go out with her again. She said she still loves him, so we're through."

"Phone her back, and try to meet somewhere and talk about it."

"That's pointless, Dave. She said that I'm moving on, God knows where, and that she's going to university, so it's better that we finish now."

Mike came downstairs and glanced over to me. "What's wrong?" he said, looking at Dave.

"Mary's finished with John. She's going out again with her old boyfriend."

"Jesus, I'm really sorry," said Mike, "I thought you were perfect for each other." He moved over and put his arm around my shoulder.

The front door opened and Pete came in. "Christ, what's the matter with you lot? It's like a bloody morgue in here."

I stood up, and looked at him. "Mary's finished with me. She just phoned a few minutes ago to tell me that we're over."

"That's a real bummer, mate. What a bitch! Still, look on the bright side, John," he said, draping an arm around my shoulder. "Girls are like budgies. You find one that you like but then it flies away, gets eaten by the cat or dies. So, when that happens, you find another one."

Furiously, I broke his grip and started punching him in the stomach. The others grabbed me, and held me firm. "Fuck off," I shouted, "Mary's not some fucking budgie. I love her. I thought we had a future together. You may treat your women like shit, but she's the only girl I've been out with that I really love. I can't believe that this has happened."

Dave glared at Pete and he disappeared into the kitchen. I sat down on the sofa. I held my head in my hands.

"None of this makes sense," I muttered. "We've got on so well, and have become really close over the past couple of months. Mary's never mentioned an ex-boyfriend. I've even been to her house and met her family. Why would she invite me there if she intended to finish with me? It just doesn't add up."

"Mary did seem very quiet last Saturday, when we all went out for a meal," said Mike.

"Perhaps," I turned to look at him, "but you've got to remember that she's a few years younger than most of us. She bound to feel a bit overawed."

"Sleep on it, John, then perhaps you can phone her in a couple of days," advised Dave. "You might be able to see her to talk things over and try to make sense of it all. She may have made a snap decision after seeing her old boyfriend after six months. She may be confused about everything. Things may go sour quite quickly, then she may feel more certain about her feelings for you. I could ask Kath to phone her if you like."

"Cheers, lads, but I don't think there's any point in phoning her back now. She sounded very keen about seeing her ex-boyfriend again, and very final about us. I'll try to get my head clear over the next few days, then maybe I'll phone her and see if she's having any second thoughts. At the very least, I should give her my home number in Preston, in case she changes her mind in the future. I still can't believe this has happened. It just feels like a fucking bad dream."

"Do you want a beer?" asked Dave.

"Yeah, why not?" I replied, "though getting pissed won't change anything."

Pete came out of the kitchen, carrying some drinks. "I'm sorry about before, John. I was a total dickhead, very insensitive. I know you cared a lot about Bluebell."

"Mary," I said, "don't fucking call her Bluebell. In fact, don't mention her name for the rest of the evening. If I have to move on, so be it. Now, haven't we got an England v Brazil match to look forward to?" I looked around the room and smiled, unconvincingly.

CHAPTER SIXTEEN
SUNDAY 7 JUNE

On Saturday I decided to phone Mary. Needless to say, the previous few days after her call had been hell for me. I had found it difficult focusing on anything apart from trying to understand why we had come to a sudden halt. OK, so I could see that Mary might still have feelings for an old flame, but for her to finish with me so abruptly seemed illogical, totally irrational. After all, we weren't just friends, but had been passionate lovers. I couldn't believe that she was prepared to throw away everything that we had between us just on a gamble that she might rekindle something better with a former lover. After three days of puzzling through all that she had said on the phone, it still did not make sense to me. Dave was a patient listener at this time. He repeated the possibility that Mary may have acted hastily, irrationally even, after seeing her ex-boyfriend again, and by now she may have had second thoughts. Why not try a phone call? What did I have to lose? After chatting things through with him several times, I decided to take his advice. My stomach was churning. I took a deep breath and phoned Mary's number.

The phone rang. Mrs Hodgson picked up the phone and said: "Hello."

"Hello, Mrs Hodgson, it's me, John," I gasped down the phone.

There was a slight pause, then she replied: "Mary does not want to speak to you ever again." She put the phone down.

I wandered back into the lounge. Dave did not speak. He didn't need to ask the question.

"Well, that was short and sweet," I sighed.

"What did she say?" Dave asked.

"Nothing. Her mother answered the phone. She told me that Mary doesn't want to speak to me. Not now, not ever."

There was nothing else I could do. I had considered trying to see Mary to ask her the question face to face, but I didn't know her address and could not remember exactly where she lived. I had only been to her house once, and it had been dark when I left. I might be able to find out her address from the phone book, but I could not just hang around in the street near her bus stop on the off chance of seeing Mary. If her parents saw me, they would probably have me arrested as a loiterer. It was now obvious that Mary had decided not to answer the phone, or had been told by her parents not to do so. I could not think of any other way of contacting her.

We were over.

There was a buzz in our house on Sunday, a buzz of anticipation shared by our friends along the street, and probably shared by the majority of the population. England had to face Brazil in the World Cup tonight.

We checked again with Andy to see if we would be welcome at his house, fully loaded, of course, with ample refreshments. He was fine with our request. The atmosphere in his house had been great at England's last match, and though we could have joined a larger crowd at one of the local pubs, we thought Andy's was the best option. After all, it wasn't far to crawl back home after the game.

Opinions were mixed about England's potential to win the match. We were World Champions after all, but had won the Cup in our own backyard in 1966. Brazil had all of the great individual players, like Pelé, Jairzinho, Rivelino and so on. Virtually all of their team were household names, and they all had outstanding skills and flair, but, some argued, England played more as a team. Furthermore, they stressed, England too had great players, like the two Bobbies, Charlton and Moore, but were they past their best? The doubters pressed on, this match is in Mexico, almost Brazil's backyard. England had it all to do. A few reminded the crowd that, even if England were to lose this match, we would still quality by beating Czechoslovakia in the final group game. Let's relax and enjoy the match!

As many had predicted, England did lose the match, but only by 1-0. There were some positives to take from this defeat. For most of the game, there was little to choose between the two teams. Gordon Banks, in goal for England, pulled off a truly memorable world-class save to keep out a header from Pelé which seemed certain to bulge the net. Andy's lounge erupted when that happened. In the end the English team was beaten by a superb strike from Jairzinho, but we had seen enough to be confident of winning the next match. We staggered the short distance home with plenty to discuss in the coming days and with most of our confidence still intact. We had lost a battle, but could still win the war. All was not over yet.

CHAPTER SEVENTEEN
SUNDAY 14 JUNE

University life was slowly winding down. Most students had finished their examinations, and were now packing and preparing to leave for their various destinations. The four of us decided to say on in Leeds until England's part in the World Cup was over. We did some packing, and spent our leisure time in saying our goodbyes to fellow students, exchanging addresses and phone numbers, making promises to meet up again soon. It was a time for reflection, and for anticipation.

Thursday evening saw England's last group match in the World Cup. After another tight match, England defeated Czechoslovakia 1-0 and we were in the quarter-finals. Our opponents were West Germany, the team we had defeated in the 1966 final. Most of us were confident that we could defeat them again.

This was the big one! Groups of us drifted to Andy's house during the afternoon and we were in good voice and good spirit when the game started. It was a warm day and all of the doors and windows in Andy's house had been opened. The atmosphere was noisy, smoky, smelly and tense. Gordon Banks, England's outstanding goalkeeper, perhaps the best in the world, was ill and could not play. Not a problem, most argued, as England had never lost a competitive match to West Germany, and Peter Bonnetti was an able replacement. The Germans had new stars, like Beckenbauer and the goal-hungry Muller, but we still had our famous names and several potential match winners. Wolfgang, our friendly German student, was with us again. He had supported England so far, but now found himself a quiet lone voice against the howling mob.

The match kicked off and for most of the first half the game was even, until, in the thirty-ninth minute, Alan Mullery scored for England. The room erupted. As the noise gradually subsided, I looked at Wolfgang and gave him a sympathetic smile. Soon it was half-time, and there was a sudden rush for the toilet. Many of us piled outside to get some fresh air, then pushed back inside to refill our drinks and settled down for the second half.

The consensus was that England needed a second goal to kill off the match. We hadn't long to wait. In the forty-ninth minute Martin Peters scored England's second goal and now we were on cloud nine. Wolfgang looked really glum. One of the pundits reminded the throng that England had never lost a match after being 2-0 up. We took heart, even though the Germans were pressing hard to get back into the match. The players were tiring in the searing heat in Mexico when, in the sixty-eighth minute Beckenbauer shot from distance and the ball somehow crept under Bonnetti's dive into the net.

"Jesus Christ," someone shouted, "Banks would never have let that one in." Many nodded or muttered in agreement. Wolfgang allowed himself a thin smile. Two minutes later, Bobby Charlton was substituted. There were howls of derision in the room.

"What the fuck is Ramsay doing?" Dave demanded.

"I guess he's saving Charlton for the semi-final," I suggested.

"Yeah," said Pete, looking worried, "but we haven't won this match yet."

After eighty-one minutes, Martin Peters was substituted to more howls of derision in the lounge then, almost immediately afterwards, Uwe Seeler somehow backheaded the ball into the top corner of England's net. West Germany were level at 2-2! We collectively held our breath until the final whistle was blown. The room emptied once more.

"That Ramsay, what a tosser," somebody remarked.

"Yeah, now we've got thirty minutes of extra time without two of our best players," another voice bemoaned.

I caught up with Wolfgang in the backyard. "I thought the match was over at 2-0," I shouted.

"So did I," he said, "but now only the strongest or the fittest side will win. Luck will now decide the result."

We felt almost as exhausted as the players as we trooped back into Andy's lounge. The confident atmosphere had vanished. Now we settled nervously to watch the remainder of the match. It was still a stalemate after fifteen minutes of extra time. We quickly grabbed another drink.

The action continued, then disaster! The ball was crossed into England's penalty area and there was Gerd Muller to smash the ball home. West Germany were leading 3-2, with little time to go. Wolfgang was grinning widely.

The tension was unbearable. As a group we were willing England to score an equaliser, but it never happened. The final whistle blew. Somehow England had snatched defeat from the jaws of victory. We couldn't believe what had happened. The inquest began at once, with lots of angry opinions being expressed, but nothing would change the result. England, the world champions, were out of the World Cup.

I shook hands with Wolfgang, then, with some others, helped Andy to put the rubbish into bags in the yard. We walked back to our house, drained and downhearted. There was little conversation. I went up to my room, and lay on my bed, thinking over the past few weeks.

My time at university was over. I wasn't sad about that, as I hadn't really enjoyed the course for the past two years. I was unsure about my future career, but I had plenty of time over the summer to decide what to do. I had developed some great friendships during my time at Leeds, but now we had to move on. I was sure that we would all keep in touch with each other in future years.

Football-wise, this season had been full of promise, but it had ended disastrously. Leeds United, in with a great chance of achieving a treble of league and cup victories, had fallen at each final hurdle and had won nothing. Preston North End, my hometown team, had been relegated again. As for England, well I thought it would be extremely difficult to retain the World Cup, but I was so bitterly disappointed at the way in which we were knocked out by West Germany. Next season had to be better, no matter which team I would be supporting.

As for Mary – that was most bitter pill to swallow. I had

found love and had it cruelly snatched away. What did I do wrong? I still could not understand how a romance so full of promise had been nipped in the bud the way it had. My head was so full of questions, but I could not find any answers. I was convinced that we both loved each other passionately. How could our love have turned so sour, so quickly? Whichever way I looked at the way we finished, it did not make sense. It probably never would.

I got off the bed and went downstairs to the hall. I phoned home. "Dad, Hi it's me. Did you watch the match? ... Yeah, it was a real bummer. I can't believe that we threw it away. Anyhow, I'm all packed and ready to come home. When can you collect me? ... Tuesday – yes that's fine. I'll be ready. Bye." I put the phone back on the hook, and looked around our lounge.

It was time to draw a line,

time to become a lotus-eater,

time to go home,

time to join the real world.

PART TWO
2012

CHAPTER EIGHTEEN
SATURDAY 28 APRIL

There are probably few more lovely or serene views in the world as the Southern Lakes of New Zealand. Beautiful in every season of the year, this area of the South Island attracts thousands of visitors from all over the world. On a calm day in autumn, the golden trees and brown landscapes fire the imagination of amateur and professional photographers alike.

I was sipping a beer at Gantley's Restaurant, taking in the majestic panorama of Lake Wakatipu and the Remarkable Mountains, which fold down to the water's edge. It was a beautiful sunny day, with barely a cloud in an azure blue sky. There was a slight chill in the air, but in such a magnificent setting, the temperature was easily forgotten. I took another sip of my beer and gazed again at the living landscape in front of my eyes.

"A penny for your thoughts," muttered my son Jason, putting an arm around my shoulder. "You look as if you're in a world of your own."

"Oh, I was just thinking how lucky I am to live in Queenstown, with such fantastic scenery and stunning views, free throughout the year. I just wish your mother had been here to share this day. We had so many plans for our retirement." My daughter Sally and her two children joined us on the terrace.

"Everything OK?" Sally asked, with a concerned look on her face.

“Fine, Sally,” I said, “just reminiscing. It’s a big day for me. It’s not every day of your life that you enjoy a retirement meal. I’m starting a new chapter of my life.”

“Come on, Dad.” Sally rubbed my back. “It’s not like you to get sad and philosophical.” By now, the rest of my family had joined us.

“Your business is in good hands with Jason, and you’ve told us that you have plans for the future. In fact, you promised to tell us after the meal what you intend to do next.”

“Yes, come on Grandad, tell us,” piped up Adam, Jason’s eldest son.

“Alright,” I smiled, “you’re right. I’ve kept you in suspense for long enough. Gather round, and I’ll spill the beans.” They all listened intently. “You already know some of my plans. First of all, I’m flying to Sydney with Sally & Co to stay for about a month. I’ve still got some friends from my days in the police force, and Nana and I had lots of friends when we lived in Australia. I’d like to catch up with as many as I can during my stay.”

“Then where?” Jodie quizzed me. She was Sally’s daughter.

“Well, then I’m going to fly from Sydney to Hong Kong.”

“Hong Kong,?” said Adam. “Why there, Grandad?”

“Years ago, I was a policeman there too. Hong Kong now belongs to China, but I still have a few ex-colleagues and friends living there, and I’d like to visit them. It will be interesting to see how the old colony has changed since the handover to China back in 1997. I’ll probably stay there for about a week."

"Australia, then Hong Kong," puzzled Ben, Sally's son. "Are you going around the world? Where next?"

"I'm going to fly from Hong Kong to the UK, back to my homeland where I spent the first part of my life. I'll stay with my brother or sister, or both, for a few weeks, and get to know their families. I've got other relatives and some old friends in England as well, so I intend to visit some of them. After that, I'm going for a walk."

""Going for a walk"," Jason gasped. "What on earth do you mean?"

I walked along the terrace. The others followed behind. "It's quite an unusual story," I grinned, "so you'll have to listen carefully." They all waited. I took a deep breath, then continued. "Many years ago, I was a student at university in England. When I was there, I had three close friends. In fact, we shared a house in a city called Leeds for about a year. My best friend from those days is called Dave. He became a teacher and lived near London for many years.

He's now retired, like me, and has moved back to the north of England, close to the town where he was born. I've only seen Dave and his wife Jenny two or three times over the past forty years, but I've completely lost touch with my other two friends, Mike and Pete. A couple of months ago, however, Dave emailed me to say that he has managed to track them down, and that they still live in England. Mike is now retired, but Pete runs a business. Luckily, Pete can take time off whenever he wants, so the four of us are going to meet up in July and we're going for a walk."

"Dad," Sally raised her arms, "surely you're not flying

halfway around the world just to go for a walk with a few friends you haven't seen for years?

"Of course not," I said, laughing heartily, "this is not going to be just a walk in the park, or something like that. In fact, it will be quite a long walk, right across northern England, coast to coast. It's a cross-country walk, over three hundred kilometres in length, and we're planning to take about three weeks in doing it."

"Where will you stay, Pop?" Leanne asked. She was Jason's wife.

"I'm not too sure, as Dave has arranged everything, but we won't be camping. I think we'll be staying in bed & breakfast cottages, farms, youth hostels, and so on."

"Youth hostels, Grandad!" Jodie exclaimed. "Do they allow old men to stay in them?"

"Yes, they do, Love," I said, smiling. The others laughed. "People of all ages use youth hostels these days."

"Dad," said Sally, "I know that you go out walking occasionally, but isn't that a long way for four men in their sixties?"

"Yes," said Jason, "and I guess there'll be a few mountains to climb along the way."

"OK, OK," I laughed, "but I'm not completely decrepit yet. I'm confident that I will be able to finish the walk. We'll be taking longer than many of the other walkers, and Dave has planned three rest days along the way. I'll be fine, don't you worry, and when I return in August I will be a lot fitter and a lot lighter!" The children giggled.

"I still can't help being a little concerned, Dad," Sally frowned. "What about your clothing and equipment, and everything else? What about the weather? Have you thought about all of that?"

"Of course I have," I reassured her. "I'm going to take my boots with me, as I'm used to them, but I will probably buy everything else I need in England. It's going to be mid-summer over there, so the weather oughtn't to be a problem. Dave's a keen walker, so he will have prepared the trip thoroughly. Don't worry, Sally, everything will be fine. Now," I continued, glancing at the Remarkables in the distance, "have you finished asking questions about my big adventure? It's starting to get a little chilly out here. Let's go back inside."

CHAPTER NINETEEN
FRIDAY 8 JUNE

I sat up and tidied my folding table as the pilot announced the plane's descent to Manchester. The flight from Hong Kong had been a lengthy one – over eleven hours – but I had slept for some of the journey and had also looked through "A Coast to Coast Walk", a book I had purchased on Amazon when I had been staying with Sally in Sydney. I had skimmed most of the book, as I knew that Dave would talk through our journey in great detail when the four of us met in St Bees, but I had read the section on Richmond several times. When Dave emailed me a few months ago he had mentioned that the walk passed through Richmond and that he intended to have a rest day there. Then, as now, my thoughts flashed back to that glorious spring day in 1970 when Mary and I had made love in the bluebell glade near the River Swale. The memory of our first passion was still very strong, but it was soured by the way our relationship had ended abruptly a few weeks later. Even now, over forty years later, I still found it difficult to accept, and understand, the reasoning behind Mary's decision to finish with me. I packed the book in my flight bag and pushed it under the seat in front of me.

During the past forty years, I had returned to England several times, mainly for family reasons. I had been in Preston for my brother's wedding, and had stayed in the city when my mother had become seriously ill. After she passed away, I stayed with my sister for a couple of weeks.

My father had died suddenly years before when I was in Hong Kong. Every time I returned to England Mary was there in my thoughts, even if I had travelled with my wife, Ailsa. The brief stays and the great distance between my home and my homeland helped me to push all memories of Mary to the back of my mind.

This time, however, it would be extremely difficult to stop thinking about her. The long walking days would provide me with lots of time to be lost in my own thoughts, and each step would take me that bit closer to Richmond, a town with precious memories for me. In many ways I was looking forward to the rest day we planned to have there, but would I be able to cope with it all? Perhaps it would be easy, as the weather might be totally different and I would not be alone. Yes, on reflection it seemed more likely that my time in Richmond would be an enjoyable step along our journey.

With my head buzzing with mixed thoughts about the coming weeks, I sat back and relaxed as the aircraft slowed and landed at Manchester Airport. Within an hour or so I would be on the train to Preston, where my brother Ian would be waiting for me at the station.

CHAPTER TWENTY
WEDNESDAY 4 JULY

The past month had been an enjoyable one for me. I had shared my stay between Ian's family, who still lived in Preston, and my sister Susan, who lived on her own in Poulton-le-Fylde, near Blackpool. It was good to spend some quality time with them, as most of my visits during the past forty years had just been fleeting stays. At the same time I had been able to catch up with a few of my old school friends from the city. I had wandered around the city centre several times, taking in the many changes that had occurred since I was a young man living there. The football season was over, however, so I hadn't been able to watch any of Preston North End's matches. As the month drew to a close, my thoughts turned ever more to meeting my old university friends and our planned Coast to Coast Walk. Needless to say, thoughts of Mary were increasingly at the back of my mind.

Dave had emailed me about a fortnight ago, sending me a list of the essentials that would be needed for our journey and giving me some directions for our reunion. He asked us to make our own way to St Bees and to meet in the café near the seafront. Once the four of us were together, Dave wanted to spend the afternoon discussing everything that would be involved with our "walk". Later on, he planned to take us to the B&B he had booked for the night, and we could then enjoy a few pints in one of the local pubs while we caught up with our lives during the past forty-odd years.

Our journey would begin on Thursday morning, 5th July!

I read Dave's list of essentials twice before shopping in Preston and Blackpool. I had only brought my tried-and-tested boots from New Zealand, together with an Australian traditional hat, but before long I had a strong rucksack loaded with spare clothing, toiletries, a small first-aid kit, a good waterproof, my guidebook, a water bottle and some snacks for the first few days. I also checked that I had charged and packed my mobile phone, camera and tablet, together with their charging leads. I thought the signal might be patchy or non-existent in parts of the journey, but I wanted to make sure that my family could contact me, and vice-versa, at regular intervals. During the ten days or so before I left Lancashire, I tramped along the country lanes near Preston to build up my strength and to get used again to carrying a pack. On two occasions I travelled to the Trough of Bowland to do some hill-walking. I felt in good shape by early July, and the weather forecast for the month was generally good.

I caught a morning train to Barrow-in-Furness, then changed for the West Coast train between Barrow and Carlisle. Just after lunch the train stopped at St Bees, a small town to the south of Whitehaven, and I alighted along with a few other passengers. I walked along the road that passed the ancient Priory, with the large imposing St Bees School to the right. A sign pointed me towards the beach, and I continued along the road. As a handful of people passed me walking towards town, I noticed another walker following about twenty paces behind me. I glanced at him a couple of times. He was taller than me, with a solid build and a bald head. As we neared the beach, he was close behind me and I looked at him again. Another Coaster, I thought, then his eyes and smile looked vaguely familiar. I stopped, and stared.

"Jesus Christ," I muttered to him, "it can't be ... Pete?"

"Yes, you ugly bastard, of course it's me. It's great to see you again, John." We hugged each other enthusiastically.

"Where have you travelled from?"

"Manchester. We were probably on the same train from Preston. Why are you speaking with that strange accent?"

"Oh, it's a long story, but I've lived in Australia and New Zealand for many years. I'll tell you more later on. Let's see if we can find the others."

We could see the café on a hillock near the beachfront, so we made our way there and opened the door. A few customers were browsing in the shop and some of the tables were occupied, but when I looked over towards the far window, I recognised Dave. We made our way to his table.

"Hey, mate, it's good to see you again." Dave stood up and I shook his hand. "Look what I found along the road." I ushered Pete towards him. The two hugged each other.

"Bloody Hell, Pete! After all these years," said Dave. "I don't know if I would have recognised you. You've put on a lot of timber and lost your hair!"

"You're no spring chicken," retorted Pete. "You've put on weight too and," looking round at me, "you've both got short grey hair."

"Well, it has been a long time," I said. We all laughed. "Let's get some coffee." I went over to the counter and ordered three coffees and some biscuits. I returned to our table.

"Mike shouldn't be too long," said Dave. "He lives near Durham now, so he's catching a train to Newcastle, then to Carlisle, then to here. He told me he'd be here by mid-afternoon."

"This is weird, surreal even," I said. "It only seems like yesterday that we were in Leeds taking final exams and watching football. Now we're almost pensioners and we're planning to walk about three hundred kilometres cross-country to the North Sea. Weird, really weird," I said, shaking my head.

"Two hundred miles, if you please," laughed Pete, "remember you're back in England now. We may have a decimal currency these days, but we've still got pints and miles."

We continued to make small talk until, just before three o'clock, a tall, wiry and bespectacled figure pushed open the café door. We all looked at him and in unison called "Mike." He gazed in our direction and waved. We stood up as he took off his pack and walked past the other tables to us. He shook hands vigorously with each of us, and the four of us stood with our arms around each other's shoulders.

"You haven't changed much," said Pete, looking Mike up and down, "still a skinny bogbrush with specs. I bet you still smoke as well."

"Sadly, I'm afraid I do," confessed Mike, "though not as much."

"Well," Dave said, as we sat down, "at least we've all arrived here safely. Now I can get started and tell you just what you've let yourselves in for." We ordered more coffees, and Dave dug into his rucksack for some sheets of paper. The drinks arrived. "I asked each of you to buy a 'Coast to Coast Walk' guidebook or to find out some details about it on the internet. I go out walking regularly, now that I'm living near the Lakes again, but I've only done a few sections of the Walk. I've modified the route to take account of our age and lack of experience, so we're going to take longer to complete the Walk than the guidebook suggests and we'll have three rest days along the way. All in all we'll be away for about three weeks. I've booked accommodation at a variety of hostels, farms and B&B's and here are all the details." He gave a sheet of paper to each of us. "As you can see, this sheet has the addresses and phone numbers of all of our overnight stays, plus the distance we're going to walk each day, and the emergency contact numbers you all sent me. Any questions so far?"

"Guess who became a school teacher?" joked Pete. We all laughed.

"Somebody's got to organise you old tossers," said Dave, pointing around the table. "Look, the main thing is that we want to enjoy ourselves, but we have to be prepared just in case something goes wrong."

"Agreed," Pete muttered, humbly. "Carry on, Dave."

"OK," said Dave, "here's a brief history of the Walk, and the itinerary I've put together for us." He pointed at the sheet. "This route was devised in the 1970's by Alfred Wainwright, who wrote a lot of walking guides for the Lake District."

"And elsewhere," Mike interrupted, holding up his hand apologetically.

"Quite," said Dave. "Anyway, Wainwright wanted to create a route across northern England that would pass through the National Parks, would use public rights of way, and would largely avoid towns and roads. He wasn't a very sociable bloke," Dave continued, looking around at us, "in fact I think he preferred sheep to people. He thought that an average walker could complete this trip in twelve days."

"Then why are we taking three weeks to do it?" Pete questioned.

"Simple," I butted in, "because we're not average walkers, and we're all old codgers." Laughter. Dave continued.

"We start here tomorrow morning," he pointed to the path on the headland to the north, "and the first week or so is going to be the toughest part of the journey. Parts of the Lake District section involve some steep climbs, that's why I've built in a rest day at Grasmere. After Shap, we'll have a few days of moorland walking, then we'll have another rest day at Kirkby Stephen. The following day we'll cross over the Pennines into Yorkshire and walk along Swaledale. Our final rest day will be at Richmond." He glanced at me. I looked away. "The last section ought to be easier, as we should be fit by then." He smiled at each of us. "We'll head for the North York Moors and finish the trip at Robin Hoods Bay, near Whitby. We'll celebrate with a few pints and the best fish and chips in the country. Any questions?"

"Have you paid for all of the accommodation, Dave?" I asked.

"No, just a deposit for each night. We can settle things up as we go along. You can pay for your own evening meals, that's if you want one every night. I think we'll be too knackered to think about food, especially for the first week or so. Let's play it by ear."

"Where's our B&B here?" Mike asked.

"Oh, it's just along the seafront," replied Dave. "We might as well go there now, dump our packs and go and find a good pub. We can have a meal and a pint before we have an early night. We need to be on our way by nine in the morning." We collected our rucksacks and left the café.

Later that evening, we were relaxing in a cosy pub after enjoying a hearty meal. Pete and I went to the bar and ordered a round of drinks. We returned to our table, and ordered some desserts from the waitress.

"So, here we are after over forty-odd years. Who's going to start first?" Pete asked.

"I guess it may as well be me," frowned Mike, "as I've probably had the most boring life and career since Leeds." We all nodded in agreement. "I've worked in the chemical industry for almost forty years, mostly in the UK but I have worked abroad as well. I won't bore you with details about the kind of work I did. For the past twenty-five years or so I was employed by I.C.I., and I have been based in Merseyside but more recently on the River Tees. That suited me because it brought me back to the North-East. Alison and I celebrated our Ruby Wedding earlier this year."

"Alison?" Dave queried, "wasn't she the one you met at

that party in Rotherham?" He looked around the table. "Remember, John, the one that was supposed to be fancy dress." I nodded humbly.

"The very same," Mike conceded.

"Have you any family?" I asked.

"Yes, five children."

"Five kids! Bloody Hell!" Pete gasped. "I didn't think you had it in you. Haven't you got any hobbies?" Laughter.

"Yeah, we've got three sons and two daughters. Two of them are doctors, and the others have done well. Two of them still live at home. Alison and I live in a large modern house on the outskirts of Durham. I retired about three years ago."

"Well done, Mike," applauded Pete, "you've done really well, but I thought you might have changed your hairstyle!"

"It's impossible," Mike shrugged his shoulders, "my hair's always been curly, and now it's grey. How about you, Dave?"

"Do you remember Katherine? Well, it didn't work out with her. I did a teaching course after university and met my wife, Jenny. She's a southerner, and after qualification we both got jobs near London. We've moved around a fair bit, and we just have one son. He's a teacher as well."

"So why have you moved back to Kendal?" I looked at him. "When Ailsa and I visited you over ten years ago you seemed settled in the South."

"Jenny loves the North, and we often went on holiday in the Lake District or in Scotland. We both enjoy walking. I finished up as a deputy head, and a year or so after I retired we moved to a house in Kendal. Jenny likes Kendal because it is close to the Lakes and the motorway, and it has a good range of shops. James, my son, still teaches in the South. He lives with his partner, but they have no children." He sat back and relaxed in his seat. "How about you, Pete?"

"I think my career has been very different to yours," he moved forward, and had a drink of his beer. We were all eating our desserts, and listening. Pete itched his bald head, and continued. "Like you, Dave, I did a teaching course, only at Manchester, not Leeds. After that I taught for a couple of years at Salford, but I decided that teaching wasn't for me."

"Why was that?" Mike asked.

"Well, if you remember, I was a good-looking bloke in those days."

"'Was' being the operative word," I quipped.

"Thank you," Pete said facetiously. "Anyway, I had one or two girlfriends," he grinned.

"One or two hundred," Dave said. The rest of us nodded in agreement.

"Whatever," Pete said, philosophically, "but it didn't work in a teaching situation. Most of the younger, and some of the married female staff wanted me to shag them, and the senior girl pupils were forever drooling over me and trying to find out where I was going out at night. I know I'm not much to look at these days," he pointed to his belly and his bald head, "but then it was like being hunted. The women were too predatory, believe me. Nowadays, I wouldn't mind a bit of female company."

"There must be a few available short-sighted women with dementia!" Dave suggested. We grinned.

"Cheers," said Pete. "Anyway, I packed up teaching and got involved in the world of antiques. My Dad dabbled a bit, and I learnt a lot from him. In the seventies furniture and pottery were in big demand, and I travelled around, buying and selling at antique fairs. Later on I built up my knowledge on a wider range of collectables, and I opened a couple of shops in Manchester. I also shipped container loads of antiques to the States. I suppose that my good looks helped at that time. I bought all kinds of things from the ladies."

"A bit like Lovejoy on the telly?" Mike asked. Pete laughed.

"Maybe. Anyway, I made a decent living out of it for a lot of years. By the nineties, the internet was becoming more important and so I gradually wound down my shops. I still have one base in Manchester, and I employ a few people who sell a shedload of things on eBay for me. I like it. It still gives me a buzz, travelling around buying and selling, going to auctions and such, and I'm not tied. I can go on long walks whenever I want!" He smiled widely at us all. "Oh, I almost forgot. I've never been married, and as far as I know, I haven't got any children. I have lived with three different women, I think, but I just couldn't settle down. Perhaps I haven't met the right woman for me. I'm not seeing anyone at the moment," he frowned.

"Jesus, Pete," I said, "I expected you to tell us that you've been married several times and have a whole brood of kids. You sound a bit lonely to me."

"I am sometimes," he admitted. "Not to worry. Now, we need some more drinks before we listen to your story – the globetrotter. I've just thought – where are your specs?"

"I started wearing contact lenses soon after I left university," I laughed. "I sometimes wear my glasses in the evening, but not every day."

Dave and Mike walked to the bar, then it was my turn when they returned.

"I don't know if you can remember," I started, "but when we finished university I was in the doldrums. I hadn't enjoyed the last year or more of the course, and didn't do well in my final exams. The football that season was a disaster – I still can't believe that England threw away that match to West Germany, and Leeds ended up with nothing. Then to cap it all Mary finished with me, just before the end of term."

"That's right," exclaimed Pete, "I do remember that. Mary... that blonde girl, I called her 'Bluebell', right?"

"Yes," Dave interrupted before I could reply, "it all really got going on the day we went to Richmond, didn't it?"

"Richmond?" Mike asked, "aren't we passing through there on this trip?"

"OK, give me a break," I said, "let me get back to my story." The others nodded and relaxed in their seats. "Right, so I was in a mess when I left Leeds. I didn't fancy a teaching career, but nothing else seem to appeal at the time, so I just went home to Preston. I got a casual job to earn a little money. I was drifting, then I decided to visit my relatives in Hong Kong and see if I could clear my mind."

"Hong Kong?" Pete spluttered, halfway through a drink, "that's a bloody long way to go just to think."

"Yes, I suppose it was but my uncle had a top job in the shipyard there and had always spoke about the good colonial lifestyle his family enjoyed. He always said I was welcome to visit, so I flew out towards Christmas in 1970. Well, to cut a long story short, I walked into a good job in the police force there and stayed in the colony for over eight years. Then I met Ailsa, an Aussie schoolteacher from Sydney. She was on holiday with a friend and I kept in touch with her and eventually moved to Australia. I transferred to the New South Wales police force, and Ailsa and I married in 1980. We visited New Zealand on holiday a couple of times and loved it, so we moved there when I was fifty in 1998. I set up a security company – burglar alarms, et cetera – in Queenstown. We have two kids. My daughter stayed in Sydney, but my son came to New Zealand and when I retired in April he took over the running of the company." I took a swallow of my beer.

"And Ailsa, how is she?" Mike asked.

"I'm afraid she contracted breast cancer. They operated, but the cancer was too advanced and she died in 2005."

"Jesus, I'm sorry, mate," Mike shook his head. The others smiled sympathetically. The conversation fell silent.

"Well," said Dave, "I think that on that note we should finish our drinks and get to bed. We have an early start in the morning and so a good night's sleep is recommended. Have any of you any questions before we head for the B&B?" The rest of us shook our heads.

"No, Colonel," Mike saluted, smiling.

"OK, then, let's go."

I slept soundly that night, but only after reminiscing about Mary and our time together. The mention of "Bluebell" and Richmond earlier in the evening had touched a nerve, and it took a little while to completely clear my mind. I forced myself to think about the day ahead and eventually fell into a deep sleep, despite Pete snoring like a pig in the other bed in the room!

CHAPTER TWENTY-ONE
FRIDAY 6 JULY

It was mid-afternoon and drizzling lightly as Pete and I trekked along a forest path in the Ennerdale valley. I glanced down through the trees towards the river but couldn't see any sign of Dave and Mike, who had decided to find their own way along the river bank. I spotted a bullfinch sitting on a branch and pointed it out to Pete. He just nodded and continued plodding along, his head down. A heron had flown lazily along the river earlier, and Pete had shown little interest then. He was grimacing a little as he walked along. I guessed that his boots were not comfortable. It was only our second day, but Pete was already struggling.

We had all been in good spirits at St Bees yesterday morning. There was a low sea-mist as we left our B&B and walked down towards the shore.

"This isn't the path, is it?" Mike enquired.

"No," said Dave, "but we have a little ceremony to do before we start our journey." He walked onto the sand and found a small pool. He dug around and pulled out a small pebble. "This is what you need to find, lads," he said. "It's a sort of tradition that you take a pebble from the shore here, carry it with you on the walk and throw it in the sea at Robin Hoods Bay. Come on, get on with it." We each found a small stone, and made our way towards the headland. The path was muddy after the spring rain and we said little as we walked along the coastal path. The mist began to thin out after we had covered a couple of miles. Foxgloves were dotted along our way, and we could hear the screeching of hundreds of seabirds on the nearby cliffs. Pete paused at one point, and I could hear sounds of him retching as we continued along the path.

"Are you OK?" I asked, as he caught up with me.

"Yeah, good," he muttered. "I guess I'm not used to eating a full breakfast on top of a few pints," he grinned.

We passed by St Bees lighthouse, and saw a panorama of Whitehaven as we left the coastal path and headed into the countryside. The walking was easy, with just one tricky marshy section to negotiate. We had a laugh when Pete, desperate for a crap, squatted by a stream and got almost caught out by a small group of ladies out on a ramble. At Moor Row we had a pleasant break when we found a baker's that sold delicious pies and beakers of tea! We continued through the village of Cleator towards a feature that Wainwright called "a small hill" – Dent Fell. We had walked over ten miles by this point and this very steep hill was challenging. We rested at the cairn on the top, unable to appreciate the view because the mist had descended again. We found our path then carefully made our way down the very steep descent on the other side. We were all tiring by this stage, but Pete was really struggling. It started to rain as we trudged along the valley, and eventually reached the farm for our overnight stay. Pete was so knackered that we almost had to carry him in.

It always amazes me how a cup of tea, a hot shower and a sound night's sleep can revive tired limbs. Pete was like Lazarus the following morning as he demolished a full English breakfast. His spirits were also lifted when he found out that there were two companies which used minibuses to transport any excess baggage to your next B&B. He quickly arranged for most of his pack to be sent to Borrowdale.

We walked down a country lane to Ennerdale Bridge, then carried on to the lake. Dave and Mike opted to tackle the more demanding route along the south shore of the lake, while Pete and I chose the easier northern path. We tested our mobiles, so that we could rendezvous later. As the forest thinned out, we could see Black Sail Hut in the distance up the valley. We put on our waterproofs while we waited for Dave and Mike to join us.

"How are your feet?" I gestured towards Pete's boots.

"A bit sore. I haven't worn these boots for years."

"Not to worry," I reassured him, "we haven't too far to go now."

About forty minutes later, we saw Dave and Mike emerging from the woods. "The weather's worsening," Dave said, looking at some dark clouds over Great Gable at the head of the valley. "Luckily we haven't far to go. Black Sail's supposed to be a great place. Let's go."

We carried on and reached the remote Youth Hostel as it began raining more steadily. The warden greeted us and showed us around the small hostel, which only slept sixteen people. The other guests were already there. We chose a bunk, and I told Pete to check out his feet. Mike had a quick smoke outside.

"Christ, they look sore," I pointed at the blisters on the bottom of each foot. "Have a word with Dave and get some plasters on them."

"Yes, I think I better get something on them. I'll be OK when I've worn my boots for a few more days," Pete said.

We were relaxing in the common room, waiting for the warden and his partner to prepare an evening meal – a curry, which pleased all of us – and we were enjoying a beer while we waited. I looked out of the door. Low cloud filled the valley, and it was pouring down. Two brightly-coloured specks appeared in the distance. "What the hell are those?" I asked, pointed along the valley. The others came to the doorway. The specks, yellow and pink, grew bigger and bigger as they neared the hostel. Before too long, the specks arrived at the hut.

"Hello," the pink speck spoke with a foreign accent, "are we near Keswick?"

"Hell, no," said Dave, "you're walking in the opposite direction. Where are you from?"

"We are on holiday from Prague." The two men were dressed in ponchos and sandals. "Can we stay here?" At that point the warden came to the door.

"I'm sorry," he said, "we're full. There's another hostel four miles down the valley. They will have room there." The two Czechs grimaced, then continued on their way. We all laughed when they were almost out of sight.

"Poor bastards," Pete remarked. "They haven't got a clue. Ponchos and sandals – I can't believe it!" We all laughed as we settled down for our meal.

CHAPTER TWENTY-TWO
SUNDAY 8 JULY

It was a warm, sunny morning as we walked steadily up the valley from Stonethwaite, a hamlet in Borrowdale. From time to time we paused for a breather, and turned to admire the beauty of the Borrowdale valley far below us. As we slowly skirted around Eagle Crag we lost sight of Borrowdale and focused our attention on Lining Crag towering ahead of us. At the base of the crag is a steep stony gully, and we carefully climbed our way to the top. Exhausted, we made our way to the scattered viewpoint on the top of the crag and found some comfortable rocks to sit on. We loosened our packs, and had a drink of water. Other walkers were already there, enjoying the wide panorama on a beautiful day. We stood up and took a variety of views on our cameras. Several women were sitting together, and Pete went over and asked one of them to take a group photo. She chose one or two different angles, returned the camera to Pete and continued chatting to him. One of the other women called to her and they made preparations to leave.

"Small world," said Pete, as he returned to our rocks, "those women are from Bolton, not far from me. They're doing the walk as well."

"Let's make a move," said Dave, pointing to the route ahead. "We've got a marshy section to get through, then we have a choice of routes to Grasmere. Let's go." He tucked his guidebook into his pack.

We carried on and carefully picked our way through the boggy fell until we reached the pass between Borrowdale and Grasmere.

"You can almost see Grasmere in the distance," Dave pointed. "There are several routes from here, but our two main choices are these. We can either go down the valley path, which is easier, or go on a ridge walk across to Helm Crag, which is more challenging but more interesting. Thorney Howe Hostel, where we will be staying for the next two nights, is on the edge of Grasmere and easy to find. You don't need to go into the village. Which route do you fancy?"

We had a short discussion. Pete voted for the valley path, but the rest of us chose the ridge walk.

"Check your mobiles," Dave instructed. "You'll probably be at the hostel before us, Pete, so get the drinks in."

"OK, boys," Pete said, "it looks as if that group of women is taking the valley path. I might tag along with them. See you later. Good Luck."

"Be careful, Pete," I shouted to him as he walked away. He turned and gave the thumbs up.

It was raining as we made the stony descent from Helm Crag and looked for the path which led to the hostel. I felt tired as we neared the hostel, and I was looking forward to a hot shower, a meal and a pint. We signed in, dumped our packs in our room and searched for Pete. He was in the lounge with the group of women from Bolton. One of them had a bandaged foot. We said Hello and joined them.

“Hi Pete. How are your feet?” Mike asked.

“Still a bit sore. I haven’t looked at my blisters yet. We’ve a day off tomorrow, haven’t we, so I might be able to get some better plasters in the village. How was the ridge walk?”

“Good,” I replied, “but quite exhausting. The path down from Helm Crag was a bit dodgy.”

Dave left the room and returned a few minutes later. “I’ve checked with the warden,” he said. “We can get a meal here and some drinks, and the warden is showing a film later. We have our first rest day here in Grasmere tomorrow, so I suggest that we relax here and have an early night. The forecast is good for tomorrow, so we’ll have a choice of things to do. Agreed?”

We all nodded our heads and left the lounge to get changed.

CHAPTER TWENTY-THREE
MONDAY 9 JULY

We woke up to bright sunshine, showered and headed for the dining room. A few of the guests were already there, having an early breakfast before setting off on their travels. It was buffet-style, so we each filled a plate then sat down to discuss how to spend our day. It soon became obvious that we would not spend it as a group.

"I haven't been to the Lake District for so long," I started the discussion, "that I fancy just being a tourist for the day. I think I'll take the bus to Ambleside, then catch a steamer to Lakeside and back to Bowness-on-Windermere. I can get a bus back to Grasmere from there."

"That sounds good to me, John," said Mike. "I don't really know the Lakes at all, so if I like the places we see, I may bring Alison here for a weekend."

"I'm going to stay in Grasmere," muttered Pete. "I don't want to do too much walking and I want to buy some better plasters or bandages in the village. There'll be enough here to keep me occupied for the day."

"In that case, I'll stay here too," said Dave. "I'll go with you to the chemist's and make sure that you'll be OK for the next few days' walking. After that, if the weather holds, I'll probably go for a walk to Easedale Tarn. It's not far, and I haven't been there before."

Mike and I walked the short distance to Grasmere, then waited for the bus to Ambleside. It was an open-topped bus, and we enjoyed the views as we travelled along the lanes to Ambleside. We got off at Waterhead and bought day tickets for our journey on the Lakes steamer.

The weather was sunny and warm, so were able to enjoy the distant views of the Lakeland Fells, as well as peering at some of the expensive houses with a lake frontage. We stayed for a short time at Lakeside, then caught the next steamer to Bowness, and joined the throngs of people in the busy resort.

"Christ, it's like Blackpool here," I called to Mike as we pushed our way along the crowded streets near the lake. "Let's get away from the front and have a drink."

"Good idea," agreed Mike. We soon found ourselves a table outside a pub in the old town, and ordered a sandwich and a pint. "This is the life," mused Mike, enjoying a cigarette.

"Yes, but don't get too used to it," I advised, "as we've got more strenuous walking to do tomorrow."

"Hmm, I almost forgot."

We wandered back to the main street and made our way up the hill. There were fewer people and shops here, but we paused to purchase a few light souvenirs for our families. A suitcase in a charity shop caught my eye.

"Hey, Mike, let's buy that suitcase. We can use that to send all of our excess baggage to our next overnight stop. The four of us can share it, so it will be cheaper in the long run."

We made the purchase, then caught a bus back to Grasmere.

It was late afternoon by the time we returned to Grasmere. We wandered around the village, looking at the pretty cottages and taking photos at the Wordsworth family grave in Grasmere churchyard. We still had time to go into a couple of the shops, and Mike bought some cosmetics for Alison. "This will prove that I hadn't forgotten about her," he joked, as he puffed on another cigarette.

We sauntered back to the hostel and freshened up. There was no sign of Dave or Pete, so we just sat in the lounge and flicked through some of the magazines. Before long, Dave joined us.

"Hi, Dave," I glanced at him, "have you had a good day?"

"Excellent, thanks, it was beautiful by the tarn. Lots of people were out walking today. How did the two of you get on?"

"Good. We've been on the Lake Windermere steamer, done a little shopping and visited Wordsworth's grave in Grasmere Church. Oh, and we bought a suitcase in a charity shop in Bowness. We thought it would be useful for sending on our surplus gear each day."

"Fine. It will be better that the old rucksack we've been using. Have you seen Pete?"

"Not since breakfast. How about you?"

"I went into the village with him and he bought some cushion bandages that might help his blisters. His feet are in a bit of a mess. He obviously did very little training for this trip."

A short time later Pete came to the lounge. He was accompanied by the woman from the Bolton group, the one who had her foot bandaged. He smiled at her and she walked back towards the dormitories. "Hi, Pete, are you up to your old tricks again?" Mike asked, smiling.

"Hi guys," Pete said, sitting down near us. "Have you enjoyed the day?"

"Yes," I nodded, "how about you? I see that you've had some company."

"She's called Karen." He paused. "Look, mates, I think you know what I'm going to say." He took a deep breath, and looked at each of us in turn. "I'm not up to this trip. I've been struggling since the start, and it's all my fault. Dave told me that I needed to do some regular walking and to wear my boots as often as I could, but I ignored his advice and just thought that everything would be OK on this walk. I didn't think it would be as demanding as it has been or that I would get blistered feet so quickly. I can only think that my blisters will get worse the more walking I do, and that sooner or later I will have to drop out. I can get back to Manchester fairly easily from here, but it will be impossible if I have problems in the middle of nowhere. I'm sorry, but I think it's for the best. I can cancel all of my bookings tomorrow," he said, turning to Dave. "Thanks for all of the hard work and preparation that you've put in."

"How much of this is to do with Karen, Pete?" Dave asked, angrily. "Surely you're not giving up on this trip just for another shag?"

"No, no, honestly I'm really gutted to have to do this. It's really been great to meet up with you all again. It's made me think a lot about my life and how much I've missed over the last forty years. You've all got families who love you, and I have nothing apart from a sackful of fleeting memories of relationships that didn't last. Look at me, I'm a fat bald mess, but I do want to keep in touch with you all and to meet up again regularly. Our friendship is still solid after all these years."

"So where does Karen fit into all of this, Pete?" I said.

"I've got on great with her. We've really clicked, and I hope it won't be a flash in the pan. We talked for hours on the way to Grasmere, and again today. She slightly twisted her ankle yesterday, so her friends have carried on to Patterdale. She thought that a rest day might help her, but her ankle is more painful today. She's phoned them to say that she can't carry on. We're going to travel back home together. She's divorced and has three grown-up children. Who knows, perhaps I'll become a family man after all? Perhaps that is what I've needed for a long time." He looked around at us again.

"I don't know what to say, Pete," muttered Mike. "It has been great to rekindle our friendship and it would have been nice to finish this challenge together, but I know you've been struggling to keep up. What do you think, John?"

"Let's be realistic about this. We're not young any more, not even middle-aged, and if Pete does carry on he may cripple himself for life. No amount of friendship or pride is worth that. As Pete says, we have got on well and I'm gutted to think that he has to drop out, but it's probably the sensible thing to do. But like you, Pete, I would like to meet up whenever we can, even if it means flying back from New Zealand. Come to think of it, why don't you all fly over to New Zealand and have a holiday in my backyard?"

"Let's get this one over first," Dave said. "We're down to three now. The others are right, Pete, you're probably right to leave now. I'm just very disappointed, not in you, but because I was really looking forward to the four of us making this trip together. I wish you luck with Karen, but with your track record ... "

"Come on," Mike said, standing up, "I need a fag. At least we're still friends, and I think it's time we had something to eat and a few drinks. Let's make this evening a celebration of our friendship, and bring Karen along, Pete. We might as well get to know her, before she ditches you!" We all laughed.

CHAPTER TWENTY-FOUR
TUESDAY 10 JULY

We had an enjoyable last evening at the hostel in Grasmere. The atmosphere was very relaxed and we focused mainly on the happy times we remembered in Leeds. We probably had too much to drink, given the fact that we had to be up early to continue on our way to Patterdale. Pete and Karen planned to catch a bus to Windermere, then to take a train south to Lancashire. They lived only ten miles away from each other.

Karen mixed very well. She was attractive, in her early fifties and a good conversationalist. She, like Pete, seemed to be genuinely gutted about having to abandon her walk. She and her friends had been planning their attempt on the Coast to Coast Walk for several years, and now it was unlikely that she would have another go at doing it.

"Look on the bright side," Dave remarked at one point, "you've met each other by chance, you seem to get on well with each other and you have plenty of free time. Lick your wounds, get plenty of practice walking in the Pennines near your homes, feel comfortable with your boots, then you can try the walk again next year, or the year after that."

"Nice idea," replied Pete, "but the main motivation for me was the four of us meeting after all the years apart and getting to know each other again. Please don't think I wouldn't enjoy walking with you, Karen," he smiled at her, "but there are lots of other things I would prefer to do with you."

"I think you said the important thing earlier on, Pete," said Mike, "in that we should keep in contact with each other. We've all got on well so far, we have more free time now, so as long as our partners get on with each other we have no excuses for not meeting up from time to time. Oh, sorry John, I forgot for a moment that you don't have a partner."

"And I don't live in England," I reminded him. "That's not to say that I won't be in England in the future. I still have a lot of family here, I have our renewed friendship and who knows, I may find a partner before too long. If Pete can manage it, with his paunch and polished head, there must be hope for me." Laughter. "Apologies, Karen, I'm only joking."

"Don't worry, John, I'm no fool. It's pretty obvious that Pete has seen better days!" We all laughed again.

We left early on this morning without seeing Pete and Karen. We had said our goodbyes the night before, with promises to meet up again soon and reflect on our walking experience. Despite losing Pete, the three of us were in good spirits and were looking forward to the rest of the walk. Ahead of us lay two more days of walking and climbing in Lakeland, with overnight stays at Patterdale and Bampton. We were feeling fitter now, and anticipated reaching the high point of our journey at Kidsty Pike on Wednesday afternoon. The Westmorland Fells, a less interesting section of the walk, faced us later in the week, before our next planned rest day in Kirkby Stephen, only a day's walk away from the halfway mark of the journey!

CHAPTER TWENTY-FIVE
FRIDAY 13 JULY

It was a bright, sunny day and the sun was beating down upon us as we descended the fell from Orton Scar. As we neared a gate, we heard an awful screaming sound and we hurried to determine the cause. Mike opened the gate and we saw a large spaniel which had caught a rabbit. The rabbit was in obvious pain and when we managed to take it from the spaniel's jaw, we realised that the poor animal's back was broken. I kept the dog at bay while Dave put the rabbit out of its misery by bashing it against the wall. The dog's owner appeared, showing little interest in what had happened and he turned and led the dog away from the scene. Then the screaming continued. We moved towards the wall, and saw a terrified baby rabbit, which quickly disappeared into a hole running under the wall.

"Poor devil," I exclaimed, "it has little chance of survival."

"Well let's hope that what we've just witnessed is our bad luck for the day – it is Friday 13th after all," Mike said, looking sad.

We continued down the fell to Sunbiggin Tarn, along some moorland to more fields of ancient settlements, then made the steep descent to the picturesque Smardale Bridge. The weather was quite hot by now. We rested and had our lunch, then Mike said: "I'm going in." He gingerly found a way through some brambles to the water's edge, stripped off and prepared to swim under the bridge.

"Bloody Hell!" I exclaimed, glancing at Mike's wedding tackle. "That looks like the last turkey in the shop!" Dave laughed, as Mike splashed around in the water.

"That's better," he shouted, "it's much cooler in here." Dave and I took some photos for posterity.

"Enjoy it while you can," I called to him, "there's a group of walkers coming down the hill." Mike quickly climbed out of the beck and dried himself on his t-shirt. He put the rest of his clothes on and strolled out from behind the bridge, trying to look nonchalant.

"Hello," we smiled at the walkers as they arrived at the old pack-horse bridge. "Warm, isn't it?" The group, mainly middle-aged women, nodded in agreement as they rested and had a drink.

"Are you on the Coast to Coast?" I asked one of the ladies.

"Yes, we're heading for Kirkby Stephen. Are you Australian?"

"No, but I did live there for some years. I'm actually from Preston. Oh, I think we're leaving," I said as Dave and Mike made their way up the hill. "Enjoy the rest of the day."

"Bye." One or two of the group raised their hands in farewell.

"That looks impressive," I gasped as I caught the others up, "over there." I pointed to the east.

"That's the Smardale Viaduct," Dave informed us. "We're in the middle of nowhere and yet there it is - a testament to superb Victorian engineering. There must have been some kind of mineral railway around here."

Several miles of gentler walking brought us to the outskirts of Kirkby Stephen, a small market town where Dave had booked accommodation for two nights. "We're going to stay in an old chapel," he announced. "It's been converted into a hostel. We'll dump our bags, take a shower then have a look around. There must be one or two decent pubs here where we can get a meal and a pint."

He was right. We soon found a hotel near the hostel, ate a hearty meal and enjoyed a few drinks. It was a relaxing evening, as we were in no hurry to get up the following morning. Tomorrow was to be a rest day, and we were going to enjoy it!

CHAPTER TWENTY-SIX
SATURDAY 14 JULY

The hostel was almost deserted by the time we all surfaced in the morning. I had slept well in my bunk bed in the dormitory. We freshened up and went downstairs to have breakfast. I peered outside the door - the weather looked fine. I prepared a bowl of cereals and a coffee and sat down with the others.

"I'm looking forward to a relaxing day here. Our rest day at Grasmere was quite hectic, but today there will be little to do apart from window-shopping, eating, having a few pints, and perhaps taking a short walk around the town. What do you reckon?"

"Yeah," Mike drawled. Neither of them looked interested.

"There doesn't seem much here," mused Dave. "Perhaps I should have forgotten about a rest day here and had two days at Richmond instead?"

"No," I said, "I think this place has more to offer than meets the eye. When we've cleaned up here, shall we..." I was interrupted by Dave's mobile.

"Hello ... Oh, hi Pete. Good to hear from you ... How are your feet? ... Good ... Is it still on with Karen? ... Excellent. I'm pleased for you. Perhaps this one is for keeps ... Really?" He laughed loudly. "Right, well keep in touch and we hope to see you again soon ... Bye." He turned to us. "That was a nice surprise. Pete's feet are healing, and he's still seeing Karen. Who knows?"

"Great," said Mike. We continued tidying the kitchen. The side door suddenly opened.

"SURPRISE!!" shouted Pete and Karen, followed by two other women. Dave grinned and hugged one of them, and I realised that it was Jenny, his wife. I hadn't seen her for over eight years. I didn't recognise the other lady, who was quite plump with shoulder-length, dark hair. She smiled in my direction, then Mike walked towards her and kissed her on the cheek.

"Alison?" I smiled at her.

"Yes, of course, it's good to see you again, John."

"God, it must be over forty years since we last met."

"And the rest. How are you? How are all of you?" she asked, looking around at the three of us.

"We're fine, really good," answered Dave. "What the hell are you all doing here?" he demanded. We laughed.

"This is all down to me," confessed Pete. "I felt so bad in having to quit the walk that I contacted Alison and Jenny and planned this little surprise. We thought it would be nice if you had some company on your rest day. I hope you don't mind, John."

"Not at all. It's great to see you all," I said, secretly thinking that it would have been nicer, no fantastic even, if Mary had walked through the door behind them. I quickly put that fantasy to the back of my mind then, stretching my arms above my head, said: "Well, we'd better decide a plan of action, folks. What are we going to do today?"

Later that morning we sat around two tables in a local

café, enjoying a coffee. We planned to have a meal in the afternoon about four o'clock. I sat next to Alison. "You're looking well," I smiled at her.

"Thank you," she said, "and you're looking pretty good as well." She glanced at my hair. "A little greyer than I remember, John." I grinned, and nodded.

"I'm afraid so. I must have had a heavy paper round." Alison smiled. "Mike told us that you have five children. They must have kept you busy over the years."

"Yes, of course," she laughed, pointing at her waist, "and altered my figure. I'm no longer the sylph-like girl you used to know in Leeds. Mike told me that you now live in New Zealand?"

"That's right, in Queenstown, and I have two children."

"But your wife's dead?"

"Yes, nearly seven years ago. She had cancer."

"I'm really sorry, John. She was too young." I nodded. She paused, and frowned. "When we last met, in 1970, you were with the blonde girl... Mary, I think. Mike said that you broke up soon after that. Why was that? You seemed perfect for each other."

"That's what I thought, Alison. Do you remember when all of us went out for a meal, just before the end of term? That was the last time I saw you. It was also the last time I saw her. A few days later she phoned me to say that an ex-boyfriend had turned up and that she still loved him. She also said that as I didn't know what I would be doing or where I would be after university, she wanted to finish with me. I was absolutely gutted. I thought we had so much together. I couldn't understand how our relationship could end that way. I still can't. It still haunts me, to be honest."

"Have you seen or heard from her since?" I shook my head. "Do you know what has happened to her?"

"No, but it would be interesting to know. I've thought about her many times over the past forty years."

"Well, there are ways these days of finding out. You know, the internet, etc." I nodded, and looked thoughtful.

"Come on you two, we've all finished," said Mike. "What have you found that's so interesting to discuss?"

"Nothing, Mike," I quickly answered, "just memories."

I have to confess that, despite feeling like a gooseberry, I really enjoyed the change of company. It was nice to catch up with Jenny, to renew my friendship with Alison and to have some different conversations. Pete and Karen looked a genuine couple, and it felt like old times, with solid friendships and compatible partners. Only one piece of the jigsaw was missing. Would I ever find it?

We parted after our afternoon meal. Alison drove east to Durham, while Pete and Karen gave Jenny a lift to Kendal, before heading south to Manchester. Dave, Mike and I headed for the pub.

CHAPTER TWENTY-SEVEN
SUNDAY 15 JULY

It was another fine day. Leaving Kirkby Stephen, we crossed the river to the village of Hartley, then climbed steadily up to Nine Standards Rigg, the impressive cairns on the Pennine watershed. We had a snack and posed for photos, then made our way through a dangerous section of peat bogs before making a gradual descent towards Keld in the early afternoon. Finally we reached Ravenseat, the first sign of civilisation since we had crossed into Yorkshire.

"This looks interesting," mused Mike, as we looked along the narrow tarmac road to the small cluster of farm buildings in the distance. There were arty signs warning of "Free Range Children" and advertising afternoon teas on the roadside. We decided to investigate. We walked down the road and crossed the bridge to the tiny settlement. Two or three children were playing around the farmyard. Some picnic tables were arranged on an area of grass. I walked to the farmhouse and clanged a small bell. A tall young blonde lady appeared.

"Hello. Can we have a pot of tea and..?" I raised my arms.

"Scones?" she said, smiling. "I've just made a fresh batch. Would you like some jam with them? "

"Brilliant," we said in unison.

"Find a seat," she said, pointing at the tables.

We sat at one of the picnic tables. A peacock was pecking around the yard. Two chaffinches flew onto the wall in anticipation of a few crumbs.

"This is great," said Dave. "An unexpected treat."

"Yeah," Mike said, lighting up a cigarette, "a bit surreal though. We've just spent hours up to our knees in peat bogs, and now we're having tea, scones and jam. It's nice, but weird." We relaxed in the sunshine and took a few photos.

Before long the blonde lady reappeared with a tray laden with crockery, a teapot and jam and scones. We busied ourselves in demolishing the scones and drinking cups of tea. The chaffinches hopped onto the table, then flew off with a crumb of scone.

"They must be the best-fed birds in Yorkshire," joked Dave.

"It's really relaxing here," I said.

"Quite," answered Dave, "but it's not going to get us to Keld. We're going to seize up if we stay here much longer." He stood up and carried the tray back to the farmhouse. When he had paid for our meal, we put on our packs and strolled back to the main path.

"I wish we had a treat like that every day," grinned Mike. His mobile rang. "Hello. Hi, Alison ... My mother? ... You think it's a heart attack? ... Yes ... Right ... Right ... OK, I'll see you there." He turned to us, a shocked expression on his face. "It's my mother. She's been rushed into hospital with a suspected heart attack. She's in intensive care. Alison's at Keld, waiting for me. I'm sorry lads, but I'll have to go to Durham and see how she is."

"God, Mike, that's really bad news," said Dave.

"Yes, terrible," I agreed. "Do you still have a father?"

"No, he died years ago," said Mike, "and I'm the only child. I need to be there with her. She's ninety-one."

"Let's get a move on," said Dave. "Where are you meeting Alison?"

"She phoned me from Keld, but she's driving along the lane, looking for us."

We continued our descent, passed a couple of deserted farms, then we crossed a bridge to a road. We could see a car parked along the road near a junction.

"That's Alison," Mike said, pointing at the car. We hurried along the road. Alison got out of the car, and hugged Mike. "Come on, Love, we'd better get a move on." He turned to us. "This is a real bummer, but I'll let you know how she is. If she's settled and recovering, I'll try to link up with you somewhere along the route, but in the meantime, Dave, can you cancel the next three or four days' bookings?"

"Of course," replied Dave. "Go on, get on your way." Mike got in the car, and we waved as the car drove off.

"Now it's just two of us," I muttered glumly. "And only two days to Richmond", I thought to myself.

CHAPTER TWENTY-EIGHT
TUESDAY 17 JULY

The good weather continued today, as we left Reeth and again followed the Swale. We headed for a hill near the ruins of Marrick Priory and climbed a series of steps which brought us to the top. We paused to enjoy the elevated view of the priory and the valley beyond.

"You know that we arrive at Richmond today?" Dave asked, "It's our first visit since, well, that day with Katherine and Mary."

"It's been on my mind," I muttered, "believe me."

"I've booked two nights at a B&B and will be staying with you," said Dave, "but I'm going to spend tomorrow with my aunt and uncle who still live in the town."

"That's fine by me," I replied, "I'll just have a look around, you know."

"Looking for what?" Dave raised his eyebrows.

"What do you want me to say ... memories and ghosts?" I snapped. "Of course, Mary will be on my mind. She has been ever since you first emailed me about this walk, and I have to admit that I've thought about little else for the past few days. Hopefully this visit will help me to exorcise a few demons."

"Forgive me, mate, I hadn't realised that you still have it bad after all of these years."

"I've never accepted the way it ended," I confessed.

"Mary was my one real love, and I guess I've been running away from it ever since." I looked at Dave. "Don't worry, my friend, I'll be OK. I'm not going to throw myself off the castle walls, or any other spectacular suicide. You can enjoy your time with your aunt and uncle, and I'll amuse myself for a few hours. I'll be fine, Dave," I grinned at him, "and I'll see you back at the digs later." We had a last look at the priory ruins, then walked through the fields, heading for Richmond.

CHAPTER TWENTY-NINE
WEDNESDAY 18 JULY

Mike phoned in the evening to tell us that his mother was over the worst. She was still in intensive care, but he hoped that she would shortly be transferred to another ward. For the time being he was going to stay in Durham, but he intended re-joining us at some point in the walk if circumstances allowed it.

Dave and I spent the evening in Richmond town centre, enjoying a pub meal and a few pints. He had chosen a good B&B and although my head was full of anticipation for today, I surprised myself by sleeping soundly. After breakfast we returned to the large market place and I watched Dave walking towards Pottergate to go and visit his relatives. He turned and waved, then I was on my own.

I suppose I always knew that I would return to the river bank then look for the bluebell glade where Mary and I had first made love. There was hardly a cloud in the sky and it was already warm as I made my way down the narrow streets to the River Swale. There were already a few dog-walkers and joggers there as I wandered along the river paths. Excited, yet slightly nervous, I walked up and down for over half an hour, then sat down on a bench and looked at the slow-moving River Swale and gentle waterfalls. My memory of that day in Richmond was so strong, yet I failed to recognise any of the setting. Of course it was over forty years since I had been here and I didn't expect to see bluebells in the summer but the layout of the paths appeared to be totally different. Furthermore, even though I explored the fringes of the woodland I could not find anything that remotely matched my memory of the clearing. I could almost hear a little boy say: "What you doin'?" but the rest of that idyllic scene had gone. Disappointed and saddened, I returned to a bench, sat back and lost myself in my thoughts.

"Mary, my pretty blonde girl in the flowery mini-dress, what have you been doing for the past forty-odd years? I can see you clearly in my mind, but where are you now? What do you look like now? Are you happy? How could we have given up that passionate love that we shared? Do you still think of me? Where are you, my love?"

I sat up straight. I had to find out some of the answers to these questions that were burning in my head. What was it that Alison said in Kirkby Stephen? "There are ways of finding out ... you know, the internet, etc." I stood up. My tablet was in the B&B, so I needed to collect it, to find a nice café and to drink lots of coffee while I searched for Mary.

An hour later I found a table in a café looking out on the market square. I ordered a cafétiere and a scone, and I made room on the table for my tablet and a notepad I had purchased in one of the local shops. I sat and thought for a few minutes. "What do I know already? What can I remember?" I began writing.

Name: MARY HODGSON

Family: father, mother and older sister (who was married?).

Names unknown. Oh, and an aunt in south

Yorkshire, perhaps Sheffield or Doncaster.

Home: Alwoodley, Leeds in 1970.

Mary's age: she was eighteen when I met her in March or April 1970, so she must have been born after August 1951 and before March 1952.

Was that all I could remember? Apart from her appearance, yes it was. Now for the internet. Where to begin? I plugged in my tablet, logged in to the café's Wi-Fi and had another drink of coffee.

I Googled 'looking for a person' and gazed at the mass of sites that this produced. Where to start? I selected half-a dozen sites and one by one studied their home pages. I tried the initial free samples that several of them offered before settling for the one that offered the options I thought I might need and looked fairly straightforward to use. I was asked for a name, and I typed in: MARY HODGSON. The site listed over 300 Mary Hodgsons born between 1837 and 2005. I now needed to pay a subscription before going any further. I logged in my credit card details and continued with my search. I referred back to my notes. Mary must have been born in either 1951 or 1952, so I used the filter to list the births for 1951, plus or minus 5 years. That produced over 75 names – too many – so I altered the filter to 1951, plus or minus one year. I now had fourteen names.

I sat back and thought. I had no idea where Mary was born, but Yorkshire would be my first choice. I selected the 'District' option, and the details for the list of fourteen came up on the screen. Four had been born in Yorkshire.

I checked my notes again. I knew that Mary had an older sister. There had been no mention of any more sisters or brothers when I visited her house. I looked at the list on the screen and pressed the 'Siblings' option for each of the four girls born in Yorkshire. One girl had no siblings, another had two brothers and three sisters. That left two girls, both of whom had one older sister, one born in 1941, the other born in 1947. I thought hard about Mary's sister. I remembered vaguely that she was of a similar age to Mary, not ten years older. I checked the site again. One older sister, Theresa. Yes, that was the one, I had found Mary!

I ordered more coffee, and opened my notepad. I noted down my new information:

MARY JANE HODGSON: born 15 November 1951 at Leeds.

THERESA ELIZABETH HODGSON: born 14 October 1947 at Doncaster.

I returned to the site. Now that I had identified the correct Mary, I could now access more family information. I clicked on the 'Parents' option, then noted down more details in my notepad:

FATHER: DAVID JOHN HODGSON, born 14 August 1922.

MOTHER: SARAH EMILY BROWN, born 17 May 1924.

MARRIED: 14 June 1946 at Doncaster.

I drank some more coffee, then contemplated the next stage of my research. I already had Mary's birth and immediate family details in my notepad. I now had to find out about Mary's life after 1970, when she finished with me. I looked back at the screen and entered Mary's details on the 'Marriage' option. I sat and stared at the information for several minutes before writing down the new details:

MARY JANE HODGSON, born 15 November 1951.

PAUL JOSEPH IRVINE, born 29 November 1948.

MARRIED on 12 June 1972 at Leeds.

So she was married, and possibly is still married. Were there any children? Another click brought me more information:

CAROLINE DAWN IRVINE, born 3 May 1977 at Leeds.

LAURA EMILY IRVINE, born 2 February 1980 at Harrogate.

Two daughters. Caroline would now be thirty-five years old, Laura thirty-two. Were they married? Did they have children? I knew that Mary's sister had been married in 1970. Did she have any children? Before trying to find out more information, I turned over a page in my notepad and began a simple family tree for Mary, noting down her parents, her husband/children and her sister. I glanced at my watch. It was almost three o'clock. I still had plenty of time to add to the tree. During the next forty-five minutes I researched and noted down details about Mary's daughters and their families, as well as similar information for Theresa's family. My family tree now had plenty of 'foliage'. I read through all of the information I had written down. So Mary was living in Harrogate when she had given birth to her second daughter. Where was she living now? Could my tablet help me again? I returned to Google.

I typed in 'how to find someone's address' and again brought up a range of sites, then typed in 'census for UK' and found more choices. I then decided which site to use, signed in and entered the Irvine family details. I could only access census information up to 2005, but this told me that Mary and her husband, together with one of their two daughters were living at an address in Warwick. I noted down this fresh information, then sat back and looked out of the window. The market square was busy with late-afternoon shoppers, groups of schoolchildren and traffic. I asked the waitress for a toasted teacake and another coffee. "Warwick", I thought. "Why Warwick?"

I ate my snack and sipped my coffee. This quest was stretching my research skills, but the more I discovered, the more I became devoured by curiosity. I felt as though I was getting to know the mature Mary and her present family situation, yet at the same time I had almost become an intruder. My long-standing uneasiness over the way our relationship had ended still drove me on. I needed to know more, then perhaps I could finally put this matter to bed.

Another thought crossed my mind. I logged into Google Earth, and fed in the Warwick address. From having only written facts in front of me, I now had a visual image – a picture of a large, comfortable modern detached house where Mary lived in 2005. Perhaps she still lived there. I quickly scanned a few of the census sites, but could not find any more recent information. I looked around, and saw that the café was closing. I logged out of my tablet, gathered my things together and settled my bill. I muttered some thanks to the waitress for looking after me during the afternoon, left a sizeable tip then exited to the market square. Before long I was back at my B&B, where I showered and waited for Dave to return.

Later that evening we were enjoying a quiet drink after doing justice to an Indian meal.

"That was great," I said, "really tasty. So how are your aunt and uncle, Dave?"

"Good, thanks, they're both well. How was your day? Have you looked around all of Richmond's attractions?"

"Not really," I confessed, "I found myself back at the river and full of thoughts of Mary." I smiled briefly. "I just couldn't get her out of my mind, Dave, so I decided that I had to find out more about her, and to know where she is now."

"Jesus," sighed Dave, "you have still got it bad after forty years. So what have you found out?"

I took out my notepad and showed Dave the family tree and the other details I had written down. "Quite a lot, as you can see. Mary has been married since 1972 and she has two daughters. She now lives in Warwick, or at least was living there about seven years ago."

"So what are you going to do now, John? Go to Warwick and abduct her, a bit like Helen of Troy?"

"Nothing, of course," I laughed, "I just had to find out. I always knew that returning to Richmond would have this effect on me. Perhaps I can finally draw a line under it all now."

"I hope so, pal. Anyway, let's have another pint and think about the next few days. We still have a walk to do, remember?"

CHAPTER THIRTY
FRIDAY 20 JULY

The good weather had held for the past two days and it was late afternoon as we walked slowly down a lane towards the village of Osmotherley. Strictly speaking, this stop was off-route, but as Dave explained at Richmond, accommodation was limited on the Vale of Mowbray and the North York Moors, a five-day spell. Osmotherley offered us a choice of B&B's, a few shops and several pubs. We continued along a street lined by pretty cottages which led to the market place.

"Jesus," I wheezed, "I'm glad that this stage is over. It's been the most boring section of the walk, with very little to scc."

"Yes, even Wainwright concedes that only farmers or people who appreciate flat rural landscapes would have enjoyed the past two days. I'm fed up of tramping along muddy paths and looking at cows."

"True, but that memorial in Bolton-on-Swale churchyard was interesting. I can't believe that anyone could live to be 169 years old. This village looks nice, however. I think I'm going to enjoy our stay here. Which way to the B&B?"

After showering, we changed and selected a pub in the village centre. It was quite busy, so we figured that the food must be pretty good. We both ordered a steak with all the trimmings, and sat down to enjoy a pint while we waited for our meals.

"I was thinking earlier on," Dave asked, "that all of that information you found on Mary was taken from formal websites, wasn't it?"

"Yes, I had a big choice, but most offered the same kind of information."

"Did you try any of the social network sites, Facebook, Twitter, that kind of thing?"

"No, I've never used any of them before. To be honest, I didn't even consider them."

"Well, I think you should, as you may not get much factual information but you might add a lot of personal details to your profile, plus some possible photos."

"Right! I'll fetch my tablet after we've eaten, and you can show me what to do. Cheers, Dave, this could be a great help."

An hour later we had finished our meal and so I returned to the B&B for my tablet. Dave ordered more drinks while I covered the short distance along the street. I sat down, had a drink and logged on. I typed in "Facebook" and completed the personal information required to join.

"At this stage I wouldn't bother listing much information on your Facebook page," Dave advised. "We only want to see what Mary has listed, assuming that she is on Facebook."

I clicked on the 'Find Friends' option, and typed in "MARY JANE IRVINE". Several names appeared, followed by more similar names, but none of the details matched those of my Mary. "Try 'JANE IRVINE'," suggested Dave, but we again drew a blank. "OK, let's keep searching. Try her husband." I typed in 'PAUL JOSEPH IRVINE'. A list of possibilities appeared on the screen.

"This one looks promising," I said, pointing at a name. "There's not a lot of personal details there, but his date of birth is '29 November 1948', which is an exact match.

"Does it say anything about his family?" Dave asked.

"No, nothing."

"OK, move over, let's have a look at him." I shifted my chair and we both peered at the photo on the screen in front of us. It showed the head and shoulders of a balding, middle-aged man grinning at us.

"Now you know your enemy," joked Dave. "Scroll down, and we'll check out his contacts." I did so, and we perused the comments and photos on the page.

"Christ," I gasped, "he obviously loves his golf." We read the various comments about golf tournaments and trips. "It looks as though he often goes on golf holidays."

"Yeah," said Dave, "but go back to the photos of his friends. There's plenty of both men and women, but no mention of Mary. What are their daughters called?"

"They are both married now. The oldest girl is called 'CAROLINE DAWN MURPHY'."

"OK, then search for her." I typed in the fresh details. Another list of possibilities.

"She's thirty-five," I informed Dave. We looked at the photos on the page. "Let's try this one," I said. I clicked on the name, and a large photo of Caroline, her husband, a young girl and a younger boy appeared. "There's no date of birth, but I think this will be the one. She has long, blonde hair and reminds me of how Mary looked all those years ago. They live in Oxford."

"Check the other photos and comments. Any clues there?" We scanned the page.

"Nothing", I said. "Lots of details about friends, but no mention of a mother or father. There is a photo of her sister Laura, however."

"Alright," Dave finished off his beer, "let's get another drink, then we'll look at the other daughter." We went to the bar for another round. I returned with a fresh drink, and typed in 'LAURA EMILY JONES'. There was no picture this time, and no personal details. There were a few photos, but not much to help with our task.

"What now," I asked.

"Type in the details of the daughters' husbands. You never know." I did so, but with little success. The only extra information that we gleaned was that Laura and her husband lived in Bristol, and had no children.

I logged out and switched off my tablet. "Well that was an interesting exercise," I remarked. "Where does that leave me?" I asked, scratching my head.

"Oh, I think we've learned a lot," said Dave. "Mary's husband is obviously a social animal who loves playing golf. It doesn't look as if he's much of a family man, as there are no photos of Mary or his daughters on his page."

"Yes," I continued, "and the lack of photos of Mary on her daughters' pages is puzzling. It's almost as if she doesn't exist."

"It may be that she just hates Facebook, or is a very private person. Or perhaps she's dead?" Dave frowned. "Switch on again, and see if you can check that out. You may be looking for a ghost." I waited for the screen to illuminate, then logged back in to the first site I had checked. I still had plenty of credit to use. I entered Mary's details, and clicked the 'Deaths' option. Nothing. Curious, I checked her mother and father's details.

"It looks as though Mary's mother is still alive. She must be about eighty-eight years old, but Mary's father died in 2006."

"Right," sighed Dave. "I think that's enough for tonight. You need to sleep on what we've found out. There's a lot to digest, my friend," he said, patting my back.

"Yes, the mystery deepens. It seems that the more I find out about Mary, the less I know her."

"Well," Dave warned, "back to reality. We've got three days of moorland walking ahead of us, so let's finish up here and get to bed."

"Good thinking." We left our glasses on the bar, thanked the landlord and walked along the street to our B&B. I lay thinking for a long time about all of the extra information I had found out today, and the many questions that remained unanswered, but eventually I fell into a deep sleep.

CHAPTER THIRTY-ONE
SUNDAY 22 JULY

It was mid-afternoon and it was hot. We were walking along the track of the former Rosedale Ironstone Railway, which had closed in the 1920's. The track is elevated above the North York Moors and there is little shelter, so we made sure that we took advantage on every hollow to have a rest and a drink of water. We had met a few other walkers along the way, some Coasters and others who were tackling parts of the Cleveland way or the Lake Wyke Walk. Our target today was the Lion Inn, a sixteenth-century moorland pub where Dave had booked a room for the night. Wiping my brow for the umpteenth time, I was thinking less of a comfortable bed and more of a cool pint of beer.

"Christ, it's hot," I muttered, as I again dried my head with an old t-shirt. "How much further, Dave?"

"I'm not too sure, John, but we have to keep on this track until we see the White Lion in the distance. Even then, it's a mile or two before we reach the inn – and our beer. It's really hard work on a boiling hot day like this."

"I hope to God that this pub hasn't run dry before we get there. I've never looked forward so much to a beer in my life," I gasped.

We trudged along a cutting which curved to the left and finally, on the distant skyline, we could see a tiny white speck.

"That must be it," smiled Dave. "Not too far now."

Actually it was a bit further than it appeared. Eventually we left the track and made our way through rising fields until we staggered into a sheltered hollow near the inn. "This is Cockpit Hill," Dave informed me, after looking at his guidebook. "It was once used for cockfighting."

"I couldn't give a toss what it was used for," I glared at him. "Where's the bar?"

We walked around the side of the inn, and saw a few picnic tables in the yard. Several guests were enjoying their drinks under large shades in the strong sunshine.

"Where have you lazy bastards been?" enquired a familiar voice. We shaded our eyes and saw Mike sprawled on one of the benches. He stubbed out his cigarette as we rushed over to him and had a group hug.

"Bloody Hell," I laughed, "it's really great to see you again, Mike, but it's even better to see this pub. We're boiling, knackered and thirsty. Get the drinks in – now," I ordered. Dave and I dropped our packs near a picnic table in the yard, and followed Mike into the pub. A few minutes later, we sat outside in a shady spot, thoroughly enjoying our beers.

"How is your mother, Mike?" I asked, after downing half a pint.

"Much better thanks. She's recovering well, and just needs to take it easy for a while. Alison is visiting her each day, so she'll phone me if Mam changes for the worse, but the doctors are pleased with her progress. Another pint?"

"No need to ask," laughed Dave. "I'm just cooling down nicely, thank you. Have you eaten, Mike?"

"No. I thought I'd wait for you two clowns to arrive, then we can enjoy a meal together."

"Oh, have you been able to book a room here tonight?" I looked at Mike.

"Yes, luckily. They had a cancellation. I've also re-booked my accommodation for the next three nights. Alison hopes to join us at Robin Hoods Bay, and we may have a night or two in Whitby if things are OK with my mother. Let's order a meal, then you can tell me all about the last week."

Two hours later, after showering and enjoying a bar meal at the inn, we sat at an inside table and told Mike about the week he had missed. Dave began the resume.

"When we got to Keld, we decided to skip the upper walk through some industrial wasteland, and so we followed the river instead. It was easy walking, and we visited a few villages on the way. We enjoyed Yorkshire Tea and cakes at Muker, and the pubs in Reeth were pretty good. We also had a good B&B at Richmond. I visited my aunt and uncle on the free day, so ... " I interrupted him.

"Before you ask, I explored on my own and yes, I did go the river bank to revive memories of Mary."

"Did you find anything?" asked Mike.

"No, but I did find out lots of things about her. I remembered what Alison had told me at Kirkby Stephen, and my tablet helped me to find out lots about her."

"Such as?" Mike raised his eyebrows.

"She's married, has two daughters and probably lives in Warwick."

"Well, that's that then. You can forget about her now."

"Not quite," chipped in Dave. "I told John to look on Facebook, and we unearthed a bit of a mystery."

"What do you mean?" Mike asked.

"Well," I took up the story, "her husband and daughters are all on Facebook, but Mary isn't. In fact, she isn't mentioned on any of their pages, and there are no photos of her. It's as if she doesn't want to be associated with the rest of her family."

"That's odd," conceded Mike. "Many people of our age probably don't use Facebook, but if her husband is on it... " He thought for a minute. "She is still alive, isn't she?"

"Yes, but faceless at the moment. I'm becoming more and more intrigued the nearer I get to the end of this walk."

"And you won't rest until you have a look?" Dave joined in.

"Maybe," I grinned from ear to ear.

"Right, let's change the record and leave John with his fantasies," Mike said. "We'll get another round in, then talk about tomorrow's walk. Dave, go and fetch your guidebook." Dave nodded.

CHAPTER THIRTY-TWO
TUESDAY 24 JULY

The three of us sat round a picnic table on a lawn outside a farm at Littlebeck. It was cloudy, but warm and the landlady had welcomed us with a pot of tea and some homemade cake. Two cats and numerous kittens played around us, and looked for food. We relaxed after the day's walking, saying little. I was sad at the thought that the walk would soon be over and that before too long I would be back home in New Zealand, facing a different future now that I had retired. I had grown used to the old friendships that we had rekindled, and I didn't want to lose them again. I hoped that they would not fade away again in the coming years. The walk had been great, but there must be other ways of maintaining the bonds. I was also wondering what to do about Mary. The temptation of trying to see her in Warwick was becoming too strong to resist.

"This is the life," sighed Mike, as he finished off his cake and lit a cigarette. "I like this place, it's really welcoming. The kitchen is very chaotic here, but I have a feeling that this lady is going to serve up a real feast later on. The rooms look comfortable too. I'm going for a shower. Dinner at seven – don't be late!"

We enjoyed a sumptuous meal, then relaxed in the lounge. Another pot of tea arrived as we lazily flicked through the pile of magazines on the coffee tables. I broke the silence.

"It was great to see Whitby Abbey in the distance and

the North Sea this afternoon. We're almost there, I guess ... only about eleven or twelve miles tomorrow, Dave?"

"Yeah," he grunted.

"You know, I've really enjoyed this trip. I wasn't sure what to expect, but meeting up with long-lost friends has meant a lot to me. The walk has been tough – especially at the beginning, when I wasn't sure if I could finish it – but we've seen some great places and met a lot of nice people. The only downer for me is that Pete didn't make it, but I think he's genuine in wanting to keep in touch with us and perhaps meet up again somewhere. What do you reckon?"

"Yes, I think you're right," replied Mike. "I think the walk has changed Pete, even though he was only with us for a few days. I think meeting up again after all these years has showed him what he's missed with not having a steady partner and a family. I might be wrong, but I think we'll see a different Pete in the future."

"I wonder if he's still seeing Karen?" Dave said thoughtfully. "That would be a good result if he is."

"I don't think we've even talked about football," I commented. "In the old days we couldn't get past three hours without mentioning it, let along three weeks."

"That shows just how much you've matured," Mike laughed.

"Oh no," replied Dave, "football is still an important part of my life. Just wait until the new season begins."

"Who do you support now?" I asked. "Leeds aren't a big team any longer."

"I used to follow Chelsea when Jenny and I lived near London but now, dare I say it, I support Man U."

"Jesus, I don't believe it!" I said, as I almost choked on my tea.

"I don't ever go to Old Trafford," Dave continued, "but I do watch some of the local non-league teams, you know, Kendal and Barrow."

"What a total waste of time," said Mike, joining in the conversation. "Football is the one thing I haven't missed in the past forty years, so don't start again now. What's happening tomorrow?"

"It's quite an easy day," replied Dave. "It's not far, as John said before. We have a nice woodland walk to start with, then a few miles on the moors." Mike and I pulled a face. "After that we head for the coast, and match the cliff walk at St Bees with a similar cliff walk to Robin Hoods Bay. We should be at the finish comfortably by mid-afternoon."

"I'll be quite sad when it's over," I confessed. "I'll miss you guys, and I feel really fit now. I think I could just turn round and walk back to Cumbria."

"Steady on," said Mike. "Remember that you were totally wrecked after the first few days."

"Yes, you're right. I don't suppose any of us will do the walk again. It's served its purpose. We've met up again and we're still friends, despite all the snoring and farting I've had to put up with!"

"Well you won't have to tonight," Dave snapped, "I'm sharing with Mike. You can have all of your farts and snores to yourself."

"On that happy note, let's tidy away and get to bed," said Mike, as he gathered up the mugs and headed for the kitchen.

CHAPTER THIRTY-THREE
WEDNESDAY 25 JULY

Robin Hoods Bay was an obscure fishing community until tourists discovered the village in late Victorian times. The quaint red-roofed cottages clinging to the steep cliffside and the maze of narrow alleys have long fascinated the day-trippers who flock here in their thousands. There are a few boats and nets at the slipway near the sea, but today's visitors are more interested in the wide range of gift shops, cafés and pubs to be found here. There is plenty of varied accommodation in 'Bay Town', as it is known locally, ranging from large hotels to B&B's and even a Youth Hostel just along the coast. The demand for a bed is strong in the school holidays, but Dave had managed to book a small B&B near the cliff walk.

We arrived, as predicted, just after three o'clock. "Our B&B is close to here, so let's dump our gear before we go down to the beach," suggested Dave.

"Good thinking," I said, grinning at him. "Almost time for the last waltz."

We soon found our B&B and received a warm greeting. We left all of our baggage in our room, which had two bunk-beds in it, and walked to the road, descending steeply to the shore. Crowds of tourists moved up and down the street. A few of them gave us looks which suggested that we had just landed from Mars.

"Cheeky buggers," rasped Mike, after a couple of children

whispered something about tramps.

We continued down the twisting road until we reached the older cottages near the shore. In the distance, on the left, we could see the Bay Hotel, where Coast to Coast walkers traditionally enjoyed a pint after completing their journey.

"There's the Bay Hotel," I called to Dave and Mike, and pointed to the old inn. "We'll have a pint there, won't we? "

"Yes, soon," said Dave, "but we have another tradition to complete first." He took out of his pocket the pebble he had collected at St Bees. "I hope you have yours with you, otherwise you've got a steep climb back to the B&B." Mike and I both dug in our pockets and held the pebbles up.

"Hey, guys, wait for me!" came a loud shout from the direction of the hotel. We looked and saw Pete and Karen waving wildly at us. We tried to walk quickly over there, as they descended the steps to greet us. Soon we were shaking hands with Pete and kissing Karen.

"Bloody Nora," exclaimed Mike, "what a great surprise."

"I hope you don't mind?" Pete muttered, as he too held up a pebble, "but I'd like to join you for this final ceremony. I know I haven't completed all of the walk like you, but I was there at the start and I've been on one hell of a journey." He smiled at Karen.

"Of course you can, mate," said Mike. "Truth be told, I missed out a week of the walk."

"Really?" Pete asked. "Why was that?"

"We'll tell you all about it later," said Dave, grabbing Pete's arm. "Come on fellas, let's do it." The four of us walked as one down the slipway onto the beach.

"Keep our seats, Karen," Pete shouted back to her. She waved as we continued walking on the beach. Fortunately the tide wasn't too far out and so we soon reached the sea. We hurled our pebbles into the water, then started dancing in the shallows and shaking hands. A few tourists stared at us, but we probably weren't the first walkers to go for a paddle that day.

An hour later, we sat relaxing at a table on the terrace of the Bay Hotel. The pub was crowded, and we recognised a few fellow Coasters. Pete glanced over at Mike.

"Why did you miss part of the walk?" Pete asked.

"We were near Keld, about halfway through the walk, when Alison phoned to tell me that my mother had suffered a heart attack and was in hospital. When we reached the main road, she was waiting to take me back to Durham. I stayed for about a week until Mam was out of danger and was recovering well. I caught up with these two reprobates at the Lion Inn."

"What have you been doing since we saw you at Kirkby Stephen?" I asked, looking at Pete.

"Nothing special," replied Karen, "just getting to know each other a bit. I've been checking out his business – if you can call it that!" We laughed.

"And I've met some of Karen's family," added Pete.

"A novel experience for you, I guess," chuckled Dave.

"Karen's going to move in with me, and we'll see how it goes. Perhaps she can tame me."

"The Best of British," I laughed, and the others joined in. "Seriously," I continued, "I really hope it goes well for both of you."

"Cheers, John," Pete said humbly.

"So what's your next move, boys?" Karen asked.

"First things first," replied Dave, "we're going to have a few more drinks tonight and a meal. We'll spend tomorrow morning in Whitby, then enjoy eating the best fish and chips in the country at lunch. After that John and I will catch a bus to Scarborough, then get a train or two home."

"I'm going to Whitby as well," Mike continued, "and Alison is going to join us for lunch. We were planning to stay on for a couple of days, but now I want to get back to see my mother."

"Listen you two," said Pete, looking at Dave and myself. "Karen and I can give you a lift to Manchester. We've been at Whitby for two days, so we'll drive over to Manchester after lunch and drop you at Piccadilly Station."

"Thanks a lot," said Dave. I nodded as well. "That'll save us some time and hassle. We would have had to change trains at York and Manchester before going north."

"What are your plans after that, John?" Karen asked.

"I'm not really sure. I still have a few things to do in the UK before I return home. I have an open return air ticket, but I'll probably fly back in the next week or so."

"John's been doing some research, some digging," Dave grinned.

"And now he has a mystery to solve," added Mike.

“I assume we’re talking about Bluebell ... sorry, Mary? Apologies, John, I’ve finished with all of those stupid nicknames.” Pete smiled at me.

“Yes, of course, but I won’t go into all of the gory details, except to say, sad git that I am, that she’s still on my mind after all of these years. I should be able to bury her ghost for good after next week. Sorry, Karen, Pete can explain everything later.”

“Did someone mention drinks and a meal earlier?” Mike queried. “Let’s go and do it.”

CHAPTER THIRTY-FOUR
THURSDAY 26 JULY

Whitby has many faces and it draws all manner of visitors throughout the year. The impressive ruins of St Hilda's Abbey and other historic buildings in the town have fascinated tourists for centuries. Other visitors prefer to browse in the wide range of quaint shops and narrow lanes on the south cliff, or to look for bargains in the antique centres and charity shops on the north cliff. Whitby's links with the Dracula story have brought an increasing numbers of Goths and horror fans to the town. Others enjoy walking along the harbour and watching the fishing boats unload their catch, or going on a boat trip along the coast. Above all else, Whitby is a popular seaside resort, and thousands of families are happy to shop for tacky souvenirs, go on fairground rides and attractions, and to eat fish and chips in one of the port's many restaurants.

After breakfast, Mike, Dave and I had caught a bus to Whitby and met Pete and Karen near the harbour. We were no different to many of the thousands of tourists in the town that morning, as we looked for souvenirs for our families, posed for photos and then queued for a table in a restaurant near the bridge. Alison had joined us by this time, having had to park her car a good distance from the centre. The meal did not disappoint, and afterwards we decided to climb the many steps which led to the ruined abbey. More photos, an ice-cream, and then it was time to go.

"Before we go back into town and leave," I spoke to the group, "I would love to see you all – and Jenny – before I return to New Zealand. Let's meet in Headingley, have a look around the old haunts, and have a meal at the Original Oak? If they don't serve food, we can go somewhere else. What do you think?"

"Great idea," said Pete, looking at Karen. "We should be OK." She nodded.

"I'll have to check with Jenny," Dave muttered, "but it shouldn't be a problem. How about you, Mike?" Alison answered for both of them.

"No problem, as long as Mike's mother continues to improve."

"Excellent!" I smiled. "That's great. I'll probably be tied up next week, but I'll decide on a date and try to give you a few days' notice."

We made the descent back into town, said our farewells to Mike and Alison, and then walked to the B&B where Pete and Karen had stayed. We piled our baggage into the boot of his car, and soon we were heading for Manchester and home. Our epic journey was over.

CHAPTER THIRTY-FIVE
SUNDAY 29 JULY

It felt good to return to my brother Ian's after catching a train from Manchester, and later that evening we enjoyed a family party in my honour. Most seemed impressed that I had finished the walk, and had returned in one piece. On Friday my thoughts turned to packing for my journey back to New Zealand, but more so to another journey I had known for some time I would have to make. I had been planning my journey to Warwick for a number of days, and found it increasingly difficult to think about anything or anyone else. We watched the opening ceremony of the London Summer Olympics during the evening. Later I explained to my brother and sister that I still had people to visit, as well as a reunion with my old university friends and their partners, and so I made arrangements to hire a car for a few days, with an option to extend the hire if necessary. I borrowed a satnav from my brother and checked the available accommodation in and around Warwick. I managed to book a room for two days in a Premier Inn on the edge of the town, as I intended to travel on Sunday afternoon and then on Monday ... well, I had no idea what I was going to do. I logged in on my tablet and searched for the last address I had for Mary and noted the details in my notepad. I checked the directions I would need to follow from the motorway and from my hotel. That seemed to be everything, so I was able to enjoy a traditional Sunday roast at a pub near my brother's before leaving for Warwick in mid-afternoon. The traffic was reasonably light on the M6 and M40 motorways, and I reached my hotel in the early evening.

After freshening up and having a drink in the nearby pub, I decided to drive round the historic town and to get my bearings. The town centre was quiet and after parking my car, I walked round this historic town. I had heard of Warwick Castle, but knew little about the area around it. When I returned to my car I entered Mary's address details into my satnav, then followed the directions to her street, or rather avenue. After parking in a nearby road for a few minutes, full of anticipation about my next move, I felt some nervous excitement as I eased my car into the road where I thought she might live. There was a variety of large houses here, mostly Edwardian or slightly later, with a few more modern constructions. Almost all of the houses that I noticed were detached. I tried to pick out an occasional house number as I drove along slowly, but many just had names. My satnav informed me that I had reached my destination, and I glanced at the house on my left. It had a generous garden and a double garage, and then I saw the nameplate, 'The Bunker'. I thought, "What a weird name", then remembered that her husband was a golf freak. That had to be it. I continued driving towards the end of the avenue, then reversed round and waited for a few minutes. I slowed down as I neared the house again, but couldn't see any sign of life. I left the avenue and parked in a nearby road for about half an hour, then repeated my earlier drive. It was dusk by now and when I glanced at Mary's house again, the lounge curtains had been closed and a soft light glowed inside. I looked more closely at the other houses this time, and noted that two of them were for sale. My initial curiosity satisfied, I made my way back to my hotel, not expecting a good night's sleep.

CHAPTER THIRTY-SIX
MONDAY 30 JULY

It was going to be a hot day. The sun streamed through my windscreen as I drove into town around ten o'clock in the morning. I found a short-stay parking place, and looked around for an estate agency. After a few minutes searching I found two shops, almost side by side. I showed passing interest in properties in Mary's area, and obtained a few brochures from each shop. I asked for a folder in the second agency, then returned to my car. I entered Mary's details in the satnav, and drove close to the avenue where I hoped she still lived. I parked, picked up the folder and glanced towards 'The Bunker' further along the road. A house near the corner displayed a 'For Sale' sign, so I stopped and looked it up and down. I pulled out a brochure from my folder and pretended to show some interest. "In a few minutes I might see Mary again, might even speak to her," I thought. My head was spinning, I had no plan of action save the pretence of being a potential house-buyer. I didn't know what I'd do if I saw her, or saw her husband, or both. I replaced the brochure in the folder, and walked slowly up the road.

I was on the opposite side from the house, about fifty metres further down, when I noticed a man weeding a flower bed in the house next to me. He appeared to be in his seventies, and he was using a kneeling pad on the path.

"Good morning," I said, smiling at him. "Hard work on a day like this? "I asked.

"I'll say," he replied, "it's going to be a hot one today, so I thought I'd make an early start."

"You've certainly got green fingers, your garden looks immaculate."

"Oh, it's not just me. My wife loves gardening as well." He put his trowel in the soil, and stood up. "You're not from around here, are you? Are you Australian?"

I laughed. "Everybody thinks that. Actually I'm English, but I've lived in Australia and New Zealand for a lot of years. I retired recently, and decided to return to England to live. I like this area, so I thought I'd look at a few houses for sale." I brandished the folder of brochures. "I noticed that there are a couple of houses for sale around here, but before viewing any houses I always like to walk around the area, to chat to residents and hopefully to get a feel for the place. Have you lived here long?"

"Oh yes, nearly thirty years. We've probably lived in this avenue longer than most."

"Well, I don't want you to tell me all of your neighbours' secrets, but perhaps you can say why you like living here so much?"

"That's easy. This is a quiet area, with good quality houses and very little crime. There's a convenient bus route, but we're also close to the countryside and the motorway." The lady of the house appeared. "This gentleman, Lorna, is looking to buy a house around here," he looked at me, "or at least in Warwick"

"We love it here," continued Lorna. "The neighbours are friendly, but not in your face. Mind you, we don't know everybody." I smiled at her.

"I quite like the house that is for sale further along the avenue, but I do wish that one or two of these other houses were for sale. That's an unusual one over there," I pointed at 'The Bunker', "with an strange name."

"Oh, that's the Irvines' house," Lorna informed me. "He's golf-mad, that's why it's called 'The Bunker'." We laughed. "He's often away playing golf somewhere. His wife Mary is very nice, but very quiet. She keeps herself to herself."

My heart began thumping at the mention of Mary's name. "Really? Are they retired?" I asked, excitedly.

"Paul hasn't worked for years, but I think Mary helps out in one of those charity shops, doesn't she, Lorna?"

"Yes, 'Age UK', near the market place, but just on Tuesdays and Wednesdays, I think." I smiled at both of them, anxious to change the conversation as quickly as possible, now that I had some useful information.

"Are there many children around here? I must admit that I've become used to a bit of peace and quiet after living in New Zealand for a few years."

"Very few," Lorna answered. "Most families with small children can't afford to live in this area." She grinned. "Do you have any children?"

"Yes, two, a son and a daughter. Oh, and grandchildren, but none of them will be coming over here to live with me."

"So just you and your wife?" asked the man.

"No, I'm afraid she died a few years ago. In some ways

that's the reason why I'm returning to the UK," I told them.

"Would you like a drink?" Lorna asked.

"That's very kind of you, but I have a few more areas to see and houses to view. Thank you for your time. You have been very kind."

"You're welcome," said the man. "I hope you find the house you're looking for." I smiled. "The woman I'm looking for", I thought.

"Goodbye," I smiled again, and walked along the avenue and turned the corner, heading for my car. "So I was right about his liking golf." I sat with my eyes closed for a few minutes, taking in the information the couple had given me, and realised I was breathing excitedly as I started the car. "I now know that Mary does still live here, and she works in a charity shop on Tuesdays and Wednesdays. That's tomorrow," I thought. "Tomorrow's the day."

I drove slowly along the avenue, waved to the couple as I passed their house and glanced again at Mary's house. "Still nobody to be seen." I continued back towards the town centre, and parked my car for a couple of hours on a car park. I had created an opportunity to see, hopefully meet Mary in the morning. I knew I would be nervous, so I wanted to make sure that I knew where everything was. I followed signs for the Market Place and quickly found the charity shop where her neighbours thought Mary worked. I walked up and down the street a few times, glancing inside the shop to gain an impression of its layout. "I've waited forty-odd years for this," I thought. "Perhaps I'll finally get some answers to those questions that have been nagging at me since 1970 in Leeds." I bought a new shirt in a local outfitters, then returned to my car and drove back to my hotel.

Later that evening, as I enjoyed a Chinese meal in town, I tried to gather all of the good memories I had of Mary. I hadn't come to Warwick for revenge, or to cause trouble, but simply because my love for her had remained so strong despite the rejection such a long time ago. I had managed to keep it buried during my self-imposed exile, but after tomorrow I could perhaps allay all of those doubts and questions about the way our relationship had finished. It was going to be a big day.

CHAPTER THIRTY-SEVEN
TUESDAY 31 JULY

It had taken me a long time to get to sleep last night. I had tried watching television, then reading a book, but with little success. Eventually, exhausted, I fell into a deep sleep and awoke feeling lousy. I had a long shower, then dressed and went down for breakfast. I was too nervous and excited to enjoy that, so I just had a little cereal and a yoghurt. The coffee tasted good, and made me feel better. I returned to my room, freshened up again, put on my new shirt, completed my packing then checked out of the hotel. My head was full of mixed thoughts, even though I knew that I would almost definitely be heading back to Preston in the afternoon.

I found a space in the same car park that I had used the day before, paid for two hours, then I walked quickly to the market place. "Christ, what are you doing here?" I saw the charity shop in the distance and headed for it. My heart was going THUMP! THUMP! THUMP! as I walked past the shop with barely a glance. I looked at my watch. It was ten forty-five, so the shop would definitely be open. I retraced my steps and looked in the shop as I walked slowly past it. Only one or two customers appeared to be inside. I wanted more people to be inside, so I crossed the street and walked around until I saw two or three other people entering the shop. "Now or never." I was perspiring – with fear? I walked across the street, took a deep breath and opened the shop door. I paused and looked around. Two ladies were examining the clothes racks, and a couple were at the rear of the shop looking at the bric-a-brac. A young woman was picking up soft toys from a large basket. An old lady, quite tiny, was behind the counter. She smiled at me. I returned her smile, then I continued looking around. I could see another older lady, rather plump, in the back storeroom, but a taller slim woman, with her back to me, was arranging paperback books on the shelves. I looked at her hair, it was shoulder-length and fair. She turned and looked in my direction, and I recognised those large eyes instantly. Mary. Older, with a fuller figure, just as attractive as ever. I jelly-legged over to the shelves, and peered at some of the titles. She was holding a small pile of books in her right arm.

"Hello," she smiled widely, "are you looking for anything particular?"

"No, thank you, I'm just browsing." I smiled back at her.

"Oh, you're Australian, aren't you?"

"Actually no, but I have lived in Australia and New Zealand for a number of years." I looked her straight in her face. Our eyes met, a flicker of recognition on Mary's face. I spoke in a more obvious Lancashire accent. "Hello Mary. It's been a long time."

"Oh My God, oh God ... John. Oh My God." She put her hand over her mouth, swayed slightly, and the books tumbled to the floor. I held her arm and steadied her, then knelt down and picked up the books.

"I'm sorry, Mary, I shouldn't have shocked you like that." I put the books on an empty shelf. "I can't say how wonderful it is to see you again."

"Oh John, what a shock. I never thought I would see you again." She looked pale.

"Do you want to sit down?" I looked around the shop. She shook her head. "Are you sure that you are alright?" Mary nodded. "Listen, Mary. I'm going over to that café across the street. I'd really love it if you'll come over and have a drink, have a talk."

"Give me a few minutes," she smiled briefly, and looked thoughtful. "You go on over. I'll be there soon."

"Are you sure you're OK?" I asked.

She nodded, "Yes, I'll be fine. I just wasn't expecting a surprise, no a shock like that." I smiled again and left the shop. I walked across the street, entered the café and ordered a pot of tea.

About ten minutes later – it seem much, much longer – Mary opened the door and came over to my table. I stood up and pulled out a chair for her. "I don't know what I'm doing here," she said sternly, and sat down. I ignored her comment, and smiled at her.

"What would you like to drink, Mary?"

"A vodka," a quick smile. "No, just a cold drink, a lemonade, please." I called the waitress over, and ordered Mary's drink.

"Oh, John," Mary said, shaking her head. "What did you say? You live in Australia?"

"No, I don't live there now. A few months after I left Leeds, I went to Hong Kong and became a policeman. I stayed there for about eight years, then met an Australian teacher and got married. We lived in Australia until I retired from the police force and moved to New Zealand. I have two children … and grandchildren. How about you, Mary?"

"I have two children as well. Why are you asking how I am, John? This meeting isn't an accident. You must know all about me."

"I know that you are married and have two daughters … not much else."

Mary stood up suddenly. "I can't believe that we are sitting here having a normal conversation like this. When you finished with me all those years ago, I vowed I would never speak to you again. I didn't want to ever see you again." Her face was flushed with anger. I stood up and touched her arm.

"What did you just say?"

"I didn't want to speak to you again, or see you again."

"No, before that?" I said anxiously. "Something about finishing with me." We both sat down.

"I vowed those things when you dumped me in Leeds."

"Mary, Love, I didn't dump you. You finished with me." Mary started crying. "Honestly, that's what happened."

"You can't be so cruel," she said, wiping her eyes, "what do you mean?" I sat and thought for a minute before continuing.

"It was towards the end of term. We had that fabulous time after we had been to the baths. Oh, then we had a meal out with my friends and their girlfriends. You remember ... Dave and Katherine, and the others?" She nodded. "Well, a few days after that, it was in the evening, you phoned me and said that your ex-boyfriend had returned and that you still loved him. You said something about me going away and you going to university, and it wouldn't work. I think you even wished me Good Luck." Mary stared at me, agog.

"I *never* made that phone call. What made you think it was me?"

"It sounded just like you. You ... or whoever ... spoke very quietly. I couldn't believe what I was hearing. The voice was very insistent. You were back on with your old boyfriend, and we were over. I was totally gutted." I paused for a minute, shaking my head. "So did you get a phone call as well?"

"Yes, it must have been about the same time. You just said that I was a nice girl, it had been fun, but now you were going away, you didn't know where, and I was going to university, so it was better to finish now. I was convinced it was you. It sounded like you, though whoever made that call was speaking very quickly. I was so upset that I barely listened to what he was saying." I thought again.

"This ex-boyfriend. What happened to him, Mary?"

"He's my husband."

Silence. We stared at each other. I pushed back my chair. I felt anger rising quickly in my body. "Let's get out of here, Mary. My head's exploding, and I think I'm about to start throwing things in here. We can go somewhere more private to talk. Can you make some excuse in the shop?"

"I've already told them that I have a headache and won't be back in today. The others will manage."

"Right, let's go. My car is parked near here." I paid the bill and we left the café.

An hour later we found a bench in the gardens at Warwick Castle. The place was crowded, but few people paid any notice to us as we continued our inquest into what had happened in 1970. We had both said little on the drive to the castle, apart from Mary giving me some directions. I held Mary's hand, and started the ball rolling.

"Please tell me how this ex-boyfriend, who deceived us both with bogus phone calls, later became your husband?"

"Bear with me, John. My head's all over the place just now." She closed her eyes, then began. "Paul's parents and my parents were very close friends, and so I've known Paul for most of my life. We almost grew up together. He went away to university, but when he came back to Leeds for the Easter break in 1969, he asked me out. We went on a few dates, nothing serious, during the holidays, but I found him to be so arrogant and bossy that I finished with him before Christmas. He came to our house occasionally with his parents, but I ignored him. Then I met you in March, or April," she frowned, "and of course forgot all about him. When you finished with me ... when I got that phone call, I was terribly upset. I made a mess of my last exams, I couldn't eat and I was really depressed. During the summer holidays Paul came round more often. I didn't go out with him, but he seemed a changed person, much quieter, more pleasant. My exam results weren't good and after discussing things with my parents, I decided to take a nursing course at St James' Hospital in Leeds."

I smiled, and put my arm around her. I didn't speak, as I was reluctant to interrupt the flow of her story.

"Paul's family were very wealthy. They owned a chain of estate agents in the Leeds area, and Paul stepped in to the family business after university. He kept calling at our house and gradually I just sort of started seeing him again. I didn't love him ... I've only ever loved you, but I suppose I didn't want to have my heart broken again. My parents encouraged me in some ways, as they thought Paul could provide some security. We just drifted along, until in 1972 we married. We lived in Leeds, and in 1977 my daughter Caroline was born. We later moved to Harrogate, where Laura was born in 1980. Paul had a maiden aunt who lived in Warwick, and when she died in 1990 she left him some property here. He had enough money to buy into an estate agency here, and so we eventually moved down here." She sat back, sighed, then she smiled. Her lovely eyes looked into mine. "Now it's your turn. Didn't you tell me that you are married?"

"Yes, I was, but Ailsa died in 2005. She had breast cancer, but the treatment was too late to save her."

"I'm sorry, John." She squeezed my arm. I smiled.

"When I left Leeds, I was in limbo. I had lost you, and couldn't cope with the loss. I suppose I just ran away. I went to Hong Kong, initially for a holiday, but I liked it there and I got a job in the police force. In those days most of the inspectors were British, and I had my degree, so I just walked in to a job. I was there for about eight years. Then I met Ailsa. She was an Australian teacher, and was on holiday with her friend Claire. We kept in touch, I got a transfer to the New South Wales police and moved to Sydney. We married in 1980. Ailsa was a lovely woman, very kind, with a good sense of humour. She had short dark hair," I touched Mary's hair, and smiled, "nothing like yours. We had a good marriage, but the love I felt for her was nothing like the love I had with you. When I retired early from the police force, we moved to Queenstown in New Zealand and I set up a security business. I have a daughter, Sally, who is also a teacher in Sydney, and a son, Jason, who took over my business this year." I paused and looked at Mary. "I've told you about my marriage. Now you can tell me about yours."

"I've told you the facts about my marriage. I guess you want me to tell you what my marriage is really like, don't you?" I nodded, and smiled. "At first things were alright. As I said before, Paul seemed to have changed, and we got on reasonably well. Money wasn't a problem, in fact it never has been a problem as he walked into the family business, but things began to turn sour after Caroline was born. He became even more distant after Laura was born. He wanted little to do with bringing up our daughters, and he spent more and more time on his work and his passions."

"His passions being ... ?"

"Golf and philately, you know, stamp collecting."

"I knew about the golf, but stamp collecting?"

"Yes, he has a valuable collection of British and Commonwealth stamps. He has a shelf full of albums in his study, but he keeps his most valuable stamps in the safe."

"So how often does he play golf?"

"Oh, virtually every day. He's either playing or watching big tournaments. He hasn't needed to "work" for years, so he has plenty of free time to do it. I've never been interested. We don't have a lot in common, and increasingly we've led separate lives. He's very popular, people think he's a great bloke, but really he's very selfish and arrogant."

"Christ, Mary, why on earth have you stayed with him all of these years?"

"I don't know. Habit, I suppose. I was a good mother to my daughters and spent lots of time with them. In fact, I do stay with their families from time to time, like a holiday."

"Do you go on holiday with him?"

"Oh no, we haven't really been abroad since the girls were teenagers. Paul goes away on golfing holidays. He's going away on Saturday for a week ... to Spain, I think. A crowd from the club go away quite regularly."

"Has he another woman?"

"I haven't a clue, probably not, or nobody permanent. He just likes company, to be the life and soul of the party."

"Your daughters are grown up now, with families, so why have you stayed? You've got nothing here, Love."

"My mother is still alive, and she did live with us for a few years, but she has dementia and now is in home near

Warwick. I visit her most days."

"Oh, I'm sorry to hear that. I only met her that one time in your house, but I remember her as a nice lady and a good cook!" We both laughed.

"Yes, she was proud of her cooking." Mary smiled, then went quiet. "We'll have to leave soon, John. I don't want this time together to end." She took my hand.

"Neither do I," I leaned over and kissed her, "and it doesn't have to end. I lost you forty years ago, but now that I've found you I won't lose you again. I think you once said "We have all the time in the world". Well, we still have, if we both want it. I know you have to go now, but I want to see you again tomorrow." We got up and started walking hand-in-hand towards the car park.

"Yes, so do I," she said, nodding her head, "but let's meet away from Warwick. Where are you staying?"

"Nowhere at the moment. I checked out of my hotel this morning, but I can find a hotel in ... say, Stratford-on-Avon."

"Yes, that would be great. It's not far from here." She turned, and looked serious. "Look, John, we still have a lot to discuss."

"Yes, I know ... I know. Here's my mobile number." Mary entered it into her phone. "Where shall we meet tomorrow?"

"I'll meet you outside Shakespeare's House, about ten o'clock."

"I don't know where that is, but I'll have a look around

Stratford tonight."

"You can't miss the house," she laughed, "there'll be millions of tourists there!"

"I just love to see you happy and laughing. That's how I've remembered you all of these years."

"I feel alive again, and happy ... so happy."

"Well we've both got a lot of things to think about tonight. I didn't know what to expect when I drove down here, but this has been the best day of my life. I'm overjoyed to find you again, but underneath I'm furious that we were deceived by your husband. He's deprived us of forty happy years together." We reached my car, hugged each other and got in.

"Please don't dwell on that for now, John. Let's concentrate on us. We're still strangers, but hopefully not for long. We've got plenty of time to work out what to do with him."

"I don't want to let you go," I said, as I drove back to Warwick.

"Trust me, Darling. I'll be there tomorrow," and her large eyes reassured me.

CHAPTER THIRTY-EIGHT
WEDNESDAY 1 AUGUST

It was the height of the summer season, and Stratford-on-Avon was very busy, full of tourists. On Tuesday afternoon, I tried several hotels without success, but eventually found a room in a smaller hotel nearer the town centre. I booked and paid for two nights initially, telling the receptionist that I might stay for longer. To kill time, I wandered around the town centre, easily locating Shakespeare's House, and walked along the banks of the River Avon for a while before returning to town to look for a restaurant. An Indian restaurant looked inviting, but I decided to go for a traditional pub meal instead. I enjoyed a couple of drinks there, then drifted around for an hour or so, my thoughts full of the excitement of finding Mary earlier today and of the anticipation of seeing her tomorrow. Later in the evening, I walked back to my hotel and watched some of the Olympics on television.

Mary was already waiting for me at Shakespeare's House, even though I was early. She was dressed very smartly, wearing a light green summer dress, brown sandals and a brown shoulder-bag. She looked absolutely stunning, and I held her and kissed her. "You look fantastic, absolutely beautiful," I said, as I stood back and admired her.

"Thank you," she said, and we both could not stop smiling.

"Yes, really stunning," I continued, "not bad for a

pensioner!" We both laughed heartily, relaxed in each other's company.

"You always were a cheeky devil," she grinned. "Where shall we go?"

"Let's have a coffee, then perhaps we can go for a walk along the river. It's another beautiful day."

"Yes, that would be nice. I know a good coffee shop. Follow me, cheeky boy." I was grinning now. "Hold my hand, just in case I fall over." Laughing, we walked towards the town centre.

The coffees arrived, and I added sugar to mine while Mary took a sip of her Americano. "What brought you to England this summer, John?"

"It was really down to Dave, my friend from Leeds. I've seen him a few times since I've lived abroad, but I'd completely lost contact with Mike and Pete, my other two mates who shared that house in Headingley. Dave emailed me just after New Year and suggested that the four of us meet up and go for a walk."

"Go for a walk?" Mary said, looking puzzled. "Where?"

"Well it was quite a long walk, from the Cumbrian coast, through the Lake District and the Yorkshire Dales to the Yorkshire coast near Whitby. We were away for nearly three weeks."

"How did you get on with each other? You all must have changed a lot in that time?"

"We got along pretty well, much better that I thought we would. We are different people now, but there was still enough between us to keep us as friends."

"You must have seen some lovely countryside?"

"Of course, especially in the Lakes and the Dales. I spent a day on my own in Richmond."

"No, really?" Mary exclaimed, "My God! That brings back some memories."

"Happy ones I hope."

"Of course," she smiled. "That was where ... " She stopped.

"Yes, I know, and I even looked for our bluebell glade."

"Did you find it?" I shook my head.

"It was when I was in Richmond that I determined to find out as much as I could about you ... on the internet, that is. That's how I knew about your family and where you lived."

"So why did you come to look for me in Warwick, if you knew I was married?"

"It was Facebook. Dave told me to look for information on that site, and I could only find pages on your husband and your daughters. There wasn't a mention of you and not a single photo. That struck me as being odd, as if you weren't part of the family, or didn't want to belong to it. Something like that. Anyway, you've been at the back of my mind for over forty years, so I just had to investigate and find out the truth."

Mary smiled widely. "I'm glad you did." I touched her hand across the table.

"Me too." Shall we go for a walk, then we can have some

lunch afterwards?"

"Yes, it's too nice day to waste."

I paid the bill and we headed for the river. We sat on a bench watching a pair of swans on the river. Lots of people were enjoying the sunny day, passing us this way or that, but we took little notice of them. I thought for a minute.

"Mary, I was thinking last night about those bogus phone calls. There was something that just wasn't right, I felt, then I got it. I think it is sinister, smacking of betrayal." Mary looked mystified. "Do you remember that we discussed how your husband must have got a couple of friends to pose as us and deliver the calls?" Mary nodded. "It would have been easy to make that call to you because your families were friends and you went out with him a few times so he knew your phone number, but how did he know *my* number? We weren't in the phone book, and in those days there were no recall features on phone sets. Where did you keep my number, Mary?"

"It was in my diary, hidden in my bedroom."

"So your parents wouldn't know it?"

"No, definitely not."

"I don't suppose that Paul would be allowed to wander around your house, so if you didn't tell him, that only leaves one person who could access my number."

Mary looked puzzled. "Surely not my sister, Theresa?"

"Who else? She would know most of your secrets. I'm sure that you discussed a lot of things with her. Right?"

"Yes, we were close in those days. We're not now, and we

hardly ever see each other. She and Brian still live in Leeds, and they have a disabled son. I can't think of any reason why she would want to betray me and try to force us apart – you and I, that is. Can you?"

"I only met her twice, the second time was when we went to the cinema. I seem to remember that she kept pushing her leg close to mine, but it's a long time ago. I'm probably mistaken."

"She did say that you were dishy, or something like that."

"Perhaps she was jealous, and wanted to split us up. I never responded when she touched me. Did she like Paul?"

"She got on alright with him. As I told you yesterday, our families were close, but Theresa's a year or so older than him."

"Whatever her motive, I'm convinced that she helped Paul with the phone calls."

"The thought of that upsets me, John. Can we change the subject? Let's have a little lunch. Does your hotel serve food?"

"I think so," I muttered, as I got up from the bench. I took Mary's hand. "Come on, my dear. Let's make a move."

My bedroom in the hotel was quite small and modestly furnished. It had a good-sized double-bed, but the bathroom was tiny and the décor was tired. I closed the curtains and turned to Mary. "You deserve a 5-star room or a four-poster bed at the very least, but I'm afraid that this is all I can offer you, Love."

"This is fine, John. Remember, we made do with a bluebell bed once!" We both laughed.

"I do remember, and it was fantastic," I whispered, drawing her towards me. I eased her onto the bed. We began kissing, gently at first, then with more passion. Mary pulled apart from me.

"That beautiful slim young woman is long gone, Darling. Didn't you call me a pensioner before?"

"That was just a silly joke. We could always laugh together. You're still a very beautiful woman, Mary, and always will be to me. It's not only physical. I felt comfortable with you yesterday, just after we had met, and I feel even closer now. I'm not interested in how old you are, I'm interested in you. I was madly in love with you then, and nothing has changed. I still feel the same now."

Mary put her arms around my neck, and we began kissing again. "Be gentle with me, John. It's been a long time." I caressed her hair, and ran my hands slowly down her body. I could feel her nipples hardening under the thin summer dress, and I eased the zip down at the back. Mary unbuttoned my shirt and kissed my chest. I eased up and took off my shirt, then helped her out of her dress. It fell to the floor. I turned and saw the small green heart pendant nestling between her breasts.

"You kept it all those years."

"Yes, even though I believed that you had rejected me, I couldn't bear to throw it away. It was the only memory I had that I could touch from that first time."

I unfastened her bra and buried my head in her breasts. She moved her hand onto my groin, unfastened my belt and unzipped me. She gripped me as I hardened to her touch, and I slid my hand into her panties. We eagerly helped each other undress, then moved under the sheets. We began kissing and touching each other, slowly and gently at first, then with more frantic passion. I caressed the tops of her thighs as Mary moved more quickly, moaning slightly as I guided myself into her. We were now as one, thrusting together, moving faster, our minds totally empty as we came to a climax together. The thrusting movements eased, we gradually slowed down until we came to a stop. We lay still for a few minutes, then I shifted slightly, caressed her forehead and kissed her lips. She put her arms around me, flickered her lovely large eyes and smiled widely. We both stifled our laughter on the duvet.

"If I'm a cheeky devil," I whispered, "how have I managed to get into Heaven?"

"Perhaps you're an angel in disguise?" We both lay back.

"If this is Heaven, I've no intention of ever leaving, as long as you are with me. Mary, I want you to come away with me to a new life. Queenstown, where I live in New Zealand, is a lovely town, and if you liked the scenery in the *Lord of the Rings* films, you'll love the South Island. But I don't care where we live, New Zealand, England, or wherever, as long as I am with you. I've erased from my memory the years we've spent apart. I want to spend the rest of my life with you."

"I feel exactly the same as you, Darling, but before we

can plan our future there are some things that I must do here first. I need some time to get them done, so you must be patient with me. Paul is going away on Saturday for a week. I won't be seeing much of him, but I won't be able to spend hours during the next two days with you. You'll drive yourself mad if you stay here, so I think it will be best if you go back to Preston for a couple of days. Do some packing, say goodbye to family and friends, then come back here on Saturday. I need to think and to see a few people in the next two days, and perhaps early next week. We can plan things together over the weekend. You must trust me on this, John. I have to do things my way."

"Yes, of course, if it has to be this way. I trusted you yesterday and you came to meet me this morning. I know you'll be there at the weekend. We've got too much to lose, and so much to look forward to, haven't we?"

"Of course, Darling. We'll meet again around ten o'clock at Shakespeare's House on Saturday morning. Don't be sad," she said, looking at my glum face, "it's a long time since I had a devil in my life and I rather like it!"

CHAPTER THIRTY-NINE
SATURDAY 4 AUGUST

After Mary left on Wednesday I decided not to return to Preston, but instead extended my hotel booking until the following Tuesday. I explained to the receptionist that my wife would be joining me on Saturday, so she made the necessary alterations. I spent the next couple of days being a tourist in Stratford, visiting the National Exhibition Centre near Birmingham and watching lots of Olympics action. I also phoned my friends from the walk, and made some tentative arrangements to meet in Leeds the following week. Providing that everything went well with Mary, I had a schedule in my head, and hoped that Thursday would be convenient for them. There didn't seem to be any problems, and so we agreed to meet at the Original Oak at one o'clock, unless I cancelled the arrangement. I told them nothing about Mary, though Dave did ask some questions. I gave him some non-committal responses.

On Friday I skyped my son and daughter and told them that I planned to return home in about two weeks' time. I described the Coast to Coast Walk in detail, but said nothing about Mary. Everything was fine with both of them, and they were looking forward to seeing me again, after my big adventure.

I was at Shakespeare's House early on Saturday morning, but Mary was about ten minutes late. I was relieved to see her, and told her so after we had hugged and kissed each other. "I'm sorry to have kept you waiting, John. It's not like me to be unpunctual, but I just couldn't find a parking place."

"Don't worry, Love, I'll forgive you this time." I grinned. "The most important thing is that you've arrived here safely. You look great, by the way." Mary was wearing slacks and a pink top.

"Thank you," she smiled, "I'm not used to getting compliments. Anyway, "Ye of little faith", I told you I'd be here," she laughed, and pinched my arm."

"Did you manage to get everything done that you needed to do?"

"Most of it, I think. I'll probably need some time on Monday to finish off. What have you done for the past two days?"

"I decided not to go to Preston. I had already done nearly all of my packing before I came to Warwick, and said most of my goodbyes. There wasn't much left to do, so I've done a few touristy things around here and watched a lot of the Olympics. Oh, and I also contacted my son and daughter."

"Did you say anything about us?"

"Not a sausage. I want it to be a big surprise for them. I phoned my Leeds friends too, but didn't tell them anything as well. I want us to meet them in Leeds next week and surprise them with our news, so I've made some provisional arrangements."

"Well let's just enjoy ourselves today, like a 'normal' couple, and we can discuss the future tomorrow."

"That sounds good to me. What do you mean by "normal"?"

"You're taking me shopping," she laughed.

Later in the afternoon we returned to our hotel, dumped our shopping, undressed and made love on the top of the bed. We were now much more at ease with one another, and getting to know what we each enjoyed. Afterwards we lay in each other's arms for about fifteen minutes, then showered and changed to go out for a meal. Mary put on a lilac blouse I had bought in the afternoon, and a tight skirt, looking very smart. I wore a black Kiwi t-shirt and jeans, not looking smart. We enjoyed drinks and a meal at a Thai restaurant, then returned to our hotel bar and watched the days' highlights from the Olympics. It had been 'Super Saturday' for Great Britain, with gold medals for Mo Farah in the 10,000 metres, Greg Rutherford in the long jump, and Jessica Ennis in the heptathlon. We joined in the applause from the other guests in the lounge when each event was won and the medal presented. When the programme finished, we walked up the stairs to our room.

I switched on one of the bedside lamps and undressed in the semi-darkness. Mary sneaked up behind me and, as I turned, she reached down for me and I reacted quickly to her touch. "Come on, you big boy," she whispered, grinning widely, "let's play angels and devils again." She pulled me over to the bed, and I obeyed.

CHAPTER FORTY
SUNDAY 5 AUGUST

I awoke around nine o'clock, hopped out of bed and switched on the kettle. I made a black coffee for Mary, and a tea for myself, and put them on the bedside tables. Mary had awoken, and we sat up in bed and sipped our drinks. "Everything alright?" I smiled at her. She nodded. "We can have these, then nip downstairs for some breakfast," I suggested.

"I'm not feeling very hungry, John," she said, looking a little glum.

"Are you sure you are OK?" I asked again. For all I knew, perhaps Mary was not a "morning person". I put down my tea, and put my arm around her.

"I'm sorry ... I just seem to have a lot on my mind."

"It's probably my fault. Are things moving too quickly for you?"

"No, Darling, it's not that."

"Have you changed your mind about me, about us?" I frowned and looked very concerned. She shook her head, and held me tightly. "There's something you haven't told me, isn't there?"

"Yes, and I'm frightened to tell you."

"Look, Love, you can talk to me about everything, anything at all. I don't want us to have any secrets. I sensed that when you told me about changing your mind about university, and then the reasons you have stayed with Paul for all of these years," I paused, "that there was something else."

"I've told you the truth about everything, John, honestly I have, believe me," she started crying.

"Come on, come on," I reassured her, "everything's going to be fine. We've got so much to look forward to in the future, nothing, I repeat nothing, is going to spoil that." I went into the bathroom to get some tissue, and Mary wiped her eyes. "Better?"

"Yes, I think so. John, I love you so much, you must believe that."

"I know you do. We're so strong together. Nothing, and no-one is going to change that. We can get through anything, can't we?"

Mary sniffed and took a deep breath. "Hold me close, I need you right now. Please don't let me go."

"I'm not going anywhere. Come on, Mary, what is it?"

"When we finished in 1970 ... no, when I received that phone call, I was absolutely devastated, so upset. I loved you so much, and you had rejected my love. My parents were very angry, and they told me to forget about you and not to try to contact you. My Dad wouldn't let me out of the house for over a week, or to use the phone. That's why Mum wouldn't let you speak to me when you phoned. About a week or so later I went to the city with my friends, and got off the bus near the Original Oak and walked to your house, but it was empty. You had all gone home." I squeezed her arm, caressed her back and smiled at her. She smiled back, still close to tears.

"I had been out with Paul a few times in the previous year, as I told you, but it wasn't serious and I had finished with him. In the summer he was still coming to our house, and he kept asking me to go out with him again, but I told him repeatedly that I wasn't interested. I'd finished my exams by then, and felt lost, really lonely. I just wanted you to turn up on my door and tell me that you wanted us to see each other again." Mary paused, and I saw her big eyes filling up with tears. She wiped them again, and then looked at me straight in my face. "Then in late July I found out I was pregnant." She began sobbing uncontrollably. I held her firmly until she stopped shaking.

"Mary, my love, come on, everything is going to be fine. Oh my God, pregnant, you must have been terrified, Love. I'm so sorry, Mary, I would have been there with you if only I had known."

"You're not angry with me?"

"Not at all. I'm only angry with myself. If I had only persevered with trying to see you, or contact you ... I was such a fool, and a coward."

"Don't blame yourself, John. You weren't to know."

"Oh, Mary, there must have been some terrible times for you." She eased herself up, and stopped crying.

"It was awful. I didn't know what to do, or who to turn to. I could only really confide in Theresa, my sister. When I told her that I was pregnant, we talked for a long time and she advised me to tell Mum and Dad. She came to our house when I did. It was the worst day of my life. Dad was furious, he went mental. Mum was so upset, and couldn't stop crying. We were all crying. Gradually we calmed down and discussed what to do. Getting rid of the baby was out of the question – we were a Catholic family. I suggested trying to contact you via the university, but Dad wouldn't have any of that. He said that you had ditched me, so there was no way that you would want me and a child. After a lot of discussion Mum and Dad advised, no, told me that I had to go to my Auntie Joan's in Doncaster when the baby started showing and to give birth there. Then we would have the baby adopted."

"No!" I stifled a shout. "Oh no, Mary, our baby ... adopted? Oh Christ, I'm so, so sorry. What a bastard I've been. How could I put you through so much pain and embarrassment? I should have been there with you ... would have been there with you all the way, if only I had known. Oh God, I can't believe this." I was now close to tears. "Go on, tell me the rest."

"I went to live with my aunt in October. Theresa came to see me a couple of times, but my parents didn't really want to know. "Out of sight, out of mind" I think." She started sobbing again. "I was there over Christmas, and I gave birth on the fourth of January."

"I'm frightened to ask. Was it a healthy boy or girl?" Mary paused, and put her hands on her head.

"It was neither, John. You're the father of healthy twin boys. I named them Mark and Matthew." I jumped off the bed, and paced around the room.

"Twin boys, oh God! Two babies." I sat down again.

"Where are they, Mary? Who adopted them? What did they tell you?"

"I had our boys for just six days, John. After that the Social Services people came and took them away. I don't know who adopted them, where they live now or what they are called. The Social Services people wouldn't tell me anything. They wouldn't even tell me if our boys were adopted as twins, or if they were separated. I haven't a clue where they are today. I only know that if they are still alive, we have two forty-one-year-old sons somewhere in the world."

An hour or so later, we were walking by the river. We had skipped breakfast and lunch – neither of us had any appetite. When the tears had dried, we showered and dressed, then left the hotel to get some fresh air. The walking helped to clear our minds and make us feel more relaxed. We were discussing things more logically now.

"Mary," I asked, "how did you get involved with Paul again?"

"He found out that I was pregnant before I went to live with my aunt. I always assumed that my parents told his parents, but knowing what we do about the phone calls, perhaps Theresa told him. As I said the other day, he seemed a changed man, and he showed a lot of sympathy and support. He told me that he still wanted to go out with me, despite my pregnancy, and after I returned to Leeds I started to see him more often. I hadn't done very well in my A-levels, so I did go to St James Hospital to train as a nurse. As you know we eventually married, and it was only later that I realised that he hadn't changed at all."

"You said that you stayed with him because of the children, and later your mother, but you stayed because of your guilt, didn't you?" Mary nodded her head.

"Yes ... yes, I suppose I did. He kept telling me that I should be grateful to him for marrying a woman who had shamed her family, and he's always said that if I ever tried to leave him he would tell our daughters what a slut their mother had been. He also said that if we did split up, he would disinherit Caroline and Laura." We sat down on a bench.

"Mary, you have nothing to feel guilty about. He was the one who tricked us into parting. If he hadn't done that, we would have still have been together and would have stayed together to bring up our sons. You have no reason to stay with him now. We need to be together so that we can search for our boys."

"You are right, John. I understand that now. I was just terrified that I might lose you when I told you about our sons."

"No way, we're stronger than ever now. I love you, Mary, and won't lose you again. We have a lot of decisions to make about where we live and that kind of thing, but they don't have to be made right now. We have plenty of time for that. We just need to think about our immediate future today. I know we can have a new life together, a happy one at that. This is the ideal week to start, while your husband is away and we have plenty of free time. Are you going to ride away with me into the sunset?" I smiled.

Mary paused and pretended to think about it. "Go on then, let's give it a go," she joked. "Of course I'm coming away with you, even though I haven't a clue where or when we're going."

"This week, Mary, it's all going to happen this week. We just need to discuss and agree what needs to be done in the next few days. Shall we have something to eat, then we can decide what to do next?"

"Yes," she said, standing up and reaching for my hand, "I feel a little peckish now."

After our meal, we returned to the hotel where we could discuss things privately. Mary started the ball rolling.

"I decided soon after we met and found out about Paul's trickery that I would leave him, irrespective of whether we got together again. My marriage has been dead for years, and as you said I'd only stayed with him through habit and guilt. Meeting you again woke me up, and made me realise that life was passing me by, all too quickly. On Thursday, when Paul was out on the golf course, I selected the clothes that I really want to keep. Tomorrow I'll pack them into suitcases, one of which I'll keep for travelling, the others I'll leave at friends' houses. I also had a brief meeting with my solicitor, who outlined everything I'm entitled to when I divorce Paul. I'll see the solicitor again tomorrow afternoon. On Friday, I transferred half of our available savings to a new account in my name. I'm sure that I will be entitled to a lot more money in the future, especially after our property has been sold, but I'll leave it to the legal people to deal with."

"You needn't worry about money, Mary. I have enough for both of us to enjoy a good lifestyle."

"That may be, but I want to claim as much as I can from that pig. I owe it to my daughters to do that, if nothing else."

"Have you said anything to your daughters?"

"Not about us, but I did phone Caroline and I told her that I want to see them both soon, probably this week. I want them to meet you then. I also need to visit my mother's retirement home, to tell them that I may be away for a little while."

"Won't she miss you, as you visit her each day?"

"Mum has dementia. She no longer knows who I am, and isn't aware of my regular visits. I want us to see her before we go away, but I also need to discuss finance and other issues with the staff. Is there anything you need to do, apart from collecting your luggage from Preston?"

"Yes, I've tentatively arranged to meet my friends from Leeds at the Original Oak next Thursday lunch. I want us to meet them together."

"They'll get a surprise."

"A shock more likely!"

"That reminds me. I need to visit Theresa, just briefly. She still lives in Leeds, so we can kill two birds with one stone."

"Are you going to tell her about us?"

"Definitely not, but there's something I need to take from her house."

"What's that?"

"I'll tell you later, if I manage to get it."

"Is there anything else, Mary? We seem to have thought of most things. I can't believe that we're planning this big getaway after knowing each other again for just over a week!"

"No time to lose, I say."

"Oh, I almost forgot. I need to make all of the flight bookings for us. Hell, I've just thought. Have you got a current passport? We also need visas for you for Australia and New Zealand."

"God, a passport. I haven't been abroad for years, but I think I did renew my passport a few years ago."

"Well, you better find it and check that it is still current, with at least six months to run, otherwise I'll just have to go on my own." We laughed.

"No way, Jose," Mary chuckled. "You're not getting rid of me that easily. You're stuck with me for good now!"

"Stuck like glue, and very pleased to be. Right, let's make out a timetable for action." I found a piece of notepaper and began to write:

Monday: Mary – solicitor, luggage,
phone daughters, visit Mum,
phone Theresa.
John – flight bookings and visas, confirm with friends.

Tuesday: drive to Oxford to meet daughters, stay in hotel there.

Wednesday: drive to Leeds, visit Theresa, stay in hotel there.

Thursday: see old haunts, meet at Original Oak, drive to Preston.

Friday: meet my family, final preparations.

Saturday: fly into the sunset.

I showed Mary the piece of paper. "Can you think of anything else, Love?"

"No, I think that's the lot. This is just like an exciting adventure. I can't believe that all of this has happened in just a fortnight or so. Talk about coming out hibernation ... ! By the way, where is the "sunset"?"

"That's my surprise. You'll have to wait and see."

CHAPTER FORTY-ONE
MONDAY 6 AUGUST

We had an early start after breakfasting in the hotel. Mary drove back to Warwick to complete her packing and to see her solicitor. She phoned me after returning home to tell me that her passport was still valid, and had about eighteen months to run. I noted down her passport number and other details which would be needed for visas and flight bookings. We arranged to meet near the M40 junction for Warwick around three-thirty, so that we could visit her mother together.

Meanwhile I phoned my friends to confirm our proposed meeting at the Original Oak on Thursday lunchtime, and told them that I was booking flights to return to New Zealand on Saturday. I then ordered and paid for visas for Australia and New Zealand for Mary, and scoured the internet for the various connecting flights for our 'ride into the sunset.' I soon decided that it was a little too complicated, especially given the shortage of time, so I visited a travel agency in Stratford to get the job done more quickly. I had a bite to eat at a nearby restaurant, then returned to the agency to double-check all of the flight details and hotel bookings and to collect the necessary vouchers and boarding cards. My planned work done, I enjoyed a coffee before leaving for Warwick.

The 'Dales Retirement Home' is a short drive out of Warwick. We travelled in Mary's car, and parked close to some impressive, well-kept gardens. A few of the residents were seated on benches or in wheelchairs.

"That's a nice touch," I said to Mary, "finding a home with a Yorkshire name for your mother." She smiled.

"You probably won't recognise my Mum. She's a little old lady now, and is in a world of her own. She doesn't know who I am these days, but I still like to visit her regularly. I need to see the Matron or one of the senior staff to tell them that I will be away for some time. I just need to check that the financial arrangements are secure, and that they have some contact details for me. I also want to make sure that if Paul comes here to find out where I've gone, they won't reveal any details. We won't stay too long. Just hover in the background if you feel awkward, Darling."

We left the car park, glanced around the gardens to see if Mary's mother was there, and entered the building. I was impressed by the quality of the surroundings, and the friendliness of the staff. Mary spoke to a senior nurse, whom she obviously knew well, and went into an office to arrange the matters we had discussed. When she came out, we walked to the lounge to look for her mother. She was seated next to another resident near the large bay window.

"Hello, Mum," Mary smiled widely as she sat next to her mother. There was no response. "How are you today?" Mary continued. This time her mother stood up slowly, with Mary's help, took hold of her walking stick and came towards me. She looked up at my face.

"Hello," she said in a quiet voice, "have you come to look for your boys?"

I was thunderstruck, and Mary had to sit down. We both

looked at each other in amazement and shook our heads. Mary was close to tears. Meanwhile, Mary's mother had wandered away, smiling at one or other of the residents. She never spoke to me again.

"How do you explain that?" I asked Mary as we headed for her car.

"I haven't a clue," she said, "that was really strange. Just to say that out of the blue. It's almost as if she knew what we were doing, yet she exists solely in her own little bubble. I'm absolutely gobsmacked."

Mary drove back towards Warwick, and I collected my car. Mary had brought all of the luggage she had packed for her travels, and I transferred it into the boot of my car. I then followed Mary to a friend's house in another part of the town, where she parked her car in the garage. After chatting to her friend for about ten minutes, Mary walked to my car and I drove back to our hotel in Stratford. "Is everything arranged for tomorrow, Mary?" I looked across at her.

"Yes, another big day tomorrow. You're going to meet my daughters in Oxford," she smiled at me briefly, "and I haven't a clue what they'll say."

CHAPTER FORTY-TWO
TUESDAY 7 AUGUST

Mary had arranged to take her daughters out for an evening meal in Oxford. Caroline and Laura both worked so it was not possible to see them during the day. They were curious when their mother asked them to come along, but she refused to give anything away. "All will be revealed tonight," I heard her say to one of them.

We drove to Oxford late in the morning, parked at our hotel and went for some lunch. Afterwards we strolled around the city's narrow streets and colleges, and visited a few shops. "Is this all I have to look forward to in the future?" I joked, as we stepped inside yet another department store.

"I'm making the most of it," Mary replied. "For all I know you might live in the middle of nowhere in New Zealand!"

We returned to the hotel, made love, showered then dressed for the evening. I looked in the mirror and thought that we looked good together. I had realised by now that Mary always liked to look smart and well-dressed.

"How are we going to play this tonight, Love?" I asked, as we were leaving the hotel.

"Good question. I'm not too sure, but I think I'll tell them at the outset that I've left Paul and plan to go away with you. I'll break the news about their brothers," she paused, "half-brothers later on."

"How close are they to their father?"

"Well, there's never been much love lost between them.

He wasn't around a lot as they were growing up, and he has rarely visited their families. Still, he is their father so there might be a few tears. I had thought of meeting at Caroline's house, somewhere less public, but if one of them does get upset, it won't last for long." She stopped, and kissed me. "You'll be fine, John. Just be yourself, stay relaxed, but go easy on the cheeky comments." She waggled her finger at me. "At the end of the day, this is our decision, but I'm sure that the girls will be happy for us when they know the whole story."

We arrived first at the restaurant. "This place serves a wide range of food," Mary informed me. "Laura doesn't like very exotic food, but she's been here before and enjoyed it." We sat in the lounge area, ordered some drinks and waited for Mary's daughters to arrive. When they entered the restaurant, I almost gasped. It was almost like turning back the clock forty years, for they both had long blonde hair and reminded me of the Mary I had known in Leeds. We both stood up and Mary hugged and kissed her daughters, then she turned to me. "Caroline, Laura, this is John." I didn't know whether to offer a hand, or a kiss, but in the end we just said "Hello".

"Caroline, Laura, what would you like to drink?" I asked, and called the waiter over. They both ordered a glass of wine, and we all sat down. Caroline looked at her sister, looked at me then spoke to Mary.

"Well, Mother, are you going to explain what is going on here?"

“I was waiting for that,” Mary answered. “There’s no beating about the bush with you, is there?” We all smiled, and relaxed a little. Mary took a deep breath. “I’ve left your Dad.”

“I gathered that,” said Caroline. “You should have left him years ago, but,” looking at me, “ who is John?”

“John and I went out together in Leeds over forty years ago,” Mary continued. “We were very much in love then, and he’s just found me again.” A waitress gave us a menu each, and we spent a few minutes selecting our meals. The waitress took our orders, then we continued our conversation.

“How has Dad reacted to this?” Laura asked.

“He doesn’t know yet,” Mary told her. “He’s on a golfing holiday. I’ve left him a note.” Laura looked upset. The waitress ushered us to our table.

“I’m a bit confused,” said Caroline, glancing at Laura. “We’re a bit confused. Take it from the start, Mum.”

“I’m sorry, girls. There wasn’t an easy way to do this. As I’ve just told you, John and I went out for a few months in 1970, when I was doing my A-levels and he was nearing the end of university. Then I had a phone call from John, as I thought, to tell me that he was finishing with me. I was really upset.” Caroline and Laura looked at me.

“About the same time, I received a similar phone call from your Mum, but both of the calls were fake. We weren’t able to contact each other again, and so we had to go our separate ways.”

"Why would anybody want to play such a nasty trick?" Caroline asked, looking puzzled.

"We're pretty sure that it was your Dad," Mary continued. "He'd been asking me to go out with him for a while, but I told him he wasn't interested. He must have asked two of his friends to make those calls. After John and I split up, he kept on calling at our house and eventually I agreed to go out with him. He seemed a nicer man then. Eventually, as you know we later married."

"In the meantime," I chipped in, "I went to live abroad. I was married in Australia and I have a son and a daughter. My wife died over six years ago. I retired recently and met up with some of my university friends over here, and I used the internet to try to find out what had happened to your mother. Something made me travel to Warwick to meet her again."

"I know you haven't been happy for a long time," Laura said, "but isn't this happening rather quickly?"

"Meeting John again has woken me up, a bit like Sleeping Beauty." We all laughed. "Your Dad is only interested in golfing and his hobbies. He's not bothered about me. I'm just one of his possessions."

Caroline leant forward. "When did you meet up again?"

"Just over a week ago," Mary replied. "On Saturday we are flying to New Zealand."

"New Zealand? Bloody Hell, Mother! Are you planning to return at any time? I need another drink." I called the waitress over and ordered more drinks. We had finished our meals by now, and we all seemed to have lost our appetite with the tension of the occasion. No-one wanted a dessert.

"Let's go back to the lounge," I suggested. "It's a little more private there." We picked up our drinks, walked through to the lounge and found a quiet corner.

"Look, girls, I know you've had a bit of a shock," Mary said quietly.

"Not as much of a shock as the one Dad's going to get when he comes back home," Laura interrupted angrily.

"I agree it's a little messy, but there isn't a perfect way to do these things. I've been unhappy for many years. Your father doesn't love me. I've thought long and hard about this, and I'm going to live with John. We won't be away for ever, and if it doesn't work out I'll have no regrets. You know what your father's like," Mary looked at Caroline and Laura in turn, "my marriage to him has been dead for a long time."

Laura sighed. "I know what you're saying, Mum, and it's true. It's just very sudden. In some ways I'm relieved, however. When you phoned me and told me that you had something important to discuss with me and Caroline, I thought you had cancer or some other terminal illness." We all laughed heartily, and the tension eased.

"I fully understand why you are concerned, but your mother and I would never have parted all those years ago. I promise that I will look after her and bring her back safely, once she has met my family in Australia and New Zealand." I ordered some coffee, and I made some polite conversation while Mary went to the toilet. She returned to the table, sat down and sipped her coffee. Looking serious, she smiled briefly at me the addressed her daughters.

"There is something else that we haven't told you, another reason why John and I will returning soon. You'd better brace yourselves for another surprise."

"Or shock," Caroline muttered. "Oh God, what next?"

"In the summer of 1970 I found out that I was pregnant." Laura put her hand to her mouth. Caroline almost choked on her coffee.

"Pregnant?" Caroline exclaimed, wiping her mouth. "I bet Nana and Grandad went berserk."

"Yes they did. It wasn't the best day of my life, believe me, when I told them. In those days having a child out of wedlock was not really accepted. They decided that I should go to my Aunt Joan's in Doncaster to have the baby, and so I did." Caroline and Laura both leaned forward anxiously. "On January 4th 1971 I gave birth to twin boys." Mary wiped her eyes. "A few days later they were adopted, and I haven't seen them since."

"Oh Mum," shouted Laura, crying. She stood up and hugged Mary. Caroline stood up and did the same. They sat down and the tears continued for a few minutes more. A few of the customers glanced in our direction. Caroline, evidently the less emotional of the two sisters, pulled herself together and spoke.

"So let me get this right. Laura and I have two half-brothers and we don't know what they are called or where they are. Were they adopted together, Mum?"

"I don't know, Darling."

"OK, so somewhere in the world we have two half-brothers, and if you both stay together we also have a step-brother and a step-sister on the other side of the world. We have a Dad who is golfing somewhere and doesn't have a clue about any of this." Mary and I smiled meekly at her. "Oh, and we have a Nana, who is in a home. What is going to happen to her, Mum?"

"Nana will be fine, Caroline. She is being well cared for and she's in her own little world. She hasn't recognised any of us for a long time. I've checked everything with the staff at the home."

"Does Auntie Theresa know anything about all of this?" Laura asked.

"No, but I'm going to see her tomorrow."

Caroline looked thoughtful. "Does Dad know about your twins?"

"Yes, he does. He was fine about it before we married, but after you were born he refused to even speak about them. When we've argued, he's called me a slut and threatened to tell you about them if I ever tried to leave him."

"He may be my Dad but he's certainly not a pleasant man," conceded Caroline.

I sensed an opportunity to join the conversation. "It's been quite an evening, hasn't it?"

"You can say that again," said Caroline, and Laura nodded.

"I think your mother deserves a good holiday after all that she's been through for many years, so we are going to enjoy ourselves for a few weeks and she'll meet my family. After that we will return and start the search for our long-lost twins. That's not going to be easy, and we'll need all the help we can get. Looking ahead, we don't know where we will live in the future. We're keeping an open mind about it and won't decide for quite some time. We may decide to spend part of the year in New Zealand and part in England. The important thing is that we're together again and that we love each other. We always did, but we were cruelly separated. As you said before, Caroline, you are now part of a much larger family and hopefully in the not-to-distant future we'll have a big gathering and you'll be able to meet all of your new relatives!"

"I'm glad I'm staying at your house tonight, Caroline." Laura slumped in her seat. "I don't think I could attempt to drive home. What a night! My head's buzzing."

"Wherever I am, you'll always be my daughters and I'll always love you," Mary said, as we got up and prepared to leave. "John and I will keep in touch every step of the way. John will give you a new mobile number to use, and we'll skype you often. Don't worry about me," she smiled at me, "I'm in safe hands, and we'll be back faster than you think." She held hands with both of her daughters and we left the restaurant.

CHAPTER FORTY-THREE
WEDNESDAY 8 AUGUST

We left Oxford after breakfast, heading north on the M40, then making our way to the M1. We discussed the meeting with Caroline and Laura and decided that it gone reasonably well. Both daughters seemed to have accepted the course of events, but we couldn't be sure how much they would tell their father when he returned from his golfing trip. Mary didn't appear too worried, however. She was more concerned about her impending visit to Theresa's. She was reluctant to discuss exactly what she planned to do, though she reassured me that it wasn't going to be some kind of revenge mission.

We lunched at a motorway services, then I continued driving north into Yorkshire. When I passed the exits for Sheffield and Rotherham, I began to think of my links with Yorkshire over the years.

"A penny for them," Mary remarked. "You've been quiet for a little while."

"Sorry, Love. I was just reminiscing about my many links with this county over the years. It's been an important part of my life."

"I know that you'll have a lot of memories from your time in Leeds, but what else is there?"

"Well, we've just passed the turn for Rotherham. Not long before I met you, my friends and I were invited to what we were told was an all-night fancy dress party. It was a girl on our course – she was celebrating her twenty-first birthday. Well, it was a bit of a disaster because we were the only ones in fancy dress." Mary smiled. "To make matters worse," I continued, "the party finished about one in the morning and we had to spend the night in Dave's car. It was bloody freezing, if I remember correctly." I grinned at Mary. "One good thing did come out of that evening. Mike met Alison there, and they been together ever since."

"Alison, yes, I remember her vaguely from our time in Leeds."

"She'll be there tomorrow, I hope, with the others at the Original Oak."

"So what about your other Yorkshire memories?"

"Lots of things from Leeds, of course, mostly connected with you. Some bad times." I frowned briefly. "Then we can't forget Richmond."

"Why, what happened there?" Mary teased me, smiling.

"My other memory is the Coast to Coast Walk, when I spent about a fortnight tramping through Yorkshire, including my second visit to Richmond. So you see, Mary, Yorkshire's been very important to me."

"Hmm," she said quietly. "We're not far from Leeds now. Let's find our hotel first, relax for a while, then we'll drive to Theresa's house."

"How will you introduce me?"

"I won't. You'll have to wait somewhere near the car."

After unpacking in our hotel, I followed Mary's directions and drove to Pudsey. Theresa and Brian lived in an old semi-detached house with a small garden, and I parked about fifty metres along the street.

"I don't think I'll be too long," Mary said. "I spoke to Theresa the other day, and we've discussed the item I want to collect. Give me the car keys, please, then walk around the block two or three times. I don't want Theresa to see you."

"Thank God it's not raining," I muttered. "Why the secrecy, Mary? Theresa won't recognise me after all of this time."

"I know, John, but I don't want any complications. The keys, please." She held out her hand, and I passed them to her.

"See you later, then," I said as I walked away, but Mary had already turned around and headed for Theresa's house. I continued walking slowly along the street, lingered on the corner for a few minutes, crossed the road, then turned around and walked along the other side of the street. I looked around occasionally, hoping that I wasn't being followed by a group of local vigilantes. After completing three circuits, I noticed Mary leaving her sister's house and walking to our car. She was carrying a large cardboard box. She opened the boot and put the box inside, then waved at a woman at the front door. She then got into the car and drove slowly along the street and turned the corner. "This is a bit cloak and dagger," I thought as I retraced my steps and walked to the end of the street. Mary was parked a few metres away. I opened the driver's door, we swapped places and she walked round to the other side.

"Mission successful?" I asked.

"Yes, but I didn't enjoy that one bit. I couldn't stop thinking about the way she helped Paul in 1970. I managed to stay polite and pleasant, but only just. Brian was there – he's OK – and their son, James. He's disabled and is in a wheelchair."

"Oh, that's sad. What's wrong with him?"

"He had a really bad motorbike accident when he was a teenager, and he's been left paralysed from the neck down." We sat quietly for a couple of minutes.

"Are you going to tell me what's in the box?" I smiled.

"It's full of photo albums and paperwork from Auntie Joan's. When she died it was passed on to Mum, and when she moved to Warwick, Theresa kept it. I'm not sure why it ended up with her, but I told Theresa that I wanted to look through the photo albums and papers to see what I could copy to help Mum remember some things from her childhood. I told Theresa that I would return the box when I've finished with it, but that won't be for some time, if ever. Can you store it at your brother's when we go away?" I nodded. "Good. When we return we can look through the box and see if there are any clues about our sons."

"Oh, I see, that's why you were so secretive. Well done, Sherlock. Let's hope it will help our task." Mary smiled and took my hand.

"I'm sorry I have been so moody since we arrived back in Leeds, but I wasn't looking forward to seeing my sister again. I'm glad that's over. Now we can relax and go and have a meal somewhere. I wonder if that Indian restaurant is still in the city centre."

"I doubt it, but it doesn't matter, and we agreed to do some exploring tomorrow. Right now I'm starving and we're going in the first decent place we see!"

CHAPTER FORTY-FOUR
THURSDAY 9 AUGUST

We had breakfast in our hotel, then packed and drove around the city, looking for familiar places. I parked the car several times and we walked to Mary's old house in Alwoodley, her former school and the old university campus. I noticed lots of changes as I had been away from Leeds for over forty years, but even for Mary some places were not as familiar. To kill more time until our lunchtime meeting we walked around the city centre shops, then drove to Elland Road football ground, where I had spent many a happy hour, as well as some big disappointments. Finally, just after midday, I parked my car near the house I had shared at Headingley.

"The old house still looks pretty much the same," I said, with a wry smile on my face. "Can you still remember this place, Mary?"

"Only vaguely, I'm afraid. I think I only made two or three brief visits here."

"Does anything stick in your mind?" I grinned.

"Yes, you devil, it does. I think you took advantage of me here." She gave me a playful dig.

"Oh I can't remember that," I muttered, pretending to think, "though I do recall a blonde girl who had the hots for me."

"Pig!" Mary laughed. "I should have ignored you in that charity shop."

"Huh! Fat chance. You knew you were on to a good thing when you saw me."

"I'll let you win this time. Look," she said, pointing at her watch, "we need to make a move." I took her hand.

"Remember what we discussed before?" She nodded, and we walked towards the Original Oak. It was just after one o'clock, and I hoped that the others would already be there. I kissed Mary, and entered the pub on my own. I walked through to the lounge, and saw a familiar crowd seated around a large table. Pete waved, and got up.

"About time," he remarked. "This lunch is for your benefit, remember?"

"Yes, sorry I'm late, folks. I just got a little delayed with last-minute packing, and so on." I moved around the table, shaking hands with my old friends and kissing Alison, Jenny and Karen.

"Sit down, John, while Mike gets you a drink," Alison said. "We're all eager to find out what you've been doing since we last saw you at Whitby." I smiled at her, then glanced at the door.

"Er, not much really. You know, saying goodbye to my friends, visiting long-lost aunts, looking for … "

"Come on, John, we know who you've been looking for," Alison said, leaning forward, "so are you going to tell us if you found her?" I smiled blankly and looked at her, then at the others and glanced again at the door. I could just see it opening.

"Well, I haven't anything really to tell you, I'm sorry."

The others sighed collectively. I looked towards the door. It was a glass collector. "God," I thought, "where is she?" I glanced again, watched Pete pass over two or three empty glasses, then was relieved to see Mary standing behind him. I grinned widely and turned to the others. "As it happens, this lady might be able to tell you something." I pointed to Mary.

"Good God ... Mary?" Alison asked, then stood up and hugged her. The others followed suit. I did the introductions.

"Mary, Love, do you remember Dave?" they kissed, "and Pete?"

"Of course I do," Mary smiled at Pete. "I'm Bluebell."

"Really?" Pete replied, pretending to look astonished. "I don't use nicknames any more. It's very childish, don't you think? Mary, this is my partner Karen." The two kissed. Mike had returned by now, and he gave Mary a hug. Finally Dave came over and introduced Jenny. Everyone was smiling and Dave looked at Mary, and shook his head.

"Well, folks," he addressed everyone, "this is one story that must be worth hearing. Fire away, Mary." She took a deep breath, then started.

"You are right, Dave, there is a lot to tell, but I'm only going to give you the short version. John can fill in the other details later. Stand by for some shocks!" They all sat, fully concentrated. "John tracked me down in Warwick, just over a week ago. I was working in a charity shop, and he gave me the shock of my life." We all laughed. "We went to a café for a chat, and quickly realised that we had been tricked in 1970. You see, I never made that phone call finishing with John and around the same time, someone pretending to be John phoned and finished with me." Gasps of disbelief around the table.

"But who ... ?" Alison asked.

"We're convinced it was my husband," Mary continued. "He kept pestering me to go out with him at the time. He knew I was madly in love with John. He must have persuaded a couple of his friends to make the calls. Anyway, when John and I found this out we acted quickly." She paused.

"You haven't killed your husband, have you?" Pete asked, smiling.

"Shut up," Karen said sternly. "Carry on, Mary."

"Nothing quite that drastic, Pete, but I've left my husband and I'm going to live with John. We're not quite sure where we'll live, but on Saturday we're going to fly to New Zealand."

"Stopping a few other places on the way," I added.

"Brilliant ... Great." A chorus of approval.

"There's more, I'm afraid," Mary silenced us. "A couple of months after John and I split, I found out that I was pregnant. My parents more or less forced me to go to my aunt's in Doncaster to have the baby." Open mouths and a few shakes of the head.

"In January I gave birth to twin boys."

"Bloody Hell!" somebody said.

"But a few days later I had to have them adopted." Mary

started crying. She wiped her eyes, as Jenny and Alison comforted her. "John and I haven't a clue what their names are now, or where they live. We don't even know if they are together, or even if they're still alive."

"Jesus, that's terrible," Pete sympathised.

"Yes, but listen," said Alison. "Look John, I told you that you could use the internet to try to find Mary. You could do the same to track down your sons."

"That's right," added Karen. "I watch that programme, you know, 'Long Lost Family' and that's the kind of thing they do, even after forty or fifty years of being apart."

"We can help," Dave reassured the group. "I'm sure that one or two of us have good IT skills. Enjoy your holiday, Mary, and fall in love again. If there's no-one suitable, John will do." Our laughter broke the tension. We decided to order some food and another round of drinks.

Later on in the afternoon, some of us were having coffee. We were more relaxed by now, and Mary was enjoying her new friends.

"Have you any more children, Mary?" Jenny asked.

"Yes, I have two daughters, both in their thirties." She took out her mobile, and showed Jenny some photos. Others leaned over to have a look.

"Christ!" Dave exclaimed. "They both look like you did in Leeds!"

"So between us we have six children," I explained. "We just have to find the other two. I don't know where to begin."

"As someone said earlier, with a holiday," Jenny advised. "After that, you'll have a team of helpers."

Early that evening, driving west on the M62, we reflected on the afternoon reunion.

"I really enjoyed this afternoon," Mary moved position in her seat. "It was nice to see that the four of you have remained good friends after the years apart, and your recent walking adventure." She smiled across at me. "I was also pleased at the way Jenny and Karen have fit in with the group."

"And you, Mary. You seemed to be totally at ease."

"Well, I was after I told them about our meeting and our lost twins."

"In an hour or so you'll have it to do all over again ... in Preston. My sister Susan is coming over from near Blackpool, and of course Ian and Sophie are already waiting. Don't worry ... there won't be a need to tell everything tonight. We have all day tomorrow to relax and finish catching up."

"Yes, I want to speak to Caroline and Laura at some point, and I suppose you'll need to contact Jason and Sally before we fly."

"It's like a magic carpet ride, isn't it Mary?" I grinned at her. "On Saturday we will be flying. The past few days have been packed with planning, packing and meeting people. I'm really looking forward to just thinking about us."

"Me too, Darling. Just the two of us. By the way, you snore a bit. Did you know?" I could sense her teasing me.

"The motorway's busy, isn't it?" I laughed and looked straight ahead.

CHAPTER FORTY-FIVE
WEDNESDAY 15 AUGUST

On a hot summer's day the island of Burano is idyllic, with its terraces of colourful houses, quaint mini-canals and an array of gift shops and restaurants. There were lots of tourists here, of course, but the atmosphere was much more relaxed that the frantic pace at the island's big sister, Venice. Mary and I had spent over two hours just meandering around the narrow, pretty streets and browsing in some of the shops. We had purchased a few souvenirs for the younger members of our families, and were now hot, tired and ready for something to eat. We selected a restaurant with a good view along one of the canals, chose a table with plenty of shade and waited to be served.

We had flown to Marco Polo airport, just outside Venice, on Saturday morning and had taken a vaporetto, a local water-taxi, to our hotel on the Lido. I hadn't visited Venice before, and didn't know if Mary had, but I knew it was supposed to be one of the most romantic cities on the planet. It seemed the perfect place for lovers and even if Mary had been there before, she hadn't been to Venice with me. As it happened, the city was new to both of us. I had selected an expensive, modern hotel where I hoped Mary and I could relax after the upheaval of the past two weeks.

We spent much of our time doing the things and visiting the places that all tourists must do in Venice – an outrageously-priced coffee in St Mark's Square, a gondola ride, browsing in the maze of narrow streets and alleys, taking photos of the Bridge of Sighs, the Doge's Palace and St Mark's Church, eating too much food, and so on. We usually returned to our room tired, but not so worn out that we could explore and develop our love for each other. We existed in an exclusive bubble, even though we were generally surrounded by hordes of strangers. We even had our first tiffs and disagreements, nothing serious, and laughed and loved after the issue was resolved. After all, we were two normal people who just hadn't been able to see each other for an abnormal length of time. It didn't seem like that, however, as the lost years soon counted for little.

Yesterday, Mary had asked me for my plans for our journey. She had left the entire itinerary to me. I told her that we were going to spend the day at Burano, one of the islands in the lagoon, and would have a relaxing day for a change, as it was our last day in Venice. She tried to get me to tell her our next destination, but I told her that all would be revealed at Burano. We got up in good time, breakfasted then caught a vaporetto to the lagoon. We saw other islands on our journey – the cemetery island, Torcello, and Murano, famous for its glass-making. Finally we arrived at Burano and followed the stream of visitors to the island's canals and shops. I took more photos here than anywhere else. The weather and setting seemed to be perfect, and Mary looked gorgeous in a plain black cotton dress. She was even starting to get tanned.

The waiter arrived and we ordered cold drinks and a light meal – tortellini for Mary and lasagne for me. I lounged back in my seat.

"This is the life, isn't it, Love? I know that's a bit of a cliché, but it's absolutely glorious here. You'll have a job on your hands to drag me out of this seat."

"Yes, I know, but you told me that we have other places to see. In fact you said that you would tell me all about them today. So ... " Mary's mobile bleeped as a message arrived. "So, there's no time like the present."

"Saved by the bleep. Are you going to read that message?" I smiled.

"Hmm, I suppose so. Bear with me for a minute or two." She clicked on her mobile and started to read. After a few minutes she began to smile and finally burst out laughing. She flicked through the message again, then turned to me. "It's from Maureen, one of my neighbours. She's sent a text to tell me that she and her husband thought my house was on fire, but when they investigated further they saw Paul in the back garden. He was cutting up and burning my clothes, together with what appeared to be photos and my album of postcards."

"That's awful, not funny. Why were you laughing so much, Mary?" Our food arrived, and we began to eat. Mary continued with her explanation between mouthfuls.

"I'm not bothered about the clothes. They were mainly things that I didn't wear and would have taken to the charity shop eventually. I've got a large suitcase of clothes with me, as you know, and I also left some other suitcases with friends in Warwick. Most of the photos I left were memories I want to forget. I've kept the ones that mean something to me."

"And the postcards? I didn't know you collected them."

"Well I do. I have a nice collection of Edwardian postcards of children's art, you know, nursery rhymes, pixies and fairies, that kind of thing. I kept them in a modern album. That's what Paul thinks he's destroyed." She grinned at me, but I continued to frown and look puzzled.

"Go on, there must be more." I carried on eating my lasagne.

"Before I visited my solicitor in Warwick, I photocopied all of my postcards and put the copies in the album. I placed the real cards in a shoebox, and left them, along with a suitcase of clothes, with a friend." Mary smiled and nibbled at her food.

"So he's burnt the copies. Very clever."

"More than that, John. I think I told you that Paul has a valuable stamp collection?" I nodded. "He kept his rarest stamps on postcard-sized stockcards in a box in the safe. Well, I removed them from the safe and placed each one behind a photocopy in my album. He's just burnt thousands of pounds' worth of his precious stamps. The whole bloody lot's gone up in smoke." Mary laughed again, then suddenly looked serious. "He'll be more upset at losing them than in losing me. The selfish pig. I hate him." I leaned across the table and held her hands.

"Come on, Mary. Don't get upset. It's all over now." She looked close to tears, and searched in her bag for a tissue.

"It's OK, I'm alright. I'm sorry, finish your meal."

"I've had enough. It was delicious, but I'd like a small

dessert, or some ice-cream. Are you sure that you're alright?" She smiled and nodded. "Good. Just remind me not to start collecting stamps!" Mary slapped my leg playfully under the table, and laughed.

Half an hour later, the meal was over and we were enjoying a coffee. I smiled across at Mary, and asked her again if she was no longer upset.

"Oh, I'm fine now. I must have been more angry than upset, because thinking about him was spoiling the perfect day ... perfect few days that we've had here. I'd forgotten about my past life until I read that text. Anyway," she continued, glancing along the canal, "we're going to enjoy what's left of today. It's your turn now. Where are we heading next?"

"Ok, Mary, I promised to reveal all today. When I was planning our trip, I didn't know how much travelling you had done in recent years, so I've booked a series of, what you might call 'stepping stones to the sunset.' Do you want to know more?"

"Of course I do, silly," Mary replied. "Come on, spill the beans."

"Well, New Zealand is a long way from England, so Venice was a first, romantic stop. Next on the list is Dubai. You won't have seen anything like it. If Venice has fabulous buildings from the past, then Dubai has the buildings of the future."

"I've seen programmes about Dubai on TV, and now we're going there. Lead on."

"The other thing about Dubai is that it has the largest

shopping malls in the world, but you won't be interested in them, will you?"

We both laughed.

"As if," Mary said, looking in her handbag. "I'm just making sure that I have all of my credit cards."

"Hold on," I said, pretending to look thoughtful, "I'll be footing the bills from now on." I smiled again. "We'll be staying in Dubai for three nights, then we're off to Singapore!"

"Wow!" Mary shrieked. "This is just like winning "The Price is Right" or one of those other silly game shows. I think there might be some more shops there, John."

"Maybe, but we are staying on an island resort, so we'll be relaxing as well."

"How long are we staying there?"

"Four nights, then we're flying to Sydney. I've told my son Jason to fly over from New Zealand, and to meet us at Sally's. They're probably thinking that I have some terminal disease, like Laura did!" We both smiled at the memory.

"So we have another session of family shocks and surprises in Australia?"

"Well, yes, but as you said when we were at Oxford, there's no easy way to break the kind of news that we have. Remember, Sally and Jason are about to find out that they have twin half-brothers and two potential step-sisters. It will be my turn to deliver the news, and to introduce the love of my life."

"I'm not sure how they will feel about that, John. I'm

sure that they really loved their mother, and you must have loved her as well. You said that you had a happy marriage, didn't you?"

"Yes I did, Love. It was different to the love that I've felt for you, both in 1970 and today, but Ailsa was a lovely person and well-liked. Having said that, she has been dead for over six years, and I'm sure that Sally and Jason will be happy that I have a new lady in my life. They'll love you, I can guarantee that, and they will tell you how pleased they are that I've moved on." Mary nodded, but looked thoughtful. I took her hand, and continued. "You have more grandchildren to meet, Nana."

"God, we're going to have a huge family, aren't we?"

"Yes, and I am sure that some of them will want to help in finding our lost twins." Mary was quiet for a minute or so.

"How far is it from Sydney to New Zealand?"

"I'm not sure about distances, but the flight is only about two hours. We'll be flying to Christchurch, then I'll drive to Queenstown. That will give you a better idea of what one of your new homes is like."

"After that, can we rest for a while?"

"Of course, Love, there won't be a hurry to do anything. I want you to get to know some of my friends over there, and to see more of the country. You'll love it, I'm sure. They even drive on the left-hand side of the road!"

"So where do you think we'll spend Christmas this year?"

"Good question, Mary. Heads or tails? Let's play that

one by ear. Christmas in New Zealand is lovely, but you must remember that it is in the middle of the summer. You might find that quite weird. Wherever we are, we'll be with friends and family." Mary stood up and hugged me. I turned and kissed her. "Then after New Year, my darling, we're going to find Bluebell's Boys."

PART THREE
2013-4

CHAPTER FORTY-SIX
TUESDAY 19 FEBRUARY

It was a bitterly cold winter's day. We had spent much of the day driving along the motorways from Preston, maintaining a steady pace and taking several breaks. It had not been a pleasant drive, given the poor weather and heavy traffic, and we were relieved to see the exit sign for Oxford. Within minutes, we had left the motorway and were heading towards the city centre and our destination – Caroline's house. We had arranged to stay with her for four nights, before travelling to Laura's where we would have another short break. It was nearing dusk as we turned into the avenue where Caroline lived, and parked on the road outside her house. The lights in her house promised a warm welcome. A face appeared at the window – Caroline's daughter Jessica – and she waved at us. We waved back. I opened the boot and took out our case, then Mary and I walked to the front door. It opened as soon as we reached it, and we were instantly hugged. Even their dog, a springer spaniel called Jess, made a big fuss. We stumbled inside the hall, out of the cold, and someone closed the door.

Later that evening, after we had eaten and the children had gone to bed, we relaxed in the lounge with a drink and chatted to Caroline and her husband, George. Caroline turned to her mother.

"Well, Mum, last Christmas was the first time ever that we haven't spent some time together since I was born, so tell us, what have the pair of you been doing for the past six months?"

"We've skyped you regularly, haven't we?" Mary said.

"Yes, but we want much more than that. We want all of the details, and I want Mum's impressions, John, not what you think I want to hear!"

"Oh alright, I'll start with our first journey together. I've brought a small album with photos and captions, so you and the children can look at it at your leisure. Venice was wonderful. We saw all of the main sights, but we stayed in a nice hotel and had time to get to know each other again." Caroline looked at me.

"You look just like a Cheshire cat, John." We laughed.

"It was a special time," I said bashfully. "Carry on, Love."

"Dubai was next and, oh Caroline, it was shopping heaven. You, Laura and I must have a holiday there sometime."

"Sometime when we have an empty credit card," George joked. I smiled in sympathy.

"We took a tour on an open-topped bus," continued Mary. "The buildings there are out of this world, aren't they, John?" I nodded in agreement. "Our hotel was fabulous too. You'll see in the album. After Dubai we went to Singapore, another fantastic city, so clean. We stayed at a relaxing resort, but there were a few more shops there as well." She looked at me and smiled. I raised my eyebrows and sighed.

"Then it was the first reality check. We flew to Sydney and met John's daughter Sally and his son Jason, and their families." Mary paused.

"Was it as traumatic as our meeting here in Oxford?" Caroline asked. Mary looked at me for help. I answered the question.

"In some ways, probably not. After all, the first thing that you heard was that Mary had left your father. My wife had died several years before, but Jason and Sally were surprised to meet me with a new lady in my life. They were disgusted when we told them about the trickery that had forced Mary and I apart, but I'm not sure how they really felt when they found out that your mother and I had been lovers in 1970. They both had a loving relationship with my wife Ailsa, and were terribly upset when she died at a relatively young age." I paused as Caroline sat up and looked at her mother. "They were certainly as shocked as you were when we told them that they had twin half-brothers somewhere. It didn't take long, however, for them to get excited about the idea of having two step-sisters, and of searching for their lost brothers. You can empathise with how they felt, I'm sure. It was a lot to take in."

"Sally and Jason's families really made me welcome," Mary smiled, "and I quickly felt part of John's family on the other side of the world. I was quite upset when we left them to return to England."

"So how was Queenstown?" George asked. "Did John live in a straw hut?"

"No, silly, John has a lovely house, much bigger than this one." Mary stuck out her tongue at George. "Queenstown is a beautiful city surrounded by mountains and a lake. The views take your breath away. You can take a cable-car to the mountain top overlooking the city, and the views from there are even more fabulous. I've never been anywhere quite like it. New Zealand is a beautiful country, by the way, very scenic. We've brought you some brochures so that you can see."

"Well, the big question is ... where are you going to live, Mum?" She glanced at me.

"We haven't decided yet. I was in Queenstown in springtime, and I'd like to see it during the other seasons. Sydney was nice, too. It's going to be awkward, because we have family over there, and family here."

"And two members of the family still to find," I interrupted. "It's likely for now that we'll spend some of the year in England, and some in New Zealand and Australia. Even if we eventually settle in England, where do we live? You and Laura live in the south, my family and friends live in the north. We could decide to live near you, then you might move a short time later."

"We definitely would!" Caroline joked. Laughter.

"So, for the time being," Mary added, "we are renting a house in Preston. Any leads that we get on Matthew and Mark," she looked at Caroline and George, "our lost twins, are likely to be in the north."

"How is the search going?" George asked.

"Not very well, I'm afraid," I took over the conversation. "We seem to be at a standstill, at an impasse. A few of our friends and family, including both of you, have been very helpful with suggestions and research on the internet, but we keep hitting a brick wall. The major problem that we are facing is that we don't what our twins were called after they were adopted, or where they were brought up. Our main hope is that we can find some clues from your great-aunt Joan's keepsakes, or from one of her neighbours. We drew a blank with the records at Dewsbury and Yorkshire Councils. They won't divulge any information relating to adoptions. Neither will the National Archives. To access any of the existing adoption records, we'll probably have to employ an Adoption Agency, and pay for their search."

"Even then," Mary continued, "we may be no further forward. If one of their agents locates one or both of our twins, they have to give their consent for us to contact them. If the twins don't want to have any contact with us, that's the end of the matter. They have the final say."

"God, that's awful," Caroline said, frowning, "but I suppose that's only fair for the adopted child. They've grown up with a different family and with a new identity, and they may not want to know their birth parents."

"We may eventually decide to employ an agency, even if we can't contact one or both of the boys. If the agency is successful in tracking down our sons, they are allowed to tell us something about their personal circumstances and possibly a vague idea of where they live. At the very least, we would know if they are alive or dead."

"Christ, it's very complicated, isn't it?" George scratched his head. "I thought that with the internet and so on that it would be a relatively straightforward process." We fell silent for a minute or two.

"Coffee, anyone?" Caroline asked.

"Please," I said, and Mary nodded.

"I'll give you a hand," Mary said, and followed Caroline into the kitchen. George looked across at me.

"You've been on a hell of a ride, haven't you, John?"

"God, yes, but it's been worth it. I still have to pinch myself that I managed to find Mary again. We've still a long way to go, however, you know, searching for the boys as well as reaching some kind of settlement with Mary's husband."

"Did I hear you mention my Dad?" Caroline enquired, poking her head through the door.

"Big Ears," George smirked. "You can't keep a secret in this house, John." I laughed, as Mary and Caroline placed a tray of coffee and some biscuits on the low table. Caroline poured some drinks, and we settled down again.

"Dad has actually phoned me a few times, but he's said little about you, Mum. He seems to getting on with his old life, golfing and such, just as if you didn't exist."

"Yes, that's what my solicitor has told me. Paul isn't interested in a divorce. He's dragging his feet on everything. He could obtain a divorce against me, but I haven't any obvious grounds to divorce him. There's no evidence of adultery, he's been very selfish for most of our marriage, but is that cruel? Probably not. Has he been unreasonable? Many would say that he hasn't, and that I've enjoyed a good standard of living. As for his deception in forcing John and I apart, well we've no hard evidence about that. He's not likely to admit it, anyway. So I have obtained a Separation Order, but have to wait two years to apply for a divorce, and that's only if Paul agrees to it. If he still refuses, then I'll have to wait for another three years. In the meantime, we can't sort anything out financially and, given his obstinacy, that will probably have to be decided by a judge. It's a mess, but we're not going to allow it to interfere with our lives, are we, John?"

"No, we are not. We've got more important things to worry about, such as finding our sons."

"Talking about my brothers," Caroline smiled and looked thoughtful, "did you mention something earlier about my great-aunt Joan's things, Mum?"

"Yes, there's a cardboard box full of miscellaneous paperwork, photo albums, documents ... that kind of thing, which was passed on to Nana after my aunt Joan died. When Nana came to live with me, the box was given to your aunt Theresa for safe-keeping. John and I collected it last August before we went abroad, and left it with John's brother in Preston. We had a quick look through it all when we came back to England before Christmas, but there didn't appear to be anything of significance."

"What did you hope to find?" George asked.

"Well we knew that wouldn't be any birth certificates or anything like that, but maybe some kind of letter from Doncaster Council with a name." Mary shrugged her shoulders. "We were just grasping at straws, really."

"I would look through it again, Mum, or get someone else to do it. You never know. The tiniest of clues would help, wouldn't it?"

"Of course," I said. "We'll see to it when we return to

Preston."

"It's getting late, Mum. George and I have work in the morning. What are you planning to do for the next few days?"

"John doesn't know the Oxford area, so we're going to be tourists, even if it stays freezing. We hope to spend some time with the children at the weekend, then on Monday we're going to Laura's."

"For another inquisition?" Caroline asked, with an impish expression on her face.

"Probably," replied Mary, nodding her head. "Probably." She smiled at me.

CHAPTER FORTY-SEVEN
WEDNESDAY 3 APRIL

Despite the threat of an inquisition, our stay with Laura and Stephen in Bristol had been an enjoyable one. They both worked during the day, so Mary and I took the opportunity to visit some of the nearby attractions. I hadn't visited the area before, so Bath and Bristol had plenty to offer. We took Laura and Stephen for a meal on one for the evenings, and visited the theatre on another. I had thought that Laura was more affected by the break-up of her parents' marriage, but by now she had accepted it. I found her easier to get on with than Caroline, and by the time we left I felt that I really was part of Mary's family. Laura, like her older sister, had had little contact with her father. He hadn't travelled to Bristol to see her.

Laura held out little hope of ever finding our lost twins, but she was keen to meet her step-sister and step-brother on the other side of the world. She and Stephen had no children, so they had more time and money to go on a long-haul holiday. They spoke eagerly about plans they had to visit Australia in the next two years and to meet up with Sally and Jason. Laura had skyped Sally several times since the previous autumn. We gave them a similar photo album to the one we had left with Caroline, but they seemed most interested in the photos and brochures relating to Australia and New Zealand. Mary and I wondered if their projected holiday in Australia was more to sample the lifestyle over there before considering a permanent move. Only time would tell. It was beginning to look as though Mary and I would spend the rest of our lives wandering around the planet either looking for or staying with the various members of our family. Neither of us was used to such a Bohemian lifestyle.

On our journey back north, we called to visit Mary's mother at the Dales Retirement Home. Mary would often go quiet when we visited Warwick, but she never asked to call at one or other of her friends. She did keep in touch with them regularly, but only via her mobile or the internet. She rarely mentioned Warwick to me, and I felt that she wanted some conclusion with her husband before she felt comfortable in that town. Mary's mother enjoyed good physical health, but she still remained in her own little world, and always ignored us when we visited. Her comments on my fist visit continued to intrigue me.

In March we enjoyed a 10-day holiday in Tenerife, then later in the month stayed for a long weekend in Kendal with Dave and Jenny, and amongst other things, enjoyed a walk around Grasmere. Dave and I suggested that we retrace the route we had taken the previous July, but Mary and Jenny preferred the gentler track round the lake, followed by some shopping in the village. The ladies won the day, and we were grateful later in the afternoon when it poured down. The following day we visited the market town of Skipton, and Mary and Jenny spent much of the day shopping around the outside market while Dave and I visited the old castle. He was naturally keen to find out how our search was progressing, but disappointed when

I told him that there were no fresh leads. He suggested having a reunion during the coming month, where our other friends might be able to suggest other sources of information. We returned to our rented base in Preston, and spent a day or two catching up with my family.

We were just watching some television in the evening when my brother Ian rang the doorbell. He and Sophie were at a loose end, and after a drink and a chat Ian asked if we had checked more thoroughly through the box of material left by Mary's aunt Joan. We hadn't, as it happened, and so we decided to spend an hour or so re-checking the miscellany of paperwork and photos in the cardboard box. In our first search, Mary and I had looked for any paperwork with an obvious link to the adoption, and had found nothing. This time we looked more carefully for any slight connection.

The photo albums were quickly dismissed, as they mainly contained old family photographs, carefully labelled by Mary's aunt, or holiday memories. Mary selected some of them to take to her mother, in the hope of triggering some long-forgotten memory or of sparking a brief recognition. There were two small boxes of slides amongst the loose photos. Both were labelled 'Family Occasions', but without a projector it was difficult to recognise anybody or to work out what the occasion was. Ian knew a photographer in Preston, and he offered to take the boxes to him to see if they could be developed into photos. Mary thanked him for his offer.

The paperwork took much longer to examine. There

were bundles of greetings cards, insurance documents, household bills and summaries, family birth and death certificates, lots of letters and newspaper cuttings. We each took a bundle and sifted through its contents carefully. None of the official certificates were of any use to our task. Mary read through most of the letters, as she knew some of the people who had written them or who were mentioned. Ian and Sophie checked through the household documents, while I read the greetings cards. We said little, as we piled paper after paper on our unofficial 'reject' heap.

"This is a strange one," I suddenly broke the silence and held up an old Christmas card. "There's no writing in it, just a loose photo of a small boy."

"Is anything written on the back of the photo?" Sophie asked. I turned it over, and showed it to them.

"No, not a sausage. This card is still in its original envelope. Look, Mary." I picked up the envelope from the carpet. "This was addressed to your aunt, and it was posted in Sheffield."

"What's the date on the postmark?" Mary reached for the envelope.

"Let me have a look. The cancellation is a bit blurred, but it looks like 20th December, 1975." Mary looked at me, a thoughtful expression on her face. "Our twins would have been nearly four years old. Where's that photo?" I handed it to her. "This boy looks about the right age to me. What do you think, John?"

"Yes, I think so. Ian, Sophie?" I passed them the photo. Ian nodded in agreement.

"Could be," he said. "This might be our first big clue. Perhaps one of your boys was adopted by a family in Sheffield?"

"But how can we find out more?" Mary pleaded, looking desperate.

"Well," Ian thought for a moment, "you know that we won't get anywhere with the local agencies. The only other source might be the local *people*."

"Explain what you mean, brother," I said. "Keep thinking, you're doing well."

"Mary, when you lived with your aunt Joan before you had your babies, did you meet any of her friends? "

"Yes, of course, Ian. I wasn't locked in the attic or chained in the basement." Ian and I smiled. "I don't think I can remember any names, but one or two of her friends used to call and see her, and she was very friendly with a few of her neighbours."

"Can you remember their names?" Sophie asked.

"Er, no, not off hand, but I might recognise where one or two of them lived. I certainly know the street where Aunt Joan lived, and although it's over forty years ago, I bet some of her neighbours are still living there now."

"How old would your aunt have been if she was still alive?" I asked Mary.

"She was a couple of years older than my Mum, so late eighties, I suppose, or ninety."

Ian thought hard again. "Well there's a slim chance that one, maybe more, of your aunt's neighbours is still alive and living in Doncaster, possibly in the same street. They may have sons or daughters living in the same house, people who were living there around 1970, people who knew your aunt, people who may even have known you, Mary. You must go to Doncaster and talk to people who live in the street where your aunt lived. Do a 'house-to-house search', just like the police. It's your only chance."

"And the photo of the little boy?" I asked.

"If that's one of my boys," Mary said, "the person who sent the card must have either known my aunt, or known someone who was close to my aunt. There's nothing written on the card, but to me, it is saying "he's alive and well." There must be a link here. We've got to find it."

We quickly looked through the rest of the papers, then put everything bar the Christmas card and the two boxes of slides back in the box. I made some coffee while Mary chatted to Ian and Sophie, and thanked them for their important contributions. We had taken our first big step.

CHAPTER FORTY-EIGHT
THURSDAY 11 APRIL

We began to make plans for our visit to Doncaster, making notes of everything that Mary could remember from her brief stay there. We were eager to make a start, but we had a prior arrangement with Karen and Pete, who were travelling from Manchester to stay with us for a few days. They hadn't visited Preston before, even though it was no great distance from where they lived. Daytime was shopping time as far as Karen and Mary were concerned. I could never understand the female obsession with large fashion shops, particularly the ones that they could visit in any large town or city.

"Ooh, look, there's Primark," Karen would point enthusiastically, or "there's River Island", or "there's New Look", or countless more.

"Karen," I interrupted her after her third point at another department store, "oh look, there's the Hanging Gardens of Babylon." Mary prodded me disapprovingly, while Karen continued looking round for the new store. Pete and I laughed.

"I think it's time that we did our own thing, John. There's must be some junkshops or bookshops where we can escape, aren't there? Let's meet outside M&S at four o'clock, then we can have a coffee. Have fun, ladies." We checked our watches, and looked up. Mary and Karen had already gone.

We got on really well with Karen and Pete, and we did enjoy a more leisurely day at Blackpool. I gave Pete a tour around Deepdale, Preston North End's ground, which he thoroughly enjoyed. It was just like the old days.

Pete and Karen left us on Monday, but as we were having a last coffee Pete smiled at Karen and looked at us. "Before we go," he grinned, "we have a bit of news for you. Karen and I are getting married." I jumped out of my seat.

"Bloody Hell! You're getting married, Pete? I don't believe it." I scratched my head. Mary pushed me out of the way.

"That's wonderful news, congratulations!" She kissed both of them. By now I had recovered from the initial shock, and hugged Karen, and then Pete.

"Jesus, I still can't believe it. When? Have you set a date?"

"No, not yet, but it will be soon," Karen said.

"We'll have to let the others know as well," Pete added.

"Just make sure that you warn them that they're about to get a shock," I advised Pete. "God, you getting married. Well done, Karen!"

We parted in good spirits, with a wedding to look forward to.

Yesterday, while we were packing a small case for our visit to Doncaster, my brother Ian called round. Mary brought in a tray of coffees and cake, then Ian quickly came to the point of their visit.

"You'd better have a look at these," he said, handing Mary an envelope full of photos. "I've had those boxes of slides made into photos. I think your aunt was keen on preserving important family occasions."

"Yes," Mary replied, glancing at the first few photos, "I think she must have had a slide viewer or projector, and just used a blank wall to view her slides. There are a few of her husband."

"I didn't know that she was married," I said.

"Not for long, I'm afraid, Derek was killed in a road accident. Aunt Joan was upset for a long time, and she never married again. I don't think she even went out with another man." She continued looking through the photos. "There are some of my Mum and Dad, and of Theresa and me when we were little. There's also a few wedding photos, but I don't know who they are. Here are some more of Mum. I'll take them when we next visit her. A few are of Aunt Joan with a friend, but none of them look familiar." Mary came to the last few photos and went quiet.

"Mary," I patted her on her shoulder, "is everything OK?" She slowly turned to me, and handed me two of the photos.

"Here are our sons, John." She gasped. "Oh God, I don't remember my aunt ever taking a photo of me when I was staying with her." I stared at the photos in disbelief. Both of them showed the Mary I had remembered, looking radiant and holding a baby in each arm. Aunt Joan had taken the photos from different angles. "I never knew these existed," Mary had recovered somewhat, "and I bet my parents never saw them."

"These are the only photos I've seen from around the time

we were together. You look absolutely beautiful, Love."

"Hmm, not bad, considering I'd just had twins," Mary smiled. She thought for a moment or two. "Thinking about it, I don't think I have many photos from my late teens. We didn't bother much in those days. I have got a photo album from my wedding," she looked at me and I grimaced, "but that's probably still at Warwick, or burnt. I did remove a couple of photos before I left him, however. They're probably in one of the cases I left with my friends."

"Hey, thanks very much for sorting out those slides," I shook my brother's hand. "They're the only image we have of our sons ... your nephews." We all smiled.

"You're welcome," Ian said, "but you owe me one." We laughed.

"These are really great," I said, looking at the photos once again, "but sadly they won't help in our search. Nevertheless, we'll treasure them, won't we, Mary?"

"Do you need to ask?" Mary said, shaking her head.

We left just after nine in the morning for our trip to Doncaster. I booked a hotel on the edge of the town for just one night, as we felt we would need to wind down and enjoy a relaxing meal following a days' search for more clues, rather than driving back to Preston drained and tired. The Christmas card in its envelope and the photo of the little boy were our only real clues, so we brought them with us, together with the photos of Mary and the twins. We had no idea if we would meet or speak to anyone with a link to Mary's aunt over forty years ago, but we had to remain positive and optimistic. Mary had her aunt's old address, but we would need some help in locating the street. We were just praying that it hadn't been demolished, and the former inhabitants scattered. After stopping for a snack at a motorway services, we headed for the M18 and Doncaster.

Locating Mary's aunt's former street was straightforward. The first person we asked gave us easy-to-follow directions, and we were there in no time. It was a street of larger terraced houses with small front gardens, once fashionable, now rather tired. Mary double-checked the number, ninety-seven, and in a minute or two I managed to park close to her aunt's old house. We looked at each other, kissed, then got out of the car.

"Are you sure that this is the right one?" I was keen to ask Mary before she rang the doorbell.

"Well I don't recognise the house, John, but it's the right number. We'll soon find out, won't we?" She pressed the bell, and a minute or so later a young woman carrying a baby girl appeared. "We're sorry to bother you, but I wonder if you can help us? My aunt used to live in this house, and we're trying to track down any of her friends who may still live in this street."

"Oh, I don't know, my partner and I have only lived here for just over a year. There are one or two old ladies who still live near here. I don't know them to speak to, but one of them lives a few doors away." She stepped out into the street, and pointed. "That house, with the green door, that's where she lives."

"That's great," I smiled at her, "many thanks for your help."

Mary and I walked along the street and knocked on the green door. An elderly lady opened the door.

"Yes, can I help you?"

"I hope so," Mary said, smiling. "My aunt Joan used to live at number ninety-seven, and we're trying to speak to any of her neighbours who might remember her."

"Joan Roberts? "

"Yes, she was my aunt."

"You'd better come in and then you can tell me why you need my help. I'm intrigued." We followed her into the house. She led us into her lounge and we sat down. "I'm Vera, by the way."

"Mary, and this is my partner John."

"Would you like a drink?" Mary looked at me.

"Tea would be lovely, thank you." The old lady went into the kitchen and switched on her kettle. "Can you give me a hand with the tray?" Vera asked me.

"Of course." I returned with a pot of tea, milk and some biscuits.

"Help yourself," Vera said, pointing to the tray. I poured two cups of tea. "Now, what's this all about?"

"Just over forty years ago, in 1970, I came to live with my aunt for a few months. I was pregnant. In January I gave birth to twin boys." Mary showed Vera the two photos of her holding her babies. Vera smiled.

"What lovely babies."

"Yes, they were, but a few days after I had these babies, I had them adopted. John is their father."

"Did you just call John your "partner"?"

"Yes, I did, because we've only been together again for about nine months."

"And now you're looking for your boys?"

"Exactly, how clever of you." She smiled at Vera.

"I think I remember you," Vera nodded, holding one of the photos and glancing at Mary. "You were very pretty, but big." She pointed at her stomach. "I don't think I saw your babies, however."

Mary took the Christmas card out of her handbag. "Someone sent this card and photo to my aunt in 1975. It was posted in Sheffield. Do you know who sent it, Vera?" Vera studied the card.

"No message, strange," she mused. "I'm sorry, Mary, but I can't help you. I didn't know anything about your babies, and I don't know of any friends that Joan had in Sheffield."

"We don't think it was sent by a friend. We think that a lady who adopted one of my sons sent it."

"Oh, I see. Let me think. Audrey Parsons who lives further along the street was Joan's best friend around here. She might be able to help you more."

"Really?" Mary said excitedly. "Which is her house?"

"I can take you there, but Audrey isn't at home. She's in hospital."

"Oh dear, I'm sorry to hear that. What's wrong with her, Vera?"

"She's been having dizzy spells, and I think she's quite ill. Mind you, I'm going to visit her this afternoon. I can take your photos, if you like, and see what she can remember. Pop round after tea, and I'll return your photos and pass on any information I've gained from her."

"That's very kind of you," I said. "Do you need a lift to the hospital?"

"No, thank you, my daughter usually takes me there."

"Well, here are the photos, Vera. Thanks again for your help." Mary giggled. "You're a proper Miss Marple, aren't you?" Vera smiled and took the photos.

"I'll see you later."

We killed time in the afternoon in the Meadowhall shopping centre in Sheffield, then returned to Vera's to see if she had found out any more information.

"I showed your photos to Audrey and she did remember you, Mary, and your babies. She was very interested in the Christmas card. She told me that she had a cousin in Doncaster who adopted a boy around the time your babies were born. She and her husband moved to Sheffield a couple of years later. Your aunt Joan must have mentioned the babies two or three years after they were adopted, and Audrey asked her cousin to send anonymously a recent photo to show that her boy was well. Oh, she did also tell me that her cousin was called Doreen, but that's all she could manage to tell me. She was too tired to have much conversation. I told her that I would visit her again on Sunday. I'll try to find out more then."

"Thanks very much, Vera. You've been very helpful," Mary said. "If you can find out her cousin's full name that will give us a real chance of tracking down one of our boys."

"Yes," I continued, "but now we do know that our twins were adopted separately. We're making progress, thanks to you." I smiled at Vera.

"Oh, you're welcome. How long are you staying in Doncaster?"

"Only tonight, I'm afraid, but if you give me your phone number, Vera, we'll call you again on Sunday night." Mary took a pen and notebook out of her handbag. Vera reeled off a number.

"Many thanks again," I touched Vera on her shoulder. "You've been very kind and trusting. Mary and I live at Preston, but we'll be back over here once we have more information to continue our search. It looks as though we'll have to look in Sheffield next."

"I'll do my best," Vera said as she showed us to the door. "I hope to hear from you on Sunday."

We drove to our hotel in a confident mood. Mary was bubbling about the progress we'd made, but I was trying to remain realistic.

"In some ways we're no further forward, Love," I muttered cautiously. "We need the cousin's full name before we can start searching in earnest, and even then we still haven't a clue about our other son."

"Stop being a killjoy," Mary snapped. "We're nearer than we were yesterday. Now let's have a nice meal, then you can entertain me afterwards." She grinned mischievously.

"Can't you switch on the TV yourself?" I chuckled. Mary poked me in the ribs.

"Drive on, devil."

CHAPTER FORTY-NINE
SUNDAY 14 APRIL

We were tempted to stay on at our hotel in Doncaster for two or three more days, but decided that we would have too much time on our hands, so we returned to Preston. I took the opportunity to skype Sally and Jason and to tell them something about our progress. I didn't mention the information we had obtained in Doncaster, preferring to wait until we had all of the details and were nearer to finding at least one of our sons. Mary adopted the same approach with Caroline and Laura. I also contacted Dave and Mike and found that, like us, they had been very surprised but delighted about Pete and Karen's forthcoming wedding. We were all eagerly awaiting a date.

Alison was particularly keen to see if we had made any progress with our search, and we did tell her that we thought we were close to obtaining a name in the Sheffield area. She reminded us that she was there to help if we needed any more specialised assistance with the internet. For the time being, however, Mary and I were coping well. We were just on tenterhooks to see if Vera had found any more information.

Mary phoned Vera around six-thirty in the evening. After exchanging pleasantries, Vera delivered the bad news.

"I'm sorry to tell you that Audrey passed away yesterday afternoon. I didn't have an opportunity to speak to her again."

"Oh, Vera, I'm terribly sorry to hear that news." Mary was visibly upset. "It must be awful for you to lose a friend so suddenly."

"Of course," Vera agreed, "but Audrey did look ill on Thursday when I visited her, and when you reach my age, as Audrey had, sometimes you have to expect the worst. I'm just sorry that I couldn't find out any more information for you."

"Don't worry, Vera, helping us should be the last thing on your mind." Mary was calmer now. "You need this time to grieve for your friend."

"Yes, I know, but life must go on as well. Anyway, don't give up hope, Mary. Audrey's daughter Molly called at my house today. She lives near Barnsley and she just wanted to check her mother's house. When she was here, I briefly mentioned your quest, and Molly gave me her phone number. She asked me to tell you to phone her after her mother's funeral, which will be on Tuesday next week. By then, she will be in a better position to think about other things, and she's pretty sure that she will be able to help you." Vera paused for a minute or two, then read out Molly's phone number. Mary noted it down.

"Well, thank you again for everything, Vera. John and I are really grateful, and we'll call and see you when we're next over in Yorkshire. Goodnight." Mary put the phone down and turned to me. "How awful, passing away like that. Vera didn't sound too distressed, but it must have affected her."

"Of course, but I suppose that when you reach old age, death isn't quite so shocking. I remember my grandfather saying that his main hobby was going to funerals."

"Aren't you the cheerful one? Oh well, we'll have to wait a couple of weeks before we can contact Molly. Vera said that Molly was pretty sure that she can help us, so let's hope that she can. She's our last chance."

CHAPTER FIFTY
TUESDAY 30 APRIL

Two weeks can seem like an eternity when you are as anxious as we were to get some more clues. The days were really dragging, so we decided to have a short break. We phoned Mike and Alison to see if they had any free time, and they were more than happy to show us around the north-east. They also insisted that we stay at their house, a large modern family home near Washington. We met Mike's mother, who was continuing to keep good health, and divided our time between shopping in Durham and the Metro Centre, and sightseeing in Durham and on the Northumberland coast north of Newcastle. Mike was keen to relive some of his boyhood memories at Whitley Bay and Alnwick. This area was new to Mary and myself, and the travelling and good company helped to take our minds off the search for our boys, though Alison did grill us thoroughly on a couple of occasions. She again reminded us of her offer of help with the internet.

I phoned Molly just over two weeks after the death of her mother, introducing myself and asking if Mary and I could see her at her home or her mother's house. Mary and I felt that we would gain more information with a face-to-face meeting. Molly was happy to see us, but preferred to meet at Vera's house if she was agreeable. On reflection, I thought that a meeting at her mother's house would be too raw, and to suggest it was inconsiderate on my part. I offered to contact Vera, and we settled on a date and time. I booked for a two-night stay at the hotel we had used before near Doncaster, as we planned to stay the night before the meeting.

Molly proved to be a very chatty lady in her late fifties. We warmed to her immediately when we met at Vera's, and the four of us spent the first hour in just chatting about life in general. Mary had chosen a large bouquet for Vera, and after tea and cakes she went into the kitchen to arrange the flowers in two vases. Mary and I took the opportunity to involve Molly in our search. After briefly outlining our relationship, Mary showed Molly the photos of herself and our babies, then the Christmas card with the photo of the little boy.

"Vera told us that your mother remembered me and my babies, and said that one of the boys," she pointed at the photo in the card, "was adopted by her cousin. She thought that she and her husband moved from Doncaster to Sheffield around 1973, and this Christmas card was sent in 1975. She also mentioned that her cousin's name was Doreen. I think that's all that Vera told us after she visited your mother in hospital."

"Yes, I think that all that you have said is correct. I can tell you some more, but it is quite a sad story, so brace yourselves. Doreen and her husband were a nice couple who had been married for over ten years. I can't for the life of me remember her husband's name, or their married name ... I'm sorry." She smiled briefly at Mary. "They had no children, so they applied to adopt a child. They lived in Doncaster at the time, and my mother recalled that they were given a boy soon after you gave birth at your aunt's.

I'm pretty sure that he was called Alan." Mary and I looked at each other, smiling and nodding. "A couple of years later they moved to Sheffield and lived near Hillsborough – you know, the football ground. Doreen's husband had a decent, steady job but sadly he died about three years later. Alan, the boy, must have been around seven years old. Doreen must have found it difficult bringing up the boy on her own, but within two or three years she had married again. Her new husband was called Bill Chambers, and he liked a drink. We didn't like him, and that's when things started going downhill for Doreen. She began drinking as well and before too long they moved to a poorer, rougher part of the city, near the centre. To be honest, I think my mother lost touch with Doreen after she married again, but the stories we heard weren't good. They may have just been rumours, but they told of violence, drink and drugs. I think Doreen and her husband separated more than once and she died around 1990. You can probably get more accurate details on the internet." Molly paused, looking apologetic.

"And the boy, Alan, do you know what happened to him?" Mary asked anxiously.

"I don't have any hard information, as I said we completely lost touch with them. Life must have been tough for him, and someone once told me that he left home a few times. Perhaps he didn't get on with his stepfather? That often happens, doesn't it?" Molly fell quiet. I thought for a minute or two.

"There's more, Molly, isn't there?"

"As I've told you, I don't know for sure what has happened

to him, but there were whispers about drugs, about prison," Molly paused, "only whispers, however. You'll have to try to find out the truth about him."

"Thank you for your honesty, Molly. We really appreciate your help, don't we Mary?"

"Of course," Mary muttered tearfully, "of course." She wiped her eyes. "We'll find him, Molly. Everything will be fine."

Later that evening, we lay in each other's arms in our hotel room, reflecting again on the meeting with Molly. We were so close to finding out the identity of one of our twins, yet apprehensive about the kind of person he may prove to be. Nevertheless, we had to know the reality of his situation, and be strong enough to help in any way that was necessary.

"The next step, finding out Doreen's first married name, and thus Alan's name, should not be too difficult," I looked at Mary, "but it might be advisable to ask Alison for her help in finding out about Alan's background and where he might be living now. What do you think, Love?"

"You're probably right, John. I think we can find out some of it ourselves, but Alison has superior skills and technology and will do a better job than us. She's always offered to help, so perhaps this is a good time to take her up on her offer. We know her a lot better now, and I think I would be comfortable in discussing delicate matters with her. Agreed?" I smiled and nodded.

"OK, we'll phone her tomorrow. Three heads are better than two. Then we'll return to Preston. We may need to pack for a longer stay in Sheffield this time. Let's relax and have a good night's sleep. I've a feeling that we aren't going to get many of those for a long time."

CHAPTER FIFTY-ONE
WEDNESDAY 8 MAY

Alison was delighted to hear about the progress we had made, and was more than happy to assist in the next stage of our search. She suggested that we continue with our independent research for the next week or so, then to meet up and share our findings. Alison was confident that she would find enough material to collate on the computers at her house, and so Mary and I agreed to travel to Durham and stay overnight with her and Mike. After that we could then make plans to stay in Sheffield or wherever else the research took us.

As predicted, Mary and I were able to access the internet sites I had used to locate her to identify our son. We cross referenced the information and established that Doreen's first husband was called George Benson, who had died in July 1977. Their son, our son, was Alan Mark Benson. We attempted to find Alan's present address, but we were unable to produce any recent information.

From there, simply googling Alan's name revealed a number of references to criminal activity reported by various news agencies. Mary and I quickly decided that we didn't have the stomach to catalogue the many reports that had appeared in the news agencies. This would be better left to our impartial friend Alison. We were confident that her summary would be less upsetting that reading the same, or similar information over and over again. We waited for her phone call.

Alison phoned on Monday evening. She asked how far our research had progressed. We told her that we now knew Alan's identity, and that his life story would not make pleasant reading. We had abandoned our search when it became too distressing for us, preferring to see what she had found.

"I could continue searching for another week or two, but I think I have enough information for you at this stage. There's only so much that you need to know, and if you do manage to meet Alan, he can tell you the rest. Is that alright?"

"That's great," Mary said. "Many thanks for your efforts so far, Alison."

"Good, then why don't you come over tomorrow? We can relax in the evening, and share our findings on Thursday morning. After that, you're on your own!"

"OK, we'll see you after lunch. Bye."

"That was a lovely meal last night," Alison said, ushering the three of us through to her study. "Mike and I haven't eaten there before, but I think we will again. There was no need for you to treat us."

"Nonsense," I said, "you're giving us free accommodation," I paused, "aren't you?" Mike and Alison laughed. "Plus you've done loads of research for us, so buying you a meal is the least we could do. Anyway, it's about time you stayed with us in Preston."

"Or wherever you may be," added Mike. "It sounds to me that you might be moving to Yorkshire."

"Yeah, you could be right," I conceded.

"Let's get started," Alison said, pointing to a table. Four piles of paper were laid out. "Grab a seat." We all settled down. "I've copied a few documents here. You can read them at your leisure, but I'll give you a summary. You now know, of course, that one of your sons, Alan Mark Benson, was adopted by George and Doreen Benson in January 1971. The family lived in Doncaster, then in Hillsborough, Sheffield, where the father died in July 1977. I've stapled together the various documents relating to the Benson family." She held up a small bundle.

"OK so far," I said.

"The next group of papers relate to Doreen and William Chambers, Doreen's second husband. They too lived in Sheffield, in Attercliffe. I managed to find a couple of news clippings reporting William Chambers being arrested for drunken behaviour and later fined. Doreen died in February 1991."

"Yes, that was just after Alan's twenty-first birthday," Mary added.

"It makes you wonder what kind of life he had after George Benson died, doesn't it?" Mike commented.

"Well, according to her cousin's daughter Molly, Doreen and her second husband had a tempestuous relationship. She thinks they separated more than once, and both of them had drink problems. All of this must have affected Alan badly." Mary looked really sad.

"Poor kid," Mike said. "He must have gone through a lot."

"I've got a news clipping here from November 1989. Alan and two other youths were convicted of theft from a working men's club, and given suspended sentences." Mary put her hand over her mouth. "It gets worse, I'm afraid. I'm sorry, Mary. May 1993 convicted of theft again, sentenced to six months in prison; August 1996 fined for being drunk and disorderly; March 1997 convicted of theft again and given a twenty-eight month sentence. He was probably released in the summer of 1998. All of those offences were in Sheffield. There are more details on these two sheets."

"This is awful," I said, glancing at the papers. "I find it hard to believe."

"Alan seems to have settled down for a while after his spell in prison," Alison continued. "I can't find any criminal references for over ten years. I think that for much of this time he was living with a woman called Ann Callow. I haven't found any marriage certificate, but they had a daughter, Louise Ann, in May 2005 and a son, Daniel Mark, in August 2007."

"You're kidding," I exclaimed, as Alison shook her head, "so we have two more grandchildren, Mary. They must be about eight and six now."

"There's more sad news, I'm afraid. Ann Callow died in September 2011 from a drug overdose." Alison waved a sheet of paper. "Alan's had two more convictions since then for drunkenness and possession of drugs."

Oh My God," Mary cried out, "how much more is there?"

"Just one more piece of bad news, I'm afraid. Alan's children have been in care since late 2012." Mary slumped forward on the table holding her head in her hands.

"I'll make some coffee," Mike stood up. I followed him into the kitchen.

"What a fucking mess," I muttered to him. "My lad's been through the mill, and so have his kids. If only Mary and I had stayed together in 1970, well, you know." I paused, deep in thought.

"You can't blame yourself for this, John. We all know what happened in 1970, but you can't change that. The priority now is for you and Mary to find Alan, and to see if you can get him on the straight and narrow. Then he might get his children back." He prepared a tray of coffee and biscuits, and carried it through to the lounge. He returned to Alison's study. "Come through to the lounge, ladies. It's more comfortable there." Alison guided Mary to the lounge, then excused herself to go to the toilet.

"Alison's done remarkably well," I commented to Mike.

"Fantastic," Mary added. "She's given us a lot of food for thought."

"She's a bloody good researcher," Mike nodded to both of us, then he turned to Alison as she entered the room. "Aren't you, pet?" Alison looked puzzled. "A good researcher."

"Oh," she laughed, "well it was my career, but I still enjoy being a detective." Mary and I smiled.

"You've done so much," I spoke to Alison, "but have you any idea where Alan lives now?"

"I assume he's still in Sheffield. When he lived with Ann, they were in an area called Manor, but I don't know where he is now. I can't access very recent census records, and in any case when he was convicted after Ann died, his address was 'no fixed abode'.

"It looks like we have another house to house search, John," Mary looked across at me. "We'll have to start with his last known address, and see if anyone knows where he is now. I think he'll still be in Sheffield. We'll find him, don't you worry."

CHAPTER FIFTY-TWO
FRIDAY 10 MAY

We enjoyed a light breakfast at Mike and Alison's, then made a booking for two nights at a Premier Inn just outside Sheffield. We had an emotional departure from Durham, thanking Alison again for all of her efforts on our behalf.

"You're more than welcome, in fact I really enjoyed doing it. Good Luck in Sheffield, and let us know straightaway when you find him."

"Don't worry," Mary said, "you'll be the first to know." She hugged Alison and I shook hands with Mike.

"See you at Pete's wedding," Mike called as we walked down the drive.

"Right," I waved back at him, and we got into our car and drove off.

We made good time on the A1 and M1 motorways and arrived at Sheffield too early to check in to our hotel, so we found a nearby pub and had lunch. Later we left our luggage in our hotel room, and changed into casual jeans and tops. I bought a street plan of Sheffield at a local newsagent's, and marked an 'x' on Alan's last known address. This was a street in Manor, an area close to the city centre. We found a parking space in a central multi-storey car park then continued by foot. In twenty minutes we had reached our destination, a street of tired-looking terraced houses. We looked for number seventeen, and found ourselves outside a plain brown door with a small diamond-shaped window near the top. The door was badly in need of a fresh coat of paint. There was no doorbell so I knocked hard on the wood. After a few minutes the door was opened by a scruffily-dressed man in his thirties. Could this be Alan? The man looked at me.

"Yeah?" he muttered.

"Sorry to bother you, but we're looking for a man called Alan Benson. We know that he lived in this house until about four years ago."

"Can't help you, mate," and he closed the door.

"That was a promising start," I smiled at Mary.

"Well at least that wasn't Alan," she said. "What a state to be in! The house looks awful."

"You'd better brace yourself, because it could get a lot worse," I cautioned, as I moved to the next front door. I rang the bell. An Asian woman half-opened the door.

"We're looking for Alan Benson," I said, "he used to live next door." The woman shrugged her shoulders and closed the door. I turned to look at Mary.

"Next," she said. We tried the next two doors, but there was no reply. "Let's cross the street." There was no reply again at the first house we tried, but the neighbouring door was opened by a middle-aged woman.

"Hello," she said, "can I help you?"

"We hope so," Mary answered, "we're looking for Alan Benson, who used to live across the road."

"Oh yes, I remember him. He lived with a pretty, younger woman, a blonde," she paused. "I can't remember her name."

"Ann," Mary reminded her.

"Yes, that's right, Ann. She was very pretty, but she and Alan both had problems - drugs, you know. It's a shame because they had two little children, but Ann died from a drug overdose and Alan moved away after that. I heard that his kids were taken into care." She shook her head, and looked sad. "Young people today, it's really bad. I see a lot of problems like that around here. It used to be a good working-class area, but now, well you can see for yourselves. I don't know what's happening to this country."

"Yes, it's terrible," I agreed with her, thinking that was the correct strategy. "I don't suppose you know where Alan lives now, do you?"

"I'm sorry, I don't. I'm not even sure if he still lives in Sheffield, but he was quite friendly with the man who lives at number twenty-eight, just along there." She pointed to a house.

"Do you know of any other friends around here?" Mary asked.

"Not really. I'm sorry I can't help you more."

"Not at all," Mary reassured her. "You've been most helpful. Thank you very much." She smiled at the woman. "We'll try that house now." We walked along to number twenty-eight, a house with another shabby door. The front window had a large crack in it. I frowned at Mary, then rang the bell. A very tall shaven-headed man appeared. He had tattoos on his neck and on his head. He didn't say anything or smile. He just looked at both of us in turn. Mary spoke first.

"I wonder if you can help us? We're looking for Alan Benson." She turned and pointed. "He ... "

"Lived over there." He nodded. "Who wants to know? Are you police?"

"No, no," Mary shook her head. "We're his parents."

The house smelt of smoke and a few other unpleasant things, and at least three cats were in the front room where we had been invited to sit. Clothes were strewn around. We both smiled as the giant came in with two mugs of coffee. The mugs were both chipped, but we still smiled. The man sat down, and stroked one of his cats.

"Right," he said forcefully, "you've got some explaining to do. I knew Al's mother Doreen and that drunken bastard of a stepfather, so whose parents are you?"

"What's your name?" I asked the giant.

"John," he replied. I laughed.

"So am I, another John." The giant even managed a brief smile. "It's a long story, John, and I won't bore you with all the details, but the basic facts are these. Mary," I raised my arm in her direction, "and I went out with each other when we were students in 1970. Everything was going fine until we both received bogus phone calls saying that the other wanted to finish the relationship. I've lived abroad for most of the forty years or so since then but what I didn't know was that Mary was pregnant. In January 1971 she gave birth at Doncaster to twin boys. They were adopted soon afterwards." I paused. "One of those boys is Alan."

"He knew that he was adopted. He always said that he was happy until his Dad died." He looked at me. "His adopted Dad."

"Last year," I continued, "I returned to England and decided to try to find out what had happened to Mary. We met up again last summer and we've been together since. When she told me about our twins, we determined to find them."

"Not easy, I guess."

"No," Mary said quietly. "We've been lucky with clues about Alan, but we've no idea where our other son is, or if he's still alive."

"Well, I'd better tell you something about Al. He's a great bloke, but he's had it tough for most of his life. Things got bad after his Dad died, and he never got on with his stepfather. He was a drunkard, and he ruined Doreen's life. Al hated him, and he ran away a few times. He was a bright lad, but he missed a lot of his schooling and got into trouble with the police." He paused. "Petty crime, and such."

"We've been able to find out some information on the internet," I said, "so we're not shocked. We know he's been to prison a couple of times." The other John nodded.

"Yeah, not for anything serious. Things got better when he met Ann. She was quite a few years younger than him, but they were good together and they've got two nice kids."

"But Ann died, didn't she?" Mary asked, a concerned look on her face.

"Hmm, she was a druggie, heroin mostly, but her father got John a steady job for a time and things were good. Then she died and it all went pear-shaped. Al got depressed, got into more trouble with the police, and now he's lost his kids.

"We know all that," I sat up and continued, "but if we can meet Alan, support him and get him back on an even keel, he might be able to rebuild his life and get his children back."

"OK, then you'll need my help. I don't know Al's present address, but I think he is still living in Sheffield. I know some of the pubs where he used to drink. If you come back here about eight o'clock tonight, I'll help you find him. You'll be safer with me." He looked at Mary. "Don't bother getting dolled up. You'll do as you are."

"Tell me, John, what does Alan look like now?" Mary asked.

"He's very untidy, he's got big eyes like you, and he has hair. He's not a freak like me." We all laughed.

Mary and I were on cloud nine as we walked back to our car. We were still on the edge of the unknown, but now believed that we would meet Alan. After that, well it would depend on him. We, of course, were prepared to go the ends of the earth to help him, but the big question was ... would he want our help?

I drove to our hotel where Mary showered, then we made love, and relaxed afterwards. Later on we both showered and dressed according to Big John's instructions. We were really too excited to eat, so we just snacked in one of the fast food outlets nearby. The time dragged, but eventually it was time to return to the centre, park our car and walk to John's house. He was waiting for us.

"This is not going to be a night on the town," he warned us. "You're going to visit some shitty dives and meet some nasty people. Stay in the background if you can, and keep close to me. I hope you're prepared for a late night or early morning." We both nodded, looking serious. "Al may not even be out tonight. We'll just have to see. Ready? Let's go."

We followed John to his first port of call, a pub two streets away. A few customers here hanging around the doorway, smoking. One or two looked at Mary and I as if we were Martians, but nobody said anything. We went into the pub. A few men at the bar nodded in greeting to John, and he spoke to a couple of them. I asked him what he wanted to drink.

"I'm fine, thanks. We won't be staying here. You can buy me a pint in the next pub. Al hasn't been in here for weeks."

We followed him for about five minutes until we reached a big pub nearer the city centre. We went inside and I ordered some drinks. I bought two pints of bitter for John and I, and a vodka and tonic for Mary. We sat down while John moved around, speaking to various people. He returned to our table and took a deep drink of his beer.

"Any luck?" I asked.

"Al's not here tonight, but he has been here a few times during the past month. Someone told me that he's moved back to Attercliffe, but I don't have an address. Don't worry," he smiled at Mary, "the night's young. Another drink?" John asked, draining his pint.

"I'm OK, thanks," I said.

"I'll have another vodka and tonic, please," Mary smiled at John. She turned to me. "It will help me to relax."

"Has your missus got a drink problem?" John laughed.

It was now almost ten thirty and we had tried three more pubs without success. I was starting to think that we were wasting our time when John's mobile rang. He went outside to answer the call, then returned and spoke to us urgently.

"Al's in that second pub we visited. Drink up quickly. Let's go." I left my beer, but Mary downed her vodka with some aplomb. I gave her an astonished look, and she grinned. I was beginning to see another side of her.

Ten minutes or so later we were back at the pub John had mentioned. He told her us to follow him inside and find a table. We sat down while he whispered to a woman at the bar, then he disappeared into another room. A few minutes later he returned with another man, a man with large eyes and dark hair. They walked across the room to our table. Big John turned to the other man. "I'd like to introduce you to Mary and another John," he said, smiling.

"Hi," smiled the other man, then turning to Big John. "Who are they – your grandparents?"

"No, Alan," Mary stood up, shaking slightly, and spoke firmly, "we are your parents."

Half an hour later, the four of us sat in a Chinese restaurant, giving our orders to the waiter. When he left, Alan turned to Mary and me.

"This is a massive shock, you know. Bloody Hell! I knew

that I was adopted, but I never thought in a million years that I would meet my real parents. You'd better tell me what you are doing here. Christ! I can't believe this is happening, mate." He turned to his friend. "I only came out for a quiet drink." Mary, fortified by the vodkas she had drank, took the lead.

"John and I met in Leeds in 1970 and we went out together for a few months. We were very much in love when we were tricked into separating."

"Tricked?" Alan said, puzzled.

"Yes, tricked. We'll explain another time. John left Leeds soon afterwards, and then I found out I was pregnant. My parents sent me to my aunt's in Doncaster to give birth, and in January 1971 you were born." She looked Alan full in the face. "Together with your twin brother."

"Jesus Christ," Alan wiped his mouth. "A fucking brother. Sorry Mary, Mam ... God I don't know what to call you. What a shock. I really have a brother?"

"Yes, you do," Mary continued, "but John and I haven't found him yet. We had some clues to look for you, but we've got nothing for him. He may not even be alive."

The waiter arrived with our food. We spent a few minutes loading our plates, then Mary carried on with her story.

"John, your Dad, didn't know anything about this until he and I met again last summer."

"I've lived abroad since 1971 and was as surprised as you are to find out that I have twin sons."

"So I guess that you both have been married to other

people?" Alan asked, chewing some curry and rice.

"Yes," Mary replied, "John was married in Australia and has a son and a daughter, and I lived in Warwick until recently and have two daughters."

"Hell," Alan laughed, "talk about an instant family. So, let me think, I have a full brother and another half-brother and three half-sisters. That's going to be expensive at Christmas," he joked.

"We know that you have a son and a daughter, Alan," Mary continued in a more serious tone. Alan stopped laughing and nodded, saying nothing. "We also know that they are in care. Well I can tell you now that we're going to help you get them back. I don't know what needs to be done, but we're going to do it."

We all paused to continue eating our meals, and I ordered more drinks. Alan suddenly stopped eating.

"I think I've had enough news, shocks even, for tonight. I'm going to finish my meal, probably have another drink somewhere, then sleep on everything that's happened tonight. Where do you live?"

"We're renting a house in Preston for now, but we have a hotel in Sheffield booked for tonight and tomorrow night. We're free all day tomorrow." Mary looked around. "Let's meet somewhere, or we can pick you up, then we can get to know each other a little better."

"OK," Alan muttered, "and you can tell me who tricked you into splitting up."

We finished our meals without revealing more secrets,

then Alan and John prepared to leave. I thanked John for his help in locating Alan for us, and Alan wrote down his mobile number and the address where he was staying. We exchanged mobile numbers with Big John as well. We arranged to meet Alan outside City Hall at ten o'clock the following morning. Alan hugged and kissed Mary and shook hands with me before he left with John. We paid the bill, walked back to the car park and drove back to our hotel. We were on a high, so excited that finally we had tracked down one of our sons, yet somewhat apprehensive as we thought about the difficulties that lay ahead with him. It took us both a good while before we managed to get to sleep.

CHAPTER FIFTY-THREE
SATURDAY 11 MAY

It was a warm sunny morning and Mary and I arrived early for our meeting with Alan. We paced around nervously waiting for him to arrive. Finally, just before ten-fifteen, we saw him walking briskly towards us. He looked as though he had made an effort to dress a little more smartly.

"Hi," he said, kissing Mary, "sorry I'm a bit late, but John and I had a few more drinks after we left the restaurant."

"We thought you might," I smiled. "It was quite a traumatic evening for you, wasn't it?"

"You can say that again. It still feels like a dream to me."

"It's lovely to see you again, Alan. It still feels like a dream to me. I keep pinching myself to make sure that it's real." Alan smiled, and put his arm around his mother. "Let's go for a coffee," Mary suggested, "then we can decide where to go for the rest of the day."

"Alright. Is a Costa OK for you?"

"You know the city, Alan," I touched his shoulder. "Lead on."

Alan carried a tray of coffees over to a quiet table in the corner of the restaurant. He passed a drink to Mary, and I took another. He smiled shyly at us.

"Where to start? This is weird."

"Well, I've brought these to show you," Mary brought out the three photos she had found in Aunt Joan's possessions.

"These two photos were taken by my aunt just after you were born. As far as I know they are the only photos of you and your brother together that exist. I'll get them copied for you." Alan stared at the two photos.

"Thank you. My daughter Louise is only eight, but she has a look of you. She has long blonde hair too."

"This other photo was sent in an anonymous Christmas card to my aunt in 1975. We believe that Doreen sent it, and that it is you."

"I'm sure that I've seen another photo similar to this. I have got a few photos and other bits and pieces from my childhood, but I think a lot was lost when my mother, that is Doreen, was married to that drunken bastard Chambers. I hated that time of my life."

"Was that when you started to get into trouble at school and with the police?" I asked. "You don't have to tell us if you'd rather not do so."

"There's probably not a lot that you don't know about me already, is there?" Alan laughed. "I bet you know more about me than I do myself. I haven't done much in my life that I'm proud of. The only things that really meant anything to me are my kids, and now I've lost them."

"But surely there must be a way of getting them back?" Mary smiled sympathetically.

"I don't know. The state I'm in, I've got no chance. When I was with Ann, things were much better. We had our drink and drugs problems, but at least I had a job and the kids were really happy. Now they've gone, and I can't see any way of them living with me again."

"Look, Alan, you can't give up so easily. When we have some time, as soon as we can, John and I will have a meeting with the local social services department, or child welfare, or whatever and find out how to bring your children out of care. I can assure you that you'll have our full backing. After all, they are our grandchildren and we're not prepared to let them go." Mary looked very angry. We finished our coffees. Alan looked up.

"I'd like to find out more about you both, how you got together, how you found each other again. Oh, and how you were tricked. That puzzles me. I want to find out everything about you, my Mam and Dad, but can you do me a big favour?"

"Name it," I said.

"It's such a beautiful day. Do you mind if we leave Sheffield and drive to my favourite place ever? It's really peaceful there, and we'll be more relaxed."

"Of course, as long as you know the way," I said. "Where is it?"

"Monsal Head, in Derbyshire. You'll love it."

I drove from the city centre, following Alan's directions, until we reached the Derbyshire border. Our route then took us along countryside roads.

"So what is Monsal Head, and why is it so special to you, Alan?" Mary was sitting in the back with Alan.

"Monsal Head is a famous viewpoint in the Peak District. It's very popular with tourists, and there's a big car park there, a hotel and a café. The view along the valley is fantastic. There's an old railway viaduct, and you can see for miles. We'll be able to get some refreshments there, and to find somewhere quiet to talk."

"And why so special?" Mary reminded him.

"Oh yeah, sorry, I forgot. When I was young kid, a bit like that photo you showed me, my Mam and Dad used to take me out regularly in their little car at weekends. Sometimes we'd go to the seaside, you know, Bridlington or Scarborough, resorts like that, but I preferred it when we went into the countryside. I've lived in the city virtually all of my life, but I love the open air and the space. I feel free and can forget all of my problems for a little while. I do like the Ladybower reservoir on the road to Manchester, but the Peak District is my favourite, and Monsal Head is my favourite place there. Mam and Dad often brought me here, and Ann and I brought the children here several times."

"I think you'd love New Zealand, Alan," I turned briefly to glance at him, "where I have lived for about ten years. The South Island is especially beautiful, with fantastic views and hardly any people. You loved it there, didn't you, Mary?"

"Yes, it's certainly a beautiful part of the world. Perhaps we'll take you there someday, and you can meet your brother Jason and his family?"

"That seems like a dream just now. I am looking forward to meeting all of my brothers and sisters."

"We still have one to find, remember," I said.

"Look, Alan," Mary took his hand, "a lot of things are

going to be possible once we get you back on track. We can help a lot, but mostly it will be down to you. If you really want it, you can do it."

"Of course I do. Just a minute, Mary. I need to concentrate on helping John to get on the right road."

Half an hour later, I drove into the car park at Monsal Head, found a space near the back and paid for a ticket. The site was busy with day-trippers who were enjoying the good weather and the superb views. Alan was keen to act as our guide and to show us the main places of interest. He took us around the other side of the old hotel and the café where we had the best view of the valley below and the old railway viaduct, now a concreted path for walkers. He pointed to the impressive viaduct to our left: "When I was a little boy the railway lines were still on the viaduct. The line had only been closed for a few years. In recent years they made concrete pathways on the top of the viaduct for walkers to use."

"It's really beautiful here, Alan," Mary said, touching his arm. "Now I can understand why it means so much to you."

We stood for a few minutes watching cattle and a few geese in the meadow far below us, as groups of walkers were making the descent using well-made pathways behind the sturdy protective stone walls on the edge of the lane. I took some photos with my tablet, and then we found a table at the café to have a snack. Once we were settled, Alan started asking questions.

"You promised that you would tell me all about

yourselves, how you met, where you went, about your romance." He laughed. "I don't need to know where I was conceived, that's if you know." We laughed as well. It was good to see our son so relaxed in our company. "Then I need to how why you separated. That's very important to me, because it led to a lot of my problems." He held up his hand. "Don't worry, I'm not blaming either of you, but I need to know who was to blame." We went quiet for a minute or two. "Finally it would be interesting to know how you got together again. You must have been a real Sherlock Holmes, Dad!" Mary smiled at his recognition of his father. She started answering Alan's questions.

"Dad and I met at a pub in Leeds. I was eighteen, studying for my A-levels, and Dad was at the university. My father was very strict as he wanted me to do well at school, but John and I managed to see each other every week and our love for each other steadily grew. We have some happy memories from those early days. One of them was a day spent in Richmond, in the Dales, where you and your brother may have been conceived in a bluebell wood."

"Bluebells. Bloody Hell," Alan roared. "I'm glad I'm not a girl. You might have christened me Bluebell." We laughed as well. Mary continued our story.

"A few weeks after that, John and I both had phone calls saying that the other wanted to finish our relationship. An ex-boyfriend of mine, more a family friend really, kept pestering me to go out with him again. I wasn't interested, but your Dad and I are convinced it was he who set up the bogus calls."

"Who was this evil bastard?" Alan asked angrily.

"He's called Paul Irvine. He's my husband. I married him a couple of years after John and I split up."

"Your husband? I don't believe it. You married the man who split you up?"

"It's a lot more complicated than that, Alan. I never loved Paul, but he did support me after I found out I was pregnant. He was OK at first. It was only later in my marriage that things became more unpleasant, and our relationship became a sham."

"Where does he live now?"

"He still lives in our old house in Warwick. He refuses to divorce me, so I have to wait for another four years or so before I can finally sort things out and get him out of my life." Mary sat back, emotionally drained. Alan looked at me.

"So you've been abroad for a lot of years?"

"Yes, for most of the time since I left university. I was a policeman in Hong Kong, then in Sydney in Australia."

"God, my Dad was a policeman!"

"I married an Australian teacher and we have a son and a daughter. My wife Ailsa died about seven years ago."

"Do you have any photos of her?"

"Not with me, Alan, but I'll show you some another time. We had moved to New Zealand before she died, and I owned a security company there, in Queenstown. My son Jason runs it now."

"Perhaps he can give me a job?" Alan laughed.

"Maybe," I said, smiling at him. "Anyway, just before I retired, three of my old university friends contacted me, and I returned to England to do the Coast to Coast Walk."

"I've heard of that. It's in northern England, isn't it?"

"Yes, it starts in the Lake District, and crosses Yorkshire, finishing at Robin Hoods Bay."

"And you managed that at your age?" Alan asked, a wry smile on his face.

"Cheeky bugger. Yes I did." We laughed. "The walk goes through Richmond, and when I was there I decided to try and find Mary on the internet."

"Your Bluebell girl, right?"

"Exactly, and I found out lots about her, when she got married, her children, where she probably lived, that kind of thing. The rest of her family was on Facebook, but Mary wasn't, so I thought I'd drive to Warwick and take a look. We met in a charity shop where she worked."

"A charity shop? How romantic."

"He nearly gave me a heart attack," Mary confessed.

"Well, it didn't take too long for us to realise that we'd been tricked into splitting up in 1970. Mary decided more or less straightaway to leave her husband, and we've been together ever since."

"Wow. Some story." Alan thought for a minute or two. "Let's walk a little. There's a lot for me to think about, but it can wait. We should enjoy the views while we are here."

At the hotel bar later that evening we reflected on the day's events.

"It's been one hell of a roller-coaster ride, Mary," I scratched my head. "What a day! So, what do you make of our son?"

"He's very bitter at the past. He's got a massive chip on his shoulder, but he does seem glad that we've found him. He doesn't appear to blame us for any of his misfortunes."

"I agree, so I think it's most important that we support him every step of the way, as much as we possibly can. He's very fragile, but having said that, we can't be with him every minute of the day. If he genuinely wants to have his children back, he must rid himself of his alcohol and drug addictions and build up a steady routine in his life. It will be interesting to hear what the Social Services people have to say."

"Yes, we must make an appointment tomorrow. I think we can best help Alan if he moves away from Sheffield, far away from the temptations and bad influences he has here, and perhaps persuade him to live with us for a while. He wants to meet the rest of his family, so we can spend some time travelling to meet our various relatives, maybe to go to Australia and New Zealand. What do you think, John?"

"Good thinking, Love, but let's not rush things. It's got to come from him. We'll have to help him crawl before he walks. If he does move to Preston to live with us, we may be able to find some work for him. He has a few days now to think things over, to consider his future, and when we see him later in the week we can agree a plan of action."

"I'm whacked, Darling. Let's drink up and go to bed."

CHAPTER FIFTY-FOUR
THURSDAY 16 MAY

On Monday morning Mary phoned Sheffield City Council and made an appointment with the Health and Social Care Department for two o'clock on Thursday afternoon. She then phoned Alan and told him about the meeting. She advised him to dress smartly, and then arranged for the three of us to meet for lunch. Mary and I thought initially of returning to Preston after the meeting, but on reflection decided to stay overnight. We felt that we needed to see Alan's reaction after the meeting, and we also had an opportunity to talk to him about a whole range of issues. How did he feel about his new family? Was he ready to meet other members of his family? Did he want to move to Preston to live with us? How did he feel about looking for a job? There were so many questions that we could ask, but we were anxious not to rush him into making any rash decisions. It was still early days.

Alan was waiting for us by the City Hall, and he took us to a nearby restaurant where we enjoyed a light lunch. He seemed a little anxious about the meeting, but Mary just advised him to relax and to listen to everything that was discussed. It was important for him to remain as calm as possible, and not to lose his temper if there seemed to be too many obstacles to bringing his children out of care. This was only a first meeting, she said. The situation had changed dramatically, as Alan now had a supportive family and a potentially better environment for the children.

Nothing would be decided or would change today, however. It might just be the start of a long road.

After lunch we walked to Moorfoot and spoke to the receptionist, who gave us directions to the meeting room. When we arrived there we were met by a middle-aged lady who introduced herself, ordered some coffees and ushered in the room. We sat down, and Mrs Sanderson opened the meeting.

"I understand that you wish to discuss the situation regarding your children, Mr Benson? As you are aware, they are currently subject to a Care Order and are with foster parents."

"Yes, I know that," Alan said, "but my personal circumstances have changed and I want to know what needs to be done to have my children returned to me."

"Please explain how your circumstances have changed."

"Just over a week ago, I met my real parents, John and Mary." He turned to us. "I was adopted as a baby, and my adopted mother died some years ago. I had a difficult childhood, but when I was with Ann, the children's mother, things were stable, were good. After she died, I lost my job and my problems returned, but now I have a new family and I think we can provide a stable environment for my children."

"Hmm." Mrs Sanderson turned to Mary and myself. "I'm puzzled. Why did you have Mr Benson adopted? What prevented you from bringing him up yourselves?"

"It's a complicated story," Mary smiled at Mrs Sanderson, "but John and I were very much in love in 1970. We were both students in Leeds, but we were tricked into splitting up and going our separate ways." Mrs Sanderson raised her eyebrows. "It's bizarre, but it happened. Soon afterwards I found out that I was pregnant, and my parents forced me to stay with my aunt in Doncaster, to have my baby there and to have it adopted. In fact, I had twin boys, so John and I have another son somewhere."

"Oh dear, what a sad story," Mrs Sanderson frowned. "So I take it that you had several years apart, and now that you are together again you have been looking for your boys? Are you married? Where do you live now?"

"We were apart for over forty years." I continued the story. "Mary and I met again last year. We aren't married, but we've lived together ever since we met. I lived abroad for many years, and Mary lived at Warwick. We have six children between us, and at least eight grandchildren." Mrs Sanderson smiled. "At the moment we are renting a house in Preston while we decide where to settle down. We are actively looking for Alan's twin brother." I sat back in my chair.

"Well this is a most unusual situation," Mrs Sanderson looked thoughtful. "The Care Order may only be lifted if we feel that the children will be going to a stable, secure environment. That doesn't mean that they have to live with Mr Benson. In cases like this the children may be homed with another member of the family, such as a brother or sister, or grandparents." She looked at us. "As I see it, and I would have to discuss the situation with my colleagues, the children cannot be moved at this moment. Ideally we would prefer the children to be returned to you, Mr Benson, but given your recent history of problems this cannot happen at present. Your children cannot be placed in the care of your parents, as they have only been together for a relatively short time and they do not have a fixed home. Do you have any brothers or sisters living in England?"

"I have two step-sisters here, and possibly my twin, if we manage to trace him."

"Do you know your step-sisters well?"

"No, I haven't met them yet."

"Well, I think you'll agree with me that we are at the beginning of a journey, possibly a long one, but there is a good chance that we may be able to re-home your children within your extended family at some point in the future. I will write a summary of this meeting and discuss matters with my colleagues, then I will write to you, and your parents, suggesting ways forward. I can give you a certain amount of advice here, I think. Mr Benson, you can help this process by finding a more stable lifestyle, looking for a permanent job and ridding yourself of your addictions. You also need to meet other members of your family and to see if you can become part of this family. As for your parents you need to inform us when you have decided where to live and when you have purchased a house. If you plan to live with your parents, Mr Benson, then your cause will be helped if they can provide a permanent home. My Department and the police will, of course, have to carry out a range of background checks to ensure that any potential new home is safe for your children. Most important of all, your children will have to meet your extended family and to have say in where or when they move, if at all." Mrs Sanderson sat back and smiled sympathetically. "As I said before, we are only at the beginning. Do you have any questions?"

"Is there any time limit to this process?" I asked.

"When a Care Order is implemented it normally takes a year or more for a judge to make the new arrangements permanent. We have time to monitor your progress, Mr Benson, but there is still much to do. Don't delay."

"Thank you for your advice," Mary smiled at Mrs Sanderson. "So can we assume that you are optimistic for our chances?"

"This is an unusual situation, quite complicated," Mrs Sanderson stood up, "but everything is possible." She smiled as we left the room.

We walked back to the centre and found a café. Alan was quiet, a man with a lot on his mind. I ordered some drinks, and we looked back on the meeting. Alan sat with his head in his hands.

"I think my chances of getting my children back are very slim." He took a sip of his coffee. "I've got too much to do ... get clean, get a job, get a life. I can't see that happening quickly enough. I don't know if I've got the willpower to do it." He looked really down.

"You've got to at least try, Alan." Mary smiled and held his arm gently. "You know you'll have a lot of support from us, and, once you've met them, the rest of the family."

"I suppose that was the one positive thing from the meeting," he seemed to brighten up. "Even if I can't look after my kids on my own, they may get the chance to live with you or one of your daughters, Mary. That way, at least they'll still be part of the family and I'll get to see them often."

"True," I said, "and I am sure that when Louise and Daniel meet us and the rest of the family they'll want to be part of it."

"Let's see," Alan said, "the journey starts today."

CHAPTER FIFTY-FIVE
THURSDAY 30 MAY

We returned to Preston on Friday morning and spent some time over the weekend in phoning Mary's daughters and our friends to tell them everything about Alan. Caroline and Laura were, of course, very keen to meet their brother and Caroline suggested that the three of us should travel to Oxford one weekend to meet members of the family there. Mary and I felt that this would give Alan an opportunity to meet all of Mary's family in one go. We could even visit Mary's mother, Alan's grandmother, on the way. Alan, we thought, would need time to decide whether the time was right for him for such an important gathering, but we were pleasantly surprised when he agreed more or less straightaway. We phoned Caroline and Laura and settled on the last weekend in May. Caroline's children were on their half-term holiday, and so would be around to meet their new uncle.

We contacted Alan to confirm the date, and suggested that he stay with us in Preston for a few days beforehand. This would give him the opportunity to meet some of my family. Again he was agreeable, and he told us that he would travel through on Tuesday. I offered to drive to Sheffield to collect him, but Alan told me that he preferred to come on the train. I suspected that he didn't want me to see the house where he was living. We met him at Preston station, and lunched in the city. Mary was keen to buy Alan some new clothes, so we shopped for a time in the centre before driving to our house. During the afternoon Mary and I raised the delicate question of money. Did he have any savings? Could he manage on his weekly benefits? Did he have any money for the weekend trip to Oxford?

We suspected that the answer to all of these questions would be 'no', and grudgingly Alan admitted that he was always short of money. We told him that we were prepared to give him money to help him with family events, to buy more new clothes, to give him a little independence, but not to pay for boozy nights or any other of his addictions. We felt that we had to show him that we trusted him, but expected to be let down more than once. We had to try, and see how he responded.

Yesterday we spent some time in Blackpool, where Alan met my sister Susan, and last night we called at my brother's house and enjoyed an evening with his family. So far, so good. Alan appeared to be enjoying spending time with his new family. He seemed comfortable, relaxed, at ease and, perhaps more importantly, Ian, Sophie and Susan liked him.

We packed after breakfast for our journey to Oxford. We were in no hurry, so we left in mid-morning when the motorway traffic was lighter. The services were busy when we stopped for lunch, but there were no major hold-ups as we headed for Warwick.

"I think I've told you that your grandmother has dementia, haven't I, Alan?" Mary turned to ask him. "She hasn't recognised me for ages, so don't worry if she totally ignores you."

"That's not a problem," Alan smiled at Mary, "I'm not expecting a hero's welcome, or anything like that. I'm just happy to meet her. I wish I'd met her years ago."

As expected, Mary's mother seemed oblivious of our visit, and continued to be happy in her own little world. Mary saw one of the senior nurses, and she confirmed that Mary's mother continued to enjoy good health. Her dementia was benign, and she showed very few signs of aggression, unlike many other elderly people with her condition. We stayed for about an hour, then returned to our car.

"Before we leave Warwick," Alan spoke to Mary, "can I see the house where you lived?"

Mary looked at me, and I nodded. She turned back to Alan. "Of course, I can't see a problem with that. My husband doesn't know this car, but he's unlikely to be around. He's always out playing golf." She turned back to me. "Do you want me to drive, John?"

"No, it's OK, Mary. Just remind me of the way."

Within a short time we reached the avenue where Mary used to live. I thought briefly of the time I had spent there talking to Mary's neighbours, trying to find a way of meeting her. I drove slowly along the avenue, and Mary gave a running commentary on some of her former neighbours and their homes. When we neared her old house, she went quiet for a few seconds, then touched Alan's arm. "This is my old house, 'The Bunker'."

"What a weird name," Alan said, then added almost immediately, "oh, of course, the golf connection. I thought at first it was something to do with Hitler!" Mary and I laughed, then she added caustically.

"Well there is a connection. They're both pigs." She paused in thought. "Keep going, John. I feel sick."

"Turn around at the end of the road, Dad, and drive past again. You can drive faster, but I want another quick look." I did a three-point-turn, and drove past Mary's house again. "Thanks," Alan said, eyeing up the house. He sat back in his seat.

By late afternoon we had reached Oxford, and I drove to the hotel we had used on our last visit. We relaxed, showered and changed, then had a drink in the bar before going to Caroline's. She had promised to have a buffet meal ready for Alan's meeting with all of the family based in the south.

It was almost seven o'clock when I parked outside Caroline's. There were one or two faces at the window. I turned round to look at Alan. He was smiling.

"I'm fine, Dad. Let's go in." Alan followed us to the front door, which was opened immediately by a small boy.

"Hello Nana and Grandad, "he chirped, "and ... ?" He peered at me.

"Alan," he said, "I'm called Alan, and I'm your new uncle." The boy smiled shyly as Caroline came to the door.

"Hi everybody. Please, come in." She ushered us in to the lounge, where everyone else was waiting.

"Hello everyone," Mary smiled at the group, then turned to make sure that Alan was in the room. "I'd like you to meet Alan." The others stood up. Mary continued, glancing at Alan. "Alan, here are your sisters and their families. This is Caroline, my oldest daughter, and her husband George, daughter Jessica and son Jack." Alan moved forward and kissed Caroline, shook hands with George and nodded to the children. He mouthed Hi in their direction. "Then over here we have Laura, my younger daughter, and her husband Stephen." Alan repeated the process with them.

"Find a seat, Alan," Caroline said. "You too, Mum. The men can talk amongst themselves for a few minutes while we get to know Alan. George, get some drinks, please." Stephen and I followed him into the kitchen.

The evening went well. Once the ice was broken, Alan relaxed and chatted to everyone comfortably. The children bombarded him with questions, but he managed to fend off the more awkward ones and satisfy them with his other answers. They were keen to know more about Alan's children, especially as they were of a similar age, but Caroline spotted the danger and shooed them away. The buffet was enjoyed by all, and Mary complimented her daughter on the spread she had prepared. Caroline sent her children to bed around nine-thirty, and the questioning became a little more personal. Alan didn't appear to be upset by any of it.

"I'm aware that you know about some of the problems I've had," he said philosophically. "You two," he pointed at Caroline and Laura, "were lucky to have had a comfortable upbringing, even if your father didn't do as much as he should have done. I don't want to say anything out of turn, but I don't like what I've heard about him. Good or bad, at least you had a father around some of the time. I've done a lot of stupid things in my time, and now I've lost my children, but I really do want to get my life back on an even keel and I'll need all the help I can get. It's not going to be easy, believe me." He sighed deeply, and Caroline and Laura came over as one and hugged him.

"Don't worry, big brother, we're behind you all the way." Laura looked at Caroline. "We're so happy to have you in our lives, and we're really positive about the future."

"Yes, we are," added Caroline, "and I hope that we'll find our other missing brother. Then our family will be complete." There were a few tears.

We left just after midnight, emotionally drained, but looking forward to spending more time with our family over the weekend. It was another positive step forward.

CHAPTER FIFTY-SIX
WEDNESDAY 5 JUNE

We left Oxford on Monday morning, after looking around the city on Saturday then taking the children to Longleat on Sunday. Alan was in good spirits, and quite optimistic about his future. He told us that he was beginning to appreciate being part of a supportive family again, and was only sorry that this change had come too late to prevent his children being placed in care. He knew that the ball was in his court, and fully understood the importance of continuing to strive for personal stability.

On the return journey on the M40, we again took the Warwick exit and made a brief visit to Mary's mother. The visit was almost a carbon copy of the one we had made the previous week, but there was so much going on in our lives at the moment that we did not want to miss the opportunity to see her again. After leaving the home, we travelled north to Sheffield and dropped Alan off in the city centre. We discussed the possibility of meeting his children, so Alan promised to contact Mrs Sanderson from the Social Services department to see if something could be arranged for the following weekend. Mary and I agreed to keep the weekend free so that we would be available if a meeting was arranged. We told Alan that we would phone later in the week.

Around three in the afternoon, the phone rang. I expected Alan to be on the end of the line, but was surprised to hear Pete's voice.

"How are things, John?" Pete asked. "Any more progress with Alan?"

"Oh, hi Pete. Good to hear from you. Thanks for asking about Alan. I think we're making some progress. He's met Mary's daughters and their families, as well as my brother and sister, and got on well with everyone. They all seem to like him. We've also had a meeting with an officer with Sheffield Social Services, so Alan now knows exactly what must be done if he wants his children back. We're behind him all the way, and if it doesn't work out with Alan, it may be possible to have his children living with other members of our family. We've some way to go on that one." I paused briefly, then continued. "Anyway, enough of us, how are you and Karen getting along? Have you set a date yet?"

"We certainly have, pal. That's the reason why I'm phoning you. We're going to take the plunge on Saturday 6th July."

"That's great news, Pete. I can hardly believe it. God, Pete, the great womaniser, finally getting hitched. That's amazing. So where is this going to happen?"

"It's a place near Bolton, where Karen lived when I met her. It's called the Last Drop Village. We'll be sending out the invites and so on as soon as possible."

"That sounds an interesting place. Are you sure it's not the Last Chance Saloon?" I could hear Pete laughing at the other end.

"Bastard. Look, my life has changed since we all got together again, and I met Karen. If it wasn't for you all this never would have happened."

"And Karen would have been happy ever after! Only joking, mate. Don't worry, we've all seen the change in you. You've got a good one there, even if you don't deserve it." We both laughed.

"Right, I can't spend all day chattering to you. I need to contact the others, then Karen and I have a million things to do."

"Such as finding a suit that fits you." I chuckled again.

"This is getting worse, John. Just wait until it's your turn. I'm off. We'll be in touch."

"See you, Pete. Great news." I put the phone down and shouted through to Mary. "You need to find a new frock, Love. Pete and Karen are getting married on the 6th of July." Mary appeared in the hall.

"Hey, that's great news. We're going shopping tomorrow. Where do you want to go – Manchester or Liverpool?"

"You choose, Mary. The shops all look the same to me!"

Mary phoned Alan after tea. Much to her surprise he had contacted Mrs Sanderson and arrangements were being made for the three of us to meet Alan's children on Sunday. Mary was delighted, and told Alan so. He promised to phone as soon as the meeting was finalised. She asked him how things were going in Sheffield, and he told her not to worry, everything was finc.

CHAPTER FIFTY-SEVEN
SUNDAY 9 JUNE

Alan phoned on Friday to tell us that a meeting had been agreed for the following Sunday. Mrs Sanderson and the carers felt that a lengthy meeting would not be advisable at this point, so it was agreed that we would meet Alan's children for a meal at the McDonald's in the city centre at four o'clock. This made sense to us and though the restaurant would not have been our first choice, we thought that the children would feel more comfortable there.

We met Alan an hour earlier at a different café. A few matters needed to be discussed before we met his children ... our grandchildren.

"How much do they know about us, Alan?" Mary asked after we had been served by a surly-looking waitress.

"Not very much, I think. This might be a little confusing for them, because I think that I told them that my mother was called Doreen. Mind you, that was a few years ago, so they have probably forgotten. Of course, they never met her, anyway."

"It might be easier if we tell them that we have lived abroad for a long time," Mary suggested, "and have just returned to England?"

"Yes, that should be OK," Alan said, "but don't tell them anything about the rest of our family, especially that I have a twin brother. That would be really confusing for them, and difficult to explain for us."

"Of course," I replied. "We'll try to keep the conversation very general, and ask questions about them. Let's hope that they won't be too shy."

"I don't think that will be a problem. Louise is quite a confident little girl, despite all that she and Daniel have been through. She'll be like the Spanish Inquisition once she gets to know you, don't you worry."

As we were waiting outside McDonald's, Alan pointed along the street where we could see Mrs Sanderson with two children. They carried on walking towards us, then Louise and Daniel sprinted towards their father and gave him a big hug. It was all smiles, and good to see. A minute or two later they broke off and Mrs Sanderson spoke to Alan, as the children looked at Mary and me. Mrs Sanderson smiled at us, then spoke to the children.

"I'll see you later, Louise, Daniel, probably about six o'clock. Enjoy yourselves. Bye."

Alan held hands with his children, then brought them over and spoke to us. "Mary and John, here are your grandchildren, Louise and Daniel." We both smiled widely.

"Hello," said Mary, "Grandad John and I are really pleased to meet you both." I nodded in agreement.

"I didn't know we had a Nana Mary and Grandad John," said a puzzled Louise, a pretty blonde-haired girl. "Dad has never talked about you before."

"That's because we haven't lived anywhere near you," I quickly intervened. "Shall we go inside and have something to eat?" Daniel came to life at the mention of food. He was a good-looking little lad, with his father's eyes. We all piled inside and found a table.

"What would you like to eat?" Mary asked. "You'll have to tell us what's nice, because Grandad and I don't eat in McDonald's very often."

Daniel stood up. "Come with me, Nana. I'll show you what there is." Mary stood up and followed him.

"I'll just have some kind of burger and fries, Mary," I told her. "Have you got some money?" She nodded.

"Same for me, please," Alan said. Louise stood up and walked with Mary to the counter.

"Nice kids," I turned to Alan. "They seem very polite. No difficult questions yet." Alan grinned.

"There's plenty of time yet, Dad."

We stood and waved as Mrs Sanderson walked away with the children. Alan turned and grimaced. I put my arm around his shoulder.

"Come on, Alan. Everything will be fine. It's been a good day."

"You're right, Dad, but it's difficult, you know."

"I'd like a coffee somewhere," Mary said. "Are there are any cafés still open, or do we have to go back to McDonald's?"

"It's Sunday, Mam, but Costa will still be open. Let's go there."

We walked to the nearest Costa, bought some drinks and found a table. Mary looked at Alan.

"I've really enjoyed meeting Louise and Daniel. They're

great kids. I think we've made some progress today, and I'm sure that you'll be able to arrange to see them again next week."

"Yeah," Alan said, looking thoughtful, "Louise and Daniel seemed to accept you naturally. I expected Louise to quiz you a lot more. Perhaps she will next time."

"Yes, and make sure that there is a next time, Alan. Phone Mrs Sanderson for their reactions, and make arrangements for our next meeting, perhaps on Sunday again. See if we can meet for a longer time."

"OK," Alan replied, "I'll get it sorted."

"John and I have been thinking about other things for the future. How would you feel about moving over to Preston to live with us for a while? Your Uncle Ian thinks he may be able to find a part-time job for you, if you think you are ready."

"Let me think that one over, Mam. I know why you consider it to be a good idea, but I'm not sure if it's the right time for me. Give me a few days, and we'll talk about it again. What kind of work would it be?

"In one of the large chain stores, Alan. Ian knows a manager."

Alan placed his knuckles on his cheek, and moved his eyes around in thought.

I gave him a few minutes before speaking. "We were also wondering if you'd like to visit the rest of your family."

"I thought I'd met them all. Oh, do you mean your sister, Mam?"

"No, we meant your brother and sister's families in Australia and New Zealand."

"Wow, really? That would be great, but I could never afford anything like that."

"Don't worry about the expenses," I said. "We would take care of that. Anyway, we need to go to New Zealand to make sure that my house is alright."

"Is it just empty?"

"Oh no, one of Jason's employees has been renting it. He'll have to find somewhere else for a couple of weeks. That won't be a problem."

"Well in that case, yes, of course I'd love to go. When are you thinking of going there?"

"We haven't fixed a date yet," Mary said. "Pete and Karen's wedding is on the 6th of July, so it would have to be after that. Perhaps mid to late July, and we'll go for about three weeks."

"What about my kids?" Alan asked. "It's their school holidays."

"Hmm, I hadn't thought of that," I said. "OK then, we can go a little later, perhaps mid-August. That would give you, or us, some time to take Louise and Daniel away, if Mrs Sanderson will allow it."

"It might be nice to take them to Oxford to meet Caroline and her family, possibly Laura as well. If not, we could always visit Bristol for a day and see Laura and Stephen then."

"I like that idea," Alan smiled. "I'd also like to take them to the seaside, you know, Scarborough or Bridlington, somewhere like that."

"Well you've got a few days to think things over," I said. "By the way, have you got a passport?"

"Christ, no I haven't. I've never been abroad."

"Then you'll have to get a form from the Post Office and apply as soon as possible. It can take two or three weeks to have a passport processed," Mary said. We sat back in thought, then finished our drinks.

"Before we go, Alan, there's one last thing. Mary and I have found you, and everything is going well so far, but we still have someone else to find."

"My brother, yes I know. I've been thinking about him quite a bit recently, what he's like, where he lives, what kind of life he's had. That sort of thing."

"We had one or two clues which helped us find you," I continued, looking more serious, "but as far as your brother is concerned, we have nothing. We've given it a lot of thought, and the only chance we have is to employ an Adoption Agency."

"How does that work?" Alan leant forward.

"We need to look into it more fully, but I think that these Agencies can access adoption records confidentially. They would be able to find out what your brother is called now, and perhaps to trace him."

"That sounds great."

"Hmm, but it's not as straightforward as that. If your brother is traced, he may not want to know any details about the three of us, or to have any contact with us. That's his prerogative, and if that's the case, the agent is not allowed to tell us any personal information, such as his name or his address. He's only allowed to tell us if your brother is still alive and if he's healthy, not much more, I think."

"Well I would like to meet him, so if this is our only chance, go for it." Alan paused. "Oh, I never thought, I suppose this search would cost?" I nodded.

"A lot of money, we think, but we're not too concerned about that. It's more how we would deal with the possible disappointment if your brother isn't traced, or worse than that, if he doesn't want to know us."

"Well you won't know until you try." Alan smirked at me.

"We'll have to go, Alan," Mary said. "We've got to drive back to Preston tonight, and you have a lot of thinking to do. Don't forget to contact Mrs Sanderson soon." She waggled her finger.

"Do you get nagged like this?" Alan asked me.

"All the time, son, all the time."

CHAPTER FIFTY-EIGHT
SATURDAY 29 JUNE

June had been a good month for us. Following our first meeting with Alan's children, and our heart-to-heart talk with him things had progressed well. After some thought, Alan decided that a break away from Sheffield would be good for him, so he took up our offer to live with us in Preston. Ian's friend also interviewed Alan for some part-time work, with the possibility of full-time work in the future if Alan fitted in well and trade continued to improve. The manager was aware that Alan had booked a holiday in Australia and New Zealand in August/September, and he told Alan that he would arrange cover while he was away. I thanked Ian for his efforts on our behalf, and checked to make sure that his friendship with the manager was not being compromised too much. Alan's working hours were flexible, so he was able to maintain contact with his children at weekends. We decided not to see our grandchildren every weekend, thus allowing Alan more private time with them. He usually travelled by train, but Mary told him that he could borrow her car if he planned to take his children on a day out somewhere.

I phoned Mrs Sanderson to see how she felt about our plans to take Alan's children on a family trip to Oxford in the summer holidays. She seemed fine with that, and told us that she was generally happy with the progress that had been made. She hoped that Alan's move to Preston and part-time work would bring more stability in his life.

Looking ahead, however, she could foresee some difficulties as Alan's children were settled at school and had lots of friends, and so were reluctant to leave Sheffield. We told her that we would move to Sheffield if necessary, but were still unable to purchase a house until Mary's divorce had been settled or some of her joint finances with Paul had been released. It was still early days, so Mrs Sanderson told us that she would continue to monitor the situation and to let us know if any concerns were raised.

Mary and I had begun the process of looking at the various Adoption Agencies on the internet, making notes on the services they offered, on their charges and on their track records. We were keen to access any feedback before we made a decision over which agency to employ. We had plenty on our plate at this time – Pete and Karen's wedding, our proposed visit to Oxford, and the trip to Australia and New Zealand – so we weren't in a hurry to decide. We therefore agreed to employ one of the agencies just before our visits to Sally's and Jason's, hoping that while we were abroad for three weeks or so, some progress might be made on the search for our other son.

The countdown to Pete and Karen's wedding had begun. Mary had gone to Bolton on Thursday for Karen's hen party, and yesterday I travelled to Leeds for a stag weekend with Pete. It was good to see Mike and Dave again, as well as to meet some of Pete's friends from Manchester, including his brother Tony, who was going to be his best man. Needless to say, we visited most of our old haunts, having a heavy drinking session in the city centre on Saturday evening before enjoying a more sedate Sunday. We lunched at the

'Oak' where my friends were keen to catch up with my news.

"So, John, how is everything going?" Mike asked eagerly. "Alison's been pestering me to find out all the details about your quest to find your boys."

"Pretty good, so far," I said, "at least I think so. Alan seems to have settled well with us at Preston and he's even got some part-time work. We've met his children. They're good, level-headed kids, and Mary and I have got on well with them. We're hoping to take them to Oxford in the holidays to meet Mary's daughters and their cousins. We're also planning to take Alan to Australia and New Zealand to meet my family out there."

"That sounds great," Dave beamed. "I'm really pleased for you, John. It looks as though everything is going well."

"We're not counting any chickens just yet. We've managed to draw Alan away from his temptations in Sheffield for the time being, but I think he's still fragile. He's more optimistic about his chance of getting his children back, but I don't know how he'll react if that doesn't happen. We'll just have to see what happens. Mary and I are staying strong for him, so fingers crossed."

"How are things going with your search for your other twin?" Mike asked. "Alison's really frustrated that she hasn't been able to help there."

"No, I'm afraid not. We're resigned to the fact that we will have to get some kind of agency help to trace him. We're going to set things in motion before we leave for Australia, and hopefully they'll have some answers when we return in September." I paused, and sat back. "Anyway, that's enough about me. How about the rest of you?"

"Oh, our lives are dull in comparison to yours," chuckled Dave. "That's why we're so interested."

"Cheers for that," I muttered. "Come on, Pete, you're almost a married man. Are you really ready for that ball and chain?"

"Well, I never thought I'd say this, but I couldn't be happier. Karen and I get on so well. I find it difficult to understand why I've never felt like this before, given the number of girls I've been out with. Hand on heart, I'm so looking forward to next Saturday."

"That's one of the blessings of dementia, Pete!" Dave quipped."

"Cheeky bugger," Pete retorted. "Just wait until I see Jenny."

CHAPTER FIFTY-NINE
SUNDAY 7 JULY

Yesterday had been a great day for Pete and Karen. Everything had gone so well. The weather had been perfect, and the afternoon ceremony had gone smoothly. My friends and I were quite surprised to see Pete looking so nervous, as he had always been the confident one at university. When it was his turn to make his vows, he stammered through his lines and the registrar had to repeat one sentence. I smiled widely, but Mary elbowed me and whispered: "Just wait until it's your turn." Karen looked beautiful in a pale peach dress. In fact all of our partners looked stunning. Mary wore a plain blue dress that reminded me of the one she had worn when we first dated all those years ago. Only the white boots were missing.

Later on, after the meal, Pete seemed to have recovered most of his old confidence. He delivered an amusing speech, and spoke about our friendship and the debt he owed us for bringing him and Karen together. "If we hadn't agreed to get together after forty-odd years and Dave hadn't organised our Coast to Coast trip, Karen and I would never have met. At the same time," he joked, "I've not forgiven them for showing me up as a middle-aged, overweight pudding during the walk!" He spoke in moving terms about his love for his new wife, and about how much he was looking forward to spending the rest of their lives together. It certainly wasn't the Pete we used to know.

A lively evening followed, with a local disco and an

enormous buffet. Mary and I spent most of the evening with Dave, Jenny, Mike and Alison, plus occasional dances with the bride and groom.

Exhausted, we staggered to bed in the hotel after one in the morning. "I wonder how long we're going to have to wait for this day," I thought aloud.

"Years, probably, as Paul will no doubt keep dragging his feet. In the meantime, my little devil, you're not too tired, are you?" She grinned in the half light.

We awoke to another beautiful morning and went downstairs for a late breakfast. A few of the stay-over guests were there, but most still had to surface. We joined Dave and Jenny at their table, and soon afterwards our other friends appeared.

"What are your plans for today, Mary?" Alison asked.

"Oh, I think we'll have a look around here for the rest of the morning. It's an interesting place, with its old-fashioned shops and cobbled streets. After that we'll probably visit a garden centre or something like that on the way home, then wait for Alan coming back from Sheffield."

"Has he gone to visit his children again?" Jenny sipped her coffee.

"Yes," Mary replied. "How about the rest of you?"

"We'll stay until all of the guests have left," Karen replied, "then we're going home to pack for our honeymoon."

"I've forgotten," Dave said, "where are you going?"

"For a cruise around Italy, then a few days at Venice."

"Very romantic," Jenny smiled, turning to us. "Didn't

you go there, John?"

"Hmm, it was alright I suppose."

"How on earth did I end up with you?" Mary asked, poking my side.

"You just got lucky," I smirked. The others laughed.

At lunchtime Mary and I were browsing in one of the shops when my mobile rang. I went outside to answer it.

"Hello."

"Hi. Is that John?"

"Yes, who's calling?"

"Big John, you know, from Sheffield."

"Oh, good to hear from you John, what's up?"

"It's Alan. He must have come through to Sheffield yesterday, because he's been on a real session and he's totally out of it."

"Christ, no!" I called out. "Where is he?"

"At my house. He crashed out there, but I don't know what he's been on. He's out for the count."

"Bloody Hell, and things have been going so well. Oh Jesus, he's supposed to be meeting his kids this afternoon. I'll have to phone Mrs Sanderson and make an excuse. Look John, Mary and I are at a wedding do in Bolton, and we've both been drinking over the weekend. Neither of us can drive today. Can you look after Alan until he comes round, then contact me again?" Mary appeared, looking concerned. *What's wrong?* she mouthed.

"No worries," Big John said. "I'll phone you later."

"Thanks a lot, John. You've been a good friend, thanks." Mary came over and clutched my arm. I switched my mobile off.

"Well, what's happened, John?"

"It's Alan, Mary. He must have gone to Sheffield yesterday and he's totally drunk, or worse. He's at Big John's."

"Oh God, no." Mary bit her lip, and thought for a moment. "What about the children? He's due to meet them any time."

"I know. I'm going to phone Mrs Sanderson." I switched on my mobile and scrolled down to her mobile number.

"Hello, Mrs Sanderson? ... it's John Newby, Alan's father. I'm sorry to mess you around at short notice, but he's been ill and we've had to return to Preston ... He's in bed, I'm sorry ... Can you apologise to the children, please, and tell them that we'll see them next weekend? ... Oh, thank you very much. They're starting their summer holidays, aren't they, and I know that Alan was planning to take them to Bridlington. The weekend after that we're going to Oxford. ... Apologies again, Mrs Sanderson, but he'll make up for it next week ... Bye."

"That didn't sound very convincing, John."

"Hmm, I'm not sure if she believed me. We'll just have to see. It should be alright, as long as it doesn't happen again. Now what do we do?"

"Didn't you say that Big John is phoning you back? We'll have to wait for his call, then take it from there. I hope to God that Alan hasn't used my car."

“He told me that he was going by train on Saturday morning. We’ll soon find out when we get home. Anyway, we can’t do anything else now. Let’s re-join the others and enjoy what’s left of today.”

CHAPTER SIXTY
TUESDAY 6 AUGUST

Our reunion with Alan following his misadventure in Sheffield was not an easy one. The trust we had built up in him had been severely dented, and we knew it would take some time before it could be restored. Nevertheless, we had always expected setbacks at some point and so we were ready to support Alan again and give him another chance. In some ways the incident was "swept under the carpet", and daily life quickly returned to its pre-Sheffield routine. Alan contacted Mrs Sanderson and the weekend meetings with his children were restored. He genuinely appeared to be enjoying his part-time work, and was pleased to tell us in mid-July that he was taking a fellow worker, Cheryl, to the cinema. More dates followed. Cheryl was a divorcee, about eight years younger than Alan, with a young daughter. She lived on the other side of Preston and Alan stayed over a couple of times.

Alan's children were now on holiday, so he was able to take them on day trips to Bridlington and to Monsal Head, a place which they also enjoyed visiting. We travelled to Oxford towards the end of July and stayed for two nights in a hotel. Alan's children got on very well with Caroline's, and there were a few tears when it was time to return home. We believed that Louise and Daniel were now starting to feel part of our family, and looked forward to the growing contact they had with their father and other family members. Things were going well again by the beginning of August, and our only real concern was maintaining this progress after we returned from New Zealand in September.

Alan now had a passport, and I booked flight tickets for the three of us for Tuesday 20 August. I had planned an itinerary and then discussed it with Mary and Alan before making the bookings. We were flying first to Bangkok, where we would stay for two nights, then on to Sydney, where we would stay at Sally's for about a week. After that we would take the short flight to Christchurch and hire a car to travel for a few days in the South Island before reaching Queenstown. Jason had made sure that my house would be available for our week-long stay there. At the end of our trip we would return to England via Singapore, where Mary planned to visit a few shops for a change! As Alan became more and more excited about this trip as the departure date loomed, his first journey abroad, I tried to think back to my feelings in 1970 when I travelled out to Hong Kong.

After much research and discussion, Mary and I had finally settled on an agency which would act as an intermediary in our search for Alan's brother. One of their agents, Colin Barnes, phoned us and we arranged a first meeting at our house in Preston for today. Mary and I wanted this meeting to be just between us and the agent, so we selected a day when Alan was at work. Mr Barnes arrived around ten-thirty, and after the usual formalities and coffee we began our discussions. Mary spent half an hour describing our relationship in Leeds, explaining how our twins came to be adopted, then outlining how she and I had got back together last year and eventually found Alan.

“Thank you, Mary,” Mr Barnes said, relaxing in his chair. “Yours is a most unusual story. You have been quite fortunate in tracing your son Alan, but from what you have told me there are still several issues to resolve.”

“Yes,” Mary replied. “Alan is keen to find his brother, but at the moment he is more concerned about getting his children back. That is why John and I are concentrating on the search for his brother.”

“Understood,” Mr Barnes paused. “I’ll run through the various processes as thoroughly as I can, but I will say from the outset that you will have to prepare yourselves for some possible emotional upsets and disappointments. Nothing is certain, and even if we do manage to locate your son, he may decide not to have any contact with you.”

“We realise that, Mr Barnes,” I said. “We have carried out a lot of research.”

“Please call me Colin,” he said, smiling. “OK, let’s make a start. I can access confidential adoption records and find out your son’s new name. That’s the easy part. Assuming that he’s still alive, and you must be prepared for the possibility that he has died, locating him could be much more difficult. He may have moved abroad, for example, and searching in other countries can be complicated, and expensive. I would, of course, tell you if we have drawn a blank in the UK before starting to search elsewhere. You may call a halt to the whole process if you feel that it is becoming too emotionally draining for you, or if it is costing too much. Are you with me so far?” We both nodded. “Good. Do you have any more coffee?”

"Of course," Mary said, and went to the kitchen to prepare another pot. Mr Barnes continued when she returned. It was obvious to me that he preferred to go through the process in small stages.

"Before we begin the search, we would like you to write a letter to your son, perhaps outlining your relationship and his adoption, describing your family and, of course, telling him that he has a twin brother. You also need to provide some contact details. You don't need to write the letter today. Include some recent photographs as well. Take your time, and post it to me when it's ready. If we trace your son, I can explain to him why you want to meet him, and give him your letter. At this point, your son can then decide whether or not he wants to have any contact with you." Mr Barnes paused and drank his coffee. Mary looked close to tears, and I spoke to her.

"Are you alright, Love?"

"Yes, I'm OK. I was just upset at the thought that he might not want any contact with us. Does that happen very often, Colin?"

"That's difficult to say, as every case is different of course, but it does happen occasionally. After all, your son has been brought up by a different family and will probably have a lot of love for them. He may feel that you rejected him soon after he was born, and so doesn't want anything to do with you. You have to be prepared for that possibility. If he does decide that he doesn't want any contact with you, he can make that decision legally binding, or he can leave it open just in case he changes his mind at some future time. I would leave your letter, contact details and photographs with him so that he is able to contact you if he does change his mind." Mr Barnes paused again. Mary and I sat thinking.

"So, Colin, if it is a 'no contact' decision, what are you allowed to tell us about him?" I asked.

"Not very much, I'm afraid. You are not allowed to have any personal details. I would have to discuss with him the information that I think ought to be passed on. That could include his general health, for example. He has the right to know if there are any hereditary ailments in the family. You would, of course, know that he is alive and well. I could also give you a rough idea about where he lives, let's say southern Scotland, the Midlands, and so on. I'll probably also be able to tell you if your son is married and if he has any children." He paused again. "Any questions?"

"Thank you, no," I replied. "You've outlined roughly what we expected. Let's be positive for a change. What happens if you do trace him and he is willing to meet us?"

"In that case I would normally act as an intermediary and arrange a meeting at a place and time convenient to you both. This would not be at one of your houses, but at a neutral venue. You may wish to choose a location where you would have some privacy, as a meeting like this can be extremely traumatic and upsetting. Further meetings can then be arranged to suit the needs and wishes of both parties. After that we would expect that more family contacts and relationships might result." He smiled and paused again. "I think that's about there is to it. I believe that potential fees and expenses were outlined to you when you first enquired about our services?"

"Yes, that's true," I replied.

"So have you any more questions?" Mary and I looked at each other.

"No," Mary said, "I think that's everything, thank you. I'll write a letter in the next few days and send it to you with some photos."

"Good," Mr Barnes replied. "Hand-written letters are better, more personal." He smiled. "I think that's all for today."

"Before you go, Colin, you do know that we are taking Alan on a trip to Australia and New Zealand, don't you? We are leaving England on the 20th of August."

"Yes, I was told about that. If our search is concluded while you are away, I will email you to arrange a meeting soon after you return. I won't give any details about the search and its outcome in the email. We prefer to discuss everything face to face."

"Of course," I said. "We prefer that too. Thank you for your time, Colin. Let's hope that you have some good news for us when we return."

"Quite," Mr Barnes smiled again. "Keep your fingers crossed, and have an enjoyable holiday. I hope to see you again next month." Mary brought Mr Barnes his coat and saw him to the door. We waved as he walked down the drive.

CHAPTER SIXTY-ONE
SATURDAY 17 AUGUST

Mary and I spent the days following Mr Barnes' visit in discussing the implications of the information he had given us, and in making lists and buying odds and ends for our holiday. We made sure that Alan would have everything he needed for his first trip abroad. Alan had arranged to see his children at Sheffield on Sunday, so we decided to write our letter then, when we had some privacy. On reflection, we could have done this task sooner, as Alan was often out during the evenings seeing Cheryl.

We agreed that Mary should write the letter and that it should only be a single sheet of A4 paper. I made some notes while Mary prepared several drafts, then we agreed on the final version. Mary folded the letter and placed it in an envelope, then we studied the photos we had prepared. In the end we decided to enclose just one photo, taken when Mary and I were in Venice the previous year. I posted the envelope via recorded delivery on Monday morning.

Dear Son

Your father and I were very much in love in Leeds in 1970, but we were cruelly forced to part and go our separate ways. John did not know that I was pregnant, so I had to go and live at my aunt's in Doncaster where you were born on 4 January 1971. You will not be aware that you have a twin brother who was also adopted a few days after being born. I was terribly upset when I had to give you up, and I have never stopped thinking about you both ever since.

John and I met again in August last year and he was shocked but delighted to find out that he was the father of twin boys. We have been searching for you and your brother since then. In May we were overjoyed to find your brother Alan alive and well in Sheffield. He has two children and is now living with us in Preston.

We are desperate to find you and to finally reunite our family. Apart from Alan, you have two step-sisters in England, a step-sister in Australia and a step-brother in New Zealand. They, and their families, are also longing to meet you.

We understand that this letter may come as a shock to you, as you probably have a happy life with your family wherever you live and never thought to hear from your birth parents. Now you have the chance to be part of a much larger family who will love you as much as we will surely do.

John and I sincerely hope that we can meet you in the near future. We are so looking forward to that day. Until then we will continue to love you in our hearts.

Your loving parents, John and Mary.

Alan drove to Sheffield this morning, collected his children and brought them to our house for a weekend stay. We made a fuss of them when we arrived, then the four of us went to the city centre, where Alan had arranged to meet up with Cheryl and her daughter. The three children were shy at first, but after a lunch in KFC, it was difficult to keep them quiet. It was good to see them enjoying themselves, particularly as we would not see them again for a month. This holiday gave Alan the opportunity to meet my family on the other side of the world, yet at the same time it could strain the developing relationships he had in Sheffield and Preston. That was the risk we had to take.

We decided to travel with Alan to Sheffield tomorrow afternoon and say goodbye to Louise and Daniel, before returning to do our final packing for our big trip to Australia and New Zealand. Our flight was early on Tuesday morning.

CHAPTER SIXTY-TWO
THURSDAY 12 SEPTEMBER

Looking back, we had a really enjoyable holiday, with no mishaps and plenty of happy memories. For three weeks or so we could put our difficulties and worries to the back of our minds, and enjoy being tourists and meeting family. Alan proved to be a good traveller, and became very excited as we began each leg of our journey.

Bangkok was a new experience for both Alan and Mary. They were fascinated by the hectic pace of life in the Thai capital, and we managed to cram a lot of sightseeing into our brief stay there. We spent the days looking around temples and markets, travelling between them by the quaint and hair-raising tuk-tuks. On our first evening we enjoyed a meal in a street restaurant, followed by a ladyboy show in one of the opulent hotels. Our second evening was spent looking around a night market, where we saw a wide choice of fake designer clothes and handbags and met people trying to sell us a bewildering variety of sexual entertainment. I think Alan would have been happy to stay in Bangkok for a week, but we had to move on to Sydney.

Sally was the perfect hostess during our stay in Sydney, but she and her husband Ricky had to work for much of the time. As at Oxford, Alan was accepted warmly by Sally and her children and he clearly relished meeting more of his relatives. We visited all of the sights so loved by tourists, and walked over the top of the Sydney Harbour Bridge. Alan was very much at home with the Australian way of life, the friendliness of people that we met, the sport and the pubs – he felt it was almost like being in England, but with a better climate. All too soon, our stay in Sydney was over, and we took the short flight to Christchurch in New Zealand.

I hired a car at the airport and drove to the west coast. It was early spring, and we enjoyed fine weather as we travelled along the coast and then inland towards Queenstown. I made a detour to Milford Sound, hoping that the fine weather would hold, and it did. The views, as always were breathtaking. Finally, after three days we arrived at my house, where Jason and his family were waiting to greet us. Alan was treated as a long-lost friend and quickly settled in my former home. We divided our time between family and sightseeing, driving to Dunedin on Tuesday. Our holiday was drawing to an end, and our thoughts were starting to turn back to England and whatever waited for us there.

We awoke to a beautiful morning, perfect for our visit to Bob's Peak, high above Queenstown. We travelled up on the gondola cable-car, and just paused at the top for ten minutes or more to take in the fabulous panorama that stretched before our eyes. Lake Wakatipu was so blue, and the snow-capped Remarkables completed a stunning backdrop. Alan commented that the view reminded him of Monsal Head. Later we enjoyed a Maori show, where Alan was dragged onto the stage to see if he could push his tongue out as far as the performers. Mary took some great photos. It was now lunchtime, so we enjoyed a meal in the cliff-top restaurant while we absorbed the view out of the window. When we had finished, we strolled around the walks on the heights.

Alan halted, and put his arms around both of us. "You know, Mam and Dad, I can't thank you enough for everything that you have done for me." Mary began to protest, and he stopped her. "Honestly, a few months ago, my life was going down the pan, but meeting you has given me so many opportunities that I don't deserve." I pulled a face.

"Alan, you've done so much for us as well. Finding your mother again and then searching for you has made our lives much more meaningful. We've had our problems, and no doubt will come across many more, but if we support each other and stick together we can overcome everything that life throws at us."

"True, but I've let you down so much. I've been so weak, and without you would have gone under, but the past couple of months and this holiday have made me realise that I've got a lot to live for. I love my family, I do feel that I belong, and things are good with my kids and with Cheryl. In some ways I'm a bit frightened about going back, in case things go wrong again and I can't handle it." He looked close to tears.

"Alan," I said, hugging him, "don't forget that we will always be there, well at least for long enough to get you properly settled." We laughed. "You're not the only one who is apprehensive about going back. Don't forget that Mary and I will be getting some news soon about your brother. He's the last piece in the jigsaw, but we may be returning to bad news. We just don't know." We continued walking along the clifftop.

"We've said it many times before, Alan," Mary joined in the conversation, "that we have to remain positive and optimistic. You're not going to face any problems on your own. We will also be there for you, and the rest of your family will feel exactly the same."

"I'm so fortunate to have parents like you," Alan muttered.

"Well you might be now," I said, "but for many years you've had to face a lot of demons on your own, and you are still here. You are much stronger than you think." Alan paused, and pointed.

"Strong enough to do that?" Alan beamed as we watched some tandem paragliders on the cliff edge. A linked couple staggered to the edge as the wind took their sail, then they were off, floating out above the void, heading slowly for Queenstown in the valley below. We could see two or three more pairs drifting downwards, like feathers in the wind. "That's fantastic," Alan enthused, "I'm going to have a go. Where do I pay?"

Just over an hour later Mary and I watched Alan jogging along the path towards us. He was beaming all over his face, just like an excited child. He reached us and hugged us wildly.

"That was absolutely fantastic," Alan couldn't stop smiling, "the best experience of my life, bar none. It was like being on top of the world. I felt like a majestic bird, wheeling around the air pockets, then slowly flying down to my nest in the valley below. Bloody Hell, that was great, unbelievable. Why don't you have a go, Mam?"

"Not on your Nellie," Mary laughed. "I'm terrified just going on the cable-car."

"There are some bungee-jumpers over there, Dad. Why don't you try that?"

"Come on," I said, taking Mary by the hand, "we're off before he persuades us to do something we might regret." Alan followed us laughing, glancing occasionally at the paragliders as they floated like butterflies in the breeze.

CHAPTER SIXTY-THREE
TUESDAY 24 SEPTEMBER

Last Friday we had a phone call from Colin Barnes to tell us that he had some news for us. As he had warned us, he refused to say any more on the phone. We arranged to see him again this morning, on a day when Alan was at work. Mr Barnes arrived about ten-thirty and settled down in a chair, until Mary came into the lounge with some drinks. Mary and I waited anxiously as he took a sip of his coffee, then he smiled briefly at us.

"I expect that this moment was at the back of your minds all of the time you were on holiday?" Mr Barnes remarked. I managed a half-smile. Mary looked as if she was going to burst into tears. "So," Mr Barnes continued, "I'd better put you out of your misery. It's a mixture of good and bad news, I'm afraid. First, the good. We have managed to trace your other son, and he is well and living in the south of England." Mary smiled briefly, then relaxed in her seat.

"Is he married?" Mary asked.

"Yes, but he and his wife have no children. When I first contacted him, he was very surprised to find out that you had been looking for him, and shocked to discover that he has a twin brother. Later on, when I went to visit him, he told me that he knew that he was adopted as a baby, and that he had a very happy childhood. Both he and his wife have good jobs."

"You haven't mentioned a name, Colin," I said ominously.

"No, I'm sorry, I'm not allowed to do so. Your son doesn't want any contact with you. I'm sorry, Mr Newby." Mary broke down in tears, and I went over to console her. After a few minutes she stopped crying and wiped her eyes.

"Didn't you show him my letter, and the photos?" Mary asked angrily, still on the verge of tears.

"Yes, of course, and he seemed to be quite moved, but as I told you before, Mrs Irvine, he's had a very happy life so far and didn't want any complications."

"Complications!" Mary shouted, "We're his family."

"Of course, my apologies," Mr Barnes held up his hand. "I've expressed that badly. Forgive me. He's content with the family that he has already. Sometimes an adopted person reacts like this. I suppose it's a case of better the devil you know ... " We fell silent for a couple of minutes.

"So that's it, then?" I asked.

"Not quite," answered Mr Barnes. "He didn't want to close the door shut and tell me that he would never want any contact. He certainly doesn't want any contact now. In a way, I have left the door open for him. He has your contact details - your address and phone numbers. The ball is in his court now, so if he does change his mind and wants to contact you he can do so easily. You must remember that he has received some traumatic, quite shocking news and sometimes it takes time, perhaps a long time, to come to terms with that news. He has a lot to think about. You will have to remain patient, and optimistic, and hope that in time he will change his mind. You, and I, can do no more." Mr Barnes sat back and drained his mug.

"Well, thank you for all of your efforts on our behalf," I said.

"Not at all," Mr Barnes replied. "I ought to have added that your son has my contact details as well. Sometimes, in these circumstances, an adopted person who has requested no contact but then changes their mind will act through an agent like me, rather than contact you directly. If that does happen, I will of course get in touch with you straightaway."

"We'll just have to keep hoping that contact will be made. We can't do anything else, can we?" Mary was still very upset. Mr Barnes nodded in sympathy. He stood up.

"I think you need some time on your own, so I'll leave you in peace, but please remember: Never say never."

"Thank you, Colin," I said, "I'll see you to the door."

Later in the afternoon, when Alan returned home from work, we asked him to sit down in the lounge.

"You've had some news, I guess?" Alan said, looking at Mary.

"Yes, your brother has been found, and he lives in the south. He's married, but has no children." Mary looked sullen.

"And he doesn't want to see us?" Alan knew the answer.

"Yes," I muttered.

"Was he told that he has a brother? "

"Yes, he was," I continued, "but he hasn't totally rejected us. He may change his mind when he's had more time to think about the situation, and he has our contact details."

"Is he well?" Alan continued to press.

"Yes, and apparently has a good job," I told him.

"So he doesn't need us then, does he?" Alan looked angry. "What's for tea, Mam?"

CHAPTER SIXTY-FOUR
TUESDAY 10 DECEMBER

The autumn had been uneventful, a kind of limbo, waiting for the news that did not arrive. We had settled into a routine, with regular contact with Alan's children, but with no decision about their future. Mary visited her mother every couple of weeks, and on one occasion she made an appointment to see her solicitor about her divorce. As expected, nothing had changed there. Paul remained adamant that he did not want a divorce, and was prepared to stick it out for the remainder of the five-year period. As a result, we could not move on, to sort our finances and perhaps make a final decision on where to live.

We heard nothing from our other son, and we were beginning to accept the fact that he would never want any contact with us. We knew that he was well and happy, and would have to make do with that knowledge. "Never say never", Mr Barnes had said. For how long could we cling to that hope?

We still had a large extended family, of course, and we kept in touch with all of our relatives, making plans for some kind of reunion at Christmas. In October, we spent a few days at Kendal with Dave and Jenny. Pete and Karen travelled from Manchester on one of the days, and the six of us had an enjoyable day at Carlisle. Mike and Alison kept in regular touch. They were both well.

Alan came in from work in a foul mood and stormed

upstairs. He didn't come down for over an hour, so Mary went upstairs to make sure that everything was OK. She came down twenty minutes later and gave me the bad news. Cheryl had finished with Alan, and she had left work for another job. "And another bloke," Alan had added. Alan appeared a little later, still looking really down. He sat down and put his head in his hands.

"First my brother rejects me, now her," he muttered. "I don't know if I can take much more." He put his head in his hands.

"Come on, son," I tried to console him, "relationships break up all the time. You know that. As for your brother, that wasn't personal. He doesn't want to see any of us."

"Everything was going so well," Alan said. "I've had a great year so far."

"We all have setbacks, Alan," Mary smiled sympathetically, her large eyes moistened. "Think about what happened to John and me, but it all turned out well in the end."

"Life has to go on, Alan," I continued. "Something, someone will turn up and all of your problems will be forgotten. You've got to try to stay strong. You have so much to look forward to - Louise and Daniel, your family, you know."

"I'm sorry, Dad, but just at the moment it's difficult to be positive. There are only so many knockdowns I can take."

"Christmas is just around the corner. Soon it will a new year, and things will get better, I promise you."

Alan just looked at me, staring. "We'll see, but I don't

know what I've done to deserve all of this misery. It's been like that all through my life - my first Dad dying, that drunken pig my Mam married, trouble with the police, drugs, Ann dying, now this. I know it's not your fault that we haven't been together for all my life. If only that bastard of a husband of yours hadn't tricked you into parting. God, I'm so angry. It can't go on like this." Alan looked at Mary.

"You're hurting now, Alan," Mary said, "but things will be different soon, believe me."

CHAPTER SIXTY-FIVE
SUNDAY 29 DECEMBER

Alan had been in the depths early in December, but as Christmas drew near he seemed to have recovered more of his normal cheery self. Cheryl was not mentioned, and gradually Alan began to enjoy his work routine again. He even helped to organise a staff night out in Blackpool on the Thursday before Christmas. He returned early on Friday morning without any apparent ill effects, and spoke about a woman called Linda he had met in one of the pubs.

Just before Christmas, we were busy making preparations for entertaining the family at our house in Preston. Caroline and Laura were going to travel with their families on Christmas Eve, and Alan had arranged to collect his children around three o'clock on Christmas afternoon. We borrowed some sleeping bags and mattresses so that all of our guests would have somewhere to sleep. We bought a large tree from one of the city stores, and Alan threw himself into arranging all of the decorations in the house. It was good to see his childlike excitement, and to feel that he was putting his troubles behind him for a while. When Mary commented about the change in Alan, we suddenly realised that this was due to be the first big family Christmas he had ever witnessed.

The weather was appropriately cold as Caroline's family arrived early on Tuesday afternoon. We made a big fuss of Jessica and Jack, and they were disappointed not find Alan's children, Louise and Daniel, at home with us.

Alan explained that they would be with us on Christmas afternoon. Laura and Stephen arrived about four o'clock. We ate out at one of the local pubs, then played a few games with the children before they went to bed ... very excited, of course.

As expected, Caroline's children were up at the crack of dawn, and they made such a racket that everybody was forced to get up and to go downstairs to watch the children open their presents. Mary and Laura made some drinks and toast while the room slowly filled up with small piles of torn wrapping paper. The adults opened some of their presents, and left the rest under the tree so that Louise and Daniel could unwrap their gifts along with the rest of us. We then got dressed and went for a family walk in the nearby park. Jessica and Jack each took a bag of bread to feed the birds. Groups of people, wrapped up against the cold, were walking around, exercising their dogs and feeding the birds by the pond. It was a typical Christmas scene, though without much snow.

When we returned to our house, Mary and her daughters went to the kitchen to prepare the Christmas dinner, while the men played video games with the children. I made sure that everyone had a drink, apart from Alan who soon left for Sheffield. We played more games and watched the usual festive mix on television while we waited for Alan to return. He was back with Louise and Daniel just after four o'clock, and we endured another half hour of excitement as the rest of the presents were opened. By the time everyone had calmed down and had tidied the room, our Christmas dinner was ready. A meal that had taken hours to prepare was demolished in a matter of minutes, and the men were volunteered to clear everything away, to fill the dishwasher and to rinse the rest. The four children were amusing themselves in the back room as the adults enjoyed a drink or two and watched some more television. Within a short time the men were asleep, and the women could chat among themselves. Such is a happy Christmas.

Our families stayed on for Boxing Day, a time for battling with the crowds in the city centre looking for bargains in the sales and for watching football at home. We enjoyed another family walk just after dusk, before watching more festive television back at the house. It was late before the last of us stumbled to our beds and sleeping bags. On Friday morning our guests packed their cases and bags of presents into their cars and then they were off – Caroline's family to Oxford, Laura and Stephen to Bristol, and Alan and his children to Sheffield. It had been a most enjoyable Christmas and for a few days all of our cares were forgotten.

Mary and I had a lazy Sunday morning. Alan had arranged to meet Linda at the Winter Gardens in Blackpool for lunch, so he was busy getting ready. He had phoned her a couple of times since meeting her on the staff night out, but couldn't remember exactly what she looked like. Mary and I waited until he left, then shopped at a nearby supermarket before returning home for some having a snack. We then settled down for a lazy afternoon watching a DVD. I had nodded off, but woke to the sound of my mobile in the hall. I hurried out to answer the call.

"Hello."

"Hello. Is that John Newby?"

"Yes, speaking. Who's calling, please?"

"I think you had better sit down. This is your son William."

"William? I don't have a son called William. You must have the wrong number."

"No, I'm your son. You employed an agency to find me in August. I'm your missing twin."

"Good Lord." I sat down on the stairs. "Hell, what a shock, I mean a great surprise. Just a minute while I switch the phone to loudspeaker and get my wife." I dashed into the lounge and gestured Mary to switch off the television. "It's our missing boy, Love," I whispered." I sat down next to her. "Hello William."

"Hello again. I am sorry to shock you both like this. I have been thinking about getting in touch with you for a few weeks now, but I just couldn't decide when. How are you both?"

"We're well, really well," said Mary. "I'm your mother Mary. Hello William. What a lovely late Christmas present."

"Hello, Mary. It's good to speak to you."

"I can't tell you how pleased I am to finally hear your voice," Mary said, smiling widely. "Mr Barnes has told us that you are well, that you are married and live in the south. Oh, and that you have no children. I think that's all he told us, wasn't it, John?"

"Yes, that was all," I continued. "How much do you

know about us, William?"

"Not a great deal beyond the letter you wrote. I was very surprised to find out that I have a twin brother."

"Yes, he's called Alan. He is staying with us in Preston at the moment, though for most of his life he has lived in Sheffield."

"That's a coincidence, because I lived in Sheffield after I was adopted. My parents moved south when I was six, and they retired to Cornwall almost twenty years ago."

"May I ask, William," I said, "what made you change your mind?"

"When I first met Mr Barnes, I was very much against it. I've had a really happy childhood and a successful career, and I suppose I didn't feel that I needed any more family in my life. My wife Miranda asked me several times to reconsider and my parents weren't opposed to the idea of contacting you, but I think what finally changed my mind was the really nice Christmas we've spent with Miranda's sisters and their families. That made me more curious about my natural family."

"There are quite a lot of us," Mary warned him.

"I gathered that from the letter you wrote." He laughed softly. "So, the big question is do you still want to meet me?"

"Yes, yes, of course," we both answered together. "When, and where?"

"I've thought about it for the past couple of days. I assumed that we all would be busy at New Year, so if you're able to do so, can you travel to Oxford on Thursday the 2nd of January?"

"Yes, perfect," Mary said, "we know Oxford well. One of my daughters lives there. Do you live there as well, William?"

"No, but my wife was brought up near there, and I studied at Oxford University. Shall me meet at the Carfax Tower, say around noon, then we can have some lunch together? I'll bring the photo you sent."

"That's fine with us," Mary said enthusiastically. "I can't begin to tell you how happy I feel just now, William."

"Me too, Mary. Until Thursday then."

"We'll see you on Thursday, William," I joined in again. "Take care, and thank you so much for your call."

"Goodbye." The phone went dead. Mary and I looked at each other, then stood up, hugged each other and danced around the lounge.

"Can you believe it, Love?"

"Pinch me," Mary whispered in my ear. "My heart's beating so fast. I'm in dreamland."

Alan returned twenty minutes or so after William's call. He looked at the pair of us, thought for a moment, then said: "Have you won the lottery, or something? You look like a pair of Cheshire cats."

"We had a phone call just over an hour ago, Alan." She paused. "It was from your brother ... your twin brother, that is."

"Really?" Alan exclaimed. "God, that's out of the blue,

isn't it? What is he called?"

"William," I told him. He grinned. "He's called William, his wife is called Miranda and they live in the south."

"Did he tell you anything else about himself?"

"I don't think so," I said, turning to Mary, "did he?"

"He went to Oxford University, and his adopted parents live in Cornwall."

"Oh yes," I said, "it's been quite a shock, Alan. Anyway, he wants to meet us, so we're going to Oxford on Thursday."

"Hmm," Alan spoke softly, "the last piece in the jigsaw. I didn't think he'd ever get in touch. That's great news for you."

"And for you, Alan," Mary added, "and the rest of our family." She paused. "How was your day? How did you get on with Linda?"

"Oh, she was nice enough, but she's married. I've got enough complications in my life without adding to them. I won't be seeing her again."

"That's a pity," Mary frowned, "but there are plenty more fish in the sea, Alan. You'll soon find one that's right for you."

"Maybe, we'll see. Anyway, I'm grabbing a bite to eat, then I'm going out for a couple of pints with some friends from work. Perhaps I'll catch that fish tonight?" He smiled as he went into the kitchen.

CHAPTER SIXTY-SIX
THURSDAY 2 JANUARY

We packed an overnight holdall on Wednesday night, just in case we had to stay in Oxford after our meeting with William. We told Alan that we planned to make an early start, but would give him a ring after we had met his brother. I don't think either of us slept well, as we were so excited at the prospect of finally meeting our other lost son. We awoke early, showered and breakfasted, and were ready to leave by seven o'clock. Alan was still fast asleep, so we quietly closed the front door behind us and got in my car. It was a chilly day, but the roads were fairly quiet as we left Preston. Many people were still on holiday, of course. I soon reached the M6 and we were on our way south.

We arrived at Oxford with plenty of time to spare, found a central car park then walked to the Carfax Tower. It was only just after eleven-thirty. Another half hour to wait! Mary and I paced up and down, glancing along the connecting streets, looking for a man with similar features to Alan. It began to drizzle, so Mary put up her umbrella and we continued to move around, occasionally stamping our feet to keep out the cold. Twelve o'clock sounded somewhere, then at five-past a familiar-looking man walked round the corner. He smiled at us, and Mary ran to him, hugging him. I walked over and we shook hands.

"Just a minute," he joked, looking at a photo, "I think I had better check that you are the people I'm looking for." We laughed. "I'm William, by the way. William Newton."

"Not too far from Newby," I thought.

"Well I'm your father John, and this is your mother Mary. We're both over the moon to meet you at last." It was all smiles. Out of the corner of my eye, I noticed a dark-haired woman peeking around the corner. She moved forward and touched William's sleeve.

"Oh, and this lady is my wife, Miranda." I shook hands with her, and Mary kissed her. Miranda smiled widely, then put up her umbrella.

"We're very pleased to meet you too, Miranda." It was raining more heavily.

"Shall we get away from this bad weather and find a nice restaurant?" William suggested. "Do you have any particular preferences?"

"No, we like most things," Mary said.

"I know a good Italian restaurant near here," William continued. "Will that be fine for you?"

"Of course," I said. "Please lead the way, William."

By half-past one we had finished our meal and were enjoying some coffee. Most of the conversation had been polite, with hardly any personal questions. I sat back in my chair, and smiled at my son.

"That was an excellent meal, William. A good choice."

"Yes, Miranda and I often eat here when we are in Oxford." William sipped his coffee. "This is rather surreal, I must say, and a little uncomfortable. Do you mind if I just call you Mary and John for now? I've been calling two other people "mother and father" for over forty years, and it seems strange to have two more." We laughed.

"Not at all," I said. "Mary and I didn't expect anything else."

"William and I have so many questions that we'd like to ask," Miranda joined in, "and I expect that you are the same?" We both nodded our heads.

"Tons," Mary said, smiling at Miranda.

"Well, William and I discussed this before we arrived in Oxford. It isn't very private here. Do you have any plans for the next day or two?"

"No, not at all," I said, looking at Mary. "We are both retired, not quite pensioners, but nearly there." Miranda laughed.

"In that case, would you like to stay at our house for a day or two?"

William asked. "Miranda and I are free until Monday, then work beckons, I'm afraid."

"That would be lovely," Mary smiled at William. "Thank you so much. Do you live near here?"

"No, we live in Surrey, about an hour away. Is that alright?"

"No problem," I replied. "I'll just follow your car. The roads ought to be fairly quiet today."

"That's good," William said, "we'll be much more comfortable at home. Just give me a minute or two, please." He stood up, walked to the counter and paid the bill. I realised what he was doing, and walked over to protest. He waved his hand. "It's my treat, John." Turning to Mary and

Miranda, he asked: "Do you need ... you know, before we go?"

"I think we better had. Come on, Mary." They walked to the toilets. I looked at William.

"Yes, we should go as well," he said. I nodded in agreement.

I followed William's car, a top-of-the-range Mercedes, down the M40, to the M25 and past Heathrow, until he signalled to exit the motorway. The traffic was fairly light and we made good time. I had heard about Surrey's leafy lanes, and now I was driving along them, following signs for Guildford. William slowed, turned off the main road and drove through a prosperous-looking village. "There's some money around here," I smiled at Mary. "It's beginning to look as though William has everything, while Alan has nothing."

"William hasn't any children, Darling. I think that's one of the reasons why he has contacted us, because he doesn't have any family."

We had reached another village by now, and William slowed down and stopped, indicating right at a driveway to a large detached house. A car went past on the other side of the road, then William drove in and I followed. I parked behind him on the gravelled drive, and Mary and I got out of our car. We looked around at the extensive gardens, then at the impressive house, and I turned to William and said: "Very nice, William. It's almost as big as my house in New Zealand." We all laughed.

"New Zealand, eh," Miranda smiled, "I've always wanted

to visit there. Have you any luggage?" I opened the boot and took out my holdall. "Please come inside. Let's get warm."

Miranda had taken us around the house and showed us into a large en-suite bedroom, where we left our coats and holdall. We freshened up, then William gave us a guided tour around the well-kept gardens at the rear of the house. Miranda prepared some soup and sandwiches for tea, and afterwards we relaxed in a large lounge with a roaring fire. William poured some drinks for us.

"Well," he said, sinking into a comfortable chair, "I think it's time that you told me your story. I'm particularly interested to know why you separated in Leeds, I think," he raised his eyebrows and Mary nodded, "why you had me adopted, and why you are together again now. Miranda and I are good listeners."

Mary and I took turns in relating the now-familiar story, emphasising Paul's deception in Leeds, Mary's agony over the family decision to have her twins adopted, and my exhaustive search for Mary last year. William and Miranda were as good as his word. They were captivated, and didn't interrupt us once. I sat back and had a drink after I had finished relating the last part of our story.

"Wow!" Miranda exclaimed, "that is some story. I think you ought to write a book about it! Really amazing." Turning to her husband, she said: "What do you think, William? You are very quiet."

"Yes, sorry, Dear," William smiled at Miranda. "There's an awful lot to think about. It's odd really. You were most unlucky to lose each other, and Alan and me, but you've also been very fortunate to find each other again and to trace my brother and me. What an unusual story! I think it will take a few days to sink in."

"It's your turn now, William," Mary looked at him. "Tell us a little about your life, and how you met Miranda." Then she turned to me.

"I've just thought, John. Hadn't you better phone Alan before William begins his story?"

"Oh yes," I said, standing up. "Please excuse me for a minute or two." I went upstairs for my mobile and called Alan's number. There was no reply, as it went to voicemail. I left him a brief message telling him that all was well and that we were staying with William for a day or two. We would be back for his birthday. I returned to the lounge. "No reply," I looked at Mary. "He must be out with some friends." I sat down again. "Now, William, we are all ears."

"I'm afraid that my story is rather dull compared to yours." He smiled at both of us. "When I was adopted I lived in Sheffield until I was about six years old. My parents were in their late thirties when they adopted me. My father was a lecturer at the university, then he was offered a new post at the London School of Economics, so we moved to Enfield. My mother also worked in the city as a journalist, so I was sent to a private school. I later read Classics at Oxford, but secured work in the City in the banking world. I'm now an executive for an investment bank in London. My parents moved to Cornwall soon after I left home. I don't really see much of them these days, I'm sorry to say. Life is so busy."

"And Miranda?" Mary asked.

"I was born in Banbury ... you know, 'ride a cock horse to Banbury Cross' and so on. It's not far from Oxford. I went to a local comprehensive school and afterwards followed a career in publishing. I moved to London and met William at an office party. We've been married for over fourteen years now, haven't we, Darling?" He smiled. "I have two sisters, and both of them have three children, so, as you can imagine, Christmas was very hectic."

William continued with their story. "Not a lot to say, is there? We lived in London for a few years, then bought this house just over seven years ago. It's really too big for us, but we enjoy living in the countryside, away from the bustle of the city. It can be a little lonely here at times, however."

"The important thing is whether you feel that it is your "home"." Mary sat forward in her seat. "I am sure that there are lots of people who are happier living in little terraced houses in somewhere like Wigan than some of the folk around here living in large mansions."

"Do you intend staying in Preston, John?"

"We haven't really given it a lot of thought, William. I still have a house in New Zealand, and Mary part-owns the house in Warwick. When that situation is sorted out, we'll decide where to purchase a house in England. We would like to have a base here and one abroad, but we may decide in the end just to live here and stay with my family when we visit Australia or New Zealand. Much will depend on Alan, when he finally decides what he wants to do."

"So, tell me about Alan. He lives with you and his children

are in Sheffield, so I take it that he has experienced some difficulties in his life. I've been the fortunate one, right?"

"That's exactly it," Mary said, a sad expression on her face. "I won't go into all of the gory details, but Alan was adopted by a good family in Doncaster. They too moved to Sheffield when he was little, but after his father died things began to go wrong. He's had many problems with stepfathers, drink, drugs, the police, you name it, but he does have two lovely children. They are in care at the moment."

"Where is their mother?" Miranda asked.

"She's dead, I'm afraid," Mary continued. "Drug overdose."

"How awful," Miranda frowned. "Will he be able to get his children back?"

"We hope so, but there must be a settled family environment before that can happen. We are working on it."

"How is Alan with you?" William asked. "He's had an awful life, judging by what you have told us. Does he blame you for that?"

"No, he says he doesn't," I replied, "and we do get on well with him, but he has a lot of anger buried inside him. Sometimes we feel that life with him is like sitting on the edge of a volcano." We fell silent for a minute or two.

"Coffee, anyone?" Miranda asked.

"Please," Mary and William answered together. I put my thumb up and smiled.

"Please excuse me," I said. "I want to try Alan again." I returned upstairs to make a call, but there was no reply.

"Any luck, John?" Mary asked. I shook my head. Miranda came in with a tray of coffee and biscuits. We helped ourselves.

"I think I'll go to bed after this," Mary sighed. "It's been a very eventful, but thoroughly enjoyable day. I'm so happy, I keep pinching myself, but at the same time I feel quite exhausted."

"I'm not surprised," Miranda smiled. "I think we all could do with a good night's sleep."

CHAPTER SIXTY-SEVEN
FRIDAY 3 JANUARY

After breakfast, William asked Mary and me how we would like to spend the day, and I told him we needed to do a little shopping. I had already mentioned to Miranda that Mary wanted to buy birthday cards and presents for both William and Alan, so she suggested that we pass an hour or two in Guildford. It was only a short drive to the centre and Miranda and Mary managed to sneak away for long enough to buy the cards and gifts. William and I contented ourselves with some leisurely window shopping along the cobbled main street, and with a few gentle questions we found out a little more about each other.

"So how about sport, John? If you've lived in Australia and New Zealand you must be sport mad."

"Oddly enough," I replied, "I still prefer watching football to anything else. I used to play to a modest level at university, and my friends and I supported several league teams. Living in a country like New Zealand, it's difficult to ignore sport, but I enjoyed hiking and walking most of all. There's some fabulous scenery over there."

"I have watched the *Lord of the Rings* trilogy, so I must admit that the locations the director used were stunning. Perhaps Miranda and I will visit there in the future."

"You'll be welcome any time. You can use my house and remember, you have a half-brother and his family living there!"

"Family," William said thoughtfully, "it's difficult getting my head around the fact that I now have such a huge family. Brothers, sisters, nephews, nieces, they go on for ever. I'm actually looking forward to meeting them all." Mary and Miranda returned to the street, complete with new carrier bags. "You've been busy, "William said, smiling.

"Time for a coffee, I think," Miranda said. "Mary and I need to re-charge our batteries."

"Before doing some more shopping, I presume?" I grinned. William led the way to a nearby coffee shop.

Half an hour later we were finishing our drinks when Mary paused, deep in thought. "I've been thinking, we're all free over the weekend, so why don't we all go to Preston and surprise Alan? We can have a big birthday celebration tomorrow and Miranda and William can return at their leisure on Sunday. You might have the chance to meet your Uncle Ian and Aunt Susan as well while we're there. What do you think William?"

I urged a little caution. "We've had a big couple of days, and it's been great, but we don't want to rush you into meeting all of your lost family, William. Do you think you are ready to meet your brother?"

"Well, I've met you both and survived, so why not? Are you game, Miranda?"

"Why not, after all we are on holiday. It surely won't harm us spending a day or so in the frozen north!"

"Steady on, Dear. Don't forget, I'm a northerner too." William turned to us. "Come on then, shopping's over, we need to go home and pack a few things."

"You'll have to be prepared to rough it, you two. We only have a small spare room."

"We'll survive," Miranda said. "Let's go."

Within the hour we were on our way, travelling in two cars. We had considered just using William's car, but that would have meant Mary and me returning to Surrey and driving back to Preston late in the day. It was easy enough to communicate by phone as we drove along the motorways. We planned to stop halfway on our journey to have a break in one of the service areas. Mary and I had just passed the exit for Oxford when my mobile rang.

"Hello," I said, expecting to hear William's voice.

"Hi, it's Big John, you know, from Sheffield. I'm phoning about Al."

"Oh God, what's happened now? I've tried his mobile a couple of times, but just thought his battery was dead." I switched to the loudspeaker.

"No, it's much worse than that. He's been on a real bender over here. I haven't seen him, but a friend of mine said he's right out of his head. He's also caused trouble at the foster home where his kids are staying."

"Oh no," Mary cried out. She looked horrified, and started to cry.

"Do you know if his children are alright?"

"My friend told me that Al didn't get into their house. I think the police were called, but by the time they got there Al had gone. I don't think he harmed anyone, just frightened a few people."

"Where is he now?" I asked.

"I haven't a clue. Nobody knows."

"Listen, John. Mary and I are on our way back to Preston. He's probably gone home, and we'll ring you when we get back. In the meantime, please phone me if you hear any more."

"OK, I'll do that. I hope you find him quickly."

"So do I, John. Thanks a lot for letting me know." I turned to Mary, who had stopped crying. "Give William a call, Mary, and tell him to stop at the next services. We need to tell them about this."

Twenty minutes later, the four of us sat at a table in a motorway Costa. I had told William and Miranda about Big John's call.

"Look, William, Mary and I will understand fully if you decide to turn around and go home. This was supposed to be a birthday surprise for Alan, not a family crisis involving a brother you haven't met." William and Miranda whispered among themselves.

"No, we're with you," William decided. "We're family now and hopefully Alan will just be sleeping it off when we reach Preston. If not, then we're there to help you sort things out. I'm sure that everything will be fine. Things must have been too much for Alan over the Christmas period."

"Yes, he has had some disappointments," Mary added. "He seemed to have a promising relationship with a woman called Cheryl, but that collapsed just a few weeks ago, and he always gets wound up over his children at times like this. It seems as if he can only take so much for so long, then he erupts. Afterwards, things are calm again until his next crisis. We definitely need to settle his children's future soon."

"Trying to gatecrash their foster home won't have helped his cause," I muttered sadly. "Drink up, everybody. Let's get back home, and we'll take it from there."

We arrived back in Preston just before six o'clock. I advised William to park further along our road, until we had checked our house to see if Alan was there. There were no lights on, and a quick look around confirmed that Alan wasn't at home. I walked to William's car, asked them to come inside and ignited the gas fire while Mary made drinks for all of us. I was just about to take a sip of my drink when I realised that something was missing.

"He's taken your car, Mary. It isn't on the drive or on the roadside."

"Why don't you call the police?" William suggested. "I hate to say it, but he may have had an accident."

"I don't want to cause further trouble for him," I said, after thinking for a few seconds. "It's most likely that he's sleeping it off somewhere in Sheffield, and he'll turn up tomorrow when he's recovered. He knows that we were planning some birthday celebrations for him, and that we were meeting you. He was excited when you had contacted us, and was dying to find out all about you. I'm sure that he won't want to miss all of that."

"Could he be staying with a friend in Preston?" Miranda

asked.

"That's unlikely, I think," I replied. "Our best course of action is to stay put here, and not to have the police chasing around everywhere looking for him. He's bound to turn up soon. After all, where else can he go? If he's been involved in a traffic accident, the police would have been here by now. I'll arrange for a meal to be delivered, then we can pass the evening looking at some family photos and suchlike. If Alan returns tonight, all well and good. If not, let's try to have a good night's sleep, then decide what to do in the morning. Does anyone have any alternative suggestions?" The others looked blank.

"Well, it looks as though we're in his hands," William said philosophically. "I vote for a Chinese." He smiled at the rest of us.

CHAPTER SIXTY-EIGHT
SATURDAY 4 JANUARY

Sleep is difficult in times of crisis, and the four of us were up and about before eight o'clock. I quickly checked the drive and the road to see if there was any sign of Mary's car, but I sensed that it would not be there. When I went back into the house, Mary and Miranda were congratulating William on his birthday. I had completely forgotten. He opened his cards and presents, and smiled when he discovered that Mary had bought him some family multi-photo frames.

"It will be fun filling these," he chuckled. "I have so many relatives to choose from now." Miranda had given him some book and DVD vouchers.

"I didn't have a lot of time to think about William's present this year," Miranda confessed. "Vouchers are always a good fallback."

No-one had much to say. Alan was on all of our minds, and we ate breakfast without much enthusiasm. We helped Mary to clear the table and tidy away the pots, then sat down in the lounge. Mary came in and sat down next to Miranda.

"I'm preparing some coffee. Now we've got to decide what to do about Alan. I suggest that we give him until lunch to show up, then to contact the police. You can discuss that while I make the coffee." She went into the kitchen, returning with a tray five minutes later.

"I think we're all in agreement, Mary," I spoke for the others. "Alan's had long enough to show up, and he knew that we wanted to spoil him on his birthday. If he was at Sheffield last night, he has enough time to get here before noon." William nodded in approval.

"Help yourselves," Mary said. "I don't know how you like your coffee yet," she smiled nervously.

It was a cold, crisp morning, so after finishing our drinks I suggested that we go for a walk.

"That's a good idea," William said. "Blow a few cobwebs off, and all that."

"What if Alan phones the landline?" Mary looked worried.

"Oh, I hadn't thought of that," I muttered. "Look, Mary, you take William and Miranda around the park, and I'll stop here. We have our mobiles. If Alan shows up, I'll call you. If he contacts you, give me a ring." Mary looked hesitant. "Go on, the fresh air will do you some good. Take some bread for the ducks, William. I'll see you later."

They had only been gone for about ten minutes when they suddenly returned to the house. I ran to the door when I heard it open. I must have looked disappointed. Mary looked awful.

"It's not Alan. I've had a text from Maureen, you know, my neighbour at Warwick. You need to have a look." She handed me her mobile. I read the message:

Hi Mary. We're a little worried. Late last night Thomas noticed your car on Paul's drive. We thought that you've returned without telling us, then Thomas saw your car leaving the drive around nine this morning. Hope all is well. Let me know. Love, Maureen.

I quickly read the message again. "For God's sake, what on earth is Alan doing in Warwick, John?" Mary asked anxiously.

"Look, this is serious. You know that Alan hates Paul, and blamed him for all of his troubles. We know that he's been out of it, perhaps high on drugs, for the past couple of days. Get on the phone to Maureen in Warwick, and ask Thomas, and maybe someone else, to use the spare key to go in your house and check that Paul is alright. Quickly, Mary."

Mary dialled a number. "Maureen ... It's me, Mary. I've just received your text. I'm in Preston, but my son Alan has my car ... Yes, I have a son. I'll explain another time. Please, this is very urgent. Can you ask Thomas to use the spare key to enter my house? Make sure that Paul is there and that he is OK ... Thanks, Maureen, ring me back as soon as you can." Mary collapsed into a chair. "Oh God, John, he's done something terrible, I just know it." The minutes ticked by.

"How does Alan know where Paul lives?" William asked.

"When we went to visit Caroline in Oxford," I explained, "we visited Mary's mother, your grandmother, in her retirement home near Warwick, then Alan asked to see Mary's house. We just drove past it, that's all, but he must have remembered the address."

Mary's mobile suddenly rang. She lunged for it. "Hello." She listened intently for a couple of minutes. "Are you sure?" Another pause. "Thanks, Maureen. I'll phone you soon." She turned to us. "There's no-one there. Both the front and back doors were unlocked. Thomas went right through the house, but there's no sign of Paul. He said the house looked tidy, there was no sign of a fight, or anything like that. He checked the garage as well. Paul's car is still there. Oh God, what's going on? Where has Alan gone?"

I though hard for a few minutes. "What time is it now, please?"

"Ten past ten," Miranda replied.

"Right," I said forcefully, "he has more than an hour start on us. We need to get moving fast." We stood up and looked for our coats.

"Where are we going, John?" William asked.

"Look, it is Alan's birthday today. What do people do on their birthday? Answer: they do things or go to places that they really like. Where is Alan's favourite place?"

"Oh no," Mary screamed, "Monsal Head."

"That's right, Monsal Head. He's taking Paul there, and Christ alone knows what he's going to do to him. I'll drive. Let's go."

The journey from Preston to Monsal Head normally takes about an hour and a half – in good weather. I drove as quickly as I could to the M6, then put my foot down on the motorway. The road surface was good and the traffic was light, but I ignored the speed cameras without taking too many risks.

"Do you know the best way from here, John?" William asked.

"I know we need to take the M61 and M60, then follow

the Sheffield roads. After that I'm not quite so sure. Mary and I have only been there once before, and that time we travelled from Sheffield."

"I've got it," Miranda said. "I'm using my iPhone, and I've just typed in the postcode – DE45 1NL. That should lead us there."

"As long as the Derbyshire roads are passable," I replied. "They get a lot of snow up there."

"Shouldn't we phone the police, John?" Mary asked, a worried look on her face.

"What and tell them that we've got a drug-crazed son who's kidnapped someone and is going to kill him at Monsal Head? The police will have an army of marksmen who'll shoot him on sight. I think we should try to get there first. We might be able to save the situation. If not, then we can call the police."

"Alright," William looked thoughtful, "you've probably known Alan better than anyone recently. I think it's unlikely that he has any weapons."

"Maybe a golf club," I said sarcastically.

We were now leaving the M67 and heading on to ordinary roads. I drove through Glossop, heading for Chapel-le-Frith and beyond. It was a fine day, and the road surface appeared to be clear of snow or ice, though there was plenty of snow on the hills of the Peak District as we headed deeper into Derbyshire. The gritting wagons had evidently been busy, because I scattered tiny stones each time I took a corner too quickly.

"Be careful, John," Mary warned, "we need to get there in one piece."

It was now eleven-fifteen, and we were nearing our destination. There was hardly any traffic on the road, but I almost drove past the hotel and car park at Monsal Head. I screeched to a halt, reversed the car slightly and drove into the car park. Only a handful of cars were there. I stopped the car and we got out and looked around. There was no sign of Mary's car. The four of us walked gingerly to the edge of the car park, peered over the wall then carried on along the road by the hotel. As we reached the corner we saw Mary's red Clio on the small car park opposite the hotel. I could see the smoke from the car's exhaust, and could just make out a driver in the front and a figure sitting in the back seat. I shouted: "Alan!" The others called as well. I began to walk towards the red car, but William put out an arm to stop me.

"Not this time, Dad," he said solemnly. "You've done all that you can for him. It's down to me now." He walked slowly across the road towards Mary's car, and we heard him shout: "Alan, it's your brother, come out and talk." We held our breath. William walked closer to the car, and stopped again. The front door swung open, and we saw Alan climb out. The two brothers looked at each other for what seemed to be an eternity. William moved to the other side of the car and we could see that they were talking to each other, but couldn't hear what was being said. They spoke for a few minutes, William appearing calm with gentle arm movements. Alan was swaying slightly, and looked very agitated. We could hear their voices being raised. Suddenly Alan moved forward, and stretched out his hand. William did the same and the two brothers shook hands. More words were exchanged, then Alan violently pushed William to the ground and jumped back into the car. He released the brake, and moved off at speed.

William staggered to his feet and began to run after Alan's car. We ran as well, and someone began screaming loudly. Alan drove the car through a narrow gap in the wall on the side of the lane and we saw the car lurch up as it hit a small mound, almost flying for a split-second before pitching over the edge and down the steep slope. I glanced back and saw that Mary had stopped screaming, and was standing with her head in her hands. Miranda stood alongside her.

I ran again and caught up with William by the wall and we watched as the red car somersaulted through some bushes and trees, bouncing downwards, igniting as it hit an outcrop, then tumbling and cartwheeling inexorably towards the valley bottom. There was a loud crashing noise as the car finally came to a halt upside-down in the meadow far below us, frightening the few grazing cattle, and we stood in silence, watching the burning car as the breeze blew a column of black smoke slowly curling around us.

Back in Preston, later that evening, William, Miranda and I sat in the lounge, saying little. Mary was in bed, heavily sedated. Earlier in the day at Monsal Head, someone in the car park had phoned the police, and soon we heard the sirens of police cars, a fire engine and an ambulance. We spent most of the next three hours being interrogated by the police. The paramedics saw to Mary, then we were allowed to return to Preston. We were exhausted by the time we reached home.

I broke the silence. "I have to ask you, William. What did Alan say to you?"

"I can't remember everything. He said something about "it was like looking in a mirror" when he got out of the car and looked at me. I tried to speak calmly to him, but he was so agitated, so excited. He muttered something about the fact that you had helped him, and now he was going to get rid of Mary's problems. I tried to reason with him, but he wasn't listening. I do remember quite clearly what he said next. He said: "This evil bastard is going to ride tandem with me, just like I did in New Zealand." He then said that it was good to meet me at last, and that's when we shook hands. As he pushed me to the ground, he shouted: "Look after my kids." That's all I can remember." He wiped his forehead, then looked at me. "I'm so sorry, Dad. I should have been able to stop him." His head drooped forward. Miranda put her arms around him.

"Don't feel guilty, William," I said calmly. "We all tried our best to help him. His demons were always there, just under the surface. I think that at the end he realised that he would never defeat them, and would never get his children back. He'd reached the end of a long road. Nobody could have saved him."

EPILOGUE
2015

CHAPTER SIXTY-NINE
THURSDAY 26 MARCH

The morning service at the St Augustine of Canterbury Roman Catholic Church on Harehills Road in Leeds had been a simple, and I assumed, a traditional one. Most of the congregation was made up from Mary's family – her sister Theresa, husband Brian and their son James; Mary's daughters Caroline and Laura with their families; William, Miranda and Alan's children; and Mary and me. Our old friends, Pete, Mike, Dave and their wives had travelled to Leeds yesterday, as we had, and we spent an afternoon and evening with them, catching up on our recent lives and visiting old haunts. Apart from those familiar faces, Mary recognised a few of her mother's neighbours from Alwoodley, and two of the staff and two of Mary's mother's friends had made the long journey from the Dales Retirement Home in Warwick.

After the service the cortege made its way slowly to the Roman Catholic cemetery on York Road, and in bright sunshine Mary's mother was buried alongside her husband. The committal was brief, and tears were shed as the coffin was lowered into the ground. Mary, Theresa and some of the other mourners threw handfuls of earth onto the coffin lid, as others stood around in silent contemplation. The priest reminded all of the mourners that they were welcome to join the family for light refreshments. Most of those who been at the cemetery then drove to a hotel near Alwoodley on the outskirts of Leeds. The atmosphere became more relaxed as we bought drinks and sat down to eat the generous platefuls of sandwiches, sausage rolls, cakes and so on. The afternoon drifted along pleasantly, as Mary and I spent time chatting to the various groups of mourners.

It was good to see our grandchildren again, as Mary and I now lived in Richmond. After Alan's tragic death we decided to take our time before deciding where to live in England. Once Mary's financial affairs were settled we then looked around more seriously. Our family and friends were scattered all over England – Mike and Alison near Durham, Dave and Jenny in Kendal, Pete and Karen near Manchester, my family in Lancashire, Mary's sister in Leeds, her daughters in Oxford and Bristol, and William's family in Surrey – plus my son and daughter on the other side of the world. Most of our family lived in the south, so we thought about buying a house there, but where to choose? There was no guarantee that the family member would still live in the same town in several years' time. In the end we voted with our hearts. Mary was brought up in Leeds and I had many happy memories from Yorkshire, so we decided to stay in Yorkshire and we chose Richmond. We liked the town and of course, it had special memories for us. Richmond also lay close to the A1 and motorways, within two hours' travelling for our friends.

I still had my house in New Zealand, and Mary and I had holidayed there last autumn. Our friends reminded us that they were expecting a wedding invitation, but we had yet to set a date and a place. The events of the past two years had been very traumatic for us and the scars were taking a long time to heal. Finding Mary again, searching for lost family, Alan's tragic death, settling his children in a new home with William – it had been one Hell of a roller-coaster ride. Actually tying the knot now seemed unimportant when compared to everything that we had been through. Mary had once said that we had all the time in the world, and now we no longer needed to make hasty decisions.

The hotel was in a pleasant setting, with its gardens adjoining farmland at the rear, and groups of cows were quietly munching away in the neighbouring fields. Some of us drifted outside to enjoy our drinks in the sunshine, before the late afternoon became too chilly. I saw Brian standing on his own, and went over to catch up with him. Mary and I hadn't seen Theresa and Brian since she visited their house to collect her Aunt Joan's box of paperwork.

"I guess this is the end of an era, Brian," I said whimsically.

"Yes," he replied, "Theresa's mother was the last of her generation. We're in the firing line now." I smiled. "Have Alan's children settled in well in their new home?"

"Oh, very well, I think. They had always wanted to stay in Sheffield, but following the awful publicity after Alan and Paul's deaths, they wanted to move away. They were being bullied at school, and had lost some of their friends. William and Miranda hadn't any children of their own, so they quickly set the ball rolling and adopted Alan's children last year. Louise and Daniel love their new home. It's in the countryside, very different from Sheffield, and they are very happy. So are William and Miranda." I glanced over to the fence, where Mary and Theresa were deep in conversation. "How is James?" I asked.

"Just the same, I'm afraid," Brian replied. "It's not easy, you know. I think he'll have to have more specialised care soon." We both looked away as we could hear raised voices. Mary and Theresa appeared to be getting quite agitated. We walked over towards them, and stood a short distance away.

"Well just make sure that you get it sorted out quickly, Mary." Theresa looked furious. "Brian and I need the money. How much do you think is left?"

"I've no idea," replied Mary. "I've always left it to the solicitors to sort everything out. The fund had a sizeable sum from Mum's savings and the sale of her house. I know she's been in the home for a few years, but there must be a lot of money left."

"Just get the solicitors to sort it out quickly. It's alright for you. You've never been short of money. Brian and I have always struggled. I bet you did alright out of that fund when Mum lived with you."

"Don't start accusing me of any wrong-doing," Mary said angrily. "I didn't take a single penny out of the fund when Mum lived with me."

"I don't believe that for a minute. I've never trusted you," Theresa bristled.

"You're a fine one to talk about trust," Mary snapped, flush with anger. "John and I know that when Paul tricked us into separating in 1970, you helped him by giving him John's phone number. I've said nothing before, but now you know. So much for trust." Theresa laughed loudly.

"I've said nothing as well, nothing about how sick I was of you when we were growing up. You were always the pretty one with blonde hair, getting the attention. Then Mum and Dad pushed you at school because you were the bright one with prospects. They weren't bothered about me. When you turned up for dinner with John, who was then a good-looking bloke with a good future ahead of him, I'd just had enough."

"So that was why you told Paul, you bitch," Mary fumed.

"You're not that bright, are you, you spoilt cow? Paul didn't trick you. *Brian and I made those phone calls.*" Brian looked away in embarrassment. I looked at Mary, stunned. "It was my idea. Paul knew nothing about it. I thought we would just rock the boat for you, but when you split up I was chuffed. Then when you found out you were pregnant, result! Little Miss Perfect up the duff. Brilliant! I loved it, and even more when you eventually ended up with that selfish pig."

"I can't believe what I'm hearing," Mary stormed, staring at Theresa in disbelief. "Betrayed by my own sister, you're evil."

"OK, I was wrong to do that, but I've been punished ever since then. Brian's never been able to get a decent job, and we've always been short of money. Then when James had his accident," she looked over to the hotel where her son was in his wheelchair talking to his cousins, "we're stuck with him for the rest of his life, or ours."

"God, I can't believe all of this," Mary was shaking her head.

"Oh, give over playing the great martyr," Theresa continued. "You may not have had a happy life, but you've had a comfortable one, even with that selfish bastard of a husband. But I tell you this, Mary. By convincing yourself that Paul had tricked you all those years ago, you've caused his death and that of your son Alan. It was your fault that they died. You're guilty. That's the cross you'll have to bear for the rest of your life."

Theresa turned and watched in silence as the cattle grazed in the meadow.

THE END

Lightning Source UK Ltd.
Milton Keynes UK
UKHW012207190522
403229UK00001B/54

9 780993 467912